THE SALAMANDER— LEGENDARY BEAST THAT THRIVES IN FIRE, SYMBOL OF MAN'S SURVIVAL

Moving from the glittering society of wealth and high finance to the grimy underworld of Rome, Milan, and Venice, *The Salamander* reveals a complex web of plots and counterplots leading deeper and deeper into the inferno of Italian politics. It explores lives touched by the passion, treachery, and evil bred in a sordid and seething world.

"A kind of fascination unequaled in any of his novels since *The Devil's Advocate*" —*America*

"Thoroughly exciting and absorbing" —*Newsday*

MORRIS WEST

The Salamander

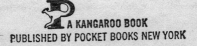
A KANGAROO BOOK
PUBLISHED BY POCKET BOOKS NEW YORK

Author's Note

This book is a work of fiction. The events herein recorded are analogues and allegories. The characters are products of the author's imagination.

Grateful acknowledgment is made to Mr. Stefan S. Brecht for permission to quote eight lines from the Epilogue of *The Resistible Rise of Arturo Ui*, by Bertold Brecht. Adapted by George Tabori. Samuel French, Inc., New York, N.Y. Copyright © 1972 by Stefan S. Brecht.

POCKET BOOKS, a Simon & Schuster division of
GULF & WESTERN CORPORATION
1230 Avenue of the Americas, New York, N.Y. 10020

For
SILVIO STEFANO,
wise counsellor, honest advocate,
friend of my heart

If we could learn to look instead of gawking,
We'd see the horror in the heart of farce,
If only we could act instead of talking,
We wouldn't always end up on our arse.
This was the thing that nearly had us mastered;
Don't yet rejoice in his defeat, you men!
Although the world stood up and stopped the bastard,
The bitch that bore him is in heat again.

BRECHT: *Arturo Ui*

BOOK I

*Scrupulous people are not suited
to great affairs.*

—TURGOT

BETWEEN midnight and dawn, while his fellow Romans were celebrating the end of Carnival, Massimo Count Pantaleone, General of the Military Staff, died in his bed. A bachelor in his early sixties, a soldier of spartan habit, he died alone.

His servant, a retired sergeant of cavalry, brought the General's coffee at the accustomed hour of seven in the morning and found him lying on his back, fully clothed, gape-mouthed and staring at the coffered ceiling. The servant set down the coffee carefully, crossed himself, closed the dead eyes with two fifty-lire pieces, then telephoned the General's aide, Captain Girolamo Carpi.

Carpi telephoned the Director. The Director telephoned me. You will find my name on the Salamander dossier: Dante Alighieri Matucci, Colonel of Carabinieri, seconded for special duty to the Service of Defense Information.

The Service is usually called by its Italian initials, SID (Servizio Informazione Difesa). Like every other intelligence service, it spends a huge amount of taxpayers' money perpetuating itself, and somewhat less in scavenging information which hopefully will protect the Republic against invaders, traitors, spies, saboteurs and political terrorists. You will gather I am skeptical about its value. I have a right to be. I work in it; but every man who works in it becomes disillusioned in some fashion. The Service encourages the loss of innocence; it makes for pliable instruments of policy. However, that's a digression. . . .

Massimo Count Pantaleone, General of the Military Staff, was dead. I was appointed to stage a clean exit for the corpse. I needed help. The Army supplied it in the shape of a senior medical officer, rank of colonel, and a military advocate, rank of major. We drove together to the General's apartment. Captain Carpi received us. The General's servant was weeping over a glass of grappa in the kitchen. So far, so good. No confusion. No neighbours on the landing. No relatives yet informed. I had no great respect for Carpi, but I had to commend his discretion.

The medical officer made a cursory examination and decided that the General had died from an overdose of barbiturates, self-administered. He wrote a certificate, countersigned by the military advocate, which stated that the cause of death was cardiac arrest. It was not a false document, simply a convenient one. The General's heart had stopped. A pity it hadn't stopped years ago. A scandal would benefit no one. It might harm a great many innocent people.

At eight-thirty a military ambulance arrived and removed the body. I remained in the apartment with Carpi and the servant. The servant made us coffee, and while we drank it, I questioned him. His answers established a series of simple facts.

The General had dined out. He had returned twenty minutes before midnight and retired immediately to his bedroom. The servant had secured doors and windows, set the burglar alarm and gone to bed. He had risen at six-thirty and prepared the morning coffee. . . . Visitors? None. . . . Intruders? None. The alarms had not been triggered. . . . Telephone calls, in or out? No way to know.

The General would use the private line in his bedroom. Certainly the domestic telephone had not sounded. . . . The General's demeanour? Normal. He was a taciturn man. Hard to know what he was thinking at any time. That was all. . . . I gave him a pat on the shoulder and dismissed him to the kitchen.

Carpi closed the door behind him, poured two glasses of the General's whisky, presented one to me and asked a question:

"What do we tell his friends—and the press?"

It was the sort of question he would ask: trivial and irrelevant.

"You saw the death certificate, signed and notarized: natural causes, cardiac arrest."

"And the autopsy report?"

"My dear Captain, for an ambitious man you are very naïve. There will be no autopsy. The General's body has been taken to a mortuary where it will be prepared for a brief lying-in-state. We want him seen. We want him honoured. We want him mourned as a noble servant of the Republic—which in a certain sense he was."

"And then?"

"Then we want him forgotten. You can help us there."

"How?"

"Your patron is dead. You did well for us. You deserve a better appointment. I'd suggest something far away from Rome—the Alto Adige, perhaps Taranto, or even Sardinia. You will find promotion a lot quicker in places like that."

"I'd like to think about it."

"No time, Captain! You pick up your transfer papers this morning. You deliver them, completed and signed, by five o'clock this afternoon. I guarantee you will have a new posting immediately after the funeral. . . . And, Captain?"

"Yes?"

"You will remember that you are in a very delicate position. You accepted to spy on a superior officer. We of SID are grateful, but your officer colleagues would despise you. The slightest indiscretion would therefore damage your career and might well expose you to great personal danger. I trust you understand me?"

"I understand."

"Good. You may go now. . . . Oh, a small matter."

"Yes?"

"You have a key to the apartment. Leave it here, please."

"What happens next?"

"Oh, the usual routine. I examine papers and documents. I file a report. Please try to be sad at the funeral. . . . *Ciao!*"

Carpi went out, wrapping the rags of his dignity around him. He was one of those weak, handsome fellows who always need, and generally attract, a patron, and who will always betray him to a more potent one. I had used him to report on Pantaleone's movements, contacts and political activities. Now he was a redundant nuisance. I poured myself another glass of whisky and tried to set my thoughts in order.

The Pantaleone affair had all the makings of a political time bomb. The irony was that you could shout the name up and down the Corso and not one in a thousand of the citizens of the Republic would recognize it. Of those who did recognize it, not one in ten would understand its potency or the magnitude of the conspiracy which had been built around it. The Director understood; so did I. I had dossiers on all the principal participants. For a long time I had chafed at my impotence to do anything about them. They were not criminals—at least not yet. They were all high men—ministers, deputies, industrialists, service officers, bureaucrats—who looked to a day when the confusions of Italy—unstable government, industrial unrest, a faltering economy, an inept bureaucracy and a very frustrated people—would bring the country to the brink of revolution.

On that day, which was closer than many people imagined, the conspirators hoped to seize power and present themselves to a bewildered populace as the saviours of the Republic and the conservators of good order and human rights. Their hope was tolerably well-founded. If a junta of Greek colonels had done it, there was no good reason why a much larger and more powerful group of Italians could not do it better . . . especially if they had the support of the Army and the active cooperation of the Forces of Public Security.

Their figurehead had been named for a long time: that noble soldier, onetime junior aide to Marshal Badoglio, passionate patriot, friend of the common man, General Massimo Pantaleone. Now the General had removed himself from the scene. Why had he done it? Who, or what, had nudged him towards the final act; and why again? Was there a new man waiting in the wings? Who was he? When and how would he reveal himself? And was the day already at hand? I was commissioned to answer all these questions, and the margin for error was very slim indeed.

Even a hint that an investigation was in progress would split the country down the middle. If the press got half an idea that a dubious document had been notarized and uttered by the Army, there would be headlines in every newspaper in the world.

Conspiracy is endemic to Italy, always has been, since Romulus and Remus began horse-trading from Tiber Island; but if the dimension of this plot were made known and the very real possibility that it might succeed . . . *Dio!* There would be barricades in the streets and blood on the tram tracks within a day; one could not rule out even mutiny in the armed services, whose political loyalties were deeply divided between left and right. I had made no idle threat to Captain Carpi. If he tried to sell himself or his information to new masters, an accident would be speedily arranged for him. Meantime, I had my own work to do.

I drank the last of the whisky and began to comb the apartment for papers. I opened drawers and cupboards and tested each one for secret hiding places. I went through the pockets of each garment in the wardrobe. I shook out every book in the library and removed the blotting paper from the desk pad. I made no attempt to examine what I found, but simply piled it into a heap. There would be hours of work to sift and analyze it all—

and very little value at the end. The General was too old a fox to have left dangerous documents lying about his house.

Still, I could not afford to take risks; so I moved pictures and mats in search of a concealed safe. Then I made a final circuit, lifting ornaments, upending cups and vases, prising up the felt beds of the jewel cases which held the General's orders and decorations. Even so, I nearly missed the card.

It was lying on its edge against the baseboard, behind the bedside table; a small rectangle of stiff pasteboard with a design on one side and an inscription on the other. Both the design and the inscription had been done by hand in black India ink. The design had been executed at a single stroke, in a series of intricate whorls and flourishes. It showed a salamander with a coronet on its head, couched in a bed of flames. The inscription was four words of perfect copperplate: *"Un bel domani, fratello."*

"One fine tomorrow, brother. . . ." It was a very Italian phrase which could preface a variety of sentiments: a vain hope, a promise of reward, a threat of vengeance, a rallying cry. The word *brother* was ambiguous, too, and the salamander made no sense at all, unless it were the symbol of a club or a fraternity. Yet there was no association with any sign or code name in my dossiers. I decided to refer it to the specialists. I went back to the study, picked up a clean envelope, sealed the card inside it and put it in the pocket of my jacket.

Then I decided it was time for a private chat with the sergeant of cavalry. I found him in the kitchen, a dejected old man ruminating over an uncertain future. I consoled him with the thought that the General had probably remembered him in his will and that, at least, he was entitled to severance pay from the deceased estate. He brightened then and offered me wine and cheese. As we drank together, he became garrulous, and I was happy to let him ramble.

". . . He didn't have to be a soldier, you know. The Pantaleone always had money running out of their ears. Not that they were free with it. Lord, no! They looked at both sides of a coin and wept before they spent it. Probably that's why they stayed rich. Lands in the Romagna, apartment buildings in Lazio, the old estate in Frascati, the villa on Ponza—of course, she's got that now."

"Who has?"

"You know—the Polish woman. The one he had dinner with last night. What's her name? . . . Anders—that's it—Anders. She's been his girl friend for years. Although, I must say, he was pretty close about it. He never brought her here. Funny, that . . . He didn't want people to think he was enjoying himself. Like we used to say in the Army, he was born with a ramrod up his backside. I knew about her, of course. I used to take her calls. . . . Sometimes I went to her place to deliver things for the General. Good-looking woman, not over the hill yet, either. Which reminds me . . . Someone ought to tell her what's happened."

"I'll do that. Where does she live?"

The question was a blind. I knew the answer and a great deal more about Lili Anders.

"Parioli. The address is in the General's pocket book."

"I'll find it."

"Hey! Now that's a thing! You're not taking any of the General's stuff away, are you? I'm responsible. I don't want any trouble."

"I'm taking all his papers, and I'll borrow a valise to carry them."

"But why?"

"A matter of security. We can't leave confidential documents lying around. So, we'll go through the lot, take out the ones that belong to the Army and return the private ones to his lawyer. You won't have any trouble, because I'll give you an official receipt before I leave. Clear?"

"If you say so. . . . Wait a moment! Who are you? I don't even know your name."

"Matucci. Carabinieri."

"Carabinieri! . . . There's nothing wrong, is there?"

"Nothing at all. . . . Normal procedure with an important man like the General."

"Who's going to make all the arrangements, tell his friends, that sort of thing?"

"The Army."

"So, what do I do? Just sit around here?"

"There's one thing you could do. People will telephone. Take their names and numbers and we'll arrange for someone to call them back."

"I'll still be paid?"

"Don't worry. You have to be paid. It's the law. . . . I meant to ask you something else. Where did the General dine last night?"

"At the Chess Club."

"You're sure?"

"Of course I'm sure. I had to know always where he was. Sometimes there were calls from Headquarters or from the Ministry. . . . Another drop?"

"No, thanks, I'll be on my way."

"And you're sure about the money?"

"I'm sure. And you'll remember to record the telephone calls?"

"Trust me, friend. The General did. I never let him down. You know, he was as cold as a fish, but I'll miss the old bastard. I really will."

The fellow was becoming maudlin now and I was ready to be quit of him. I scribbled a receipt, picked up the bag of documents and walked out into the thin spring sunshine. It was ten minutes after one. The shopkeepers were closing their shutters and the alleys were busy with Romans homing for lunch and siesta.

I have to tell you frankly, I don't like the Romans. I'm a Tuscan born, and these people are first cousins to the Hottentot. Their city is a midden, their countryside, a vast rubbish tip. They are the worst cooks and the most dyspeptic feeders in Italy. They are rude, crass, cynical and devoid of the most elementary graces. Their faces are closed against compassion and their spirits are pinched and rancorous. They have seen everything and learned nothing, except the basest arts of survival. They have known imperial grandeur, papal pomp, war, famine, plague and spoliation; yet they will bow the knee to any tyrant who offers them an extra loaf of bread and a free ticket to the circus.

Yesterday it was Benito Mussolini, drunk with rhetoric, haranguing them from the balcony in the Piazza Venezia. Tomorrow it might be another. And where was he now, at this very moment on Ash Wednesday, in this year of doubtful grace? . . . One thing was sure, he wouldn't be standing like Dante Alighieri Matucci, flat-footed in the middle of the Campo Marzio.

I shook myself out of the reverie, walked half a block to my car, tossed the documents onto the seat and drove back to the office. I might have saved myself the trouble. My two senior clerks were out to lunch; number three was flirting with the typist, and the data bank was out of action because the power supply had been interrupted by a two-hour strike. There was a message from the Ministry of the Interior requesting "immediate contact on a most urgent matter." When I called, I was told that my contact was entertaining some foreign visitors and might possibly be back at four o'clock. Body of Bacchus! What an oafish lot! Judgment Day might come and go, the Maoists might even now be storming the Angelic Gate at Vatican City, but the Romans must finish siesta before they did anything about it.

I dumped the bag of documents on the desk and shouted for number three clerk to sort and collate them. Then, because the strike had put the elevator out of action, I climbed three flights of stairs to the forensic laboratory, where there had to be someone alive, even at lunchtime. As usual, it was Stefanelli who, according to local legend, slept every night in a bottle of formaldehyde and emerged fresh as a marmoset at sunrise every morning. He was a tiny wizened fellow, with wispy locks and yellow teeth and skin like old leather. He must have been ten years past retirement age, but still managed by a combination of patronage and sheer talent to hang on to his job.

What other technicians burst their brains to learn,

Stefanelli knew. Sprinkle a peck of dust in his palm and
he would name you the province and the region and even
make a reasonable guess at the village from which it
came. Hand him a swatch of fabric and he would fondle
it for a moment, then tell you how much cotton was in
it and how much polyester, and give you a list of the
factories that might have made it. Give him a drop of
blood, two nail clippings and a tress of hair and he would
build you the girl who owned them. He was a genius in
his own right, albeit a tetchy and troublesome one, who
would spit in your eye if you crossed him, or slave
twenty-four hours at a stretch for a man who trusted him.
He read voluminously and would bet money on his technical knowledge. Only a very new or a very vain junior
would bet against him. When I came in, puffing and
sour-faced, he greeted me exuberantly.

"Eh, Colonel! What have you got for Steffi today? I've
got something for you. . . . Death by suffocation . . .
green alkaloids in the blood . . . no punctures, no abra-
sions, no apparent means of entry into the blood system.
Five thousand lire if you can tell me what it is."

"Put it that way, Steffi, and I know I'll lose my money.
What is it?"

"It's a shellfish. Comes from the South Pacific. They
call it the Cloth of Gold. On contact, the fish injects
microscopic needles full of alkaloids which paralyze the
central nervous system. Case in point—a marine biologist
working with the Americans in the South Pacific. . . . If
you're interested, I'll send you a note on it."

"Thanks, Steffi, but not today. I have troubles on my
own doorstep." I fished out the salamander card and
handed it to him. "I want a full reading on that: paper,
penmanship, the meaning of the symbol and any prints
you can lift. I want it fast."

Stefanelli studied the card intently for a few moments
and then delivered himself of a peroration.

"The card itself is made from Japanese stock—fine-
quality bonded rice. I can tell you who imports it within
a day. The penmanship—fantastic! So beautiful it makes
you want to cry! I haven't seen anything like it since

Aldo the Calligrapher died in 1935. You remember him, don't you? Of course, you wouldn't. You're too young. Used to have a studio over near the Cancelleria. Made a fortune forging stock certificates and engrossing patents of nobility for fellows who wanted to marry wealthy Americans. . . . Well, Aldo's dead, so he can't help you. We have to go to the files to find who's in practice now. . . . The design? Well . . . it's obviously a salamander, the beast that lives in the fire. What it means here, I don't know. It could be a trademark. It could be a *tessera*— a member's card for a club. It could be adapted from a coat of arms. I'll put it up to Solimbene. . . . You don't know him. Old friend of mine. Works in the Consulta Araldica. Knows every coat of arms in Europe. He can read them like another man would read a newspaper."

"Good idea. In fact, why don't you do some copies now, before the others get back from lunch. I'll need one for my own inquiries anyway.".

"Where did you get this, Colonel?"

"General Pantaleone died last night. I found it in his bedroom."

"Pantaleone? That old *fascista!* What happened to him?"

"Natural causes, Steffi . . . and we've got a notarized certificate to prove it."

"Very convenient!"

"Very necessary."

"Suicide or murder?"

"Suicide."

"Eh! That smells bad."

"So, Steffi, for the present, this business is between you and me, and the Director. Keep the card in your own hands. No files, no discussion in the laboratory. Dead silence until I tell you."

Stefanelli grinned and laid a bony forefinger on his nose—the gesture of knowing and agreeing a conspiracy.

"I don't like Fascists any more than you do, Colonel —and we've got our share of them in this department. Sometimes I wonder if we've got any democrats left—or whether we ever had any in Italy—except you and me.

If we don't get a stable government soon, we'll get a *colpo di stato,* with a fascist in the saddle. The week after that there'll be civil war—or something very like it—Left against Right, North against South. I'm an old man. I can smell it in the wind. . . . And I'm scared, Colonel. I have sons and daughters and grandchildren. I don't want them to suffer as we did . . ."

"Nor I, Steffi. So we have to know who steps into the General's shoes. Get busy on the card. Call me day or night as soon as you have anything."

"Good luck, Colonel."

"I'll need it. . . . *Ciao,* Steffi."

Now I was at a loose end. I could make no sense of the Pantaleone documents until they were listed and collated with the General's dossier. The Director was the only man to whom I could talk freely, and he was out of the office. I could, of course, call on Francesca, the little model who was always available after midday. But that would leave me lulled and dozy for the rest of the afternoon. I settled for a cup of coffee in a bar and then drove out to Parioli to see Lili Anders.

Her apartment was on the third floor of a new condominium, all aluminum and glass, with a porter in livery and an elevator panelled in walnut. The place had cost, according to the lady's dossier, sixty million lire; the upkeep, according to the contract, was a hundred and twenty thousand a month. The fiscal records of the Comune di Roma showed that Lili Anders was taxed on a visible standard of living of a million lire a month. Since she paid the tax without demur, it was obvious she must be living at twice the scale assessed. I was keeping an apartment, a servant, a three-year-old Fiat and an occasional playmate on six hundred thousand a month less taxes and I thought Lili Anders was a very fortunate woman. By the time I came to ring the bell, therefore, I was feeling bad-tempered and resentful. An elderly housekeeper, dressed in black bombazine and starched white linen, confronted me like a true Roman, laconic and hostile:

"Yes?"

"Matucci. Carabinieri. I wish to see the Signora Anders."

"You have an appointment?"

"No."

"Then you'll have to come back later. The Signora is asleep."

"I'm afraid I must ask you to wake her. My business is urgent."

"Do you have any identification?"

I offered my card; she took and read it slowly, line by line, then swept me into the hallway like a pile of dust and left me.

I waited, grim and dyspeptic, but touched with a sour admiration for this ancient matron, whose ancestors had tossed roof tiles on popes and cardinals and puppet princelings. Then Lili Anders made her entrance. For a woman in her middle thirties, she was singularly well-preserved; a little plump for my taste, but still most definitely on the right side of the hill. For a woman who had just been sleeping, she was beautifully turned out: every blond hair in place, no slur in the makeup, no wrinkle in skirt, blouse or stockings. Her greeting was polite but cool.

"You wished to see me?"

"Privately, if that is possible."

She passed me into the salon and closed the door. She prayed me to be seated and then stood herself by the mantel under an equestrian portrait of Pantaleone.

"You are, I believe, from the Carabinieri."

"I am Colonel Matucci."

"And the reason for this visit?"

"A painful matter, I'm afraid."

"Oh?"

"I regret to inform you that General Pantaleone died early this morning."

She did not weep. She did not cry out. She stared at me, wide-eyed and trembling, holding on to the mantel for support. I moved towards her to steady her, but she waved me away. I crossed to the buffet, poured brandy into a goblet and handed it to her. She drank it at a gulp, then gagged on the raw spirit. I gave her the clean handkerchief from my breast pocket and she dabbed at her lips and the front of her blouse. I talked to her, quietly:

"It's always a shock, even in our business. If you want to cry, go ahead."

"I will not cry. He was kind to me and gentle, but I have no tears for him."

"There is something else you should know."

"Yes?"

"He died by his own hand."

She gave no sign of surprise. She simply shrugged and spread her hands in a gesture of defeat. "With him it was always possible."

"Why do you say that?"

"There were too many dark places in his life, Colonel, too many secrets, too many people lying in wait for him."

"Did he tell you that?"

"No. I knew."

"Then perhaps you know this. Why did he choose last night to kill himself? Why not a week ago, or next month?"

"I don't know. He had been moody for a long time, a month or more. I asked him more than once what was troubling him. He always put me off."

"And last night?"

"One thing only. During dinner a waiter brought him a message. Don't ask me what it was. You know the Chess Club—it's like being in church, all whispers and incense. He left me at the table and went outside. He was away about five minutes. When he came back, he told me he had had a telephone call from a colleague. Nothing more was said. Later, when he brought me home, I invited him in. Sometimes he stayed the night, sometimes he didn't. This time he said he had work to finish at home. It was normal. I didn't argue. I was tired myself, anyway."

I took out the photocopy of the salamander card and handed it to her. "Have you seen this before? Or anything like it?"

She studied it intently for a few minutes and then shook her head. "Never."

"Do you recognize the animal?"

"Some kind of lizard . . . a dragon, perhaps."

"The crown?"

"Nothing."

"The words?"

"What they say . . . 'One fine tomorrow, brother' . . . that's all."

"Have you ever heard them before anywhere?"

"Not that I can remember. I'm sorry."

"Please, dear lady! You must in no sense reproach yourself. You have had a grievous shock. You have lost a dear friend. And now—how to say it?—I have to distress you still further. It is my duty to warn you that from this moment you stand in grave personal danger."

"I don't understand."

"Then permit me to explain. You have been for a long time the mistress of an important man, whom certain elements have considered an explosive man. A mistress is presumed to be a confidante, a repository of secrets. Even if the General told you nothing, others will believe he told you everything. Inevitably, therefore, you will come under surveillance, under pressure, possibly even under threat."

"From whom?"

"From extremists of the Right and of the Left, persons who are trained to use violence as a political weapon; from foreign agents operating within the confines of the Republic; even—though I blush to confess it—from officials of our own Public Security. As a foreigner, residing here on a sojourn permit, you are especially vulnerable."

"But I have nothing to tell! I lived a woman's life with a man who needed comfort and affection. His other life, whatever it was, I did not share. When this door closed on us, the world was shut out. He wanted it so. You must believe that."

She was shaken now. Her face seemed to crumple into the contours of middle age. Her hands fumbled restlessly at the balled handkerchief.

I leaned back in the chair and admonished her. "I wish I could believe you. But I know you, Lili Anders. I know you chapter and verse, from your first birthday in Warsaw to your latest dispatch to one Colomba, who is a printer and bookbinder in Milan. You identified yourself, as usual, by the code word *Falcone*. All the members of your network are called by bird names, are they not? You are paid by Canarino from account number 68-Pilau at the cantonal bank in Zurich. . . . You see, Lili, we Italians are not really as stupid or inefficient as we look. We are very good conspirators, because we love the game and we make the rules to suit ourselves. . . . Another brandy? I'll have one myself, if you don't mind. Relax now, I'm not going to eat you. I admire a good professional. But you are a problem, a real problem. . . . *Salute!* To your continued good health!"

She drank, clasping the glass in both hands as if it were a pillar that would support her.

"What happens to me now?"

"Eh! That's a very open question, Lili. As I see it at this moment there are two alternatives. I take you into custody on charges of conspiracy and espionage. That means a long interrogation, a stiff sentence and no hope even of provisory liberty. Or I could leave you free, on certain conditions, to continue your comfortable life in Rome. Which would you prefer?"

"I'm tired of the game, Colonel. I'd like to be out of it. I'm getting too old."

"That's the problem, Lili. You can't get out. You can only change sides."

"Which means?"

"Full information on the network and all your activities, and a contract with us as a double agent."

"Can you protect me?"

"As long as you're useful, yes."

"I was a good mistress, Colonel. I kept my man happy and gave value for money."

"Let's try some more questions then. Who arranged your first meeting with the General?"

"The Marchesa Friuli."

"What is her code name?"

"Pappagallo."

"It suits the old girl. She even looks like a parrot. What was your directive?"

"To give early warning of any attempt at a coup d'état by neo-Fascist groups, and of actions designed to provoke it."

"Such as?"

"Acts of violence planned against the police or Carabinieri during labour demonstrations, bomb attacks that could be attributed to Maoist or Marxist groups, the spread of disaffection among conscripts and new levies in the armed services, any contacts, secret or open, between the Greek regime and officials of the Republic of Italy, shifts of influence or changes of political groups in the Italian High Command."

"Had there been any such changes recently?"

"No . . . at least not to my knowledge."

"Then why was the General depressed?"

"I don't know. I was trying to find out."

"Money problems?"

"I wouldn't think so. . . . He was never a lavish man—even to me."

"Political pressures—blackmail?"

"I had the feeling that it was a personal and not a political matter."

"What gave you that impression?"

"Things he said when he was relaxed here with me."

"For example?"

"Oh, odd remarks. He had a habit of saying something —how would you call it?—something cryptic, then passing immediately to another subject. If I pressed him to explain, he would close up like a shellfish. I learned quickly to hold my tongue. . . . One night, for example, he said: 'There is no simple future for me, Lili, because my past is too complicated.' Another time he quoted from the Bible: 'A man's enemies are those of his own household. . . .' Things like that."

"Anything else?"

"I'm trying to remember . . . Oh, yes, about three

weeks ago we met in Venice. He took me to the opera
at the Phoenix Theater. He talked about the history of
the theater and he explained the name to me. He said
that the phoenix was a fabulous bird that rose again,
alive, from its own ashes; then he said that there was
another animal more fabulous and more dangerous—the
salamander that lived in fire and could survive the hottest
flames. . . . Wait! That's your card . . . the salamander!"

"So it is, Lili. You see how far we come when we talk
like friends? What else did he say about the salamander?"

"Nothing. Nothing at all. Some friends joined us. The
subject was dropped and forgotten."

"Let's leave it then. There will be other times and
other questions. From now on you will be under constant
surveillance. There is my card with day and night numbers. You'll be notified of the date of the funeral. I'd like
you to be there."

"Please, no!"

"Please, yes! I want tears, Lili. I want deep grief and
black mourning. You will not move back into society until
I tell you. Naturally, you will have telephone calls from
your masters and from friends of the General. Your
housekeeper will want to know the reason for my visit.
You will tell them all the same story. The General died
of a heart attack. It would not hurt to confess that he had
an ailment which sometimes interfered with his lovemaking. . . . One other thing. No new boyfriends until
you are out of mourning. That would make an ugly
figure. If you find a live one after that, I'd like to check
him out before you adopt him."

She managed a weak and watery smile. "Him or me,
Colonel?"

"I admire you, Lili, but I can't afford you. If you could
make an old fossil like Pantaleone sit up and beg, God
only knows what you'd do to a hungry fellow like me.
Still, it's a thought to keep. One fine tomorrow we just
might play a little chamber music. Be good now. And
there's a prize for every tear at the requiem. . . . Where's
your telephone?"

Half an hour later I was seated in a glass booth on

the Veneto, with a sandwich and a *cappuccino,* scanning the afternoon editions of the Roman and Milanese papers. The General's death was reported only in the stop press. The terms of each report were identical, a direct quotation of the Army announcement. There were no obituaries, no editorial comments. There might be some in the final editions, but the bloodhounds would not be in full cry until morning. By that time the General would be safely embalmed and lying in state in the family chapel at Frascati, with the cadets of his old regiment standing the death watch.

◆

THE obsequies of Massimo Count Pantaleone, General of the Military Staff, made a splendid piece of theater. The requiem was sung by the suburbicarian Bishop of Frascati, Cardinal Amleto Paolo Dadone, assisted by the choir of the monastery of Sant' Antonio della Valle. The panegyric was delivered, in classic periods and ringing tones, by the Secretary-General of the Society of Jesus, a former classmate of the deceased. The Mass was attended by the President of the Republic, ministers of the Council, members of both chambers, prelates of the Roman Curia, senior officers of all services, representatives of NATO and the diplomatic corps, relatives and friends of the deceased, family retainers, pressmen, photographers and a motley of Romans, countrymen and casual tourists. Six field officers carried the bier to the vault, where the regimental chaplain consigned it to rest until resurrection day, while a detachment of junior officers fired the last volley, and the Penitentiaries of Sant' Ambrogio recited the Sorrowful Mysteries of the Rosary. The door of the vault was closed and locked by the President himself, a gesture of respect, gratitude and national solidarity not lost upon the gentlemen of the press. Lili Anders was there, heavily veiled and leaning on the arm of Captain Girolamo Carpi, who was visibly moved by the passing of his beloved patron.

I was among the mourners, too; but I was less concerned with the ceremonies than the efforts of my camera crew to produce a clear photograph of every person at the funeral, from the Cardinal celebrant to the florist who laid the tributes. I hate funerals. They make me feel old, unwanted and disposed to sexual exercise, which is a kind of defiance of my own imminent mortality. I was glad when the rites were over, so that I could drive down to see Francesca, while my colleagues were still guzzling spumante and sweet pastry at the Villa Pantaleone.

At three-thirty in the afternoon I went back to the forensic laboratory to talk to Stefanelli. The old fellow was jumping like a grasshopper.

". . . I told you, Colonel! Bet with old Steffi and you have to win! I showed the card to Solimbene and he recognized it at first glance. The crowned salamander is the emblem of Francis the First. It recurs, with certain modifications, in arms derived from the House of Orléans, the Duchy of Angoulême and the Farmer family in England. I've retained Solimbene to get us a list of existing Italian families who use the symbol. You'll have to authorize the payment. The pen work? We say it's based on Aldo the Calligrapher but probably executed by Carlo Metaponte, who used to be a forger, made papers for the partisans during the war and has been going straight ever since. The card itself . . . I was wrong about that. It's not Japanese at all. It's a very passable Italian imitation made in Modena by the Casaroli Brothers. They're supplying us with a list of their principal customers in Europe. The inscription makes no sense yet, but we're coming to it. How's that, eh? Not bad for forty-eight hours. Tell me you're happy, Colonel, otherwise I'll drown myself in the toilet."

"I'm happy, Steffi. But we need a lot more. Fingerprints, for instance."

"I'm sorry, Colonel. The only ones we've been able to lift belong to the late lamented General. You didn't expect anything else, surely?"

"I want miracles, Steffi. I want them yesterday."

"Spare us a little pity, Colonel. Everything takes time.
. . . How was the funeral?"

"Beautiful, Steffi. I cried all through it! And the eloquence! . . . 'That noble spirit snatched untimely from
among us, that dedicated servant of the Republic, that
Christian patriot, that hero of many battles . . .' *Merda!*"

"*Requiescat in aeternum.*" Stefanelli crossed his hands
on his bony chest and rolled his eyes heavenwards. "If
he's in heaven, I hope never to go there. Amen! . . . Have
you read today's papers?"

"Now, when have I had time to read, Steffi?"

"I've got them in my office. Come on! They're worth a
look."

The obituaries were, like the obsequies, an exercise in
grandiloquence. The right wing was fulsome; the center
was respectful and only mildly censorious of the General's
Fascist period; the left achieved a kind of poetry of
abuse, culminating in a pasquinade, which for form's sake
was attributed to some anonymous Roman:

Estirpato oggi,	Uprooted today,
L'ultimo della stirpe,	The last of his line,
Pantaleone,	Pantaleone,
Mascalzone.	The rogue.

I was not unhappy with the things I read. They were
good reviews for a bad score and a book full of contradictions. Not one of them called in question the official
version of the General's demise, which was not to say
they believed it but only that it suited all parties to accept
it. The pasquinade worried me a little. Take it at face
value and it was a harmless squib. The General was
the last of the Pantaleone line, and an old rogue to boot.
Read it another way and it might mean that the Left had
taken a hand in rooting him out and that happily no
successor was in sight. If one were very subtle—and I
was paid to read meaning even into blank pages—one
might see it as the opening gambit of a campaign to villify
the General and bring all the skeletons out of his family
vault. A pity if it happened, but there was nothing I could

do about it. I was still drowsy and disinclined to exert myself, so I began leafing through the journals, while Stefanelli added a spicy commentary.

". . . Now, here's a pretty thing: 'The Principessa Faubiani presents her summer collection!' You know about her, don't you? Came from Argentina originally, married young Prince Faubiani, set him up with a boyfriend and then petitioned for separation on the grounds of his impotence. That way she kept her freedom, the title and a right to maintenance. Since then, she's had a new protector every couple of years—old ones now, and all rich. They finance the collections and improve her standard of living as well. That last one was the banker, Castellani. . . . Wonder who it is this year? Funny thing, she still stays friends with them all. See, there's Castellani, next to the model in the bikini. Ah, there's the new one, in the front row, between Faubiani and the editor of *Vogue*. That's the place of honour. Ritual, you know. When the High Priestess gets tired of you, she hands you down to the models. Still, if you're sixty or over, who cares? The girls come cheaper than a whole summer collection, eh? I must find out who the new one is."

"And what's your interest in fashion, Steffi?"

"My wife has a boutique on the Via Sistina . . . high mode for rich tourists."

"You crafty old devil!"

"I'm a lucky man, Colonel. I married for love and got money for my old age as well. Also the staff is decorative and the gossip's always interesting. . . . Which reminds me—Pantaleone is supposed to have a brother floating around somewhere."

"Not in my dossier, Steffi. The old count, Massimo, had two daughters in the first three years of his marriage and a son about ten years later. One daughter married a Contini and died in childbirth. The other married a Spanish diplomat and lives in Bolivia. She has three adult children who all have Spanish nationality. The son, our General, was the only male issue. He inherited the title and the bulk of the real estate. That's the record, verified at Central Registry and from the baptismal files at Frascati."

"Well, I agree she's not as official as the Central Registry, but the old Baroness Schwarzburg has been a client of my wife's for years. She's tottering on the edge of the grave, but she still spends a fortune on clothes. She claims she knew the General's father—which is very possible, because the old boy was chasing girls until the day he fell off his horse on the Pincio and broke his neck. According to her story, the Count bred himself a bastard from the girls' governess. He paid her off and she married someone else who gave the boy a name, though what the name was the Baroness couldn't remember. She's getting doddery, of course, so it could be nothing but scandalous rumour. You know what these old girls are. They've never got over their first waltz and the time Vittorio Emanuele III showed them his coin collection. . . . Anyway, it's a note in the margin, if you're interested."

"Not really, Steffi. Now, if you could find me a suicide note or a blackmail letter that would tell me why Pantaleone killed himself, I'd be much happier. ; . . . *Dio!* It's nearly five. The funeral photographs should be ready. If they're not, I'll send you three heads for pickling. See you later, Steffi. Keep in touch."

Naturally enough, the photographs were not ready, and the Chief of Photographic Records was liverish and unhappy. Everyone understood the urgency, but I must be reasonable. Could I not see that the tanks were clogged with film, the enlargers were working overtime, and even with three photographers and two photo-file experts, it would take hours yet to identify all the personages? Even then there would be gaps. This was like an epic at Cinecittà, the whole set crowded with hundreds of extras— and how did one put names to farm labourers and three busloads of tourists?

After ten minutes of snappish dialogue, I gave up in disgust and went back to my own office. Here, at least, there was a semblance of order and efficiency. The documents I had brought from the General's flat were all indexed and filed, and number one clerk had made some interesting discoveries.

"Brokers' advice notes, Colonel. All sales. The General has unloaded about eighty million lire worth of prime stock in the last four weeks. Covering letters from the brokers, each one in the same terms: 'We have remitted proceeds in accordance with your instructions.' Question: Where did the proceeds go? Not into his bank, because there's his last statement, issued a week ago. Then there's a letter from the Agenzia Immobiliare della Romagna. They advise that though the Pantaleone property has been on open offer for more than two months, there has been no serious interest at the figure named. They recommend withdrawing the property until the credit situation in Europe eases a little and the new agricultural agreements have been announced for the Common Market. . . . Now come to this little piece. It's a handwritten note from Emilio del Giudice in Florence. You know him; a big name, a heavy dealer in important artwork. Here's what he says: 'Strongly advise against any transactions which involve you personally in a commitment to export works from the Pantaleone collection. As vendor you offer the works for sale subject to the conditions of the laws in force. After that, full responsibility for export formalities rests on the purchaser . . .'"

"So, he was trying to sell up. Any indication why?"

"Not in these papers."

"What else have we got?"

"Check stubs, household accounts, bank statements, correspondence with estate managers and renting agencies, desk directory, pocket address book. I'm still checking those against the names in our dossiers, and so far, no surprises. This is the General's key ring with a key to a safe-deposit box at the Banco di Roma. I'd like to see the inside of that."

"We will—as soon as the banks open in the morning."

"His lawyer is howling for us to release the documents."

"I'll worry about him later. I'll also have a chat with the General's brokers. I'd like to know where they remitted the sale money. . . . If you want me in the next hour, I'll be at the Chess Club. After that, at home."

❧ ☙

THE Chess Club of Rome is an institution almost as sacred as the Hunt Club. You enter it, as you hope one day to enter heaven, through a noble portico and find yourself in a courtyard of classic dimension. You climb a flight of stairs to a series of anterooms, where servants in livery receive you with cautious deference. You tread softly and speak in muted tones, so as not to disturb the ghosts who still inhabit the place, kings and princes, dukes, barons, counts and all their consorts. In the salon you are dwarfed by soaring pilasters and frescoed ceilings and gilt furniture designed for the backsides of grandees. In the dining room you are awed by an afflatus of whispers, the talk of men who deal with great affairs like money and statecraft and spheres of commercial influence. You are daunted by the cold eyes of dowagers, sour with the virtue of age. You are hounded by waiters so disciplined that even a crumb upon the shirtfront seems a sacrilege. . . . And you will look in vain for chess players, although it is rumoured that they do exist, cloistered as Carmelites in some secret cell.

I was not coming to play chess. I was coming to wait upon the secretary, who might condescend to present me to the headwaiter, who might, if the stars were in favourable conjunction, put me in touch with the steward who had served General Pantaleone on the eve of his death.

I did not relish the prospect. The Chess Club is one of those places that makes me despair of my countrymen. In the uplands of Sardinia, where I once served as a junior officer, there are shepherds who live a whole winter on cornbread and black olives and goat cheese, and turn to banditry to feed their families, while their landlords lobby senators and ministers over brandy in the Club. In the mortuary at Palermo I have identified the body of a colleague murdered by the Mafia, while the man who ordered him killed was lunching with a Milanese banker

—at the Chess Club, of course. The economists weep
tears of blood over the flight of capital from Italy to
Switzerland, but the men who put wings to the money
sit sober and respectable over lunch at the corner table.
Here, the survivors of the old order and the exploiters
of the new make truce and treaty and marriages of con-
venience, while the people, poor, ill-educated, impotent,
fume at the chicanery of politicians and the tyranny of
petty bureaucrats.

Time was when I toyed with the idea of joining the
Communists, who promised at least a levelling and a
purging and one law for all. My enthusiasm died on the
day when I saw a high Party official sharing smoked
salmon and fillet steaks with the president of a large
chemical corporation. The more things change in Italy,
the more they are the same. The scion of an old house
joins the Christian Democrats; the cadet is free to flirt
with Left or Right; and no matter who wins the last race,
the bets will still be settled in the Chess Club. . . . Eh!
Philosophers are as big a curse on the country as politicos,
and a muddled conscience is bad medicine for an investigator. Let's be done with the job and go home!

It was still only eight-thirty and the guests were sparse.
The secretary was unusually urbane and the headwaiter
was disposed to be helpful. He installed me in the visitors'
room, brought me an aperitif and, five minutes later, re-
appeared with the head porter and the steward who had
served the General's last meal. I explained my mission
with suitable vagueness. Sometime during dinner the General had been called to the telephone. For reasons connected with military security, I wished to trace the call
and contact the person who had made it. Then I had my
first surprise.

"No, Colonel." The head porter was very definite.
"You have been misinformed. The General was called
from the dining room, but not to the telephone. A senior
member of the Club had asked to speak with him in
private. He waited in the cardroom. The steward conducted the General to him. They spoke for a few mo-

ments, the General returned to his table, the member collected his coat and left the Club. I saw him leave."

"And who was this member?"

"A gentleman from Bologna. The Cavaliere Bruno Manzini. He's in the Club now. Came in about twenty minutes ago with the Principessa Faubiani."

"La Faubiani, eh?" I permitted myself a small grin of satisfaction. At least I was one up on old Steffi.

The head porter coughed eloquently. "Colonel. . . ?"

"Could you tell me something about the Cavaliere?"

"I could, sir, but—with respect—that sort of request should be addressed to the secretary."

"Of course. My compliments on your discretion. Would you give the Cavaliere my card and ask him to spare me a few moments?"

In any company the Cavaliere Manzini would have been an impressive figure. He must have been nearly seventy years old; his hair was snow-white, brushed back in a lion's mane over his coat collar; but his back was straight as a pine, his skin was clear, his eyes bright and humorous. His clothes were modish, his linen immaculate and he carried himself with the air of a man accustomed to deference. He did not offer his hand but announced himself with calm formality.

"I am Manzini. I understand you wished to see me. May I see your official identification?"

I handed him the document. He read it carefully, passed it back and then sat down. "Thank you, Colonel. Now, your question."

"You were, I believe, a friend of General Pantaleone?"

"Not a friend, Colonel, an acquaintance. I had small respect for him, none at all for his politics."

"How would you define his politics?"

"Fascist and opportunist."

"And your own?"

"Are private to myself, Colonel."

"On the night before he died, the General dined here with a lady. I understand you had a conversation with him."

"I did."

"May I know the substance of it?"

"Certainly. I am the client of an art dealer in Florence. His name is del Giudice. He had told me that Pantaleone was about to sell the family collection. I was interested in certain items, an Andrea del Sarto and a Bosch. I told Pantaleone I would like to negotiate with him directly. It would save us both money."

"And. . .?"

"He said he would think about it and write to me soon."

"You didn't press him for a date?"

"No. I could always buy through del Giudice. May I know the reason for these inquiries?"

"At this moment, sir, I am not at liberty to disclose it. Another question. The Pantaleone collection is an old and important one. Why would the General want to disperse it?"

"I have no idea."

"May I ask you to keep this conversation private?"

"No, you may not! I did not invite it. I gave no prior promise of secrecy. I stand upon my right to discuss it or not, as I please—and with whom I please."

"Cavaliere, you know the organization which I represent?"

"The Service of Defense Information? I know of its existence. I am not familiar with its activities."

"You know, at least, that we deal with highly sensitive matters, both political and military."

"My dear Colonel, please! I'm an old man. I lost my milk teeth years ago. I have no taste for spies, provocateurs or those who treat with them. I know that intelligence services can become instruments of tyranny. I know that they tend to corrupt the people who work in them. If you have no more questions, I trust that you will excuse me. . . . Good evening!"

He stalked out of the room, stiff as a grenadier, and I let out a long exhalation of relief. This was a sturdy one for a change, hard to coax, impossible to frighten. He looked you straight in the eye and gave you clean answers crack-crack-crack, knowing that you dared not gainsay him. But there were important questions still open. Why would Pantaleone, with suicide on his mind, engage in the long and tedious business of selling an estate? If he did embark on it, why not complete it? And why promise a letter he knew he would never write?

Boh! It was enough for one day and more than enough. My head was full of cotton wool and my heart full of envy for a seventy-year-old Cavaliere who could afford expensive pets like the Principessa Faubiani. I walked out of the Club into a soft spring rain, prised my car out of the courtyard and drove reluctantly homeward to a hot dinner, a tepid hour of television and a cold bed afterwards.

In fact, I had a very troubled night. Shortly after ten a colleague from Milan telephoned with the news that a young Maoist under questioning in a bomb case had fallen to his death from the window of the interrogation room. There would be headlines in every morning paper. The Left would swear he had been pushed. The Right would affirm that he had jumped. Either way, they had a martyr on their hands. My colleague was evasive, but when he mentioned the name of the interrogator, I knew the truth. The man was a sadist, a rabid idiot who didn't care how he got his evidence or where he made it stick. He also had friends in high places who would spray him with rose water at any inquiry. This was the kind of madness that bedevilled the whole country and brought the police and the judicial system into disrepute. There would be troops on every street corner for a week and this, too, would heighten the tension and polarize the factions, the one crying tyranny and repression, the other shouting law and order and an end to anarchy. *Dio!* What a nightmare mess! If I had any sense I should pack my bags and take the next boat to Australia.

At eleven-thirty Lili Anders telephoned in panic. Her network contact had called and summoned her to a rendezvous at the Osteria dell'Orso. She was due there at midnight. What should she do? I told her to keep the rendezvous, rehearsed her three times in her story and then spent an anxious fifteen minutes trying to regroup my surveillance team.

I was just about to crawl into bed when the telephone rang again. This time it was Captain Carpi's shadow. The Captain was drunk and mumbling darkly to a bar girl at the Tour Hassan. What did I want done about it? For God's sake! Let him drink himself silly on bad champagne. The girls at the Tour Hassan wouldn't leave anyway until four in the morning. After that, if Carpi was still on his feet—or even if he wasn't—bundle him into a taxi and take him home. . . . Expenses? Have them put the drinks on Carpi's bill. They'd be padding it anyway. Good night and the devil take the pair of you!

∽§ §∾

At nine-thirty next morning I sat in conference with a senior official of the Banco di Roma. He was courteous but very firm. There could be no access to the late General's safe deposit until every judicial requirement was met. He understood perfectly my position. He was sensible that matters of national security were involved. However, they were equally involved in his own case. The bank was a national institution. Public confidence depended on the rigid performance of contracts between banker and client. The law demanded it. The Carabinieri were servants of the law. Besides——he paused before delivering the coup de grace—the strongbox was empty. The General's lawyer had taken possession of its contents under an existing authority. I acknowledged defeat and went to see the General's brokers.

The brokers, an affiliate of a large American house, were much more cooperative. They had remitted the proceeds, under instruction, to the General's legal representative, Avvocato Sergio Bandinelli. So far as they were concerned, the transaction was closed at that point. They had no information as to the ultimate disposition of the funds. They were brokers only. They offered market advice under the normal disclaimers. They bought and sold under instruction. They functioned rigidly within the prevailing laws. End of conference.

Back in my office, I signed an *invito* requesting Avvocato Sergio Bandinelli to wait on me within forty-eight hours. Then I spread the funeral photographs on the desk and settled down to examine them minutely against the accompanying checklist. It was not the names or the personages which interested me so much as the juxtapositions: who was talking to whom, which group seemed the most cohesive and intimate. Sometimes, in a crush like that, public enemies were revealed as secret allies. Sometimes, by a thousand-to-one chance, one saw a sign given or a message passed from hand to hand. At the end of an hour I was left with one small surprise.

The surprise was the Cavaliere Manzini, the old autocrat from the Chess Club. He appeared in three shots, once talking to Cardinal Dadone, once with the Minister of Finance and the third time, a little removed from the cemetery vault, standing beside an elderly peasant who was listed as employed at the Villa Pantaleone. For a man who had small respect for Pantaleone, who regarded him as a fascist and an opportunist, it was a singular gesture. I wondered why he had troubled to make it. I made a telephone call to a colleague in Bologna and asked that a copy of the Cavaliere's dossier be sent posthaste to Rome. Then I called the laboratory and summoned Stefanelli to a private talk.

Old Steffi was bursting with news, little of it good. First, his wife had told him that the new protector of the Principessa Faubiani was one Bruno Manzini, a Bolognese, richer than anyone had a right to be—big enterprises, textiles, electrics, steel, food processing. Eat any pie you liked, Manzini owned a slice of it.

"I know all that, Steffi."

"The hell you do? How?"

I told him at length and in detail. Then I spread the photographs on the desk.

"Now, tell me, Steffi. What's he doing at the funeral of a man he disliked and despised?"

"Easy, my friend. The Club. Members may not like each other, but they don't insult each other either. You may not like me, but you'll come to bury me, won't you? How else can you be sure I'm dead?"

"Maybe . . . maybe. . . . What else have you got for me?"

"The Casaroli Brothers sell rice paper to wholesalers only, one in each province of Italy. The wholesalers sell to retail printers and stationers. That's the list of the wholesalers. The retailers will run into hundreds, possibly thousands."

"Body of Bacchus! Don't you have any good news, Steffi?"

"Solimbene called me from the Consulta Araldica. He'll have his list ready tomorrow morning. So far he's found fifteen surviving families in Italy who use the salamander in their coat of arms. Another paper chase, I'm afraid. . . . Did you read the headlines this morning?"

"I did."

"I'm scared, Colonel. When the police look like gangsters . . ."

"Or are made to look like gangsters, Steffi."

"Either way, there's trouble ahead. They had two thousand Carabinieri on the streets of Milan this morning. And there's another thousand on extra duty in Rome to say nothing of Turin and down south in Reggio. Right now we've got the country clamped down tight—but we're not curing anything, we're not reorganizing anything."

"It's not our job, Steffi. We're an arm of government —but we're not the Government itself."

"We don't have a government, friend. We have parties, factions, warring interests, and the man in the street doesn't know where to turn. Who represents the Government to him? A cop who walks away from a traffic jam; some little clerk in the pensions office who slams a window in his face. If things don't change soon, our man in the street is going to start shouting for a leader . . . a new *Duce!*"

"And who would that be, Steffi? Go on, toss me names! Pantaleone's dead. He's offstage. Who enters next —and from where—left, right or center? That's what I'm trying to find out."

"And when you do?"

"Say it, Steffi . . ."

"You buried an embarrassing corpse yesterday—under orders. Suppose you stumble on another embarrassment, a live one this time—a man in our own service, for example. Suppose you're ordered then to close the file and keep your mouth shut. What will you do? Tell me honestly, friend to friend."

"Steffi, I'm damned if I know. Old Manzini was right. This trade corrupts people. I know it's corrupted me; I don't like to ask how much."

"You may have to ask very soon, Colonel. Look! Last night in Milan a suspect under questioning jumped or was pushed from a window. He's dead now. He can't be brought to trial. Nobody else can, either. You and I are guardians of public security. What do we do? What does the whole service do? We absolve ourselves. Why? Because we can put ten, twenty thousand armed men in the streets to keep the people cowed and stifle the questions. Who are the real rulers of Milan at this very moment? The Government? Hell! We are—the Carabinieri and our colleagues of the police. That's a tempting blueprint, you know. Terribly tempting. We don't have to offer bread and circuses anymore; just public order, peace in the streets and the buses running on time. I told you I'm scared. Now I'll tell you why. I'm a Jew, Colonel. You didn't know that? Well, here and now, it doesn't pay to advertise the fact. I live over behind the synagogue in the old ghetto. In the synagogue we've got a list of names, three hundred men, eight hundred women and children. They were shipped out of Rome to Auschwitz on the Black Sabbath of 1943. After the war fifteen came back. Fourteen men and a woman. Do you know why I joined the Service? So that I'd know in advance if it were ever going to happen again. . . . How old are you, Colonel?"

"Forty-two. Why?"

"You were a boy when it happened. But every time I see an election poster now, I get nightmares. I'm sorry if I've offended you."

"You haven't, Steffi. I'm glad you told me. Now, why don't you go play with your microscope, eh?"

When the old man had gone, I sat a long time staring at the littered desk, the photographs, the memoranda, the tapes recorded last night in the Osteria dell'Orso. Suddenly, it all seemed irrelevant, trivial to the point of absurdity. What was at issue was not politics, not power games and the sordid ploys of espionage, but myself, Dante Alighieri Matucci, who I was, what I believed and what price I would accept for my soul—if indeed I had one.

To be a servant of the State was easy. The State was like God. You couldn't define it. Therefore you didn't have to ask questions about it. You didn't even have to believe that it existed. You had only to act as if you did. This was the difference between the Anglo-Saxon and the Mediterraneans. For the Anglo-Saxon, the State was the people. Parliament was its voice. The bureaucracy was its executive. For the Latin, the State was the *res publica* —the public thing that had little, if anything, to do with people. The Latin, therefore, was always in an attitude of defense against the State, of opposition to its directives, of compromise with its exactions. The policeman was not his servant, but the factor of his master. In England they called their bureaucrats "public servants." In Italy they were *"funzionari,"* functionaries of the impersonal State.

But I, Dante Alighieri Matucci, was a person—or hoped I was. How much of me did the State own? How far could it legitimately direct me? To toss a living man out of a window? To shoot a rioter? To stifle a citizen with papers so that he couldn't even piss without a permit? And then there was the other side of the coin: fifty million people locked in a narrow peninsula, poor in resources, rich only in sap and energy, turbulent in spirit, easy prey to demagogues and agitators. How did you stop them tearing each other to pieces if you didn't break a few heads from time to time? It was all too easy to live underground like a mole nibbling at the roots of other people's lives, never caring to stick your dirty snout into the sunlight. . . .

I was still chewing on that sour thought when the boys from the surveillance team presented themselves to report on Lili Anders. Their tapes of the nightclub meeting were almost unintelligible. I wanted to know why.

"No time to plant anything effective, Colonel. A crowded nightclub, haphazard table placement, half an hour's notice . . . no chance. Anyway, they only stayed half an hour. We followed them back to Anders' apartment. The contact dropped her there and drove off. Giorgio followed him. I stayed to get a report from the lady."

"Who was the contact?"

"Picchio . . . the woodpecker."

"What did sweet Lili have to say for herself?"

"I've got it here: Woodpecker asked what the General died of? She replied a heart attack. Had she known he was sick? No, but he did have occasional chest pains that he called indigestion."

"Good for Lili. Go on."

"Who brought her the news? A colonel of Carabinieri. What was his name? Matucci. Why a full colonel? She didn't know. She'd been wondering. How long had he stayed? Twenty minutes, half an hour. She'd been upset. The Colonel had been kind. Had he asked any significant questions? Only about Pantaleone's movements and contacts on the night of his death. She had told him the truth, there was nothing to hide. Woodpecker asked who were the General's heirs. She didn't know. She had never seen his will. Did she know the General's lawyer? Yes. Was she friendly with him? Reasonably. Then she was ordered to cultivate his acquaintance and if possible his friendship, and find out all the things she could about the General's estate. Had she ever met a Major-General Leporello?"

"He's one of ours, for God's sake."

"It shook me a little, too, Colonel."

"What did Lili say?"

"She'd never met him. Had the General ever spoken of him? No. At least not that she remembered. What would her next assignment be? Sit tight, concentrate on the lawyer, await further contact and instructions. . . .

Fade out, *fine*. That's it, Colonel. . . . And, by the way, I didn't get to bed until three in the morning."

"Poor fellow! I hope you slept well and chastely. Anything from Lili's phone tap?"

"Nothing since her call to you, Colonel."

"Good. . . . Now, let's hear about our little Captain Carpi."

"Nothing to tell, Colonel. He passed out cold about three in the morning. I paid the girl and the drink bill from his wallet and then took him home. He's a bad drunk, Colonel."

"That's something new. Anyway, he's off to Sardinia tomorrow. That should sober him up. Thank you, gentlemen. You may now resume your sleep. Make sure you're fresh and sharp by eight this evening. You're still on night roster. . . ."

They slouched out, bleary-eyed and grumbling, and I grinned at their discomfiture. This was what the Americans called the name of the game. You walked your feet off. You knocked on doors. You stood watch on street corners and cruised round smoky clubs. You waded through reams and reams of useless information until you came up with one fragment of fact that began or completed a whole mosaic. I had one now: why was Woodpecker, a Polish agent, interested in Marcantonio Leporello, Major-General of the Carabinieri?

❧ ❦

As an investigator I have many shortcomings and two special talents. The first is a photographic memory. The second is that I know how to wait. Comes a moment in every investigation when there is nothing to do except wait and let the chemistry of the case work itself out. If you try to hurry the process, to satisfy yourself or a superior, you make mistakes. You accept false premises, create fictional logic. You harry your operatives so that they make myopic observations and give you half-answers to keep you happy. You snatch at facile solutions and come up with a handful of smoke.

The Italians love bustle and brouhaha. Sketch them a scene and they will build you an opera inside an hour. They are glib; they are dilatory; they are evasive. They hate to commit themselves to either an opinion or an alliance, lest tomorrow they be held to the consequences. They would rather lose a tooth than sign a binding document. I am a colonel at forty-two because I have learned to make a virtue out of the vices of my countrymen.

The Minister of the Interior wanted action? He got it, scored for brass and tympani. NATO needed a spy scare to tighten up security? *Bene!* There were twenty scripts to choose from and authentic villains to fit them. There was a stink over a procurement contract? For that, too, there was a magic formula: sabotage by enemy agents, at source, in transit, or on delivery site. But when a big thing came up, the trick was to create a zone of quiet and sit there, visible but enigmatic, digesting the facts in hand, calm as a Buddha waiting for the next turn of the wheel of life. It was a tactic that disconcerted many of my colleagues and irritated some of my superiors; but, most times, it worked—with a little sleight of hand to help the illusion.

At that moment in time the Pantaleone affair was in suspense. The meaning of the salamander card was not yet deciphered. The General's papers and his money were in the hands of his lawyer, who would probably wait until the last moment before he answered the *invito* and then stand pat on legal privilege. The man at the funeral might mean nothing. The Cavaliere Manzini was simply a buyer of expensive art. There was nothing yet from the heraldic expert. Nothing . . . nothing . . . nothing. Except that a Polish agent named Woodpecker was interested in Major-General Leporello. It seemed an appropriate time to have a chat with the Director.

The Director of the Defense Information Service was a character in his own right. He was related on his mother's side to the Caracciolo of Naples and on his father's to the Morosini of Venice. In the Service they called him Volpone—the old fox. I had another name for him: Camaleonte, the chameleon. One moment you saw him plain,

the next you had lost him against the political under-
growth. He had the manners of a prince and the mind
of a chess player. He had a sense of history and a conviction that it always repeated itself. He was an ironist in
eight languages and had made conquests in all of them.
He played tennis, sailed a keelboat, collected primitive
art and was a devotee of chamber music, in which he
sometimes played viola. He was inordinately rich, generous to those he liked and ruthless as a public executioner
to those he did not. He insisted that I, Dante Alighieri
Matucci, was one of those he liked, one of the few he
respected. We had clashed often. He had tempted me
more than once, but I had sniffed at the bait and turned
away from it with a grin and a shrug. I made no secret of
my weaknesses, but I was damned if I could be blackmailed with them, by the Director or anyone else. And if
the Director wanted to play games, I had a few of my
own, with rather complicated rules.

I was playing one now. Major-General Leporello was
a big man in the Carabinieri. I wanted to know whether
the Director was big enough to handle him if ever there
were a need. So, without ceremony, I put the question:

"Woodpecker is interested in Leporello. Why?"

The Director was instantly alert, the old fox sniffing
a hostile air. He said evenly:

"Isn't it your job to tell me?"

"No, sir, not yet. Leporello's dossier is marked 'Reserved to Director.' "

"Forgive me, I'd forgotten. Let me see now. General
Leporello has spent the last five months abroad."

"Where?"

"Japan, Vietnam, South Africa, Brazil, the United
States, Great Britain, Greece, France."

"Who paid the fare?"

"The tour was official. The General was on a study
mission."

"Studying what?"

"Riot control and counter-insurgency."

"Do you know the General personally, sir?"

"Yes. He's a sound man."

"Vulnerable?"

"He's a patriot, a devout Catholic, a Christian Democrat and financially independent. I doubt he could be bought or frightened."

"Attacked? Assassinated?"

"Possibly."

"Seduced?"

"By what, Colonel?"

"The ultimate infirmity—ambition."

"For example. . .?"

"The man who devises the strategy of counterrevolution might decide to put it into practice on his own account . . . or on account of a potent minority."

"Any evidence?"

"Indications only. Woodpecker and his network have a commission which I quote: '. . . to give early warning of any attempt at a *colpo di stato* by neofascist groups, or of factions designed to provoke it.' If Woodpecker is interested in Leporello, we have to be interested, too."

"You're in unicorn country, Matucci."

"Half our lives we deal with fables. Sometimes the fables come true."

"In Leporello's case, I think not. However, let me play with the idea. I'll come back to you. For the moment, no action."

"Yes, sir."

"Anything else?"

"No, sir."

"Then permit me to offer you a compliment. I like your attitude to your work, careful and open-minded. That's rare, necessary, too, in these times."

"You are kind, sir. Thank you."

"Until later then."

I walked out a very pensive man. If the Director was scared, everybody else should be running for cover. If the Director was committed to a cause or a compromise, nothing would divert him but a bullet in the head. He was the perfect *cinquecento* man, with a confessor at his right hand and a poet on his left, while his enemies rotted, howling, in the dungeons beneath his feet. I was named

for a poet and needed a confessor; but I had no slightest
wish to end my days in the dungeons of official disfavor.
And yet . . . and yet . . . A man who could control rioters
and urban guerrillas might, one fine tomorrow, control
the country, especially if he were a patriot, a good Christian, and didn't have to worry about his rent or his
dinner.

I was hardly back in my office when my secretary announced that Avvocato Sergio Bandinelli had answered
my *invito* and was waiting to see me.

The advocate was short, fussy and very irascible. I
debated for a moment whether to play the bureaucrat or
the gentleman, and then decided to smother him with
courtesy. I regretted the need to disturb a busy man. I
was grateful for so prompt a response. I trusted to dispose
quickly of the few matters in question. I understood the
relationship between advocate and client. It was my duty
to protect that relationship and to discourage any breach
of it. However . . .

". . . In cases where national security is involved,
Avvocato, we both need to be slightly more flexible. I
am sure you understand."

"No, Colonel, I do not. I am here to protest the illegal
seizure of my client's papers and to require their immediate delivery into my hands."

"No problem at all. You may take the papers with you
when you leave. As for the protest, what's the profit? The
Defense Information Service works under presidential
directive and to rather special rules. Of course, if you
wish to press a complaint . . ."

"Well . . . under the circumstances . . ."

"Good! I am encouraged now to take you into our confidence, to solicit your assistance in a matter of importance."

"I am happy to assist, Colonel, provided I may reserve
my position in the event of conflict of interest."

"Of course. Let us proceed then. General Pantaleone
was an important man. His death has political consequences. I am directed to study those consequences. I am
interested, therefore, in every aspect of the General's acti-

vities. He was, for example, engaged in liquidating his estate, selling shares, preparing to disperse his art collection. Why?"

"I am not at liberty to say."

"His brokers inform us that the proceeds of his shares were transmitted to you. What were you directed to do with the money?"

"I cannot tell you that, either."

"I am afraid you must."

"No, Colonel. Legal privilege."

"Before you invoke it, let me tell you something else. Your late client maintained relations with a member of a foreign espionage network."

"I don't believe it."

"It's true, nevertheless. You yourself are under surveillance by the same network."

"Is this some kind of threat, Colonel?"

"No threat, Avvocato, a statement of fact. So . . . when you refuse to disclose what has happened to large sums of money, you put yourself in some jeopardy. Crime is involved, a threat to the security of the State. Your client is dead. You are answerable for your part in his affairs. So, I ask you again, what happened to the money?"

"I was instructed to reinvest it."

"Where?"

"Abroad. In Switzerland and in Brazil for the most part."

"And if the art collection had been sold, and the land?"

"The same instruction applied."

"Such export of funds requires approval from the Ministry of Finance. Did you have it?"

"Well, no . . . but the nature of the transaction . . ."

"Don't tell me, Avvocato. The transaction would involve intermediaries who have safe channels for currency export. They charge five percent for their services. For this, they guarantee immunity to the client. It's an old story. It doesn't hold water and you know it. You can be charged with conspiracy to circumvent the law. You're lucky I'm an intelligence investigator and not a policeman . . . But I can change my hat any moment I choose. So talk, Avvocato! Don't play children's games! . . . Why was Pantaleone exporting funds?"

"In sum, he was afraid. He had joined himself with the new fascists as their military adviser and as commander in chief in case of a *colpo di stato*. Their provocative tactics worried him. He felt they were not strong enough to risk a *colpo di stato* and that, if they tried, it would lead to civil war. All the strength of the Movement is in the South. In the North, the Left is in control and far better organized. So the Movement began to lose faith in Pantaleone. They wanted to move him out in favor of a bolder man."

"Who?"

"I don't know."

"Did Pantaleone know?"

"No. All he knew was that it was someone who was not in the Movement but who might be attracted into it when the time was right."

"A military man?"

"Obviously. If they were provoking a disturbance, they had to be able to offer military actions to suppress it. That's the whole point of provocation, no?"

"So, the General was frightened. Of a rival or of something else?"

"Of action against himself."

"What sort of action?"

"I don't know."

"Then guess."

"Damage to his reputation. Some kind of revelation of his past."

"Blackmail, in fact?"

"Yes. He had a checkered career and many enemies."

"Had he received any direct threats?"

"Well . . . in a legal sense, no."

"In common sense, Avvocato?"

"About a week ago he received a communication by messenger."

"What sort of communication?"

"It consisted of a very complete and accurate biography which, if it had even been published, would have damaged his reputation beyond repair and banished him forever from public life."

"He showed it to you?"

"Yes. He asked whether there might be any defense against publication or any means of tracing the author. I advised him there was not . . . at least not without risk of spreading the information dangerously."

"But a threat of publication was made?"

"I read it so."

"Read what?"

"A card, attached to the typescript."

I laid the salamander card on the table before him. "This card?"

The advocate picked it up gingerly, examined it and agreed. "Yes, that's the one. Where did you get it?"

"I found it in the General's bedroom. What happened to the biography?"

"He lodged it in his strongbox at the bank."

"Which you emptied yesterday."

"Yes."

"I want it. I want all his documents."

"I'll give them to you, happily—on a judge's order. Without it, no."

"This card, Avvocato, what does it signify?"

"To me, nothing."

"What did it signify to the General?"

"I can only tell you what he said."

"Yes?"

"He was a taciturn man, given to aphorisms. He said, 'Well, Saint Martin's day at last.' "

"And what the devil was that supposed to mean?"

"He wouldn't explain it. He never did. I puzzled over it for a long time; then I found the reference. It's in *Don Quixote:* 'To every pig comes Saint Martin's day.' In Spain, pigs are usually killed on the feast of Saint Martin."

"Avvocato Bandinelli, I am sure you are a very good advocate. You never tell a lie. You simply bury the part of the truth that really matters and the law protects you while you do it. However, you've stepped outside the law and put yourself and your privilege in jeopardy. You can fight me, of course. You can delay me, by tactics and quibbles, but your Saint Martin's day will come in the end. If you want to avoid it, I'm prepared to make a bargain with you. I'll forget the currency question. I'll send a man with you now to assemble every paper you hold on the Pantaleone family. He will list the papers, then lock and seal them in your safe. Tomorrow I will come to your office and go through them with you. That way you keep your privilege and I get the information I want. Agreed?"

"I seem to have no choice."

"Very little."

"Then I agree."

"Good. You can sign for the papers we hold and take them back with you. When you go home this evening, leave the key of your office with my man. He will spend the night there."

"Why?"

"Protection, Avvocato. Politics is a risky business these days."

I meant it is an irony. I was the old-line professional patronizing a civilian. I should have known better. In this trade, in this country, you are always standing on a trapdoor with a hangman's noose around your neck.

The which being said, I agree an explanation is needed. This so-called Republic of Italy, we so-called Italians, are not a nation at all. We are provinces, cities, country-sides, tribes, factions, families, individuals—anything and everything but a unity. Ask that fellow over there, the street cleaner, what he is. He will answer, "I am a Sard, a Calabrese, a Neapolitan, a Romagnolo." Never, never, will he tell you he is an Italian. That girl in the Ferrari, she's a Venetian, a Veronese, a Padovan. Wife, mistress, mother or rare virgin, she names herself for a place, a plot of separate earth. I myself, as I have told you, am a Tuscan. I serve, because I am paid to serve, the nebulous public thing called the State; but my belonging is elsewhere—Florence and the Medici and the Arno and the pines planted over the graveyards of my ancestors. The consequence? A kind of anarchy which the Anglo-Saxons will never understand; a kind of order which they understand even less. We know who we are, man by man, woman by woman. We despise the outlander because he is different. We respect him because he knows and we know who he is. So, my dilemma: I can never say, "This is the enemy, destroy him!" I must say, "This is the enemy of the moment, but he comes from my country, his sister is married to my cousin and tomorrow we may need to be friends. How must I comport myself so that the links are not broken even though the chain be stretched to breaking point?"

There are many who say that, in this system, there is no place for patriots, only for pragmatists and opportunists. These are dirty words—or are they? We have to survive: a practical problem. We have one life, one opportunity to come to terms with it. So long as the terms are negotiable, we try to negotiate. If we are forced to a base bargain, we accept it and wait for a tomorrow when the contract may be annulled or varied by mutual consent. As you see, I know it all. So there is no excuse for the follies I began to commit that afternoon.

The first was my contemptuous bargain with Avvocato Sergio Bandinelli. I judged him for a frightened and pliable man. I gave him for guardian a junior agent, one Giampiero Calvi. I issued a set of simple instructions. Calvi would accompany Bandinelli to his office. He would take possession of the Pantaleone papers, list them, lock them in the advocate's safe, seal the safe and remain in the office until I relieved him at nine the next morning. During the night he would call the duty officer at headquarters every hour on the hour. Calvi was a promising young man. I read him no lectures. I presumed on the training I myself had given him.

Then, because I was tired, I decided to mix business with pleasure. Because I was—and am—too arrogant for my own good, I elected to play out my little game against the Director. I telephoned my maid and told her that I would not be home for dinner and that I might have to spend the night outside Rome. Then I called Lili Anders and told her that, in line of duty, I would call on her at eight-thirty for a cocktail and take her out to dinner afterwards. Where? A discreet place, but elegant, where she could forget her grief and relax. My intentions? Dear madam, those of a colleague and collaborator; no more, no less.

I walked down the corridor to chat with my associate Rigoli, who concerns himself with the movements and the security of public and not-so-public officials. Rigoli is a grey, mousy fellow with a card-index mind. What he does not know he can guess with 70 percent accuracy: where the Minister of Finance can be found at three on Friday morning, what First Secretary took what flight to Venice and who had the seat next to him. He told me that Major-General Leporello was presently in Rome, lodged at the Hassler, and engaged in a series of conferences with senior service officers. I called the hotel and, after a brief passage-at-arms with a junior aide, was put through to the General. The conversation was brief and terse.

"General, this is Colonel Matucci, SID."

"Yes?"

"An urgent matter. I should like to see you."

"How urgent?"

"Very."

"I am busy until six. I can spare you half an hour after that. Call me from the lobby. Suite ten."

"Thank you, sir."

"The name again?"

"Matucci. Section E."

I put down the telephone and waited. If I judged my man aright, he would check back either to me or to the Director. If he called the Director, I was in for an uncomfortable hour. I was gambling on the fact, well known in the Service, that the Director was a very secretive fellow who refused casual contacts, even to senior officials. Sure enough, within three minutes my phone rang and Leporello came on the line.

"Who is this, please?"

"Matucci, Section E."

"This is Leporello. We have an appointment, I believe."

"Yes, sir. Suite ten at eighteen hundred hours."

"Please be punctual. Good-bye."

Boh! I might well need a little relaxation after half an hour with this hardhead. I made one more call, this time to a curious little office on the Via Bissolati which feeds to the press and to private subscribers news of the comings and goings of celebrities. I don't subscribe to it. I use it and pay my way by encouraging my colleagues at the Questura to overlook a few irregularities in procedure —German telephonists whose sojourn permits are out of date, English typists who don't pay social service contributions and the like. It's a kind of corruption, but there is a more historic name for it—*tolleranza,* live and let live, but remember always that the law has a long memory and a heavy boot. My contact is a busty Dane who lives, unhappily, with a Spanish journalist accredited to the Holy See. Her civil status is highly dubious, but her information is always accurate.

"Faubiani . . . ? Well, old Manzini's in town, so she's doing the rounds with him. Let's see . . . Yesterday Valerio was showing knitwear. Tonight Fosco is displaying jewelry and they've tied in with Lavezzi, who is launching a coffee-table book on Renaissance goldsmiths. Faubiani will probably be there. It's a buffet supper at Fosco's, eight-thirty until the champagne runs out. If you want a ticket, I can let you have mine. Claudio's working tonight, and I only get envious when I look at all that expensive junk."

"You're an angel, Inger."

"Don't tell Claudio that. He's getting demonic again. . . . When am I going to see you, Dante?"

"When I pick up the card at seven-thirty. *Ciao, bambina!*"

And so, with my evening laid out, hour by shining hour, one small decision remained: what number should I leave with the night duty officer? I gave him two—Lili Anders' and my house. Now I was ready for grooming: a change of clothes, a trim, a shave, a massage to tone up my sagging face muscles and half an hour of instructive gossip from my favourite manicurist.

At eighteen hundred hours precisely I telephoned Major-General Leporello from the desk of the Hassler. He commanded me to wait until his aide came to fetch me. The aide, I noted, was a muscular young blood with red hair and freckles and a Trentine accent. He was respectful but laconic, and he wanted to see my card before we moved from the lobby. I suspected that when he left me with the General, he posted himself just outside the door of the suite. Leporello himself was a surprise. He was a tall man, blond and ruddy, more German than Latin. His chest was broad, his belly flat. His gestures were restrained and his manner brisk and businesslike. He had no sense of humour at all.

"Your identification, please."

I gave it to him. He studied it, line by line, and then handed it back to me. "What do you wish to discuss, Colonel?"

"Matters arising out of the death of General Pantaleone."

"Such as?"

"This card, sir. It was found in the General's room after his death."

"What does it signify?"

"That's what I am trying to establish. It was attached to a set of records which were delivered to Pantaleone before his death."

"What sort of records?"

"Incriminating documents of the General's past life."

"Blackmail?"

"We believe so."

"Where are they now?"

"In his lawyer's office, in custody of an officer of SID."

"The card?"

"Is our only clue to the identity of the blackmailer."

"The symbol?"

"A salamander."

"That's odd."

"Why, sir?"

"During the war, one of the most important partisan groups in the Valpadana was led by a man who called himself the Salamander."

"What was his real name?"

"I don't know. He dropped out of sight about 1943. There was a rumour the Germans had got him."

"Did he use a card like this?"

"My memory is vague, because all my information at the time was second or third hand; but I seem to remember some talk of a calling card pinned to the chest of victims of the band."

"Was this a Marxist group?"

"Most groups in the North had real or imputed connections with the Marxists."

"Did you ever work with such groups, General?"

"I? Never. My loyalties were to the Crown. I never changed them—even when it might have been convenient to do so. I disliked the Fascists, I loathed the Germans; but even for that I could not make myself a turncoat soldier. Today I am able to be both honest and proud."

"I am sure you are, sir. You are also a natural target for the terrorists of the Left."

"I must presume so."

"Which brings me to the real purpose of my visit, which is to inform you that you are under surveillance by at least one network of foreign agents."

He gave me a thin, humourless smile. "That's hardly fresh news, Colonel. I have always assumed surveillance by all groups—foreign or local."

"The news is, General, that this group regards you as a possible successor to General Pantaleone."

"In what capacity?"

"As a military and political leader in the event of a right-wing coup."

"Which is nonsense, of course . . ."

"Of course, sir. But it does make you vulnerable."

"To what?"

"To blackmail or assassination."

I had thought to shake him or at least to interest him. Impossible. He was hard and smooth as cemetery granite.

"Blackmail, Colonel? Quite impossible, I assure you. My life is an open book. I am not ashamed of any single page. As for attempts on my life, these have been foreseen and security measures arranged to protect me and my family. I am more concerned by the suggestion—even from hostile elements—that I might have political ambitions. I have none. I believe in hierarchy and order. I see myself only as a servant of duly constituted authority."

"I understand perfectly, sir."

"A question, Colonel."

"Sir?"

"Have you discussed this matter with your Director?"

"I have."

"His opinion?"

"That no action is required by SID. I have, in fact, exceeded my brief by seeking this interview with you."

"Why did you seek it then?"

"We are colleagues, General, you and I. We are members of the same corps. I felt that a point of honour was involved. I decided to act on my own initiative and at my own risk."

"What risk, Colonel?"

"Well . . . to put it gently, the Director is a very formidable character."

"Are you afraid of him?"

"No, sir—but I have a healthy respect."

"So you would prefer I did not report our meeting to him?"

"I have not said that, sir. Nor would I say it. I have done my duty as I read it. I was, and am, prepared to accept all consequences."

For the first time, Leporello relaxed. He offered me a cigarette from a gold case and condescended to light it for me. He leaned back in his chair and surveyed me with grim approval.

"You impress me, Colonel. If you need a friend in the Service, you have one in me. I shall instruct my staff that you may have instant access to me at any time."

"That is very generous, sir."

"Not at all. We have a common aim: the security and stability of the Republic. We must cooperate whenever we can. Pantaleone was a dangerous fool and more than half a rogue. Today we need strong men who are prepared to risk themselves in public service. I judge that you are such a one. Your present experience is, of course, most valuable. If ever you felt an inclination to join my personal staff, I should be happy to have you."

"That's a great compliment."

"You deserve it. And, Colonel . . . ?"

"Sir?"

"I have no intention of discussing this meeting with your Director."

"Thank you, sir."

He shook my hand and ushered me out, commending me to the care of his athletic aide, who escorted me downstairs with a trifle more grace and favoured me with a salute as I drove away.

In the gardens of the Pincio I stopped the car and sat for twenty minutes trying to make sense of Major-General Leporello. I have an instinctive fear of characters who act as if they were first cousins to God Almighty. Their virtue dazzles me. Their ruthlessness never ceases to amaze me. Their passion for order sets them beyond reason or pity. They have all the rectitude of a grand inquisitor, and a Jesuit skill in casuistry. They are dogmatists all, and they have no hesitation about rewriting the codex to suit themselves. They attract minions and satellites and suborners who feed their ambition and bloat their conscious virtue into a legend of impeccability. In short, I loathe their guts and I am more afraid of them than of all the venal villains I meet in my trade. They make me afraid of myself, too, because they provoke me to anger and misjudgment and savage reaction.

Still there was a tenuous profit. Leporello was tempting me into an alliance, first with a scrap of information, true or false, on the Salamander, then with a promise of friendship and advocacy. An alliance pointed to a strategy; a strategy pointed to a goal. What goal? What was

the next ambition of a man who was appointed to control
ant-heap cities and their millions of volatile humans?
Even if he had not yet defined it for himself, there were
others ready to prescribe it for him. Eh! It was too late
and too early for Dante Alighieri Matucci to read the
future. I started the car and drove through the dappled
alleys of the gardens to drink cocktails with Lili Anders.

᚛ ᚜

THE apartment had changed since my last visit. The
equestrian portrait of Pantaleone was gone from the mantel, and in its place was a bright surrealist piece by Spiro,
a landscape of flowers with smiling human faces, and a
procession of musical instruments playing them into a
dance. The furniture had been rearranged, the ornaments
culled to produce an air of undiluted femininity. Lili herself was changed, in some subtle fashion that I could define only by details: the hair more softly swept, the
clothes more modish and extravagant, her manner more
relaxed and confident. Even the housekeeper was a shade
less brusque, if still suspicious and unwelcoming. When I
commented on the changes, Lili smiled and shrugged.

"I am my own woman now. Not as much as I would
wish, but a little more, anyway. What will you drink?"

"Whisky, please."

"You are changed, too."

"How?"

"More human, perhaps. Less professional. How am I
to call you, Colonel?"

"My name is Dante Alighieri."

"Dante was a very somber man. You?"

"Sometimes. Not tonight."

"What is different about tonight?"

"There is business to be done; but I would still like us
to enjoy ourselves."

"That's hardly possible, is it?"

"Why not?"

"Because, Dante Alighieri, you own me. You direct

me like a puppet. I have no choice of what or how I may enjoy. . . . Your drink, master."

"Your health, Lili."

"Where are we dining?"

"We are guests at an exhibition and a champagne supper afterwards. Fosco is displaying his new season's jewelry."

"That should be interesting. Do you like jewelry, Dante?"

"I do—even though I can't afford it."

"Would you like to see mine?"

"If you like."

"I'll show it to you when we come back. I presume you will bring me back after the supper."

"You're being rough with me, Lili."

"No. I want you to know that I understand our relationship. I promised value for money and protection."

"I'm not a whoremaster, Lili."

"Then what are you?"

"Would you believe me if I told you?"

"I might."

"It's very simple. I'm a self-indulgent bastard who likes pretty women."

"Now tell me the rest of it."

"I'm tired and I want to laugh. I'm puzzled and I want to stop thinking. I'm scared and I don't really want to ask why."

"You, scared?"

"Yes. This is the age of assassins, Lili—the age of the fanatics and the destroyers. They want a new world. They'll tear down twenty centuries of civilization to achieve it. What they don't see is that when they're sitting in the ruins, the old gang will have to come back, the technocrats to build the factories, the financiers to create a new illusion of money, the police to bully people into order, even the city ratcatchers like me. It's a madness, Lili, and I'm at the center of it. So are you. There's no escape for either of us, but I thought, just for an hour perhaps, there might be a zone of quiet in the eye of the hurricane. I was a fool. Forget it. I'm not a sadist. So, for

Christ's sake, don't be insulted! . . . Now, please, may I have another drink?"

She took the glass from me without a word, refilled it and brought it back. Then she laid a cool hand on my cheek and said, very calmly:

"Even if you mean only half of it, I'll believe you. And I'm not insulted."

I wasn't sure I believed myself; but I wanted to feel less like a pimp and more, much more, like a man who could face the sunlight without shame. I drew her hand down to my lips and kissed it lightly.

"Now, let's start the scene again. Enter Dante Alighieri Matucci, who is welcomed by Lili Anders. Her greeting is formal but not unfriendly . . ."

"Correction. Her greeting is friendly though not yet intimate."

She bent and kissed me on the forehead and then moved away to pour herself another drink. Twenty minutes later we were driving down to Fosco's, and we joined the gathering, hand in hand, like lovers.

I had not told Lili, but I knew a small something about Fosco, the jeweler. He was—still is, for that matter—a phenomenon: a young and talented homosexual who had leaped from a back-alley apprenticeship in Florence to establish himself in five years as one of the best private goldsmiths in Rome. He showed up once in our files as the friend of an Arab Embassy official; but the association lapsed quickly and we lost interest in him. We are very tolerant in moral matters but highly sensitive to Middle Eastern politics. Sometimes, because his shows attracted a motley group of titled somebodies and moneyed nobodies, I planted an observer among his guests or his security guards. But, though the exercise was profitable in minor ways, Fosco himself always showed clean: a good craftsman, with exquisite manners, and an iron-clad egotism that enabled him to impose his taste and his exorbitant price list on a wide spectrum of Roman matrons, diplomatic wives, rising film stars and vagrant notables.

The presentation of his spring collection was a gala

occasion. The best titles in Rome staged a slow pavane round the showcases. The most expensive models disposed themselves at strategic points in the gallery. A master chef presided over the buffet. An army of handsome young waiters distributed champagne and canapés; and even the security guards contrived to look like Milanese captains of industry. It was a sophisticated social ballet and Fosco directed it with considerable charm and only a hint of contempt for the performers.

We arrived in the middle of the first movement; the early diners who would come, be seen, drink a cocktail or two and leave. The serious ones, the friends of the Master, would come later, linger over the buffet and leave at midnight. Fosco received us with vague courtesy and waved us into the concourse. We snared two glasses of champagne and a pair of catalogues and began our circuit of the exhibits. One fact was immediately clear: Fosco had made a killing. Half the items were already pre-empted, some marked "Sold," others "Reserved," optioned in advance to great houses——Bulgari, Cartier, Buccellati, Tiffany. Not that he did not deserve it. He was master of every style, the baroque, the antique, the avant-garde. His designs were original, his craftsmanship superb. The poorest stones looked like gems of the first water. The best were set like sacred relics alive under the artful lights.

He was not modest about them either. He labelled every exhibit as if it were a museum piece, described the genesis of the design, the particulars of the stones and their setting, and whenever he could, the name and title of the person who had commissioned it. The older houses sniffed at such vulgarity, but Fosco demolished their snobbery at a stroke.

"I want my jewels to be talk pieces. How can a woman talk about what she doesn't know? I explain my work and thus emphasize its value. Right or wrong? Look at the result! I carry no dead stock. I am liquid after every exhibition. . . ."

After this one, it seemed, he would have money running out of his ears. We were about halfway round the

gathering when Lili tugged at my sleeve and pointed to
the catalogue. The section she indicated was entitled "A
Fantasy of Rare Beasts" and referred to a collection of
jewelled butterflies, birds and animals to be worn as
brooches, pendants, clasps, buckles, earrings and symbolic guardians of women's chastity. Lili was pointing to
Number 63, of which the description read:

SALAMANDER.   Brooch in the form of an heraldic beast.
Emeralds in pavé. Crowned with brilliants and orna-
mented with Burma rubies. Adapted from a calligraphic
design. Commissioned by Cav. Bruno Manzini, Bologna.

The piece itself was twenty feet away, laid on a bed
of black velvet, in a small showcase mounted on a pillar
of alabaster. It was not a gaudy jewel, but the craftsman
had preserved the character and sweep of the original
calligraphy, so that when I compared it with the card
there was no shadow of doubt that the designs were
identical.

I drew Lili away from the showcase into the crush of
people round the buffet. At the same moment the Cavaliere Bruno Manzini entered the gallery with the Principessa Faubiani at his side and a small retinue of friends
in attendance. Fosco greeted them effusively, snapped
fingers at his minions to bring them champagne and catalogues and then led them on his own personal tour of
the masterworks.

Immediate problem: how to confront Manzini before
he left the gallery. I had him under my hand here. Once
he left, I could be chasing him all over the peninsula. On
the other hand, with the press and the gossips of the city
turned out in force, I could not risk a scandal. Leaving
Lili at the buffet, I made my way to the entrance where
an agreeable young man was deputizing as host for
Fosco.

I flashed my card at him. "Carabinieri. Who is in
charge of your security guards?"

"Over there, by the stairwell, tall fellow with grey hair.
There's no trouble, I hope?"

"None. Just routine."

I drew the tall fellow into the shadows and showed him my card, too, but this time I made sure he read it carefully before I instructed him.

"This is important. We can't afford a mistake. You will take me to Fosco's private office. I'll give you a note to the Cavaliere Bruno Manzini. You will escort him to the office, then leave us alone. Stay outside the door and let no one in while we're talking—clear?"

"Clear. There's no trouble, I hope?"

"No trouble. I've noted your security arrangements. First class."

He was happy then. He led me to Fosco's office—a fairy bower done in Pompeian red. I scribbled a note to Manzini on the house notepaper. The text was respectful but cryptic:

> Regret intrusion but have urgent and official communica-
> tion. Please accompany messenger to office.
>
> Matucci SID

He was with me in three minutes, cool and condescending as ever. He would not sit down. He had guests waiting. He demanded that I state my business and be done with it.

"My business is still the late General Pantaleone."

"So?"

"Shortly before he died, he received a communication which was, in effect, a dossier of his past life."

"And what has that to do with me?"

"Attached to the dossier was this card. You will note the design—a crowned salamander. We have established that the design corresponds exactly with exhibit Number sixty-three in the Fosco catalogue. We are confident you will wish to explain the connection."

"Why should I wish to explain it, Colonel?"

"A matter of national security is involved."

"Is that fact or opinion?"

"Fact."

"And you could establish it as such to my satisfaction?"

"I believe so."

"Is there any suggestion of criminal activity in this case?"

"As yet, none."

"Then what do you want from me, Colonel?"

"At this stage, an informal discussion."

"When?"

"Now, Cavaliere."

"Quite impossible. I am occupied with friends."

"Afterwards then. At your hotel, perhaps?"

"My dear Colonel, I am seventy years old. By midnight I am near to dying. You would get no sense out of me at all. Say, nine in the morning at the Grand Hotel, and I'll do my best to enlighten you. Now, may I be excused?"

"Some questions before you go, Cavaliere."

"Yes?"

"The salamander, what does it signify?"

"Survival. It was my code name during the war. The rest is too long to tell you now."

"The inscription?"

"That's a long story, too."

"The beginning of it then, if you please."

"The beginning and the end, Colonel. Pantaleone was my half brother. Only he happened to be conceived on the right side of the blanket."

I stared at him openmouthed, like an idiot. He smiled at my discomfiture and made a small gesture of deprecation.

"Please! I am not trying to make theater, only to show you that we do need time to be clear with each other. Agreed?"

"Agreed."

"Now, Colonel, will you answer one question for me?"

"If I can, yes."

"Who killed Pantaleone?"

"The death certificate states that he died of a cardiac arrest."

"But that's what kills us all, Colonel."

"Exactly."

"No other comment?"

"None. Until tomorrow, Cavaliere."

"My compliments, Colonel. Good night."

Why didn't I hold him? Why didn't I hammer him with questions while I had him off-balance? I told you before, this was a very special one, the best of the breed. Off-balance? Never for an instant. I was the unsure novice, groping for handhold and foothold on a bare mountain. Besides—let me make it plain to you—this is Italy, where the law goes back to Justinian, and half of it hasn't been dusted off for centuries, and the rules of the game are written in sand. Three people in Manzini's retinue could immobilize me for a month by lifting a telephone. Twenty names of Fosco's party could consign me forever to the limbo of the retired list. And if you've ever tried to collect a debt or enforce a claim against the Republic, then you'll know what I'm talking about. In China they drowned their enemies in a bath of feathers. Here in Italy they stifle them with silence and bury them under a tumulus of *carta bollata*.

It was still only ten-thirty. I rescued Lili from the crush at the buffet and carted her off to dinner at a place I knew in Trastevere, where the food was honest Tuscan, the wine was honourable and the waiters were proud to serve you, and there was a great open fire for the winter and an arbour of vines for the summer nights. There was music, too: a skinny, plaintive fellow with a guitar, who would come to your table, when you were ready for him, and sing the soul out of your body with the old songs of the South. I was known here, but not for my trade, only because I prized the cook, and sometimes drank enough to sing and strum a song or two while the sad fellow ate his supper.

I had friends there: Castiglione, who used to be a great locksmith until the arthritis got him; Monsignore Arnolfo Ardizzone of the Vatican Secretariat of State, a cleric, knowledgeable and discreet, who had renounced marriage to serve God and adopted the bottle as the only mistress

acceptable to Mother Church; Giuffredi, the poet, who
wrote satires in Romanesco which nobody read anymore;
and Maddalena, who sold yesterday's roses at five hundred lire a bloom and was said to own a whole apartment
block on the Tuscolana. True or false? I had never cared
to inquire. This was one place where I was myself—whoever that might be. I accepted everyone at face value. I
used no one. I paid the score and was welcome in the
house. Enough! Everyone needs a bolthole. This was mine.

I tried to explain all this to Lili as we walked the last
hundred meters through lanes hung with laundry and
came out into a tiny square guarded by a dusty Virgin
in a glass case. I wanted to explain, which in my trade
is a weakness. She seemed happy to listen, holding close
to me as we stepped over foul runnels and spilled refuse,
while the cats of the quarter slunk back into the shadows.
Sometimes, when the rare light fell on her face, she
looked like a young girl. When she crossed herself at the
shrine of the little Virgin, she looked like a peasant
woman, weary from a long day in the fields. You may
not believe me, but I did not care. I was not hunting now,
I was simply glad not to be alone.

When we were settled at the table, with bread and
wine and a fresh candle, Lili leaned across to me and
laid her hands on mine.

"You look different now, Dante Alighieri."

"How?"

"At Fosco's you were tight, wary, like a fox. Now you
are loose, free. You greet people like human beings.
They, too, are glad to see you."

"This is Trastevere, my love. Across the river. You
know what these people call themselves? *Noantri*—we
others. They refuse to belong to anyone but themselves."

"I like that. For now, we, too, are *noantri*. Please, may
I have some wine?"

"I may get drunk and sing."

"I'll sing with you."

"And who will drive us back across the river?"

"Perhaps we won't go back—ever again."

It was a happy thought and we nursed it with all sorts

of fantasies through the *zuppa* and the *pasta* and the *griglia* and the *dolci*. We embroidered it with the music of the plaintive one as he perched on the stool next to Lili and played her the curiosities of his repertoire—"The Song of the Washerwomen of Vomero"; "Friend, Don't Trust the Spinster"; "The Undressing Song" and "The Tale of the Lecherous Clog-seller."

Midnight came and we were still singing. At one-thirty in the morning we were vaguely drunk and the waiters had begun to wilt, so we wandered into the square, said good night to the lonely Virgin and strolled towards the riverside car park.

Lili said drowsily, "Do you know something?"

"What?"

"I want to go to bed with you, but I don't want to go home."

"Why not?"

"Because home is yesterday. I want to forget it."

"And tomorrow?"

"Tomorrow starts when the sun comes up, and this place will be ugly and smelly and full of sad people afraid of each other, and you'll be all wise and wary again."

"So let's drive out along the ring road. There's a place I know . . ."

"Anywhere you say, *caro mio*. Anywhere you say."

"I have to make a phone call first."

"Why?"

"I left your number with my duty officer. I'll have to check in and give him a new one."

"There's no escape, is there?"

"We escaped tonight."

"So we did. But you still have to telephone . . ."

"Please, Lili."

"Please, just kiss me . . ."

In case you're hoping—as I was—for a happy tale of love and lechery, forget it The evening of liberty ended with that kiss. I called Headquarters from the corner phone booth. The time was 0210 hours. The duty officer told me agent Calvi had not made his hourly call. What did I want done about it? I ordered two cars of our mobile squadron, one to pick up Stefanelli, one to meet me at the lawyer's office. I flagged a passing taxi, bundled Lili into it and sent her home. Then I climbed into my own car and drove like a madman across the sleeping city.

ॐ ॐ ॐ

THE office of Avvocato Sergio Bandinelli was on the fifth floor of a large modern block on the Via Sicilia, only two hundred meters from the bustle of the Via Veneto. When I arrived, one car of the mobile squadron was already parked outside the entrance. The second, carrying Steffi and his little black bag, came hurtling around the corner a few seconds later. Before we entered the building, I gave a few sharp directions to the squadron leaders: this was a high-security matter; no police, no press, no curious sightseers; two men standing by the cars, one on guard with the concierge, three to accompany Steffi and myself to the fifth floor. Then we rang the bell.

The porter, bleary-eyed and grumbling, opened the door and immediately launched into a babble of questions. We flashed our cards, left him still babbling and took the elevator to the fifth floor. Bandinelli's office was in darkness, the door was closed but unlocked. I entered first and switched on the lights.

The scene was curiously tranquil. Avvocato Bandinelli lay stretched on a leather settee. Agent Giampiero Calvi was seated in a chair behind the desk, head pillowed on his arms. On the desk beside him was a Moravia novel, a loaded pistol, two ham rolls, a hard-boiled egg and a flask of coffee. The coffee was warm. The two men were stone-cold. Old Steffi sniffed the air, made a brief examination of the bodies and pronounced his verdict.

"Dead. Cyanic acid gas. Pistol or pressure pack."

I examined the safe. The seals were broken, the door was open, the Pantaleone papers gone. The immediate temptation was to plunge into action: forensic procedure, interrogation of witnesses, all the rest of it. It was a temptation hard for any man with police training to resist, but in my work it could be fatal to a sensitive project. I picked up the phone and called the Director's private number. He answered with surprising promptness.

I told him, "We're in trouble. Documents missing and two bundles of dirty linen for immediate disposal—one of them ours."

"So . . . ?"

"As soon as the situation is tidy, I'll report in person!"

"When might that be?"

"Before breakfast, I hope."

"I'll expect you for breakfast then—the earlier the better."

Steffi cocked his head and cackled at me, for all the world like an ancient scruffy parrot. "When everything's tidy! Eh! So now we're in the miracle business!"

The boys from the mobile squadron were fidgeting on their feet, waiting for me to make some decisions. The problem was that every decision carried highly explosive consequences. If I made a big scene with police procedures and interrogations, the press would come swarming like wasps to a honey pot. Once they found the Pantaleone papers were involved, they would immediately start asking questions about Pantaleone's death and hasty burial. On the other hand, if we could not interrogate freely, we would be grievously handicapped in reconstructing the events of the evening and, therefore, in our search for the Pantaleone documents. Besides, there were two bodies to be disposed of in a convincing, if not legal, fashion. Steffi was right as usual. Willy-nilly, we were in the miracle business. So it was time to get the ritual started.

The first problem was to get the two bodies out of the building without fuss or comment. I sent Steffi down to question the porter in his own cubbyhole, out of view of the entrance. Steffi's talk would hypnotize a fighting cock. I counted on having the porter so bemused that he would miss a herd of elephants six feet from his nose.

Next we emptied Bandinelli's pockets and Calvi's as well. The boys of the mobile squadron carried the bodies into the elevator, rode them to the ground floor and bundled them into the waiting cars like a pair of late drunks. One car drove Bandinelli's remains to the casualty department of the Policlinico; the other deposited Calvi at the Hospital of the Blue Sisters. In each case the story was the same; the mobile squadron had found a man lying, apparently unconscious, in an alley. They were consigning him to hospital while they pursued inquiries as to his identity. Dead on arrival? Dear me! Then give us a receipt and hold him in the mortuary while we complete our inquiries!

It sounds naïve? Then let me explain that even if your grandmother, with all her documents in her purse, falls sick on the Corso and is carried off to a public hospital by some street samaritan, it may well take you the best part of a week to trace her. We have small talent for administration at the best of times, but our public health service is a mess beyond description. Unless you go to an expensive clinic, you may find your blood report really belongs to a ballet mistress and your urine was supplied by a fellow who caught clap at Fregene. So, by all the rules of the game, two unidentified bodies should stay unclaimed until we were ready to deal with them.

While Stefanelli was questioning the porter, I drank Calvi's coffee, ate one of his ham rolls, and examined the entries in his notebook.

20.00 hrs.		Bandinelli's staff left.
20.30	"	Completed indexing of Pantaleone documents. Locked and sealed safe in presence Bandinelli. Signed receipt for papers and keys. Bandinelli left.
21.00	"	Telephoned duty officer H.Q.
21.25	"	Office cleaners arrived.
21.55	"	Office cleaners left.
22.00	"	Telephoned duty officer H.Q.
23.00	"	Telephoned duty officer H.Q.
23.36	"	Made final check of fifth floor.
24.00	"	Telephoned duty officer H.Q.
00.37	"	Bandinelli telephoned. He wished pass by office for late night conference with two

clients. He explained it as a police matter. He would not disturb me, but would use outer office for conference. Since my instructions referred only to custody of safe and contents, I had no authority to refuse him access to his own office. I agreed.

01.00 hrs. Telephoned duty officer. Asked him note Bandinelli's request and my decision.

The entries ended at that point. I called the duty officer myself. He confirmed the entries from his own log. Which left me with a vital question: had Bandinelli come to the office under duress, or had he come as an accomplice who was liquidated when his usefulness was ended? I was still puzzling over it when Steffi came back, cross-grained and unhappy.

The porter knew nothing, had seen no one. He worked strictly by the book and the terms of his contract, which stated that he would remain awake on duty until midnight or until the cleaners left, whichever was the later. After that he might go to bed. All tenants had passkeys to the front door. They had free access to their offices at any hour. Non-tenants were refused admission outside office hours unless they were identified as cleaners or contractors.

". . . So, in fact, Steffi, anyone with a passkey could bring a whole army into the building after midnight, with no one any the wiser?"

"That's the size of it, Colonel."

"Where was Bandinelli when he telephoned at thirty-seven minutes after twelve?"

"One way to find out, Colonel. Ring his house."

I lifted the telephone again and called Bandinelli's villa on the Cassia. The phone rang for a long while and then a very surly male answered:

"Villa Bandinelli! Who is this?"

"Carabinieri. We wish to speak to the advocate."

"He's not here."

"His wife then."

"The Signora is in Naples."

"Who are you?"

"De Muro, majordomo."

"Where can I find the advocate?"

"At this hour, God knows!"

"What time did he go out?"

"He hasn't been home since yesterday morning. He telephoned in the evening to say he wouldn't be home for dinner."

"No idea where he might be?"

"None at all."

"Thank you. Good morning."

He did not return the greeting. He hung up in my ear. Steffi grinned. "No luck?"

"No. His wife's away. He didn't go home for dinner."

"Which helps your little fiction about an unidentified body."

"But it doesn't tell me who did the killing and took the documents."

"Does it matter, Colonel?"

"For God's sake, Steffi! What sort of question is that?"

"A very good one, I thought, Colonel. Look! This is a professional job, neat, tranquil, simple as walking. Which do you want, the liquidators or the people who paid them? This is not police work, friend; it's intelligence analysis, an exercise in pure reason. Start from the bottom and you'll be wandering round the sewers six months from now. Start from the top and you halve the work and double your chances—believe me!"

"I do believe you, Steffi. But sometime in the next three hours I have to face the Director. What do I offer him?"

"Human sacrifice! . . ." Steffi favoured me with a gallows grin. "So why don't you pour me some coffee, Colonel, and let's discuss the candidates."

❧ ☙

THE Director's apartment was the top floor of a sixteenth-century palace just off the Via della Scrofa. The revenues from the rest of the palace—dwellings and fashionable shops—would keep him in kingly state for a lifetime. His paintings, sculptures and objects of virtue were a fortune in themselves. His library was a minor treasure-house of rare editions, specialist studies and exotic poetry in a variety of languages. The Director was an exotic himself, resplendent in a brocaded dressing gown, attended by a wiry Sicilian who was both butler and bodyguard. At six in the morning, grubby, unshaven and very unsure of myself, I was in no mood to appreciate the dramatic effect.

The Director offered me a cool welcome and an English breakfast—tea, toast, scrambled eggs and marmalade. I asked for coffee and pastry. The Director conceded the point with a smile and then proceeded to make a few of his own.

"You knew the Pantaleone papers were important, Colonel. Why did you not take immediate possession of them?"

"I needed a judicial order. To get it, I would have had to appear against Bandinelli in the presence of a judge. I thought it unwise."

"So you made an arrangement which resulted in the death of Agent Calvi and of Bandinelli himself?"

"Yes."

"Any excuse?"

"No excuse. An explanation. I was trying to scare Bandinelli into further revelations. I thought the security risk was minimal. In the event, I was wrong."

"Who else knows the facts at this moment?"

"Only SID. We had the bodies out and the place cleaned up by four this morning. We're in a holding situation for a few days at least."

"But we don't know who has the Pantaleone papers?"

"No."

"So let's guess, Colonel. Local group or foreign?"

"Local, I think."

"Right wing or left?"

"Right."

"Why?"

"The left have a lot of dirt they haven't published yet. The right have a lot of dirt they want to bury—I think last night was a funeral party."

"You don't convince me, Colonel."

"I'm not trying to convince you, sir. I'm telling you what I believe. If you're thinking of Woodpecker and his network, forget him. I had him pulled in at four this morning. I worked on him myself for nearly two hours, before I came to see you. I know what his brief is. Assassination is not part of it. Besides, he's been under constant surveillance and he doesn't have the resources or contacts to set up a job like this in half a day. Now, let's look at the other side of the coin. Bandinelli was on the right wing. He served Pantaleone. He could have sold out to a successor . . ."

"And been killed for his pains?"

"That, too."

"Name me a possible successor."

"Major-General Marcantonio Leporello."

For the first time the Director was shaken and he showed it. He set down his teacup with a clatter and sat a long moment staring at me with bleak and hostile eyes. Then he said, quietly:

"I presume you have evidence in support, Colonel?"

"Some. I interviewed the General yesterday at the Hassler Hotel."

"You what?"

"I interviewed Leporello."

"In spite of my orders that no action was to be taken with that subject?"

"Yes, sir."

"And what did you tell him?"

"That he was under surveillance by a foreign network who had tipped him as political candidate for the Right."

"What else?"

"The whereabouts of the Pantaleone papers."

"Oh . . . !"

"And the fact that I was acting against direct orders."

"And what was his reaction to that?"

"He promised to keep the interview secret—and he offered me a job on his own staff."

"I'm tempted to make you immediately available, Matucci."

"That's your privilege, sir—and, even from the point of view of the Service, it mightn't be a bad idea."

"You're bargaining with me, Matucci. I don't like that."

"And you're threatening me, sir. I don't like that, either."

"You disobey orders and that's dangerous."

"It was a risk. I took it. I think it paid dividends."

"It gave you a convenient suspect, nothing more."

"Something more."

"What?"

"I've identified the Salamander."

That brought him up short. He held a piece of buttered toast halfway between the plate and his thin lips. Then he popped it into his mouth and chewed on it pensively. Finally he said:

"And do you propose to tell me who he is?"

"Yes, sir. If I'm still in the Service at nine o'clock this morning, I'll be keeping an appointment with him. He's the Cavaliere Bruno Manzini. He tells me, and I hope to confirm it from the records, that he is the bastard brother of General Pantaleone."

"First Leporello, now Manzini. Leporello is your military superior. Manzini is one of the most powerful financiers in Italy. You're flying very high, my friend."

"And you can shoot me down now, if you choose."

"I mightn't need to do it. Whoever killed Calvi could as easily kill you."

"I know."

"So if I let you go on?"

"I want a free hand and access to the Leporello file."

"Can I trust you, Matucci?"

"You can, but you'd rather not."

"Do you trust me?"

"With reservations, yes."

"What reservations?"

"You're the Director. I know what you are commissioned to do. What I don't know is how you interpret your commission and to what secret ends you direct the activities of SID."

"Do you have any right to know?"

"Legally, I suppose not. I'm a serving officer, I do as I'm told . . . *basta!* Personally? That's another matter. If you'd asked me the same question a week ago, I'd have given you a nice, complaisant answer: bless me, Father, lead me in the way of salvation and look after my pension rights! This morning it's different. I'm middle-aged and tired and I haven't had a shave and I lost a good lad because I didn't think straight. So I don't want to be manipulated anymore. I want to know where I'm being directed and why—and if I don't like it, I'll resign my job with you and go back to desk duty or police work."

The Director drank the last of his tea and dabbed at his lips with a linen napkin. He pushed back his chair, walked to the window and stood a long time looking out at the tumbled rooftops of Rome, gold and umber and crimson in the early light. When he turned, the light was at his back and the contours of his face were in shadow. He began to talk, quietly at first, then with mounting passion and eloquence.

"You are a presumptuous fellow, Colonel. Yet I can forgive you, because I also presume too much and too often. I presume on wealth and family and myself as a product of all the alliances and misalliances of our history. In a way, I am yesterday's man; but then Italy is yesterday's country as well as today's. We build our houses on tombs. We build our prosperity on ruins and papal monuments and the genius of our ancient dead. Our law is an idiot confusion of Justinian, the Codex Canonicus, Napoleon, Mussolini and the founding fathers of the United States. Our nobility is a hodgepodge of ancient families and the last upstarts ennobled by the House of Savoy. In politics we are Marxists, Monarchists, Socialists, Liberals, Fascists, Christian Democrats—opportunists all! We have the best businessmen and the worst bureaucrats in the world. We're a nation of anticlericals and we've manipulated the Catholic Church for centuries. We shout federal republican democracy—yet every province is a separate continent. A man's country is whatever miserable village he was born in. . . . Now you, my dear Colonel, demand that I should tell you to what I am committed and to what end I direct the Defense Information Service. . . . Let me turn the question then and ask you where you would walk if you were in my shoes—as you may be one day if you are cool enough and clever enough and understand the price to be paid. . . . No answer? Then here is mine. Our problems will not be solved by an election, by a coalition of parties, by the victory of one system over another. We are Mediterranean men, Colonel. We are, whether we like it or not, a mongrel breed of Greek and Latin and Phoenician and Arab and Iberian Celt and Viking and Visigoth and the Huns of Attila. We live, as we have lived for centuries, in a precarious balance of tribal and family interests. When the balance tips, ever so slightly, we are plunged into disorder and civil strife. When the strife becomes too bloody for us all, we cry halt and beg to be delivered—by the Church, by a personal saviour—or, most pathetically of all, by politicians and bureaucrats who are as bloodied and confused as we are ourselves. The Spaniards and the Greeks and the Portuguese turned to dictators. The Arabs threw out the colonial powers and replaced them with local autocrats. We Italians have tried one dictator and made a shambles of democracy. Now we don't know what we want. Me? I don't know what the people want. I can't even judge what they will tolerate. So I manipulate information and situations to hold things in balance as long as I can. I don't want dictatorship. I don't want Marxism. I'm sure the kind of democracy we have is too unstable to last. But, come one or the other, I'll try to make it as tolerable as I can. Politics is the art of the possible. Mediterranean politics is the art of the impossible, and I understand it better than most. You're worried about Leporello, but you have no evidence against him and I'm not going to antagonize him just at a moment when we may need him. You're worried about your Salamander, who, I confess, makes no sense to me at all just now. You want a free investigation? I'll give it to you, but understand me, Matucci, when I move, in whatever gambit, I am king on the board and you are a pawn. Take it or leave it."

I gave him the answer without a second's hesitation.

"I'll take it. And I'll give you an honest report. If I don't like what you do, I'll argue it face to face. If we don't agree, I'll fight you, but I'll do it in the open."

"It's a rash promise, Matucci. I won't hold you to it. If ever you fight me, you'll have to lie like a whore and cheat like a cardsharp, just to save your skin. . . . By the way, you can't meet Manzini looking like that. My valet will show you to the guest room and find you a razor and a clean shirt."

❧ ❧

AT eight o'clock on the same spring morning, with an hour to kill before my meeting with Manzini, I rejoined old Stefanelli as he strolled whistling down the Spanish Steps. The sun was bright; the air was crisp; every tread of the staircase blossomed with girls. I had been up all night, but I felt miraculously refreshed and I could see the sap rising even in Steffi's withered trunk.

This was the best of Rome: the smell of dust and women and new bread and fresh violets; the clatter of the gossips on their way to market, the honk of taxis, the solemn parade of tourists, pale from the mists of Denmark and High Germany; the tumble of cupolas and campaniles and russet roofs crowned with clotheslines and television antennae. This was the fountain of youth that gave a man fantasies, put birds in his head and wings on his bunioned feet.

At the foot of the steps we paused so that Steffi could buy himself a carnation for his buttonhole; then we turned into Babington's Tea Rooms, where Steffi had promised to buy Solimbene tea and English muffins. Solimbene was a pedant but an amiable one who affected small eccentricities—velvet smoking jackets, fin-de-siècle cravats, gold fob seals and eyeglasses on a ribbon of watered silk. He also nourished a passion for redheaded women and English manners, though he had never in his life travelled farther than Paris.

We found him enthroned in a corner of the tearoom, clasping the hand of a blond waitress and pouring out his passion in execrable German. He let her go, reluctantly, and turned the flood of his eloquence on Steffi:

"My dear colleague! My brother in arms and in art! I have revelations for you, Steffi mine! Revelations, mysteries and scandals. Don't laugh! Your trade is horrible—blood and dust and excrement and clothing torn from the dead. Me? I live with fairy tales—gryphons rampant and unicorns couchant, allocamels and lioncels and dancing dolphins and magical swords in disembodied hands. . . . But when you need a simple little fact, who finds it? Me! Solimbene, the herald! . . . Yes, my love, my dove, tea, muffins and English marmalade. Coffee is a madman's drink. It produces dyspepsia and dries out the kidneys. . . . Now, my friends, we began with this"—he laid the salamander card on the table and stabbed at it with a cakefork—"which is not heraldry at all, but calligraphy, a monkish art. Even the crown is corrupted. However, notwithstanding, *mutatis mutandis,* I was prepared to accept a heraldic origin. Result? I found myself chasing salamanders across every escutcheon in Europe. Insanity! Total insanity! Finally I reduced the number of possibles to four. Insanity again!" He spread a set of glossy photographs on the table and annotated them. "These two families are extinct. The only survivor of this one is a monk in the Certosa of Florence. Which leaves us, my dear friends, with this last photograph. I found it listed in our files under *Curiosa and Exotica.* There is your salamander in the first and fourth quarterings; the supporters are lions rampant. It's beautifully executed, as you can see. Only one problem: it is not a coat of arms at all. It is an artist's conceit. It belongs to no known family."

Stefanelli shrugged and spread his hands in a Levantine

gesture. "So, it's beautiful and it means nothing. Why show it to us?"

"Oh, it does mean something, dear colleague. It means a great deal—fraud, fakery and scandals juicy as a beefsteak. How old are you, Steffi?"

"None of your business."

"Come now, don't be touchy. I'm doing you a favour."

"No favour, you're being very well paid—provided the Colonel here authorizes the invoice. Now, let's see the meat in the sandwich."

The waitress came back with tea and muffins and Solimbene detained her again with compliments and cajolery. Then, when she had whisked herself away, he began another comedy with notebook and eyeglasses and a new flourish of rhetoric.

"In the year of Our Lord, nineteen hundred and ten, when Pius the Tenth was gloriously reigning, and you, dear Steffi, were still wet behind the ears, there lived not a stone's throw from here a very notable lady of fashion, who called herself the Countess Salamandra. She entertained only the noble and the wealthy—among them a certain opera singer, who, as he left her house early one morning, was shot and killed, presumably by a jealous rival. There was, of course, a scandal. The lady, assisted by some of her clients, fled the country and went to live in Nice. Police inquiries revealed that the Countess Salamandra was not a countess at all, but a young Scots lady named Anne Mackenzie, who, having fallen from grace in a noble bed, decided to enrich herself by the same means. . . . How's that for a prelude, Colonel? Will you authorize the invoice now? Or are you bored already?"

"Go on! Go on, man!"

"This coat of arms was used by the Countess Salamandra. She had caused it to be forged for professional purposes."

"Is that all?"

"All?" Solimbene was outraged. "My dear Colonel, when I do a job, I do it properly. I have tramped this city in your service. I have burrowed like a badger into the files of Central Registry. I have spent hours of my life with withered old dowagers, who have almost, but not quite, cured me of concupiscence. Miss Anne Mackenzie was once in service with the Count Massimo Pantaleone, as nurse and governess to his daughter. She became pregnant by the old Count and left his service. In August, 1900, she married one Luca Salamandra, described in the marriage certificate as a circus performer, who, two days after the wedding, fell from a high wire and broke his neck. The child, a boy, was born a week after his demise and was baptized Massimo Salamandra in the Capuchin church in the Via delle Zoccolette. In proof of which I offer certificates of marriage and birth and baptism, all dated 1900. In October of the same year a lady calling herself the Countess Salamandra set herself up in the Palazzo Cherubini, just down the road there, and began to prepare her entry into Roman society. It is a reasonable guess, supported by the gossip of my dowagers, that she was financed in her venture by a generous allowance paid by old Count Pantaleone."

"And what happened to the boy?"

"His mother took him with her when she fled to Nice. After that, no record until 1923, when a young man named Massimo Salamandra presented himself before a tribunal in Rome and applied to change his name to Bruno Manzini. The tribunal approved the application and the transaction was entered at the Central Registry in Rome—which is where I found it yesterday. . . . Now, gentlemen, do I get my money?"

I didn't tell him, but at that moment he could have tripled the price without a murmur from me. When you are playing against the house, it always pays to have a spare ace in your sleeve. Even that doesn't help, of course, when the rest of the deck is stacked against you.

❧ ☙

THE Cavaliere Bruno Manzini received me in a suite large enough to house a division of infantry and still leave room for the camp followers. His morning face was

benign. His manners impeccable. He was even solicitous
for my health.

"You look a little peaked this morning, Colonel. A
late night?"

"A long one, Cavaliere. I haven't been to bed yet."

"My dear fellow! Had I known, we could have made a
later appointment."

"Kind of you, but I need, desperately, whatever information you can give me."

"Let's save time then. How much do you know already?"

"That your mother was one Anne Mackenzie, sometime nurse to the Pantaleone family. That you are the
son of her union with the old Count. That you were
baptized Massimo Salamandra in Rome in 1900. That
your mother, for reasons of business, adopted a spurious
title and a coat of arms to match it. The device of the
salamander appears in that coat of arms. In 1923 you
changed your name to Bruno Manzini. . . ."

"And how did you come by all that information?"

"Some luck, some heraldry and the Central Registry."

"What else can you tell me?"

"That depends, Cavaliere, on how much you are prepared to tell me."

"Anything you wish to know."

"Do you mean that?"

"I would not say it otherwise."

"Then why were you blackmailing your brother?"

"Blackmail? My dear Matucci, since the war I have
become inordinately rich. I could have bought and sold
him twenty times over. I was threatening him with public
disgrace! If he had persisted in this crazy politic of his,
I should have exposed him without mercy."

"Instead you killed him."

"I beg your pardon?"

"He died of an overdose of drugs—self-administered."

"A fact which was not made public. Why?"

"Bluntly, Cavaliere, for fear of a political scandal
which might lead to civil disorder."

"Now I could make the scandal."

"Will you?"

"No. It would defeat my purpose, which is the same as yours. To avoid political disruption and civil violence."

"Next question then. If the document you sent your brother fell into other hands, what use could be made of it?"

"Now that he is dead, very little. Oh, a newspaper could publish it and make a ten-day wonder, but politically—in my view at least—it would be a damp firecracker. Why do you ask?"

"Because all the Pantaleone papers were stolen last night from the offices of Avvocato Sergio Bandinelli. Bandinelli and one of our agents were murdered."

"There was no news of this in the press."

"Nor will there be, unless you choose to release it."

He stared at me in blank disbelief. Then he shook his head like a man waking from a dream and wondering where he was. He pieced out the next words, slowly, as if they were quite inadequate to express his thought.

"I do not believe . . . I cannot believe . . . that any intelligent man would . . . would be so rash as to commit himself to a stranger in this way. You have put an atomic bomb into my hands, Colonel. I could blow up the country with it. . . . My God, don't you see? You, a serving officer, have just admitted to falsifying the records of a suicide and . . . and concealing two murders! How do you know that I will not lift this telephone and call the press—some of which I own—and splash the news all over the world?"

"I don't know, Cavaliere. I'm gambling."

"Then you're a madman."

"Only if you lift the telephone. If you don't, if you place your knowledge at my disposal, then I'm the sanest man in Rome."

"But you have no guarantees, have you?"

"In this dog's world, Cavaliere, there are no guarantees and you know it. The law is no more than a thin crust over a nest of soldier ants. Even death is big business now—international business. You want someone dead in Israel, you fly killers in from Japan. You want a murder

in Venice, you phone London or Munich and your assassin arrives the next day. Hijack an airliner? Simple.
You let the contract in New York, embark your people
in Stockholm, fly the damn thing to Libya if it suits you.
. . . I have to trust someone. Let's say I trust you because
you despise the trade I'm in and make no secret of it.
. . . Now, can we go on?"

"You'll check my answers, of course?"

"As if I were the Grand Inquisitor himself."

"That's better. Please begin."

"Cavaliere, what would you expect to find in the Pantaleone papers that would be worth two lives and the risk
of the crime itself?"

He pondered that for a long while before he answered:

"In the family papers themselves, very little. There
would be title deeds, business transactions, wills, settle-
ments, old correspondence, some of it scandalous perhaps, but of interest only to the social historian. In my
brother's personal papers . . . ? Well, let's think of him
as a political soldier, playing a power game. He would
assemble dossiers on friends and enemies alike. Some of
those might be very valuable either to the subjects themselves or to political rivals. But murder. . . ? Somehow I
don't see it. You're an expert on dossiers. I use them, too,
in business. But, truly, how important are they? Everybody in Italy knows a little dirt—or a lot—about the
man next door. We're all gossips and scandalmongers,
and what we don't know, we invent. It's a social disease,
tolerable only because it's endemic—like syphilis among
the Cossacks. Our sexual morals are special, our social
ethics nonexistent. After the Fascists and the war, and
the occupation and the scrabble for world trade and
the late history of the Vatican and all the chicanery of
our recent politics, who has clean hands, anyway? No
matter what my brother wrote in his notebooks, you can
safely wager twenty other people knew it before he did.
I'm not saying the stuff couldn't be valuable. . . . But the
murder of a lawyer and a Government agent . . . ? No.
I can't see it. There must be something else."

"For example . . . ?"

"Plans, more likely. The tactics and strategy of a *colpo di stato*. The political and military organization that must be ready to take over at a moment's notice. The list of participants, active and passive. The location of arms, the disposition of available forces in sympathy with the plotters. Even your own service might do murder for such things."

"In this case they didn't."

"So now, Matucci, we are at the heart of the artichoke. We have to decide whether or no we can trust each other. Who makes the next move?"

"It's your turn, Cavaliere!"

"Before you arrived your Director telephoned me."

You know that strange sensation of disembodiment that comes in moments of shock. You are suddenly outside yourself, looking at the antics of a body that doesn't belong to you. I had it then. I watched myself tumbling into the trap which opened under my unwary feet. Then the hallucination passed and I was back in my own skin, writhing under the irony of my situation. Manzini watched me, grave and unsmiling. He went on:

"You are angry. You have a right to be. I know your Director very well. He is sometimes too clever for his own good and always as vain as Lucifer. He wanted to display his cleverness to me and also, I think, to teach you a lesson for some delinquency."

"That's true, at least. Now what, Cavaliere?"

"Now I am going to give you a piece of information which your Director does not yet possess. At eight o'clock yesterday evening I signed, on behalf of one of my companies, a procurement contract with the Government. The contract calls for the urgent supply of large quantities of riot-control equipment. The specifications were drawn up by Major-General Marcantonio Leporello, and the equipment will be used by troops under his command. . . . I have drawn certain conclusions from this situation. You may care to hear them."

"Please . . . !"

"If I were a new Fascist or an old one, if I were looking

for a new leader, I should be very ready to bargain with Marcantonio Leporello."

"Perhaps the bargain has already been struck."

"No, Colonel. Leporello was waiting on the contract which would put firepower and bargaining power into his hands. He was waiting for something else, too."

"What?"

"He would not commit himself until the Pantaleone papers were safe in his own hands."

"And he has them now?"

"I believe so."

"It seems to me, Cavaliere, you're something more than a businessman."

"I'm a salamander, Colonel—a perennial survivor. You?"

"A servant of the State. Except that I'm not sure what the State is today—and I'm scared of what it may be tomorrow."

"That makes us allies."

"In a lopsided league."

"That frightens you?"

"Yes, Cavaliere, it frightens me."

"Then let me offer you a small reassurance. I shall write you a name and an address. If you go there you will hear part of the truth about me. If it satisfies you, you will come to see me in Bologna. If it doesn't, you will still be in profit."

He took a business card from his wallet, wrote a name and address on the back of it and handed it to me. The name was Raquela Rabin; the address, a street near the Theater of Marcellus. He made no explanation. I did not ask for one. We shook hands, he led me to the door and held it open for me.

"One other thing, Colonel . . ."

"Yes?"

"Advice from an old campaigner. Always walk close to the wall, and sleep with one eye open. . . . I hope we meet again soon."

"I hope so, too, Cavaliere, Good-day!"

When I hit the street, it was exactly ten o'clock. The

bells of Santa Susanna were tolling the hour; the traffic made a dramatic discord; the vast indifference of the city was a blow in the face. All of a sudden I was maudlin tired, rocking on my feet. I climbed into my car and drove, in a perilous daze, all the way to Parioli. I hammered on Lili's door and almost fell into her arms when she opened it herself. She asked no questions but led me by the hand into the bedroom and helped me to undress. I don't know what I said or tried to say; but she hushed me like a child and drew the covers over me and let me collapse into sleep.

That sleep was a journey to the underworld, so deep I could not hope to escape from the nightmares that beset me. I was harried by faceless huntsmen, bayed through dark tunnels, stood naked in a desert under the eyes of a hundred accusers; I was arraigned in a graveyard by dead men, I was hung by the thumbs in my own interrogation room, while a masked executioner held a vial of poison under my nose. I screamed as he crushed it in his giant fingers, and woke, sweating and trembling, with the sheets knotted about me like a shroud.

The smell of my own body offended me. It was the odour of fear, damned up too long, souring the body juices, spilled like the voidings of an animal for the predators to follow. I was marked now—by the Director as an intransigent, by Leporello as a man who must be bought or seduced, by Manzini as a collaborator, useful one moment, dispensable at the twitch of an eyebrow. I was in danger because I knew too much. I was exposed because I could do too little. I was a silly goat tethered to attract the tiger—and if the tiger did not come, the marksman in the tree could pick me off at a whim.

Lili could be picked off, too: by her own people, if not mine. I had pulled in Woodpecker. His network was in disorder. Lili was compromised. In the code of the trade she was marked for liquidation. If the assassins did not get her, the Director would order her arrested, if only to teach me a lesson. I looked at my watch. Three o'clock. Siesta time still. I lifted the bedside phone and called Stefanelli's house.

"Steffi? Matucci."

"Don't you ever sleep, for God's sake?"

"Steffi, the roof's falling in. Have you got a spare room?"

"For you?"

"No. To store a very sensitive package."

"How sensitive?"

"It has to be kept away from heat and light until other storage is arranged."

"*Porca miseria!* I was up all night with you. I had breakfast with you. I've had two hours of bad sleep and I'm still in my pajamas!"

"Steffi—the package may explode and blow my head off!"

"Eh-eh-eh . . . ! Where do I collect it?"

"I'll bring it to you. Go back to sleep."

"Thank you for nothing, dear friend."

I had just put the phone down when Lili came in, frowning and solicitous. "I thought you were talking in your sleep. Earlier you were shouting and groaning."

"I had bad dreams, Lili."

"You look like a bad dream yourself. What happened after you left me last night?"

"Don't ask. Just listen to me."

"But . . ."

"Lili, it's condition red for you. I want to try to get you out of the country into Switzerland. That needs time and planning. So I'm taking you to a safe house. You stay there until I'm ready to move you. Yes or no?"

I felt the sudden tension in her hands, saw the suspicion in her eyes. "If I say no . . . ?"

"You get killed by your own people or jailed by mine."

"I don't believe it. Last night . . ."

"Last night was a million years ago. While you and I were singing 'The Undressing Song,' two men were murdered—one of them mine, the other Pantaleone's lawyer. It's not in the papers because we did some stage-management. I arrested Woodpecker at four this morning. The network is broken. You're compromised. I can't protect you more than a few days, and I'm putting myself at risk to do it."

"Why?"

"Just to prove to myself I'm not a whoremaster. Will that do? You've got fifteen minutes, which is about how long it will take me to shower and dress. After that you're on your own."

"Please . . . ! Hold me. I'm frightened."

"I want you frightened, Lili. I want you to do exactly as I tell you, and don't, for Christ's sake, try to make second guesses. Understand?"

"Yes."

"Start now. Pack a small overnight bag. Take your jewelry, your checkbooks, whatever cash you have in the house."

At that moment the doorbell chimed: four musical notes, ominous in the silence. I laid a finger on Lili's lips and whispered:

"The housekeeper?"

"Out. Her day off."

I rolled out of bed, ridiculous in my nakedness, and crept from the bedroom, through the salon and into the hallway. A letter had been thrust through the mail slot and was lying about a foot from the door. I bent to pick it up and then drew back. This was siesta time. No self-respecting postman would be on the streets at the sacred hour. I went back into the bedroom.

"Lili, do you have a kitchen spatula or anything like that?"

"I think so, why?"

"Get it for me, please."

While she was rummaging in the kitchen, I dressed. Then, incongruously armed with a fish-slice, I walked back into the hall, lifted the letter by sliding the fish-slice under it and carried it gingerly to the coffee table in the center of the salon. The address was typed. The stamp was Italian. But it had not been franked by a post office. I left it there, walked back into the bedroom, snapped at Lili to get her packing done and telephoned a friend of mine in the security section of Posts and Telegraphs. He gave me the cheerful news that a normal letter bomb contained enough explosive to kill the man who opened it and maim anyone else in a normal-sized room. He promised to have an expert on the doorstep in thirty minutes. I told him I couldn't wait that long. He told me to call the police and put a man on guard until the expert arrived.

I hurried Lili through the packing. We locked the apartment and then, avoiding the elevators, walked down four flights of stairs to the lobby. The porter was sitting at his desk, his nose buried in the *Corriere dello Sport*. The street was lined on both sides with parked vehicles. My own car was jammed beautifully between a Mercedes and a Fiat 600.

I left Lili in the foyer and walked outside. The road was deserted except for a woman walking a dog, an old street cleaner laboriously pushing a tin can on wheels and the flower seller dozing at her booth on the corner. I looked up at the buildings on the opposite side. All the windows were closed, some were shuttered. There was no place for a marksman. I walked back into the building and dialled Pronto Soccorso, the police emergency service of the Carabinieri.

Five minutes later a squad car pulled up at the entrance to the apartments and the two-man crew came in at a run. The *brigadiere* was cool and efficient. He would call the explosives squad to handle the letter and to check my car for booby traps. Meantime, if I would give him a deposition . . . ? My card convinced him he could wait for it. I needed his car and his driver to deliver the lady and myself to the Excelsior Hotel.

Senz'altro! . . . We took off at speed and he dropped us diagonally opposite the hotel. We waited five minutes window-shopping at Rizzoli's, then took a taxi to the Theater of Marcellus and walked through the maze of alleys to Steffi's house.

Steffi received us with characteristic flourish. He clucked over Lili, showered her with compliments, insisted on settling her into her room himself and then stormed downstairs to give me the rough edge of his tongue.

"Matucci, you're a madman! That little baggage upstairs is dangerous! When the Director hears of this—and he will, sooner or later—you'll be cooked, screaming, like a lobster. God Almighty! It's a ready-made case to put you away for twenty years: SID colonel sells out to Polish agent! I could write the indictment myself, blindfolded. And all this other melodrama—letter bombs and calling the Carabinieri to defuse your car. Wait till that paper work starts going the rounds!"

"Steffi, have you got a whisky?"

"For you, hemlock and soda."

"Then pour me a big one and shut up."

"Shut up, he says! The next thing you'll be wanting to sleep with the woman under my roof."

"I might at that, Steffi."

"Oh, no, you don't! This is a good Jewish house. If anybody's going to defile it, it won't be a dumb goy like you. There's your drink."

"Chin-chin, Steffi."

"I hope it rots your gullet! . . . Now, can we be serious a minute?"

"I'm serious, Steffi. I'm sweating blood."

"Good! Sweat a little more for me."

"Tell me, who is Raquela Rabin?"

"Will you repeat the question, Colonel?"

"Who is Raquela Rabin?"

"Why do you want to know?"

"I have an introduction. I'd like to know something about her before we meet."

For a moment he stared at me, blank-faced and hostile; then he sat down heavily on a chair, cupped his hands round the glass and sat staring into the liquor, an old man ravaged by time and history.

". . . Fifteen came back from Auschwitz, Colonel. Raquela Rabin was the only woman. In the ghetto, when you say her name, you say it with respect—great respect. She did not have to go away; she had powerful protectors. But when the trucks came she was here, standing in the piazza, waiting like a daughter of David. She was an artist, Matucci, an angel voice, one of the greatest of her time. When you see her, you will say she is older than I, but she is still only sixty-six. Everything that should not happen to a woman happened to her, but she is still sane and splendid as the evening star. . . . You will be very gentle with her. What she tells you, you will believe without question. You will not mix her in this stinking business of yours. You will not mix her—understand that!"

"Easy, Steffi. . . . Easy!"

"I'll take you to her, because I want you clean when you go in—clean and humble, because this is a great woman. I've done you a favor, Colonel. Your woman —and she is your woman, no?—is under my roof, at my risk. Now you will tell me, who gave you this introduction?"

"Bruno Manzini."

"Why?"

"He said that if Raquela Rabin spoke well of him I might be prepared to trust him. I need that, Steffi. You warned me once I would be put on the auction block. I'm there now, Steffi. Tomorrow or the next day someone's going to open the bids. They'll be high and tempting. I'm not sure I'll be able to resist them. . . . A wise friend would help. A strong one might lend me courage. I'm running out of it, Steffi, because I don't know what to believe anymore. I don't even know who I am."

He brightened at that, as if I had read him the best news in the world. He cocked his head in that old parrot pose and surveyed me with grudging approval. "So! History is being made. The *Risorgimento* of Dante Alighieri Matucci. So you don't know who you are? Who does? But sure as breathing, you'd better see what's being done to you."

"I see it. I don't understand it."

"Because you refuse to come to terms with yourself. You don't want to decide what you are—a patriot or a mercenary."

"Hard words from a friend!"

"True words, because I am your friend."

"I've seen too many rogues wearing too many bright labels, Steffi."

"A simple question then. Today you might have been killed. Tomorrow the risk is bigger. Why do you take it? When you stake your life, what are you staking it for— or against?"

"Maybe for a dream, Steffi . . . I don't know. Maybe against a madness I smell every day in the streets. The land is the center of it somehow. The vines greening on the terraces, the white hills and the brown stubble and the river sedge with the mist on it. My land! I will not live in it by sufferance and privilege. The people? That's another thing. I hate the crowds that jostle me, the silly functionaries who bedevil me from dawn till dark; but then I see a woman bursting like a grape with love; I am served by a peasant who says 'Salve!' and offers me wine and bread and salt as if I were his brother. . . . These are the good things, Steffi, painted on the walls of Etruscan tombs, celebrated in the songs of fishermen. . . . Boh! This is home. And I don't want it trampled by jackboots or desecrated by mindless mobs. . . . Now, let's leave it, eh?"

"I can leave it, friend. You can't. You're the man who knows the underside of politics, the cogs in the power machine. You have to decide how you will use that knowledge."

"I'm not paid to use it—only to collect it."

"You collect it, but you filter it, too. You suppress, you emphasize, you interpret. To what end?"

"For Christ's sake, what do we all want? A quiet life. Some dignity in our living and dying."

"Not enough! Not half enough! Look. . . !"

"Be quiet, old man!" Lili challenged him from the doorway, cold and angry. "Let him find his own answers in his own time."

"He has no time." Steffi was brusque and brutal. "He robbed himself when he gave it to you."

"I am here to give it back. May I sit down, please?"

Steffi pointed to the chair and she sat down between

us. She laid her palms flat on the table as if to hold herself erect and in command. She was silent for a few moments, gathering herself, then she told us:

"You are friends. I am the outsider. I accept to be here because I am afraid. I don't want to be killed. I don't want to spend the rest of my life in a Roman prison. But I am not a beggar. I can pay for what you give me."

"You were not asked to pay."

"No, but I will." She turned to me and laid her hands on mine. "You are going to be very angry with me, Dante Alighieri."

"Am I?"

"There's something I haven't told you. I might have told you last night if . . . if things had been different. Then again . . . I might not. We were still bargaining then. This morning you held my life in your hands. You did not bargain. Neither did your friend."

"So . . . ?"

"Massimo Pantaleone did not leave all his documents in the bank."

"Where are the rest?"

"In the villa on Ponza."

"What are they, Lili?"

"Microfilms and maps."

"How long have they been there?"

"He took them on our last visit to the villa—a week before he died."

"But you didn't tell Woodpecker or any of your own people?"

"No."

"Why not?"

"I had no control over what Woodpecker might do. If he stole the stuff, I was finished. Only Massimo and I could possibly know the hiding place."

"Could you decribe it to me?"

"No. I would have to take you there."

"That means new arrangements. You have to wait here while we make them. Steffi, you and I have a visit to

make. Don't leave the house, Lili. If there are any call-
ers, don't answer. We'll be back in an hour or so."

"I may never come back," said Steffi mournfully. "I
may drown myself in the Tiber. I do not want to be alive
when you try explaining this madness to the Director."

… …

HE did not drown himself. He withdrew, quite deliberately, into his own yesterdays and forced me to withdraw
with him, as if it were some rite of passage that I must
undergo before I met Raquela Rabin. As we strolled—
he would not let me hurry—through the alleys of the old
ghetto, he conjured ghosts out of every doorway: old
Marco, the furniture maker, who whittled a piece of pine
into the shape of a fearsome brigand and carved his name
on the underside; Ruggiero, the pharmacist, who once
made him privy to mysteries—a mummified hand and
waters that changed colour when you mixed them; Blasio,
the gunsmith, who showed him pistols which had killed
five men in duels of honour.

As he talked, his narrative became more vivid, his
gestures more ample and exotic. He swept away all traces
of the present and planted me firmly in the city of his
own childhood. Over there, for instance, was Salomone,
called by the folk of the quarter Salomone Vecchione. He
was so old that he looked like a twin brother to Methu-
selah, so shrunken that one more year must see him disappear altogether. He wore a long black caftan that was
green when the sun shone on it, a little black cap
perched on his wispy scalp and a silver chain with a star
pendant on his wheezy, hollow bosom. He trundled a
barrow from which he sold old prints and books with
mildewed bindings and metal tubes with scrolls inside
and clay tablets that looked as though birds had walked
on them before they were fired in the oven.

The market people were afraid of Salomone and treated
him with the exaggerated respect due a magus or a caster
of spells. When he passed they made the sign against
the evil eye and muttered, balefully, about the fire that

would consume all Jews and pagans. But to the young
Stefanelli, he was like the imp out of a bottle, with a
wonder in every pocket.

Not all of Steffi's ghosts were friends. Some were sad
traitors; some were nightmare enemies. Luca, the hunch-
back, for instance, who sat on his stool outside the hairdresser's and allowed his hump to be touched for a coin.
Luca was a police pimp who spied on the ghetto people
for the Fascists. Balbo was a ruffian policeman who took
tribute from every shopkeeper on his beat, and Fra
Patrizio was a shave-pate Franciscan who in every ser-
mon railed against perfidious Jews who crucified the
Saviour every day. . . .

"Sometimes," said Steffi moodily, "I would like to forget them all. But God is an ironist who keeps the key to
memory in his own hands. . . . Here we are, Colonel. I
will present you to Raquela Rabin and then leave. You
will come directly to the point with her and not stay
too long. She is very frail."

She was frail indeed, white-haired, pale as milk, almost
transparent, so that you felt the next *scirocco* might blow
her away. Only her eyes were alive, dark and lustrous,
and strangely pitying. She sat erect and calm, listening in
silence while I explained who I was and why I had come.
When I had finished, she seemed to lapse into meditation
like an ancient pythoness waiting for the spirit of divina-
tion to animate her. I felt oddly diminished—an ignorant
neophyte in the presence of a woman who had seen and
suffered everything. Even when she spoke—and she was
very gentle with me—there was a hieratic quality in her
tone that diminished me still further.

"Do you know why Bruno sent you to me?"

"No, madam."

"We were lovers for a long time. Not happy lovers
always, because I was famous and courted and Bruno
was haunted by his own past: a mother who was a once
famous courtesan, a father who lavished money on him
but was never prepared to acknowledge him. But the
love was there. It is still there."

"Even though you were taken, and he stayed."

"We had parted long before. I went of my own free will. He stayed to fight against those who had taken me. He is still fighting."

"How?"

"He is a strange man. He believes in forgiving. He does not believe in forgetting."

"Is there a difference?"

"He thinks so."

"You?"

"I accept what is: that I am alive and others are dead; that I cannot change it; that people must forget because they cannot bear to remember."

"Can I trust Bruno Manzini?"

"To be what he is, yes."

"What is he, madam?"

"A man who has built himself, cell by cell, from nothing. . . . He is very strong, very faithful. What he promises he will do, however much it costs him. Each year, on the anniversary of the Black Sabbath, he sends me a card. In the right-hand drawer of the desk you will find a folder. Please pass it to me."

The folder was of tooled leather made by a Florentine craftsman. On the cover, embossed in gold, was a Star of David. I handed it to her. She spread it open on her knees, took out the cards and handed them to me. The cards were identical with that which I had found in Pantaleone's bedroom. Only the inscriptions were different.

HANS HELMUT ZIEGLER
São Paulo—3 January, 1968

EMANUELE SALATRI
London—18 August, 1971

FRANZISKUS LOEFFLER
Oberalp, Austria

"What do these mean, madam?"

"They are the names of men connected, each in his own way, with what happened to me and to others in 1943. I have fifteen so far. There are nine to come.

Bruno Manzini traced them all. A labour of years, because they were spread all over the world. When he traced them, he sent each man a card and a dossier on his past."

"What do the dates mean?"

"The days on which they died."

"Who killed them?"

"They killed themselves."

"There is no date on this one."

"He is still alive. . . ."

"The difference?"

"Bruno told me that this was the best gift of all—a man who had found a way to live honourably with himself. I was very content to know that."

"Are you happy with Bruno Manzini—a man who plays God?"

"He does not see it that way."

"How then?"

"He says that every man must be allowed to judge himself, but he must not be allowed to bury the evidence."

"And you, madam?"

"I agree with him, Colonel. I gave evidence at Nuremberg—for and against those in the dock. I hate no one now. I am afraid of nothing. But the terror has come again—in Vietnam, in Brazil, in Africa, here in Europe. Is not that why you have come to me—because you, too, are afraid?"

"Yes, madam, I am very much afraid."

"Then trust my Bruno, but not blindly, because then he would have no respect for you. Argue with him, fight him, friend to friend. You may not convince him; you may even end as adversaries, but he will never, never betray you. . . ."

"Thank you, madam."

"Thank you for coming. I wish peace on your house and in your heart."

I was grateful for the blessing, but I walked out into the sunlight a very pensive man. A new conviction was crystalizing out of the murky fluid of my own thoughts.

There was no cure for the human condition because every man read the present and plotted the future in the light of his own past. There was no such thing as a clean start, because no one truly forgave and no one wholly forgot. In the end, the folk memory betrayed us all. The wrongs of the fathers were revenged on the children. I understood Manzini and his cold conviction that, even in exile, the tyrants should not be allowed to flourish. I understood the Director and his willingness to settle for a balance, however precarious. I understood Leporello and his fanatic belief that order at any price was cheaper than chaos. The only person I did not understand was myself. . . .

On the way back to Stefanelli's, I stopped in a bar and made a telephone call to Manzini at the Grand Hotel. Our conversation was brief.

"Cavaliere, I have just spoken with Raquela Rabin."

"And. . . ?"

"I am very glad we met. I should like to see you as soon as possible."

"I leave for Bologna in half an hour. I am happy to receive you there at any time. When may I expect to see you?"

"In two or three days at the latest. Sooner if I can make it."

"Good! What is your own situation?"

"Difficult. It may improve soon. I hope so, anyway."

"Good luck then!"

His wish must have had some potency because when I called the Director, his aide told me he had been called to an urgent conference at the Ministry. Was there a message? None that I could deliver safely on an open line. He should tell the Director that there were new developments in my current investigation and that I would be out of contact for forty-eight hours. I was only putting off the bad day; but if I could get to Ponza and lay my hands on the rest of the Pantaleone files, I might still cheat the headsman.

I was faced now with a problem in space and time. The island of Ponza—which is not my favourite place in all the world—lies about sixty-five kilometers southwest of Gaeta. Legend says Pontius Pilate was born there. The Fascists used it as a place of exile for political prisoners. After the war, islands being scarce and getting scarcer in the twentieth century, people started to buy land and build villas on the slopes around the shoreline. The island is served by ferries from Anzio, Formia and Naples, but whichever way you choose, it still means a road journey from Rome and a three- or four-hour sea trip, which in rough weather is a purgatory. At all costs I wanted to avoid using public transport and to cut the time of the operation to a minimum. If the Director decided to send out a panic call for me, I would be as conspicuous as a wart on the Mona Lisa.

Besides, there was another and more sinister possibility. The papers stolen from Bandinelli's office were now in the hands of persons unknown. By now it would be clear that the codex was incomplete. Conclusion: the hunters would be on the prowl again and by simple logic they must come back, sooner or later, to Lili Anders and to the villa which she had shared with Pantaleone. Postscript to the conclusion: I needed help in a hurry.

By the time I got back to Steffi's house, it was five-thirty. I put through a priority call to a certain Colonel Carl Malinowski at NATO headquarters in Naples. Malinowski is an agreeable American—sometimes too agreeable for his own good. Two years ago I managed to prise him out of an embarrassing situation which involved his Neapolitan girl friend and a Russian agent operating in the naval dock areas. Malinowski owed me a favor. I needed it now, in the shape of the big Baglietto, which he used for drinking parties and seduction and which could do twenty-five knots in any reasonable sea.

Malinowski was happy to oblige. He could write himself a leave pass. He also had a new girl friend who would appreciate the outing. If we could be at Mergellina docks by first light, he would drive us to the island himself. Better still, if we cared to come down to Naples tonight, he would feed us dinner and offer us a bed in his own apartment. The bed was matrimonial size. He presumed it would suit. If it wasn't that sort of party, I could sleep on the divan and to hell with me. The rest was easy. I hired a Fiat 130 from a rental agency, and by seven in the evening—to Steffi's infinite relief—we were out of Rome and heading south along the *autostrada* to Naples.

I enjoyed that drive: the sudden sense of relief as the city fell away behind us, the dusk gentling the hills of Lazio, the lights pricking out from the mountain farms, the processional sweep of the traffic along the highway, the rise of the yellow moon behind the crags of the Apennines, the brief but grateful privacy of man and woman in a small floating world.

Lili was tense at first, openly resenting my high-handed dealings with her person. I had leaned heavily on the dangers of her situation; but now, homeless and rootless, she could see no hopeful future, and I was in no position to promise her one. She sat, stiff and withdrawn, as if she could not bear to be near me. I turned on the radio to a session of Neapolitan music and affected to ignore her. After a while she began to nod, and when I drew her towards me, she did not resist but laid her head on my shoulder and dozed, fitfully, until we passed Monte Cassino.

She was calmer then. She sat close and we talked, quietly and disjointedly, until the mood of the first evening came on us again.

"Know something, Dante Alighieri?"

"What?"

"At this moment we really are *noantri*. I can't go home. You don't know where you're going."

"True, my love, true."

"I like your Steffi."

"Yes. . . . He's quite a character."

"He's very fond of you."

"We understand each other."

"But he's afraid you'll make wrong decisions, isn't he?"

"I'm afraid, too, *bambina*."

"I hope you don't sell out—to anyone. Once you do, there's no way back. I know. . . ."

"Why did you come into the game, Lili?"

"Haven't you got that in your dossiers?"

"The how of it—not the real reason."

"There's a whore in every woman, *caro,* and you know it. Come the low moment when she's lonely and unloved and the first crow's-feet are beginning to show, she'll sell, provided the price looks like a gift and the words are said gently, and tomorrow doesn't look too near. No excuses. No pity, thank you."

"Suppose we get you out of the country, what then?"

"I'm a bachelor girl of modest means, in the market for a man."

"What sort of man?"

"That's a private dream, and I won't have you laugh at it."

"I wouldn't laugh."

"What kind of a woman do you want, Dante Alighieri?"

"I've had all kinds, Lili—except the one I'd settle down with and make children."

"Aren't you ever lonely?"

"Often. But it's a tolerable condition. At least it has been. . . ."

"Now?"

"I don't like the fellow who lives in my skin."

"I like him—sometimes."

"You don't know him very well, Lili."

"Well enough to put a name to him."

"What name?"

"*Bufalo solitario*—the rogue male."

"Paid to protect the herd."

"From what? The Marxists, the Fascists, the Monarchists? I don't believe this 'protection,' neither do you. You're a political instrument. Any hand can lift you and use you for any work."

"Let's talk about something else, eh?"

"If you like. What do you do when you can't bear to be alone. . . ?"

"I go out and play."

"Like last night in Trastevere?"

"Like that. . . ."

"I wish we didn't have to go to Ponza."

"So do I."

"What happens when we come back?"

"It depends on what we find and how well I can hide it. . . . That's Capua over there, where Spartacus raised the revolt of the slaves."

"I know about Spartacus, *caro*. I just hope we have better luck than he did."

MAJOR Carl Malinowski of the United States Marines was a tonic for our jaded spirits. He was six feet tall, all brawn and muscle, with ham fists and a big laugh and a magnolia drawl which, although I speak tolerable English, was often hard for me to understand. He had an unshakable conviction that the world was still a Garden of Eden, full of willing Eves and congenial serpents. His apartment, furnished in American style, was a bachelor's paradise, with a view across the Bay, from Vesuvius to Capo di Sorrento, a bewildering liquor cupboard and piped music in every room. His new girl was a Swede, culled from the summer crop of tourists and blooming after the transplant. He took one look at Lili and shouted his approval to the neighbourhood.

"*Bella! Bellissima!* Dante, my boy, your taste's improving. This is a real Southern-style woman! Honey, you be good to this man now. He's the best Eyetalian I know—all heart and sex urge. Bright, too—though you wouldn't think it to look at him. Helga, why don't you take Lili and get her settled while Dante and I build some drinks." He clamped an iron fist on my shoulder and steered me to the bar. "Tell me now, Colonel, sir, is this business or pleasure?"

"Business, Carl."

"So what do you want me to do?"

"Get us to Ponza, get us back fast."

"In this weather it's three hours each way—more if the wind freshens. How long do you want to stay?"

"Two hours should do it."

"We leave at six in the morning, we're back midafternoon. Suit you?"

"Fine."

"Expecting trouble?"

"An outside chance."

"What's with you and Lili-belle?"

"Some business, some pleasure. Too much of one, not enough of the other."

"I read you, Colonel, sir. I read you loud and clear. So tonight we drink Christ's tears and have ourselves a love-in. Tomorrow we hit the beach at Ponza!"

It was a long night and a merry one. We dined like kings on caviar and beefsteak and Neapolitan ice cream. We drank two liters of Lacrima Christi and half a bottle of Courvoisier, talked the world to rights and told bawdy stories and sprawled on the rug, drowsing to taped music. Sometime after midnight we paired off and went to bed, and I must tell you there is no bed in all the world more comfortable, more apt for lovemaking, than a big brass Neapolitan *letto matrimoniale*.

It was a good night for both of us. We did what pleased us and we pleased each other. We were glad, we were grateful, and, for a while, not solitary. We slept deeply and we did not dream at all. We were awake and enjoying each other again when Malinowski hammered on the door and summoned us to breakfast.

I have told it badly; I might have used the same words for a dozen encounters, because I am—and I say it, gratefully—a man who has been fortunate in most of his women. But this time there was a difference, a sense of consequence if not yet of commitment. There was another difference, too; I was disposed to be sentimental afterwards, while Lili would have none of it.

She told me so, bluntly, as we stood together on the afterdeck of the Baglietto and watched the green cone of Ischia fade against the dawn.

"*Caro,* sometimes you treat me as if I had no brains at all. I know what's at stake. If the material at the villa

is important, it puts power into your hands. You think
it will also buy me a free passage out of Italy."

"I hope it will."

"And salve your conscience about me."

"If you like to put it that way."

"But you won't promise anything?"

"I can't."

"Nonsense! I don't need you to get me out of Italy,
Dante Alighieri."

"You think you can run the frontier guards yourself?
Don't try it, Lili."

"I wouldn't have to do that. I could hire any fisherman
on Ponza to run me into Corsica tomorrow."

"What are you trying to say, Lili?"

"That you need me, like you need the Pantaleone
records, as a bargaining card. Let me go and you rob
yourself of power, you castrate yourself. I understand
that. I accept it. But you insult me when you try to dress
the thing up like a confidence trick. Your friend Steffi
was right. You always refuse to come to terms with
yourself. . . . Now can we go inside, please? I'm cold."

It was cold. The wind was freshening from the north-
west, whipping up an uncomfortable sea, and Malinowski
was driving the boat hard, pitting his helmsman's skill
against the yaw of the high-powered craft and the short,
tricky chop. We settled ourselves in the saloon and I
tried, with a kind of desperation, to salvage the argument
and my own pride.

"Let's have it clear, Lili. I made a treaty with you. So
far I've honoured it. So far you're free and protected.
Agreed?"

"Agreed."

"Now you want to change it. You want me to turn a
blind eye while you make a run for Corsica."

"No! I want you to be sure what kind of treaty you
are making with other people, and what it will do to
you in the end."

"And why the hell should you care?"

"Poor Dante Alighieri! So many women and you've
learnt so little. What a waste!"

"At least I don't have any illusions."

"Boh! Let's not argue then. You write the script, you say the words, you pull the strings, and when the play's over Lili, the puppet, is packed up in her box. Just so we know, my love."

"And you said there'd be no blackmail! God!"

"Blackmail involves a threat, doesn't it? How can I threaten you? With the Pantaleone records? You will have those as soon as we reach the villa. With a night in bed? That's the custom of the trade, isn't it? With your promise of protection? That's the trade, too—every little policeman plays the same trick at every interrogation. So . . . what frightens you, my brave Colonel, if not yourself?"

"If that's the way you read it—fine! Right or wrong, it doesn't change anything. . . . Let's go up on the bridge."

"I'd like to be alone for a while."

"This is business, Lili."

"At your service, Colonel."

Malinowski welcomed us with a blue-eyed smile, all health and innocence, and spread on the chart table a small-scale map of Ponza. On this Lili identified the site of the villa, a small promontory on the eastern shore of the island. The villa was noted in the Pilot as a landmark for mariners: ". . . a large square building of grey stone, due east of which the pillars and arches of a Roman ruin are clearly visible. In winds W to NW the southern inlet offers fair shelter to small vessels. The bottom is sand and rock with some wood." I asked Lili:

"If we put in there, can we get to the villa from the beach?"

"Yes. There's a rough track that goes up to the ruins."

Malinowski cut in with a sailor's question. "If we anchor, we'll have to put down the dinghy and winch it up again. You'll have a wet and uncomfortable ride to the beach. Why don't we moore in the harbour itself and you take a taxi to the villa?"

"Strategy, Carl. In the port we'd be conspicuous. It's

out of season. The locals would talk. I'd rather not have that."

"'Clear, Colonel, sir. We anchor."

"The villa itself, Lili. Any servants?"

"No. Out of season it's closed up. A village family comes in once a week to clean it and turn on the heating for a few hours. But we don't have to go near the villa. What we want is there, in the ruins."

"Why the ruins?"

"You will see when you get there."

"Can you overlook the ruins from the house?"

"Only the top of them. Our domain is walled all the way around. The ruins are on Government land, part of the shoreline. The *demanio* line runs here."

"Better still. Take a look at the chart, Carl. How close in can you anchor?"

"Let's see . . . For safety, a cable's length."

"Visible from the house?"

"On the approach, yes. When we're anchored, probably not. I don't understand your problem, though. That's public terrain. Anyone can land from the sea. That's one piece of Italian law I do know."

"I'm not worried about trespass, Carl. Lili owns the villa, anyway. Let's say I'm concerned with hostile intruders."

"Those, Colonel, sir, we can take care of very nicely." He opened the cupboard under the chart table and brought out an automatic rifle. "I carry this little baby in case the sharks chase one of my girls while she's swimming bare-ass. So, while you and Lili-belle go ashore, I stand deck watch for hostile intruders. . . . Satisfied?"

"No. I can't have an American officer involved in an Italian domestic drama. So, if you don't mind, I'll take the gun ashore with me."

"Just as you like. Switch on the radio, will you? We should get the news in a minute and I'd like to catch the weather report afterwards."

"If you don't want me anymore," said Lili, "I think I'll lie down in the saloon. I'm feeling a little seasick."

"You should have told me, Lili-belle. I've got just the thing to . . ."

"No, thank you, Carl. I'll be all right. Excuse me!"

When she left us, Carl grinned and fixed me with a knowing eye. "Problems, brother? Need a little postnuptial counselling?"

"As a matter of fact, I do."

"Okay, tell Uncle Carl."

"What would you say if I told you Lili was a double agent working for me and for the Marxists?"

"I'd say half your luck—and forget you told me."

"And if I told you I might have to toss her in jail to satisfy my people?"

"I'd say you were in a nasty jam."

"And if I then asked you to keep her on board and run her up to Corsica out of Italian jurisdiction, what would you say?"

"I would tell you, Colonel, sir, that you are my very good friend, and I owe you a big favor which I am now repaying. But I would tell you also that I am a natural-born, dyed-in-the-wool Republican, that I have seen my buddies die in Korea and in Vietnam and I don't much like niggers, though I've learned to live with 'em, but Commies of any sex or breed I can't abide. And so, if you asked me—and I'm sure you wouldn't—I would have to say no sir, no thanks, no way at all. You do read me, Colonel?"

I read him so clearly I couldn't believe it. For a moment I thought he was joking. He joked about most things. The shock was that he was in dead earnest. I suppose I had never really believed that a great and vigorous people could survive on such simplistic formulas of faith. But then we Europeans had a much longer and bloodier experience and we were still not half as skeptical as we needed to be. . . .

Carl Malinowski held out his hand. "No hard feelings, eh, Dante?"

"No, Carl."

"And I'm not saying you're a Red. You know that."

"Of course."

"And I'm not judging Lili-belle either. Just ducking the issue, you might say."

"I understand."

"And I'm still with you against the hostile intruders."

"Thanks."

"Now, let's listen to the news, eh?"

The news, read in the bland, euphoric style of R.A.I., was the usual mixture: the war in Vietnam, the peace negotiations in Paris, the tribal feuds of Africa, strikes in England, strikes in Italy, another piece from the Pope on the Italian divorce law, another Italian parliamentary squabble, this time over the allocation of provincial subsidies, and finally a terse postscript: an Arab employee in the Libyan Embassy in Rome had been shot dead outside his house on the Aventine Hill. The victim was the Roman representative of the Palestine guerrilla organization, Al Fatah. The police were treating the murder as a political crime, probably organized by Israeli agents.

The item made the hair stand up on the nape of my neck. In the SID I was regarded as an expert on Arab-Israeli terrorist activities. I had built up our first files on Palestinian guerrillas, resident or active in the Republic. I had good informants among the Jordanians and the Egyptians. I knew the director of the Jewish counter-terrorist organization, a cool-eyed Lett, who, in my view, was one of the best intelligence men in the world. Once, in a very private gathering of experts, I had heard him discourse on the true nature of terror, both as a political weapon and as a social infection.

"As a weapon, it is almost irresistible. It infuses fear and doubt. It destroys confidence in democratic procedures. It immobilizes police agencies. It polarizes factions: the young against the old; the have-nots against the haves; the ignorant against the knowing; the idealists against the pragmatists. As a social infection it is more deadly than the plague: it justifies the vilest of remedies, the suspension of human rights, preventive arrests, cruel and unusual punishment, subordination, torture and legal murder. The most moral of men, the sanest of governments, is not immune from the infection. Violence begets violence; blackmailers are paid from the public treasury; reprisals fall heavily on the innocent as on the guilty. . . . You Italians made a hero of a man who hijacked an airliner. When we strike at an Arab who plants a bomb in Rome, we have to accept that we will waken all the latent anti-Semites in Italy and give a scapegoat to the new fascists. Every Marxist beaten in a police cell raises twenty recruits for the revolution. Every bomb thrown in the streets brings out a new brigade of riot police with gas guns and water cannon. Every big city has its own university of terror. And the lessons are circulated from Ulster to the Udine, from Vietnam to Venezuela, from Rio to Athens to Rome. . . ."

For me, therefore, the murder on the Aventine was more than bad news, it was a personal disaster. Here I was cruising like a tourist between Naples and Ponza, in very mixed company, while the Director would be pressing panic buttons and combing the country for one delinquent expert on Semitic affairs. If I brought back the Pantaleone papers and Lili Anders, I might just escape the rack and thumbscrew. If I came back empty-handed, he would rend me limb for limb and feed me to the lions in the zoo.

For one panic moment I thought of trying to contact him by ship's radio, at least to report myself on duty. Then I realized that this would only compound the mistakes of the last two days and broadcast my business to the whole of the Western Mediterranean. To the devil with it then. He had given me a free hand. I would nail the brief to his door like Luther's articles; if he didn't like what he read he could eat it for supper. I rather hoped it might choke him.

We raised Ponza in a squall of wind and driving rain, and we had to coast slowly right under the lee of the island before we could make any positive identification of the promontory and Lili's villa. Even the Pilot book fell short of its promise. The shelter offered by the inlet was less than fair and the anchor-hold was dubious at best. There was one small profit. If there were any watchers in the villa, they would have no better visibility than

we had. Lili and I draped ourselves in oilskins and
scrambled into the bobbing dinghy. Carl handed me the
rifle, and after the customary struggle to start the out-
board, we motored through a choppy surf to the beach.

The beach was deserted. On the promontory itself
there was no sign of life. The track which led to the
ruins was steep and greasy, and at one point we were
scrambling on hands and knees, hauling ourselves up-
ward by tussocks and the stalks of wild rosemary. By
the time we reached the top, I was breathless and irritable. I was convinced that either Pantaleone was mad or
Lili had deliberately led me on a fool's errand. I could
not, for the life of me, understand why, with a great
fortress of a villa at his disposal, any man would hide
valuable documents in a mouldering ruin, on land that
didn't even belong to him. I said as much—and heatedly
—to Lili, who burst out laughing.

"You look so silly—like a clown in a circus! And that
little popgun. What are you going to shoot with it—sea
gulls?"

She took me by the hand and led me through an archway into the shelter of a vault which had, somehow, with-
stood the ravages of the centuries. The outer walls were
of hewn stone, but the inner ones were of reticulated
brickwork thrust upwards and inwards into a shallow
dome. The floor was paved with slabs of marble, cracked,
discoloured and sagging in places, but still mostly intact.
The place smelled of stale droppings and sea spray. Lili
threw back the hood of her oilskins and stood, hands on
hips, surveying the shadowy interior.

"You think Massimo was crazy? So did I when he
brought me here. But think again. The villa is left all
winter. Servants poke into everything when the *padrone*
is away. Look around. Go on, examine! What do you
see?"

The brickwork of the walls revealed nothing. I walked
the floor testing for hollow spaces beneath it. Again nothing.

Lili stood there grinning at me in triumph. "See, Dante
Alighieri, you are not half so clever as you think you

are. And Massimo was not always so stupid as he looked. Watch!"

She moved to a small sunken patch of floor where the rain, driving in through the archway, had created a puddle, perhaps three or four centimeters deep. She knelt down and with her bare hands prised up a small triangular piece of marble. She held it up for my inspection. It was the size of my palm, coated on the underside with a thick wad of cement.

"Like a bath plug, eh, Dante? You didn't walk in the puddle, but even if you had, the floor would have sounded solid."

She plunged her fingers into the aperture and drew out a long aluminum tube such as architects use for plans and specifications. It was sealed at both ends with black adhesive tape. Immediately she removed the tube, the puddle emptied itself into the hole. Lili replaced the marble plug and handed the tube to me.

"It is exactly as we left it. The maps are rolled inside. The microfilms are in small capsules."

"There's nothing else?"

"Nothing."

"Let's go. You carry this."

"Not even a thank you for puppet Lili?"

"Thank you, puppet Lili. Now you follow me until we come to the beach track. Then you go first."

I released the safety catch on the rifle and made for the entrance to the vault. Halfway to the entrance I stopped to scan the narrow vista framed by the archway. All I could see was the rise of the land, covered with tussocks and boulders and stunted bushes and the lower courses of the wall surrounding the villa domain. So far, so good. I moved closer so that the vista widened and the upper course of the wall became visible and then the top of it, a layer of cement stuck with fragments of broken glass. Then I heard a shout, amplified and distorted by a loud-hailer.

"You, in there! Come out with your hands up. This is the Carabinieri. I repeat—this is the Carabinieri."

I turned back to Lili and snatched the tube from her.

"Now listen and understand. Stay close to me. Do nothing, say nothing, unless I tell you. Clear?"

"Clear."

"We're going out now."

I threw back the hood of my oilskins and then, holding the rifle and the tube high above my head, I walked through the archway with Lili at my heels. Twenty yards from the entrance, just outside my last field of vision, there were five men, two on one side, three on the other. Four were in uniform and armed with submachine guns. The fifth was in civilian clothes and carried the loud-hailer. I recognized him immediately: the freckle-faced redhead, aide to General Leporello. He recognized me, too, and the expression on his face gave me a singular pleasure.

The troops began to close in, guns cocked and ready. The young man followed, a little less confidently. I let them come to within five meters before I halted them in my best parade-ground style. They stopped, looking uncertainly from me to the redhead. Then I told them:

"I will identify myself in proper form. Whoever is in command will check my documents. I am Matucci, Dante Alighieri, Colonel in the Service of Defense Information. The person accompanying me is Anders, Lili, in my custody and assisting me in my investigations. Now, we shall lower our hands, and the officer in command will approach to complete the identification and explain this situation to me."

The redhead found voice and courage at last. He approached, gave me a tentative salute and presented himself. "Roditi, Matteo, Captain, aide to Major-General Leporello. May I see your papers, please, sir?"

I fished them out from under the oilskins and handed them to him. He made a great play of reading them, then handed them back.

"Thank you, sir. The situation, sir, is as follows. I am under orders from General Leporello to maintain surveillance of the Villa Pantaleone and its environs and to inhibit any attempt to remove papers or property of whatsoever kind from the premises. In pursuance of these orders I am empowered to call upon the assistance of local units. That explains the presence of the detachment."

"May I see those orders, please, Captain?"

"Certainly, sir."

He handed them to me and I took a little longer than I needed to study them. Then I quizzed him, loud enough for the local boys to hear and take note.

"It would appear, Captain, that you have misread these orders."

"Sir?"

"The orders refer specifically and exclusively to, and I quote, 'the villa and the domain dependent thereon which is called the Villa Pantaleone.' That's right, isn't it?"

"Yes, sir."

"You will note that the land on which we are now standing and the ruins at my back are outside the domain of the Villa Pantaleone and are, in fact, public property delimited by the *demanio* markers on the land and the low watermark on the shore. Correct?"

"Correct, sir."

"Therefore you have exceeded your orders. You have impeded a senior officer of the Service of Defense Information in the discharge of highly secret duties. You have placed him and the person in his custody at considerable risk. One incautious move by any of your troops might have caused a fatal accident. You do see that."

"Respectfully, I submit the danger was minimal."

"No doubt that submission will be considered at the proper time and place. Anything else, Captain?"

"I should like a private word with you, sir."

"Not possible at this moment, Captain. I suggest you return to your duties and leave me to carry out mine."

"That vessel, sir, in the bay . . ."

"Has been made available to me by courtesy of our friends and allies in NATO. Further questions?"

"No, sir."

"My compliments to General Leporello. I shall telephone him on my return to Rome. Dismiss! Come, Miss Anders. Walk in front of me, please."

It is hard to make a dignified exit with four guns at your back. It is harder still to make it down a slippery goat track in driving rain, carrying a rifle and a long tube of explosive documents. In point of fact, we slid the last thirty feet on our backsides and floundered into the dinghy like seals.

By the time we reached the Baglietto, we were both in shock. I was sweating from every pore and Lili was retching over the side of the dinghy. Helga hauled us inboard and made the dinghy fast. Carl—God bless the Marines! —had the anchor up and was charging seaward at twenty-five knots before I had poured our first brandy.

Lili, grey and trembling, lay on the settee while I forced the liquor between her chattering teeth. She stared at me as if I were a stranger. "Back there . . . they were going to kill us!"

"They didn't, Lili. And they can't touch us now."

"Not now. But tomorrow, the day after . . ."

"Finish your drink. Close your eyes. Try to sleep. . . ."

"Who was that man, Roditi . . . ?"

"You heard."

"I heard. I didn't understand."

"I'll explain later. Relax now. . . . Relax. . . ."

"I don't know you at all, Dante Alighieri. Your face changes all the time. I can't tell which one is yours."

"I'm a bad actor. That's all. Trust me, *bambina*."

"I have to . . . there's no one else."

"Another drink?"

"I couldn't."

"Close your eyes. . . . That's better. . . . *Lasci' andare, bambina* . . . let go. Let everything go."

After a while she lay quiet and the surge of the sea made her dozy. I poured myself another brandy, stripped the seals from the metal tube and examined the contents: a set of overlay maps on transparent paper, each labelled with the name of a city and references to standard ordnance maps, and half a dozen metal capsules, each containing a spool of microfilm. The maps were easy to interpret. They showed the positions of police posts, military installations, communication centers, traffic control points, military and civilian airfields. The microfilms were impossible to decipher without projection equipment. However, I borrowed the chart enlarger from the bridge and was able to establish that they consisted of documents and letters and nominal rolls, and lists of figures. I had no doubt at all that they supplied the best possible motive for the murders in the Via Sicilia and were, in fact, the blueprints of a *colpo di stato*. It would need a team of experts to interpret them accurately, and a very wise statesman to decide how to use them. I sealed them back in their container, and went up on the bridge to talk to Carl.

I found him poring over his charts while Helga stood wheel watch. I asked him, "How much fuel have you got, Carl?"

"Plenty. Why?"

"Enough to get us into Ostia?"

"Ostia! For Chrissake, that wasn't in the schedule at all!"

"I know, Carl. But could you get us there?"

"I could. Would you like to tell me why?"

"Because I've just identified a murderer and we could have been murdered ourselves."

"The Commies?"

"No, Carl. The other ones."

"So, we go to Ostia. Take five while I lay me a course."

"Can you give me an estimated time of arrival?"

"I'll give it to you firm, little brother."

"Then I'd like to make a ship-to-shore radio call."

"Can do. Sit tight now, while I play with my slide rule."

While Carl was doing his arithmetic, I jotted down the coded messages which would convey to the Director my immediate needs: a car and an armed escort to meet us at Ostia, an emergency conference immediately on our arrival in Rome, safe lodgings and an agent to guard Lili Anders until her future was decided. Forty minutes later I had the Director's answer:

"Communication acknowledged. Arrangements agreed."

We do have code words for thanks and commendations. He didn't use them. Under the circumstances I could hardly blame him.

❦

In the event, the Director was extremely civil. He was a little frosty at first; but he thawed like an ice cube in whisky when I handed over the maps and the microfilms and made my first verbal report. He approved, without reserve, my concern for Lili Anders, in proof whereof he countermanded a previous order and lodged her, in state, under a fictional name, at the Grand Hotel. He even changed the guard for a more presentable type who would not detract from the ambience.

He invited me to dinner at his apartment. He commended me for my imagination, my finesse, my courage in risking my career and perhaps my life to conclude an important investigation. He saw good sense in my suspicions of Leporello, although he was not yet ready to pass judgment. He sat with me through a private screening of the microfilms and was sedulous to weigh my opinion of the documents and the personages named therein. He read the maps with me and agreed with the major points of my interpretation. At the end of the session, which lasted until after midnight, he ordered fresh coffee, brought out his best brandy and offered me the rewards of virtue.

"This Lili Anders . . . I agree with your submission. She has done us a service. She is no longer a security risk. She could be an embarrassment. Let's get her out of the country—tomorrow."

"Thank you, sir."

"Now, let's talk about your own future. How much leave have you accumulated?"

"About four months."

"I'd like you to take it, now. After you return from leave, I propose to detach you for extended studies with friendly agencies abroad. You will have the best possible introductions, a very flexible brief, and your pay and allowances will be supplemented by a generous grant from the funds of this Service. How does that sound?"

"Like an obituary notice."

The Director smiled and spread his elegant hands in a gesture of deprecation. "My dear Matucci! You and I live in an upside-down world. You will be buried for a while but you will not be dead, just enjoying yourself while you wait for resurrection day."

"No alternatives?"

"There are always alternatives, my friend, but I do not think they would recommend themselves to an intelligent man. I could, for example, retain you on the Leporello investigation, in which case you would be at constant risk, an abrasive element, a prime target for assassination. I could, on the other hand, bow to the pressure which inevitably will be applied, to remove you from the Service altogether and return you to your own corps of Carabinieri, where you would fall under the direct authority of Major-General Leporello. He knows you for a nuisance. He may consider you a threat."

"I see what you mean."

"You see everything except the core of the apple."

"Which is?"

"You know too much. You lack the authority and—forgive me—the experience to make use of the knowledge."

"And . . . ?"

"You would not be content as passive instrument of a complicated and highly variable policy."

"Also I would not submit to pressure by a murder suspect, however high he stood."

"And you would be very unwilling to treat with political conspirators, however high they stood."

"Exactly."

"So, because I respect you and because I should like to be in a position to recall you at an appropriate moment, I immobilize you. I offer you as a propitiatory victim to the powerful people whose names we know. I buy myself time to deal with them by the classic formula: divide and rule. I told you once before, this is the only course I see as possible for Italy at this moment in history. You would polarize the factions, Matucci. You have already done it."

"That, too, is a classic formula."

"And like every formula, it has limited application. I am not blaming you, Matucci. On the contrary, since I do not often choose to explain myself, I am paying you a compliment which I believe you merit. . . . Well?"

"I'd like to pay you a compliment, too, sir. I think you're a very civilized man. I couldn't ask for a more stylish funeral."

"Excellent! More brandy?"

"Thank you."

"Now, as to details. As from this moment you are officially on vacation for four months and relieved of all duties and responsibilities in the Service—except one. You will escort Lili Anders to Zurich tomorrow morning. Your flight has been booked. A hotel reservation has been made for you at the Baur au Lac. I shall hand you the tickets and the necessary currency before you leave tonight. You will remain outside Italy for at least a month. After that you may make whatever arrangements you choose for the rest of your vacation. If you choose to divert yourself with the lady—to whom obviously you have some attachment—that is your business. The Service has no further interest in her, provided she does not attempt to reenter the Republic. It's a little rushed, I'm afraid, but I am sure you will find the financial arrangements more than generous. . . . Questions?"

"No. A minor worry. I'd hate to spend a long vacation waiting for a bullet in the back. I'd much rather stay on duty where there's a certain amount of protection."

"I thought we had covered that. The whole purpose of the tactic is to demonstrate that you are no longer a threat to Leporello or anyone else and that action against you would violate what I might call your very useful neutrality. . . . There is a danger period, however: from the moment you leave this house until you take off for Zurich tomorrow."

"I was wondering about that, too."

"So I've assigned a two-man team to cover all your movements. They've already packed your clothes and delivered the suitcases to the Grand Hotel. Your room adjoins that of Miss Lili Anders. You will leave the hotel together at eight-thirty. Much simpler from a security point of view."

"Of course."

"Now . . . two air tickets, ten thousand Swiss francs in varying denominations and an order on the Union Bank in Zurich for another twenty thousand. That's a bonus with my personal thanks. Your salary will be credited in the normal way to your bank account in Rome. . . . That's all, I think. The car is waiting to take you to your hotel. I wish you a pleasant trip and a very restful vacation. *Sogni d'oro,* Matucci—golden dreams."

We parted with a handshake, firm and fraternal. The Sicilian bodyguard escorted me to the ground floor and handed me into the care of two junior colleagues, who drove me like a visiting potentate to the Grand Hotel.

It was one-thirty in the morning. The foyer was deserted. They steered me past the reception desk and the concierge, rode up with me in the elevator and installed me in my bedroom. One of them checked cupboards and bathroom and even under the beds, while the other pointed out the beautiful job of packing, and how my suits had been pressed, and that if I wished to speak with the Signorina Anders the key was on my side of the communicating door. . . . As the Director had prescribed maximum precautions, I could sleep soundly. They bade me good night and retired like lackeys from the presence of a prince.

Perhaps they were right. I was the Prince's man, bought and endowed. His money was in my pocket. His gift was sleeping next door. His brand was on my forehead like a slave mark. Still, give the devil his due, he was a very rare specimen. He recognized merit. He enjoyed malice but never practised it wastefully. He had been scrupulously polite. He had exacted my consent with just the right amount of pressure and finesse. He was the king. I was the pawn. He had swept me off the board to wait for another game. Never once had he suggested that I was making a slave's bargain. He knew it, of course. So did I. Which is why, much as I wanted her, I could not turn the key and go to Lili, but, instead, lay dressed and wakeful until dawn, scheming revolt like Spartacus in Capua.

At dawn I abandoned the futile exercise and went to Lili Anders. With a very refined irony, the Director had kept her in ignorance of the arrangements, so that at six in the morning, sleepless and in need of loving, I was forced to explain the whole complicated play, step by step. When I explained that she was to be set at liberty in Switzerland, she was hysterically delighted. When I told her I would go with her, it was Christmas, Epiphany and all her birthdays rolled into one. After that I had no wish or heart to tell her the price. From the moment I left Italy I would be, in effect, an exile. From the moment I became an exile I would be subject to a clinical change which the Director had calculated to a nicety. For most Europeans, for all Anglo-Saxons and Americans, the word *exile* has an old-fashioned ring. Whatever crimes a man may commit, he is never deprived of his citizenship or his primal relationship with his homeland. He may be imprisoned, he may be brutalized, but he is never robbed of that essential element of his identity, his contact with the mother earth.

For us Italians, however, for us whose identity depends upon a small terrain, a tribal group, a dialectal area, exile is a constant and sinister reality. We can still be legally transported and confined to a distant province, a depressed island, to a community whose tongue and customs and history are totally foreign to us, where we will be strangers until the day we die. We cannot move from it without permission from the police. We cannot flourish in it because we are an alien corn. We exist only by sufferance and under surveillance.

The personal consequences are as deep and as demoralizing as if we had been transported to Siberia or dumped like castaways in the dry Tortugas.

The terror begins subtly with a sense of disorientation

and discontinuity. It can end with a trauma of impotence, when every act seems pointless, every step ends at a barred gate, every hope is proved an illusion.

The Director knew this because he had used it many times as a means of immobilizing men who were hostile to him. I knew it because my father had been in exile under the Fascists and I had seen him come home a broken man. But how could I explain it to Lili, who had survived her own exile and was now breaking out into freedom . . . ? Perhaps it was just as well; the loving would not have been half as sweet or our exit from Italy half as impressive.

At eight twenty-five our baggage was removed under the supervision of an agent. At eight-thirty, with no bills to pay, and as many bows as if we had paid them twice over, we were led from the foyer into an official limousine. At nine-fifteen we were conducted into the VIP lounge at Fiumicino and held in comfort and respect until fifteen minutes before takeoff. Then, spurning the crush of common travellers, we were escorted to the aircraft and deposited in a pair of first-class seats. Our agent hovered over us until the moment before the doors were closed. Then, with a final salute on behalf of a grateful Republic, he left us. Five minutes later—this being a fair and strike-free day at Fiumicino—we were airborne in the care of the Swiss. We held hands. We made foolish jokes. We toasted each other in champagne. Then I fell asleep and did not wake up until we were on the final approach to Kloten Airport in Zurich.

When we arrived at the Baur au Lac, we found that the Director had provided against all contingencies. We were accommodated in separate rooms, each communicating with a large salon, furnished already with flowers, fruit, liquor and a welcome note from the management. There was also a telegram from the Director: SECOND SAMUEL SEVEN ONE. Zurich is a sound Calvinist town, so I deciphered the joke from the Bible on my bedside table: "The Lord gave him rest from all his enemies."

Later in the day a second telegram arrived, two words only: TEKEL STEFANELLI. I didn't need the Bible for that one. I remembered the riddle from my religious youth: "Tekel: Thou art weighed in the balance and found wanting." I had to answer him and I did it with Deuteronomy I:16: "Judge righteously between every man and his brother and the stranger that is with him." By then the joke was stale and bitter. I had to make an end of it. I told Lili the truth.

The moment of telling had a curious quality about it. It was seven in the evening. We had decided to dine early in the suite, to relax after the alarms and excitements of the last few days. Lili, glowing from a visit to the hairdresser, the masseuse and the manicurist, was dressed in a housecoat she had bought to celebrate her new liberty. She had presented me with a silk shirt and a rather exotic cravat. I was mixing drinks like an amateur barman, feeling very domestic, very comfortable and yet somehow remote and passionless, as if I were recovering from a long illness. The story told itself in the same remote fashion and I heard myself speak it as if I were listening to a report from another man:

". . . Everything the Director says is true and yet it all adds up to a lie, which you still cannot disprove. He is a very great actor. He conjures you into a world that doesn't exist and yet makes you believe that every leaf on every tree is real. He shows you another self—and makes you believe it is you. . . . 'You lack authority, Matucci. You lack experience. You are an abrasive element. You polarize the factions.' All true, but true in an opposite way. . . . 'You are not dead, just buried for a while.' . . . But I knew, the moment I stepped on that plane, I was dead; because he has all my files and records now and he can reprocess history in any way he chooses. He says he wants to divide and rule. But suppose he doesn't? Suppose he wants to unite and conquer and then play Fouché to Leporello's Napoleon? I've given him the means to do it. . . . And he paid me for them: with you, with a long holiday, with a sinecure that half the men in the Service would give their eyes for. And he'll honour the payment, have no doubt of it, so long as I play the game according to his rules and wait on the word of the Lord. . . ."

"Why did you accept the payment, Dante Alighieri?" There was no reproach in the question. There was no compassion, either. She was calm and composed as an examining magistrate. "Because I was part of it?"

"No. I believe that, even if I had fought him, he would still have to let you go, if only to demonstrate that I was obstinate and unreasonable. He might even have worked to set you against me. . . . He spins webs so fine you cannot see the threads."

"So why did you consent? For me, this is freedom; for you, exile."

"Strange, but at this moment I'm enjoying it."

"If you could go on enjoying it, with me or without me, then it would be another story. Could you?"

"I don't know. . . . Yes, by God, I do know! Last night I dined with him and enjoyed him. After dinner we worked together on the documents and I respected him—because he respected me. So, when he asked me to step out of the picture, and gave me his reasons, I had to respect those, too. Then, after I had agreed, he had to show me how clever he was, how he knew in advance that I must consent. He was so certain that he had arranged everything in advance—even to this liquor and the roses in your bedroom. Suddenly I was not a man anymore, I was . . ."

"A puppet, my love! A marionette, life-size and help-less, with no manhood left at all. It's a bitter experience, isn't it?"

"I think it's funny, very funny!"

"Is it?"

"The joke of the century! Dante Alighieri Matucci, tenor castrato in the puppet choir!"

"Why don't you laugh then?"

"I'm a clown puppet, Lili. I make other people laugh. That is his final triumph, don't you see? He's spread the news all round the Service. How else would Steffi know? Why else would he send me a telegram: '. . . weighed

in the balance and found wanting.' Mother of God!
What a beautiful, beautiful comedy!"

"I'd like to see the end of it."

"This is the end, Lili. Don't you understand that?"

"It's the end he wrote. I think there's a better one."

"I'd love to hear it."

"The puppet becomes a man, scrapes off the clown's
paint and rides out to confront his enemy!"

"It's a fairy tale, Lili."

"No! It's a truth—my truth. And now that we're quits,
I can tell it. I know you for a man, much man—and not
just in bed, Dante Alighieri."

"Thanks. That helps a little."

"But not enough. Where's your wallet?"

"In the bedroom, why?"

"There's a card in it, remember? A salamander and
an inscription: 'One fine tomorrow, brother.' A good
motto, don't you think? And a very appropriate device:
the lizard that lives in the fire. Get the card, my love.
And find the telephone number of the Cavaliere Bruno
Manzini. I think you should call him in Bologna."

The idea was seductive. But I was still gun-shy and
suspicious of any new entanglement. Bruno Manzini belonged to another world, with another set of rules: the
world of the *condottieri,* the freebooters, who had taken
over the ruins of a cardboard empire and built a new
one of steel and concrete and international gold. They
dispensed enormous power, but the dispensation was in
another currency than that to which I was accustomed.
True, Bruno Manzini had invited me to trust him.
Through Raquela Rabin he had offered me proof of good
faith. But, if he betrayed me, then I was lost beyond
redemption, since the jurisdiction of money is universal
and its minions are devoid of pity.

I argued this with Lili—the new Lili who had flowered
overnight into another woman, serene, mature and wholly
confident in herself. She abolished my doubts with a
simple challenge:

"What have you to lose? Nothing. What have you to
gain? At best a powerful friend. At least an alliance of

interest that you can dissolve at will. Most important of all, you will have begun to fight. Please! Telephone him now!"

To make the call was easy. To speak to the Cavaliere was only less difficult than having a Sunday chat with the Pope. I was passed from a telephonist to a woman secretary, from the secretary to a male assistant, very efficient, very *alt'Italia,* who informed me that the Cavaliere was conducting an important conference and could in no wise be interrupted. I took a risk then and used the magical name of the Service, threatening all sorts of vague crises if the Cavaliere were not called immediately to the telephone. I waited another three minutes before he came on the line. I told him:

"Cavaliere, yesterday I recovered certain records from Ponza. I delivered them to my superior, our mutual friend. I am now on four months' leave and will later be transferred to other activities in the Service. I am under orders not to return to Italy for a month and I am lodged at the Baur au Lac in Zurich."

There was a moment's silence, then a series of brusque questions:

"Have you yourself examined the records?"

"Yes."

"Important?"

"As you suggested in Rome."

"Do you know what will happen to them now?"

"Only what may happen. There are several possibilities."

"Which you can no longer control."

"Precisely."

"Do you need assistance, financial or otherwise?"

"I need the man whom Raquela Rabin recommended to me, provided, of course, he is still available."

"He is. He will be with you tomorrow evening. . . . By the way, how is our mutual friend?"

"Very pleased with himself."

"No doubt. And you?"

"Happier. Now that I have spoken with you."

"Are you in good health?"

"Our mutual friend assures me I have nothing to fear."

"He would know, of course."

"Yes. But he never tells all he knows."

"Remember it, my friend. Walk close to the wall."

"Thank you, Cavaliere. . . . Good night."

When I put down the phone, I was trembling and the palms of my hands were wet. I was truly afraid now. The old man's parting words had demolished the last frail illusion of security. I was a stranger in a land stuffed with money and indifferent to the point of callousness. I was a member of a legal underworld, suspect everywhere and nowhere loved. I could be shot down on any street corner and the Swiss would have the blood hosed off and the traffic flowing before you could say John Calvin. I told you I am a Tuscan born. In that moment I tasted the full, Florentine flavour of the Director's revenge. Then Lili came and put her arms around me and we held each other close while she whispered the words over and over like an incantation:

"One fine tomorrow, brother . . . one fine tomorrow . . ."

Tomorrow was a gift of God: no wind, no cloud, the lake adazzle under the spring sun, snow on the uplands, the lower meadows ankle-deep in spring grass, the herdsmen moving the cattle up the slopes to a music of bells. I hired a car and we drove eastwards along the lake into the Grisons, aimless and happy as a honeymoon pair. Lili was in a rapture of contentment. She sang, she clowned, she played word games and love games and built dream houses, furnished and demolished them, plucked chickens out of nowhere and blew them away like thistledown.

Me? I was happy, too. I had been a stranger too long to this kind of simplicity. My relationships with women had been too haunted by time, too frail and feverish to issue in any kind of peace. I hunted; they challenged; we joined, we parted, tomorrow was another day and another hunt, with a tip of the hat and *ciao, ciao, bambina* at the end of it. I knew nothing of homecomings and kisses at the door and the daily loving absolution from all the

sins of my trade. I was the *bufalo solitario,* always on
the fringe of the herd, cutting out the errant females,
leaving them for other males to breed and cherish. I used
to boast of it, because this is our national pastime, to
prove that we are infinite in potency. But today, humbled
by fear, diminished in self-respect, I was, perhaps for
the first time, truly grateful to a woman.

For the first time, too—and this may sound strange
from a man who is trained to observe and fit every
human being onto an anthropometric chart—I saw her
to remember: the honey colour of her hair, escaping from
under the scarf, the high Slavic cheekbones flushed with
the wind and the excitement, the little flecks of gold in
her eyes, the half smile that haunted the corners of her
mouth, the lift of chin and shoulder and breast and the
way she fluttered her hands when she spoke, even the
first faint touch of time in the texture of her skin. She
was no girl, this Lili. She had lived too strangely for too
long. But I was no boy either; and I was tired of baby
talk and lovers' lies and all the gossip of the model
circuit.

We lunched in a mountain inn, perched high over the
valley. We ate cheese soufflé and beef fondue and drank
a thin pétillant wine, much different from the rich vintage of my Tuscan hills. The girl who served us was
blond and pink and white and dressed like a doll in
dirndl and embroidered blouse. We sat in front of a big
log fire and drank coffee and pear brandy; and we loved
the solid, smug Swiss comfort of it all. We talked of the
future and Lili assessed her own without resentment.

". . . I am on file now. Any policeman who knows my
record can harass me like a streetwalker. So I have to
be careful. If I live modestly and soberly, the Swiss will
give me temporary sojourn. They will extend it grudging-
ly; but with a good lawyer in a small canton, I may be
able to live in peace for a long while. If I married, it
would be different. I would have a new civil status and
a new life. So I have to think of that . . . but not yet.
I have money here, enough for two years of simple living. I have the villa on Ponza, which can be sold and will

bring a good price. Massimo told me he had provided for me in his will, but that is stolen now. And, in any case, there is bound to be litigation and I base nothing on it . . . especially as I cannot return to Italy ever again. . . . Still, I am very lucky. Lucky in you, too, my love. . . . I did not believe you would have so much concern for me."

"Boh! I didn't believe I would ever need a woman in this way. To be calm, to prove nothing, just to be glad that she is in the room. What would you say if I asked you to spend this month with me?"

"I would say yes. But I would also say, please leave me before you get bored; please let us have no quarrels and no bad words. Let it be as it is now, simple and easy, one hour, one day at a time."

"One day at a time. Good . . ."

"And when you go away—you must, I know that—and you find yourself lonely, come back again. We do not have to spell the words, you and I. We do not even have to say them. You must be very free now, free to risk or enjoy, as you choose. You have to begin to know the man who lives in your skin."

"I'm afraid of him, Lili."

"So one day you must confront him in the mirror. After that, please God, you will be able to be happy."

"I hope so. But there is something that must be said, Lili."

"What?"

"If a day should come when you have to choose between me and yourself, consider your own interest first. I would want that."

"I don't understand."

"Listen, *bambina!* We are not here by accident. We are not lodged side by side in a beautiful hotel because people want us to be happy. This was arranged by the Director so that we would become tied to each other, the more closely the better. Then a threat to one would be a pressure on the other. He has thought to buy me. Perhaps he is convinced he has bought me. But he is also buying insurance against a day when I may cheat on the contract. You see . . . ?"

"I do. And I want you to cheat him. Tell me something."

"What?"

"I have never heard you name this man. You speak of him only as the Director. Why?"

"A rule of the game that has become second nature. But, now that you ask, there is another reason. This is a very attractive man. He can seduce you, as he has seduced me many times, with a smile, a handshake, a show of confidence and infinite good sense. He was born with that talent. It was bred into him through twenty generations. I envy it—God, how much! I am awed by it. I have grown more and more afraid of it. So I force myself to think of him not as a man, but as a function. like the Pope or the President. That way I can cope with him. I can obstruct, inhibit, redirect, as I have often done in the past. Strange! I've never admitted that to another living soul."

"Perhaps the day will come when you will be able to name the two in one breath—the man who lives in your skin, and the other of whom you are still afraid."

"Am I so great a coward, Lili?"

"There is one fear that makes each of us a coward!"

"And what is yours?"

"The little room, the light shining in my eyes, the faces I cannot see, the questions and the blows that come from nowhere. You saved me from that, and there is nothing I would not do to repay you."

"We're both rewarded, *cara* . . . the good day is enough."

"And tonight your Cavaliere Manzini arrives. . . . Are you going to tell him about me?"

"I can hardly avoid it. Does it worry you?"

"No. But it's an odd situation. I was his brother's mistress. Now he finds me with you. I wonder what he will think or say."

"Do you care?"

"Yes. I want him to be a friend to you."

"He calls himself the Salamander. He must have paid his own price for survival. We start with the hope that he will understand ours. After that . . . who knows? There are no signs in the sky and I cannot read a crystal ball. . . . We should go back now. It's an hour and a half to Zurich."

૭ે ૬ે

AT eighty-thirty in the evening the Cavaliere Bruno Manzini received me in his suite at the Dolder Grand. Once again the setting was opulent: the vast salon, the vista of dark woodland and moonlit lake and the lights of the nesting city; yet the man himself was aloof, austere, so that you knew, if all the rest were swept away, he would still stand there, straight as a pillar, with his proud eyes and his patrician beak, and his hair like snow on a great alp. His greeting was warm and smiling, but from the moment I entered he was reading me by stance and attitude and intonation. His first comment was characteristic:

"You are changed, Colonel."

"How so, Cavaliere?"

"Every way. You wear your clothes as if you enjoyed them. You are more loose, more forthcoming. I would guess that you had found yourself a satisfactory woman and a little more courage than you had yesterday."

"Both true."

"A drink?"

"Whisky, please."

He served me himself and I noticed that he drank very lightly. He raised his glass in a toast:

"Health, money and love . . ."

"And time to enjoy them, Cavaliere."

"That above all, Colonel. . . . I have ordered dinner to be served here in half an hour. I thought you would trust me to choose the menu."

"Of course."

"Now, tell me everything that has happened since we met in Rome."

I told him. I recited all the facts without gloss or interpretation, up to, and including, my arrival in Zurich with Lili Anders and the relationship which had begun to mature between us. During the whole narrative he did not utter a word, but his eyes never left my face and I knew that he was weighing every phrase and inflection. When I had finished, he sat a long time in silence and then began to question me. His tone was curt and inquisitorial.

"You are convinced that Major-General Leporello has allied himself with the neofascists?"

"I am convinced that he was and is a candidate for such an alliance. I cannot prove he has concluded it."

"You infer, therefore, that he ordered, or connived at, the murders in the Via Sicilia and the theft of the Pantaleone papers."

"I state that there is a case to be investigated."

"And the evidence in support?"

"Leporello knew, from me, where the papers were and the steps that had been taken to guard them. If and when the papers came into his possession, he would have known instantly that they were incomplete. He would— and in fact he did—take steps to trace the remainder, to wit the microfilms and the maps on Ponza. His aide was there, armed with an authority signed by Leporello."

"And why would he be stupid enough to sign an order that would incriminate his aide?"

"The order would not necessarily incriminate him. He could justify it quite simply as an investigative measure under his own counter-insurgency program. You know how our services and agencies are organized. Sometimes they run parallel, at others they overlap; sometimes they run contrary to each other. There are rivalries between them and the ministries that control them."

"There are also internal conflicts, yes?"

"Of course."

"Conflicts of policy?"

"Always."

"What is the ground of dispute between you and your Director?"

"There are several. I asked for an investigation of Leporello. He deferred it. I disobeyed a direct order and made contact with Leporello."

"In effect you may be responsible for two murders and the theft of vital documents."

"I believe I am responsible."

"So your Director was perfectly justified in taking you off the investigation."

"If he did it on disciplinary grounds, yes."

"You suggest he had other reasons?"

"He stated them clearly: I lacked the authority and experience to deal with a complex political situation; I would polarize existing factions who would be better kept divided; I was a convenient victim who would buy him time."

"Good reasons or bad?"

"Eminently sound."

"And he has treated you very generously?"

"Very."

"So what is your quarrel with him? Why do you object to the way he has acted?"

"I have no quarrel. I have no objection that I can validly sustain. But . . ."

"But what, Colonel?"

"I said it to his face and I say it still. I do not trust him."

"His answer?"

"I quote it verbatim: 'I don't want dictatorship. I don't want Marxism. I'm sure the kind of democracy we have is too unstable to last. But, come one or the other, I'll try to make it as tolerable as I can.' "

"A laudable ambition, surely?"

"That depends on the interpretation. He himself put a gloss on it: 'I am king on the board and you are the pawn.' "

"And you don't like being a pawn, Colonel?"

"No, I don't."

"You would prefer to be king, no doubt?"

"Cavaliere, my father was an old-line socialist who spent five years of exile on Lipari under the Fascists. They let him come home to die."

"I'm sorry, I didn't know that."

"No reason why you should."

"So, what would you like to be?"

"A servant of an open society."

"But you joined a closed service, more subject than any to the corruption of secrecy. Why?"

"I was recommended, Cavaliere. I seized the opportunity."

"Why?"

"I have a talent for investigation."

"And intrigue?"

"That, too, if you like."

"And a taste for influence without responsibility."

"No. I like responsibility."

"And you resent the fact that you can no longer exercise it?"

"Yes, I do."

"And what do you resent most of all?"

"That one man can, at a whim, make me less than I am—and that the same man can, if he chooses, bury, manipulate or trade information that may determine the political future of this country. My country, Cavaliere . . . yours, too."

"How much do you know about this country of ours, Colonel?"

"Too little. And too much from the wrong side. I know criminals, agitators, propagandists, policemen, politicians; but the people—eh!—there are times when I feel like a little green man from Mars, all brain and antennae but no heart at all."

"Can you be bought, Colonel?"

"I was, Cavaliere, forty-eight hours ago."

"Can you be frightened?"

"I am frightened now. I know too much. I'm isolated. I'm an easy target."

"And who would want to eliminate you?"

"The Director for one. Leporello for another."

"Or both, working together."

"That's the real nightmare. And it could be true. Look what happened in Greece. And look how quickly the colonels have become respectable. Pantaleone, your half brother, had the first blueprints for a military coup, and they are still very formidable. With Leporello and the Director acting in concert they could be twice as formidable, very quickly."

"And when you called me yesterday, what did you think I could do about it?"

"I thought you might advise me how to stay alive and use the knowledge I have to prevent a *colpo di stato*."

"What knowledge do you have, Matucci?"

"I know every name on the microfilms. I could reproduce every document. I could reconstruct every map. I have a photographic memory, Cavaliere. I'll back it for ninety percent accuracy."

"Does the Director know that?"

"Yes."

"Then he told you the truth. You are a natural victim."

"And you, Cavaliere?"

"I, too, told you the truth. We are natural allies. But you have to accept that it will be—what did you call it? —a lopsided league."

"How will it be loaded?"

"Enormously in my favour. I will introduce you into a new world. You will have to learn its history, its language and its symbols. I have everything you lack: influence, money, friends or servants in every country of the world. Also I am old and obstinate. So I have to hold the advantage."

"I understand that and accept it."

"There is one more condition."

"Yes?"

"This Lili Anders. . . . She is a danger to you, an embarrassment for me. Pay her off and forget her."

"I can't do that, Cavaliere."

"I insist on it, if we are to work together."

"Cavaliere, thirty years ago I am sure you had many friends who gave you the same advice about Raquela Rabin. As a Jewish celebrity, she was a danger to you and a nuisance to them. What did you do?"

"I took their advice."

"Raquela Rabin told me a different story."

"I know, but mine is the true version."

"And yet you ask me to do the same thing to another woman?"

"For a different reason."

"The same reason, Cavaliere."

"You are making a great mistake."

"Probably. But you offer me the same stale bargain as the Director. Submit and be safe. I'm sorry. The market's closed. No deal."

"Another whisky?"

"No, thank you. And if you'll excuse me, I'll dispense myself from dinner."

"You will not dispense yourself, Colonel. You will stay and humour me, if only because I'm thirty years older than you and I have some excuse for bad manners."

"Cavaliere, I have excuses, too. I may be dead very soon. I should like to enjoy the time I have left."

"Sit down, man, for God's sake! The game is over now."

"I beg your pardon."

"I offered you a shabby contract, my friend. Had you consented, I would have sold you myself to the assassins. . . . Now, ring the bell, please. I think we are ready to eat."

꾿 ꯰

THE man who sat with me at dinner that night in the Dolder Grand was a phenomenon, different from any image I had formed of him. He was seventy years old, an age at which most men are content to lapse into comfort and idiosyncrasy. Not this one. He bubbled like champagne. He talked books, women, painting, money, oil, films, fashion, religion, game parks, wine and the growing of roses. He was so various that he dazzled me, and yet so complete in what he was and did that he shamed me with the waste of my own good years. It was not simply that he was eloquent or interested; he knew, and knew profoundly. He enjoyed. He savoured. He had made his own sense of the mad mathematics of creation. Above all, he still had respect for mystery, and though he judged trenchantly, there was always a touch of reserve and compassion in the verdict. Between the fruit and the cheese he opened a new line of talk:

"We are all inheritors, Matucci, and we can no more shed our past than we can slough off our skins. We are free only to make the best of what we have, in the now-time at our disposal. We send men to the moon and believe we have discovered tomorrow; but tomorrow is still growing out of all our yesterdays, and we decipher it in scraps and fragments like the arithmetic of the Incas. You and I, for instance, we have shared bread and salt and wine. We have begun a friendship. But you will never understand me unless you remember that I was born in an attic above a brothel, on the feast of the Assumption of the Virgin, the day the acrobats came to town. You are curious? . . . I'm glad. When you get to my age, Matucci, you will find that there are few left with whom you can share your past. The old go away. The young have no interest. You are there, a broken pillar in a wheatfield, the triumphs you celebrate long forgotten, the hands that raised you crumbled into dust and blown away. Let me tell you of my birthday. Most of it is true; some of it is uncertain; the rest, perhaps, I have dreamed into myself; but, nonetheless, it is part of me. Please pour yourself some wine. It may help you to be patient with my fairy tale."

And that is exactly how he told it, like a fairy tale, in old-fashioned language, with ample gestures and quite obvious enjoyment. He was playing the *gigione,* the ham actor, and watching sidelong to see how I would react to his improvisation.

". . . The time, my dear Matucci, was 1900. Victor Emmanuel the Third was king of Italy and Leo the Thirteenth was gloriously reigning as Pontiff of the Holy Roman Church. The place is the Piazza delle Zoccolette, the Square of the Little Wooden Shoes, in Rome. . . .

"I didn't see it, Matucci, but I can reconstruct it for you because I saw the acrobats many times in my childhood. . . . They came twirling and prancing and tumbling in their gaudy patchwork while the fifers tootled and the drummers made boom-boom-boom, rat-tat-tat and the mountebank tossed his ribboned staff and announced to one and all the wonders that would soon be enacted in the Piazza delle Zoccolette. . . . They set up a stage for the mummers and a booth to sell favours and cure-all potions . . . and a little theater for Pulcinella. They hoisted poles and ladders and stretched a tightwire so that the *funambolo* could do his death-defying walk high above the crowds from one corner of the piazza to another. . . . They made a square of cords to hold back the crowds and laid down bright mats for the tumblers and rolled out the great barbells which only Carlo the Magnificent could lift . . . though he would pay a gold coin to any man who could match him. And all the while the mountebank strode about distributing handbills, crying the talents of his company and the virtue of his nostrums and the surpassing beauty of his female contortionists. . . .

". . . In the old days, Matucci, there was a brothel in the piazza called, by courtesy, a house of appointment and run by a bawd called Zia Rosa. It wasn't the most fashionable place in town, yet again, it wasn't the seediest. I don't remember it, but my old nurse Angela, who was Zia Rosa's sister, would sometimes tell stories about it to the goggling maidservants in my mother's house. . . . For Zia Rosa the feast day and the arrival of the acrobats spelt money in the cashbox. The feast day meant eating and drinking and strolling by the river, and afterwards every young fellow with red blood in his veins was ready for a bout in bed. The show meant crowds and a press of bodies in the piazza; and the sight of the girl acrobats spelt money in the cashbox. The feast day meant send Saint Anthony screaming for solace from his midsummer lust. . . . I know, Matucci. I lusted after more than one myself in my salad days. . . .

". . . . On that day, Matucci, my mother was in labour in the attic of Zia Rosa's house. How she came there was simple enough; a pregnant girl, disgraced, with little money, found her way almost inevitably to Zia Rosa or to someone like her. Zia Rosa provided a double service.

Her sister Angela was both midwife and abortionist. And afterwards she recruited the more likely girls for service in the house.

"I once overheard Angela describe my mother as she was then. She called her 'an original,' a *furbacchiona*, sidelong and hard to read. She had pale skin and blue eyes and honey-coloured hair. She spoke Italian and English and Romanesco. Her clothes were good but a trifle too modest for someone who obviously knew more than her prayers. She had money in her pocket, too— at least enough for Angela to attend her at the birth; for Angela would do nothing without cash in hand. . . .

". . . Even then, apparently, my mother was arrogant and demanding, in spite of her swollen belly and her need of so mean a shelter. She wanted clean sheets and towels, and soap, and two good meals a day from the kitchen and a list of medicines from the pharmacy. She stated flatly that she would stay a week after the birth of the child and she would pay a maid to attend her during her convalescence. She was a tough one, too. Most women by this time would have been screaming and tossing and clamouring to be spared the birth pangs. Not this one, said Angela. Every groan had to be wrenched out of her as if she were a martyr on the rack. As each spasm passed, she forced herself to talk in that cool, matter-of-fact voice that made even Italian sound strange. What she said made little sense, especially from a woman sweating out her labour in the garret of a bawdy house. But then most women were a little mad at such a time, so Angela humoured her until the pains came sharper and faster and she was compelled to cry continuously. . . . Does this sound strange to you, Matucci, that I should be reliving my own birth? There is a meaning at the end of it. At least I think there is.

"Down in the piazza—and this I know, Matucci, because Angela was watching—Luca Salamandra, the wire walker, was about to begin his pilgrimage across the sky. He was dressed all in black with plastered hair and curled moustaches. Halfway up the ladder he turned and saluted the cheering crowds. Then he climbed to the little platform on the top of the pole and stepped onto the wire. There was a gasp from the crowd as they saw it sag under his weight and watched him come perilously into balance. Then they fell silent. . . .

". . . He moved slowly at first, testing the strength of the breeze and the tension of the cable under his foot soles. In the center of the piazza he stopped and began bouncing himself on the wire. Then he flipped into a somersault and landed upright on the swaying cable. He was, perhaps, five meters from the end of the wire when he stopped, staring straight into Angela's eyes. She remembers him smiling at her, beginning to walk towards her . . . At which precise moment, Matucci, my mother screamed and I poked my reluctant head into the world and Luca Salamandra toppled into eternity.

"Ten days later a woman in deep mourning, with an elderly companion, presented herself at the General Registry Office to deposit a set of notarized documents. The first was a certificate of marriage, between Anne Mary Mackenzie, a spinster, of Great Britain, and Luca Salamandra, bachelor, acrobat. The second was the surgeon's certificate of the death of Luca Salamandra. The third was a notification of the birth of Massimo Luca Salamandra, male, infant, issue of Anne Mary Salamandra and Luca Salamandra, deceased.

This extraordinary concatenation of documents was the result of a long discussion between Anne Mary Mackenzie and Zia Rosa, followed by three hours' hard bargaining between Angela the midwife, Zia Rosa, the mountebank, and Aldo the Calligrapher, an elderly forger who lived in a lane behind the piazza and specialized in the reproduction of historic manuscripts. The fact that the registry clerk accepted the documents without question was a tribute to his calligraphic skill.

"The result of the whole transaction was that Anne Mary Mackenzie became a respectable Roman widow, and I was endowed with a spurious legitimacy which would enable me to enter the service of the Crown or even to take Holy Orders, in the unlikely event that I should ever aspire to the priesthood. . . .

"Of course, I have never wanted to be a priest, Colonel, but I sometimes think I should have made a splendid Cardinal, under the Borgias, of course, when celibacy was less stringently demanded. . . . Shall I tell you what you are thinking at this moment? You are asking yourself what is the point of that long story, whether I am making fun of you or indulging myself with a captive listener. You are right on both counts. But I have also shown you a parable. I was sired by a nobleman, fathered by a dead acrobat. I am, and always have been, a contradiction. To treat with me you will need patience and as much faith as it takes to believe in the blood of San Gennaro. Now, you are the man on the tightrope. You want to save yourself and serve a very divided country and a very contentious people. You will need steady nerves, because you, too, will see monsters burning, and if you slip once you are dead. . . . I hope you understand that."

"I do. But where do we begin?"

"You are under orders not to return to Italy for a month. We use that month to establish an insurance. Tomorrow morning at nine you and Lili Anders will check out of the Baur au Lac. A limousine will be waiting to drive you by a circuitous route into Liechtenstein, where you will be lodged in a house which belongs to one of my companies. It's actually a converted hunting lodge, quaint but comfortable. There you will record everything you know of the Pantaleone affair, the microfilms, the maps . . . everything. This material will be copied and the copies will be lodged in a series of banks inside and outside Italy. During this same month you will receive other material from me. You will study it carefully, because it will prepare you for the next stage of the operation: your return to Italy. We shall, of course, remain in close personal contact. You will have two of my staff on constant call as guards and couriers."

"And when I go back to Italy?"

"You will still be on leave, an underpaid career officer with specialist qualifications. I shall, to use a cant phrase, take you up, professionally and socially. I shall offer you substantial fees as a consultant on economic intelligence.

This will be an open transaction, sanctioned by regrettable custom. Every public functionary in the country tries to supplement his income by private business. Of course your Director will hear of it. In fact, I shall make it my business to secure his approval."

"Are you sure he will give it?"

"Why not? It will give him another means of compromising you whenever he wishes. It will demonstrate that you are what he hopes you are, a venal man, easily bought and silenced. Under cover of this situation, you will continue your investigations into the new fascist movement and Leporello's connection with it. You will report your findings to me and we shall agree on a course of action. Does that make sense to you?"

"With one reservation, Cavaliere."

"Which is . . . ?"

"The Director. . . . I have seen him write the script of similar comedies. I do not believe he will buy this one."

"Nor I. But he will try to make us believe he has bought it—which is all we need. The real problem is rather different: we have to keep you alive."

❧ ❧

THE hunting lodge was ten kilometers south of Triesen, where the peaks of the Rhätikon join the Glarner Alps and the pine forests climb, haunted and dark, towards the snow line. It was built at the neck of a high valley, accessible only by a single track of bitumen which ended at a massive gate of stout pine, topped with steel spikes and slung between pillars of hewn stone. Inside the gate a paved driveway wound through tall trees to the lodge itself, a long, freestone building, raftered with logs, roofed with zinc on timber, standing squat and solid against the lift of the pines and the heave of the misty peaks.

Outside it looked cold and unwelcoming, ready to withstand invasion or avalanche. Inside it was simple but warm, with firelight gleaming on panelled walls and polished copper and peasant pottery. The house was kept by an elderly Tyrolese and his wife, and there were two other staff: Heinz, a big taciturn fellow from the Grisons, and Domenico, a swarthy young Varesino, who was garrulous in English, French, Italian and Switzerdeutsch. They were an odd, but formidable, pair: Heinz, a deadly shot with a rifle; Domenico, a circus athlete who was accomplished in pistol and karate. There was always one of them on duty, patrolling the grounds, surveying the road, scanning the high defiles for herdsmen or climbers. Each morning Heinz drove into Triesen to do the shopping and pick up mail. Each evening at sunset the gates were locked, a complicated series of alarms was set and the two men shared the night watch.

There was a telephone in the house, but we were warned not to use it. We could walk freely in the confines of the estate, but always and only with Heinz and Domenico in attendance. For the rest, there was a typewriter, papers, carbons, a copying machine, and, if I needed anything else, I had only to ask for it and Heinz would procure it, even from as far away as Zurich.

For the first few days I felt caged and restless; but Lili was as carefree as a bird, and she scolded me into relaxation and a simple routine of work. We rose early and, after breakfast, I settled down to the task of reconstructing from memory the material in the microfilms. It was a tedious job which depended on a whole series of mnemonic tricks, each of which triggered off a sequence of visual memories. With trained interlocutors and a stenographer to record the material immediately, I could have done the job in half the time. As it was, I had to interpose the mechanical labour of transcribing each sequence on a typewriter. I had therefore to reckon with a fatigue factor and stop work immediately it inserted itself into the memory equation. In effect, I could work only about four hours a day on the reconstruction. The rest of the time I spent sorting and annotating the dispatches which arrived each day by mail from Bruno Manzini.

All the dispatches were posted from Chiasso, which is the frontier town of the Swiss canton of Ticino. The information was beautifully codified and it covered a

startling variety of subjects: the organization and control
of labour unions, the location of Marxist cells, and the
pattern of their activities; charts showing the financial
and management structure of large companies, with dossiers on their principal directors; lists of contributors to
political parties, matrimonial alliances among the great
families; investment holdings by foreign organizations,
credit reports, notes on the editorial policies of newspapers and publishing houses; the activities of foreign
embassies; the names and private histories of prominent
functionaries and a schedule of their visits to Greece and
Spain; a whole set of illuminating documents on Vatican
finances and the political activities of the Vatican Secretariat of State.

I had been in the intelligence trade a long time, but
much of this material was new even to me, and it argued
the existence of an enormous and expensive organization, not merely to gather the information, but to classify
and process it for constant use. The more I read, the
more I was in awe at the complexity of Italian life and
the problem of maintaining even a semblance of order
in a modern industrial nation. The tension was so high,
the balance of forces so precarious, that even the most
sanguine could not ignore the daily threat of disaster.

I understood vividly the frustration of the revolution-
ary who wanted to sweep the whole mess out of existence
and begin again. I understood the despair of the young
who wanted to drop out, like the Poverello of Assisi,
and live in fraternal simplicity on cannabis and cornbread. I understood the seductive illusion of dictatorship:
that one messianic man, armed with plenary power, could
impose order and unity with a wave of his scepter. More
slowly, I began to see the meaning of Bruno Manzini's
belief that we were all prisoners of our genes and our
history and that our future was written by scribes long
perished.

There were days—bad ones—when memory was slug-
gish and reason balked, and I was oppressed by a sense
of total futility. I was a vain fool, shouting down the
avalanche. I was a prancing ape, crying to be a king of

humankind. What right had I to determine, however
minutely or indirectly, the text of a single line of history?
I found myself drawn with poignant yearning back to
the beliefs of my childhood: a personal God to whom not
even the fallen bird was unimportant, who would in one
grand, glorious judgment redress and stabilize and make
all things new. And then I knew that I had reasoned
Him out of my universe and that He was forever beyond
my appeal.

In those desert days Lili was an oasis of comfort. She
refused to be put out by my snappishness. She lavished
tenderness on me. She coaxed me out of the house and
walked with me through the pinewoods, forcing me to attend to every small wonder: the contour of fungus on a
tree bole, the music of mountain water, the texture of stone
and bark, the play of sunlight on the high crags. Whatever
was left of dreamer in my dried-out self she woke and
nurtured with extraordinary patience. She chided me, too,
and shamed me back into sanity.

". . . I know how you feel, my love. Everything passes.
You and I will pass, too, and the horror of the world
will still remain. But think of this—while we are still
fighting, we hold it back if only for a little while. If
everyone gave up the fight, the barbarians would take
over for another thousand years. Even if we are ignorant
and misguided, the cause is still good. You must believe
that, you must never let yourself forget it. Look . . . even
I am one small triumph for you. No, please, hear me out.
I cannot remember how long it is since I belonged to
myself. Today I do. Even when I give myself to you, I
give as a free woman. If you had not cared, even a little,
I should be dead, or locked up with the prostitutes in the
Mantellate. This is good, isn't it—this day, this place? We
should not be enjoying it if you had not made your fight
and your mistakes as well. . . . Now, why don't you take
me home and make love to me. It's much too damp out
here."

The lovemaking was always good; but it was haunted,
too, by the thought that all too soon it must end. We
talked very little about that; I was a man without re-

sources, too old to make another career in exile. She had
to be reborn out of the dark womb of the trade into another existence. I was the cord that tied her to the past.
The cord must be snapped before she could be wholly
free. There was no hope for either of us in a daydream
future; but the thought of lonely tomorrows weighed
heavily on us both, and our nights were the more desperate and the more precious because of it.

We had been about two weeks at the lodge when
Bruno Manzini came to visit us. It was a Sunday. He
arrived just after lunch, tired and brusque. He took
possession of my notes and retired to his bedroom, and
we did not see him again until he joined us for a drink
at seven-thirty in the evening. He apologized for his ill
humour and made a special effort to set Lili at ease.

"You are good for this man, Lili Anders. I am sure
you were good for Pantaleone. Please don't be embarrassed with me. Life is much too short to entertain ghosts
at the dinner table . . . and I am old enough to value
beautiful women. I've studied your notes, Matucci. Excellent! But very disturbing. Have you made any sense
out of the stuff I've sent you?"

"Some, yes. I'd like to discuss it with you after dinner."

"That's why I'm here. We will shut you out, young
lady, but you are going to forgive me in advance; because
the more you know, the more you are at risk, and our
friend here has a singular concern for you. Have you
told her, Matucci?"

"Told me what, Cavaliere?"

"That I ordered him to send you away and threatened
to withdraw my help if he refused. He defied me. Meeting you now, I am glad he did."

"Thank you, Cavaliere. He did not tell me."

"Matucci, you're a fool."

"That's old news. Let's not labour it, eh?"

He laughed, put his arm around Lili and toasted her
with old-fashioned gallantry, then launched us into a
cascade of small talk and reminiscences that swept us
from soup to coffee without a noticeable pause. After-

wards, when we were alone, with the brandy warming in our hands, he told me:

". . . Things are bad, Matucci, very bad. First we have this business of Bessarione. The police say he blew himself up while he was attempting to sabotage a power pylon. The Left say he was framed and assassinated by the Right. I knew the man: an eccentric if you like, a wealthy romantic, who was also a very good publisher. What's the truth? Who knows? But, at least, it should be open to public debate. What happens? A series of arrests of journalists and students. The charge? 'Spreading news calculated to disturb public order.' For God's sake! That's the old Fascist dragnet. I remember the day it was promulgated. Result? More division. More unrest. Tomorrow there will be another walkout from Fiat. In Rome the garbage collectors will be on strike and the city will be a dung heap in three days. After that, with Easter coming and the tourist season beginning, the hotel employees will walk out. In between we shall have a bomb or two and maybe a child hit by a police bullet. . . . You see how beautifully it works. The Fascists blame the Marxists, the Marxists blame the Fascists. Each provokes the other. Each blames the other for the consequences of violence. In the middle are the people: the students, who cannot get an education because we do not build enough schools; the housewives, who cannot get home because the buses do not run; the sick, who are lined three-deep in our hospital wards. Let me tell you something, Matucci. I am on notice to rush deliveries of every piece of riot equipment I can fabricate. What I cannot make I am to buy, borrow or steal, and no limit on foreign valuta either. The markets are beginning to panic, too. If I told how much money went out of the country last week, it would make you weep. So, how does it add up? The Marxists can, and maybe will, disrupt the country, but they are not ready to run it. I am not sure they want to run it, at least not from the Quirinal Hill. Their support is at the local level, in the cities and the communes and the provinces. They can practice terror and intimidation with urban guerrilla groups, but they cannot mount a military coup. The Right could do that, as you know, provided they had enough tacit support from the Center and from the confessional. As for outside encouragement, they would have it from America, which has huge investments in the country and the Sixth Fleet bottled in the Mediterranean playing cowboys and Indians with the Russians. They would get it from Spain and Greece and very probably from France. After that, who cares? . . . Your notes confirm all this, Matucci. But they tell more: my half brother was less a fool than I believed. He planned better than I knew. With certain modifications, his strategy is still valid today or tomorrow. . . . I have kept the worst news till last. Leporello has made his deal. He has stepped into Pantaleone's shoes."

"And the Director . . . ?"

"Has joined him. . . . They met last weekend at a house party at the Villa Baldassare."

"How do you know this?"

"I was there, too. They wanted me to join the club."

"And . . . ?"

"I agreed, of course. A natural union when you come to think of it. Heavy industry, textiles, newspapers, banking and a stable government pledged to law and order."

"Why had they never asked you before?"

"Because Pantaleone would never hear of it. And at that time they needed him more than me."

"Why now?"

"Because, thanks to your investigation and to the information in my brother's papers, the Director and General Leporello knew all about my connection with my brother's death. So the time was very ripe for a civilized arrangement. Don't you think so?"

"I think, Cavaliere, that I am going quietly mad."

"Not yet, please, Matucci. I need you very sane. I joined to be inside the conspiracy. I want this precious junta broken and brought down. Between us, I believe we can do it."

"In God's name, how?"

"Convict Leporello of murder and the Director of conspiracy with a murderer. Could you do it?"

"I'd be willing to try."

"The dangers are doubled now."

"I know."

"Hesitations?"

"Some. I think we need a new script."

"Let's discuss that in a moment. Do you have any conditions?"

"That I conduct the affair in my own way, without interference from anyone."

"Agreed."

"That I call on you for information, money and such other help as I need from time to time."

"Agreed. What about financial arrangements?"

"No financial arrangements, thank you. I'm not a mercenary and I can hardly ask you to pay life insurance in advance. I have a request, that's all."

"Name it."

"From the moment we leave this place, I want Lili Anders protected. If I succeed in the job, I want a Presidential amnesty for her so that she can be free to reenter Italy, if she chooses. Can you guarantee those things?"

"The first, yes. The second, no. But I would break my back to procure it."

"That's all, then. Now, let's talk about the script."

He sipped his brandy slowly, set down his glass, then made a small cathedral with his fingertips and smiled at me across the roof of it. He said, placidly:

"My friend, I have already sold the script to the Director."

Suddenly and unreasonably I was angry. My gullet was sour with bile and my head full of buzzing wasps. I thrust myself out of the chair and stood over him, mouthing a vehement abuse.

"You are an arrogant old man. Arrogant and dangerous. This is my life, mine! . . . You can't play knuckle-bones with it! What you do is your own business. You're rich, protected. You can buy yourself advocates, bodyguards, diplomatic privileges, immunity from everything but cardiac arrest. I can't. I have to carry my own insurance—sole risk! So you don't make arrangements

that I haven't approved. You don't close sales that I
haven't ratified. You haven't bought me, Cavaliere. Understand that. You haven't bought me! Oh, I know you're
the Salamander and you've survived longer than I'm ever
likely to do. But you wrote that history by yourself. I
have to write mine, even if it's only two words: *Hic
jacet!*"

Without thinking what I was doing, I slammed the
brandy glass into the fire, where it exploded in a rush of
flame. The flames died in a few seconds and I turned to
see Manzini still smiling at me over the tips of his fingers.
Then he stood up and faced me across the hearthrug,
still bland and benign.

"My dear Colonel, truly you underrate me. Or perhaps I am too cryptic for a late evening. When we talked
in Zurich two weeks ago, did we not agree on a strategy?"

"We did. But the circumstances are different. You are
now inside the club. That colours any public relationship
I have with you."

"May I suggest that the colours make a better camou-
flage than before?"

"You may suggest what you like. I need proof."

"Let me try to give it to you, then. When I talked with
your Director and with Leporello at the Villa Baldassare,
your name was mentioned several times."

"Who introduced it?"

"The Director first. Then Leporello. Naturally I had
comments to make, too."

"What was said?"

"The Director, with his usual delicacy, said you were
a nuisance. Leporello used the words 'grave risk!' The
Director said you were immobilized. Leporello said he
required the risk eliminated altogether."

"And you, Cavaliere?"

"I pointed out that you were a very senior and very
intelligent officer, and that if I were in your shoes I
should have taken certain precautions, for example, by
lodging documents in a bank, for publication in the event
of your death. I offered the opinion that an untimely
accident might demoralize your friends and colleagues in

the Service. I then ventured a small fiction: that after your arrival in Switzerland you telephoned me and asked whether I could find a place for you in my organization. You told me that you had been badly treated and that you were thinking seriously of resigning your commission and seeking civil employment. I told the Director I had invited you here this weekend to discuss the matter. I thought it might be a good idea if I offered you temporary employment while he still retained you at the disposal and under the authority of the Service. In sum, I managed to persuade the Director that you were safer alive than dead, at least for the moment."

"And Leporello?"

"Did not agree. The Director overrode him."

"For how long, I wonder?"

"Good question. And I don't know the answer. However, as you see, the arrangement is not yet concluded because your consent is necessary. You may have changed your mind. You may still elect to conduct this operation in secret and without any overt connection with me. I would agree to that, too, if it left you more free and efficient. For the rest, I am often arrogant, though I do not wish to be so with you. I am also old, and I can be dangerous, but never to my friends, Matucci, believe that!"

"I do believe it, Cavaliere. I was rude. But I'm tired of people playing games with my life."

"Do you often break out like that?"

"Not often."

"I'm glad to hear it. That's expensive brandy. Have another."

"Let's finish this discussion first. If I work underground, I am constantly on the run. I have to use false papers, perhaps two or three identities, and often unsuitable addresses. I've done it before. I can do it again; but I am handicapped. I should prefer to work in the open as your employee, but I may compromise your position and expose you to personal risk. So it's your decision."

"I've already taken it. You join me."

"When?"

"I telephone the Director tomorrow, tell him I want to employ you on trial and ask his permission to bring you back to Italy with me."

"So soon?"

"The answer's in your own notes. There is very little time."

"I haven't finished the notes yet."

"Finish them at my house. I'm lodging you there until you make other arrangements."

"What do I tell Lili?"

"Whatever she needs to keep her happy. I'll instruct her on the security arrangements before we leave. You concentrate on the love passages."

"Talking of love passages, Cavaliere . . ."

"Yes?"

"What is your exact relationship with the Principessa Faubiani?"

It was his turn to be angry now. He flushed red as a cock's comb. His head jerked up and the nostrils of his patrician beak flared out. He snapped at me:

"And how the devil does that concern you?"

"I have to ask, Cavaliere. I've known several good men talked to death in bed."

He stared at me for a long, hostile moment. He gulped the last of his brandy and tossed the glass into the fire as I had done. Then he relaxed and smiled and the smile made him look twenty years younger.

"Let's say that I'm a wealthy patron who has visitor's privileges whenever I'm in Rome. But I do take your point, Matucci. The arrangement isn't exclusive and the lady does gossip. Perhaps I should introduce you and let you judge for yourself. Who knows? You might even find her useful. I also have other relationships, Matucci. Do you propose to intrude on them all?"

"If my life is involved, yes, Cavaliere."

"Dio! We do snarl at each other, don't we? I don't mind. I need an argument occasionally to keep me honest. But let's not do it too often. I'll give you a thought to take to bed. Comes a moment when all you have left is sap for one good loving and courage for one good

fight. Don't waste the loving on a whore or the fight on a
paper dragon. Good night, friend!"

It was an actor's exit, and I wondered, irritably, why
he took the trouble to make it so obvious. He had nothing to prove. He commanded so much power, he had
survived so many storms, that the teasing and the mysti-
fication only cheapened him. Then I began to wonder
whether he were not trying to cheapen me, to make me
more pliant to his designs. I told the thought to Lili, as
we lay together in the dark, spelling out the hours of our
last night together.

She disagreed passionately. "You have to trust him, my
love. I think he is a rather wonderful old man, so alert,
so vigorous; but he resents the passing of time. He is
lonely, as he told you. So he preens himself to command
your interest and respect. You can be a rough man, Dante
Alighieri. You have lived an adventurous life. Manzini
has been an adventurer, too. He sees you as a friend, but
also as a rival. Indulge him a little. You will not lose in
the end."

I told her then the promises I had exacted to keep her
safe and to claim an amnesty afterwards.

To my surprise, she rejected the idea out of hand. "No!
You want to be kind. But this is not the way. Don't you
see? You tie me to the past. You tie me to yourself in a
way I do not want. When you come to me again—if you
come—you will visit me in my house, you will drink my
wine and eat at my table. I will not be empty-handed
as I am now. I need that, my love. As for the risks, I
do not care. We will arrange addresses where we can
write to each other. There's another reason, too. You will
be doing a dangerous work. You cannot do it with a
divided mind. You will need other women. You must be
free in the end to choose between them and me. I must
be free, too. . . . Please, let's not be tense and desperate.
Love me gently tonight, gently and slowly. I am so fond
of you. . . ."

Somewhere, in the small dark hours, while we were
sleeping in each other's arms, the alarm went off: a
shattering noise of bells and sirens. I leapt out of bed

and ran to the window. The grounds were lit with blazing floodlights, and I saw Heinz and Domenico loping across the open space towards the pinewoods. We threw on dressing gowns and hurried into the lounge, where we found Manzini standing, erect and calm, at the window. It was impossible to speak. The noise went on and on, a vicious assault on the eardrums, until twenty minutes later, perhaps, Domenico came hurrying back, switched off the system and reset it. A few moments later he reported to Manzini.

"We got him, Cavaliere. Up on the northern boundary."

"Alive or dead?"

"Dead. Heinz got him with the first shot."

"Who was he?"

"Italian, I think. No one we know. No papers, no identifying marks. No labels in the clothes."

"Armed?"

"Grenades, plastic explosive and fuses and a Walther pistol."

"How did he get in?"

"He had to come over the mountain on foot. We might be able to trace his route when the sun comes up."

"Not worth the trouble."

"Do we call the police?"

"In Liechtenstein? No! Bury him."

"With respect, Cavaliere, the alarm can be heard for miles."

"So far as we know, a deer fouled one of the trip wires."

"As you say, Cavaliere."

"Bury him deep, Domenico."

"Leave it to me, Cavaliere. . . . Good night."

When he had gone, Manzini poured three glasses of brandy and passed one to each of us. His hand was steady. He raised his glass in a kind of grim salute.

"Like the old days in the Partisans, Matucci, which you are too young to remember."

He meant to proclaim it like an ancient battle cry. To me it sounded like an epitaph.

BOOK II

*The practice of politics in the
East may be defined by one word:
dissimulation.*

—BENJAMIN DISRAELI: *Contarini Fleming*

WE DID not go directly into Italy, but drove by way of
Salzburg, where Manzini wanted to discuss a lumber
contract with an Austrian mill, and then down through
the Brenner to Mestre, where one of his companies was
building a graving dock for small tankers. It was a tedious
journey because the weather closed in, with heavy snow-
falls, north and south of the Alps, and the roads were a
mess of churned snow and dangerous ice.

Manzini, however, was in high spirits, determined, as
he put it, that we should divert ourselves before we
stepped into the lions' cage. He had a taste for legend
and for local history, and he understood the continuity
of it all, and how the old feudal families were still mixed
up in the omelet of modern Europe. He did not ramble
as some old men do, but talked his themes through to a
wholeness. He was a natural dramatist, and even when
he invented dialogues and situations, you were left with
a sense of concordance and probability.

Time and again he returned to his own childhood, as

if his deepest need was to purge himself of old rancours and remember forgotten joys.

"I grew up in a spacious time, Matucci, in a tolerant and cynical city. I lived in a palace behind the Condotti; a house full of doting women, from which men were never absent. I had all the illusions I needed and no guilts at all. In this, I think, I was a very fortunate child. Strange as it may seem, I was most fortunate in my mother. There were so many of her, you see—a new one for every day.

"I remember her, naked in the bath, smooth and appetizing as a peeled peach, whistling and singing and sipping champagne from a glass perched on a stool beside the bath. I remember her in corset and camisole, all ribbons and laces, pirouetting before the mirror and chattering about my uncles. . . . No boy in all the world had as many uncles as I.

"There was Colonel Melchior, who had one hand made of wood, covered with a black leather glove, because he had lost his hand in Abyssinia at the slaughter of Adowa. There was Uncle Burckhardt, who wore a gold chain across his belly and huffed when he bowed and puffed when he talked and who bored my mother to distraction. There was Uncle Freddie, who bought me my first clockwork train and taught me to play chess. He was English and his name was ffolliot-Phillimore, and the servants called him the 'Pope's angel,' because he had a high piping voice like the eunuch tenor in the papal choir. A lot of people hated him. Even Mamma hated him sometimes, because he could be very malicious. But I loved him. . . .

"He opened a new world to me. He took me down the Tiber in a rowboat. He read my first Latin and Greek with me. He showed me how to dig for shards and seals on Testaccio. He would sit with me on a tumbled pillar in the Forum and make me close my eyes and see the Vestals garlanded with flowers and the augurs telling the future from the flight of birds, and Petronius walking proud and elegant among the gossipers. . . . One day he said to me, 'When you grow up, young fellow, you must be an elegant man, else I shall be miserably disappointed in you. Look out there. That's your city. You must impose yourself on it as Petronius did, with brains and good taste and a talent for mockery. You must learn from it, too. Learn the art of survival and being reborn every day. When you have your first woman, let her be a Roman, all fire and fury, tears and tenderness. This is a rogue's city. Learn to be a rogue, too, if you must, but for God's sake be a rogue with style.'

"Strange! I remember that as if it were yesterday. I didn't know anything about style, of course. So I asked him what it was. He pointed up to the sky and said: 'Look up there. See the swifts, how they fly, riding the wind as if they owned the whole heavens. Now look over there. See that poor dumb donkey hauling the wine cart. He's a useful creature. We couldn't live without him. But which would you rather be, the swift or the donkey? . . . The swift, of course! That's style, young fellow. That's style. . . .'

"My father? Well, that's a hard one, Matucci. You see, I believed for a long time that my father was dead. I accepted it as children do, without question and truly without too much regret. Even after I had met him in the flesh, I was allowed for years to believe that he was just another kind uncle. That is one of the things I have found hardest to forgive. You told me I have too many enemies. I wonder sometimes if all the enemies are not one man: Massimo Count Pantaleone. I wonder if that is not why I hated my own brother, because he bore the name that should have been mine. And yet, given the custom of the time, given the laws of legitimacy and inheritance, I should not blame him too much.

"The first time I saw him, I was riding with Mamma on the Pincio. Uncle Melchior had bought me a pony and Mamma had given me a jacket and breeches in the English style, and this was my first day out with her. You should have known the Pincio in those days, Matucci. It was the place where you would see the most stylish landaus and some of the best horses in Rome. The Cardinals would drive up in their carriages, and they would

walk solemnly under the pines, while their retainers, all
in livery, would gossip together. The nobles of Rome
would ride and salute each other and flirt in the fashion
of the time. Not everybody saluted Mamma. Most of the
ladies held their heads high and looked through her as
if she were a windowpane. I remember she used to toss
her head and swear at them in Romanaccio: 'Old farts!
The only thing they can ever get under their skirts is a
horse.'

"Well, this morning a gentleman reined up and fell
into talk with Mamma. He was tall and bulky with a big
eagle's beak—like mine, probably—and a shock of
grey hair. He rode a black stallion with flaring nostrils
and he looked like a giant statue come to life. Mamma
was like a doll beside him, but she sat straight and smiling and held out her hand as if he were the humblest of
men. They talked for a long time. Then suddenly he
swept me off my pony and onto his own saddle and took
me on a wild gallop through the woods. He rode the
stallion into a lather and then dismounted in a small
grove—long gone!—where there was a statue of Pan
and a runnel of clear water. He put both his hands on
my shoulders and looked at me, silent and frowning.
Then he smiled and said: 'Good boy. You have good
manners and a stout heart—a trophy for any man in his
autumn days. I wish I had the courage to claim you. . . .'
I didn't know what he meant, only that he was pleased
with me. Then he took me back to Mamma. . . .

"Eh, Matucci! If you are bored, blame yourself. You
wanted to know me. Here I am! Now, let's talk a little
business. You will stay for a few days at my country
place outside Bologna. Then I suggest you establish yourself in Milan. I have a furnished apartment, which I can
place at your disposal, together with servants you can
trust. You will need a bank account and credit facilities,
and a cover story for your activities in my employ; after
that, good luck and a very active guardian angel."

"More, Cavaliere. I need a list of safe houses and two
or three sets of papers. The best forgeries."

"Surely you know how to get those?"

"How and where and how much, but I cannot appear in the negotiations."

"I know the best forger in the business."

"I know him, too . . . Carlo Metaponte, pupil of Aldo the Calligrapher. He engraved your salamander card. He's on our files."

"Still usable?"

"If you can control him, yes."

"I can control him. . . . Matucci, will you take a little advice from me?"

"Yes."

"Please try to be generous with me. I'm old enough to be your father. Strange as it may seem, I still have a conscience, because I try to live by logic and conscience is the last term of a syllogism. I have tried to examine this conscience on our relationship. I conclude, rightly or wrongly, that what divides us is not principle but history . . . the class struggle, the class image. Your father was an old-line socialist, exiled to Lipari. Mine was an old-line aristocrat, who exploited the poor and broke his neck chasing women on the Pincio. But when you were thirteen years old, Matucci, I was making petrol bombs in a barn near Pedognana. When you were fourteen, I was hung by my thumbs in a Gestapo cell in Milan. What I fought for then, you are trying to preserve now, a liberty, however precarious and imperfect. I cannot risk what you risk, because I have only the tag end of a life at my disposal. But it's still sweet and I savour every second of it. This is not a reproach, believe me. It is—how can I call it? —a plea that we should enjoy this fight. Go down, if we must; survive, if we can, singing and shouting. Can you understand that?"

"I can. I do. I'm grateful, Cavaliere."

"Please! Not 'cavaliere' anymore. I am Bruno. You are Dante Alighieri . . . *Bene?*"

"*Bene, grazie!*"

"And I want you to develop some style, my Dante. New uniforms for special occasions. A colonel should look like a colonel, not a conscript corporal. New suits, too, the best fashion, a modish cut. And don't be mean with money; spread it like sauce on spaghetti. . . . Good! That's the first time I've heard you laugh like a happy man!"

Then, because he must still play the conjurer, he hit me with a new surprise. We would stay, not in Mestre, which was a barbarous town, but across the water in Venice at the Gritti Palace—and the Director would join us for dinner. After all the charm he had spent on me, I had to take it with good grace. That pleased him almost as much as his own cleverness, and he explained the reason at length and in detail:

". . . You would have to confront him sometime. Better with me than alone. Better in his own city, where he feels most a prince. Across the water he will see some of the enterprise that makes me what I am. He will see you, too, in another light: a bought man enjoying the fruits of judicious compromise. We are at home now, where these subtleties matter. Not that you will demean yourself. Never! You will be courteous, a little reserved, but not insensible of his magnanimity. He will goad you, of course; but you will still fight back, though not so strongly as before, because you have less to lose. He will ask you about Lili Anders. You will shrug her off, a ripe peach tasted and thrown away. When you think you have had enough, you leave. You have to meet a woman in Harry's Bar. She will be there, too. Her name is Gisela Pestalozzi. She will be on your list of safe houses. . . . The barman will know her. You will say that the Salamander sent you. . . . Clear?"

"Clear. Except how you manage it all."

"It's a game, my Dante. One of the few I can still play well."

We came to Venice in the early dark. There was mist on the canals, a thick pestiferous haze, heavy with the fumes of sulfur and the exhalations of the canals. Domenico parked the car and we took a gondola to the hotel because, said Manzini, the gondoliers were all vultures, but even vultures had a right to survive. At the Gritti we were welcomed like medieval Cardinals and lodged in adjoining suites overlooking the Grand Canal.

Not that there was much to see, because the fog sat low on the water and the lights of the sparse traffic made dull yellow blotches in the murk. I shaved and bathed at leisure, while my clothes were pressed. I dressed with more care than usual and managed to make my entrance just as Manzini and the Director were settling themselves at the table.

The Director received me like the prodigal son. "My dear Matucci! I'm delighted to see you. Filthy weather, isn't it?"

I agreed it was; but Venice was still Venice after all.

"You look well and rested. That's good. Did you have a good journey?"

"Brutal!" said Manzini testily. "Chains all the way! Still, it should bring the skiers out. Did you invest in that little project I recommended at Bolzano?"

"Regrettably, no. I bought a Picasso instead."

"Rubbish! There's too much of him and more to come when he's dead. You should have waited until the Pantaleone collection came on the market. It has to, you know."

"My dear Bruno! What's the use, if you can't export the stuff when you're tired of it. Are you interested in painting, Matucci?"

"I am, sir, but I can't afford it. Not yet, anyway."

"Take my advice. Start with the young ones. If you have a good eye, you can't fail to pick at least one in ten. At that you'll still make a profit. Wouldn't you say, Bruno?"

"I want him interested in my profits first. That's the quickest way he'll make them for himself. Do you have any idea how many milliards of lire we lost a year through pilfering, large-scale theft, industrial sabotage and bad bookkeeping? Matucci here has made some intelligent suggestions. If he can put them into action, I'll be prepared to bid very high for him."

"Provided, my dear Bruno, that the Service is prepared to waive claims on his valuable talents. . . . Still, I must say I'm glad to see him have his opportunity. He deserves it. I owe you some thanks, Matucci. You behaved very

well in a difficult diplomatic situation. I don't blame you
for feeling angry. I'm glad to see you had the enterprise
to contact Bruno here. It's a situation that could work
out very well for all of us, even for the Service, because,
as you have often said, we are weak in the high industrial sector. Still, that's for another time. . . . We've made
a few changes at Headquarters since you left."

"Oh?"

"Gonzaga moves into the Middle East section and
Rampolla takes over the Balkan desk. The rest are
minor, except that we've retired Stefanelli from Forensics. He was getting much too old and crotchety. . . . Ah,
the menu! What do you recommend, Bruno?"

"My dear fellow, you should know by now, I never
recommend food, horses or women. It's the surest way
to lose friends. Wine is another matter altogether. I believe you had a very good vintage last year."

"One of our best in a decade. It's too early yet, but
when it's ready, I'll reserve you a few cases."

"Thank you. I'd appreciate it. By the way, have you
recovered the Pantaleone will yet?"

"Not yet. Which reminds me, Matucci. We were lucky
about Bandinelli. It appears the wife was having an affair
with a young singer at San Carlo. She was only too
pleased to consent to a quiet funeral with no embarrassing questions."

"I'm delighted to know it, sir. I'm afraid I didn't handle
that situation very well."

"We all make mistakes. And you were under a big
strain. Let's order, shall we? I hate having waiters breathing down my neck."

I was glad of the respite and the small talk that followed it: the talk of high men who played with power
and people as if they were coloured counters on a gaming
table. They were well matched, these two: the Director
so firmly entrenched in history that you had only to
change his costume to set him back in the Council of
the Ten; Manzini, the old technocrat, straddling the past
and the present and the future like a colossus in a business suit. But the language was the same and the power

was the same as in the days when one galley a day slid
down the slips and half the treasure of Byzantium poured
into Venice of the Doges. For a while they ignored me,
and I was very content to listen and begin to learn the
stylized language of this other world.

After a while, inevitably, the talk became spicy and
scandalous: who was taking advantage of the new divorce
law and who was not and why. Then, without warning,
the Director tossed a question to me.

"By the way, Matucci, what happened to the Anders
woman?"

"I took your advice, sir."

"Oh, forgive me, Bruno, I forgot there was a family
connection."

"Please! I am not in the least concerned. I only hope
Matucci enjoyed himself."

"Did you, Matucci?"

"Briefly, sir."

"Where is she now?"

"She was talking of going to Klosters for a while. I
didn't inquire too closely. You know the way it is."

"Do you think she'll go back to the trade?"

"Not our trade, sir. I think she has marriage in mind."

"Any prospects?"

"Not with me, I assure you. Which reminds me, if
you gentlemen will excuse me from coffee, I have an
appointment with another lady."

"By all means, unless Bruno here . . ."

"No, no! Go ahead. Enjoy yourself while you can.
You'll have little enough time later."

"Oh, before you go, Matucci . . ."

"Sir?"

"This dual employment of yours. I'm quite happy about
it, of course. I'm glad to oblige my friend Bruno here.
But you will be discreet about it, won't you? It's faintly
illegal and I'd hate to raise discontent among your Service
colleagues. You do understand?"

"Perfectly, sir. And I'm very grateful. Good night,
gentlemen."

"Good luck with the lady."

"It's a dirty night," said Bruno Manzini, with a grin. "Don't fall into the canal."

❧ ❧

IT was a fair warning and I took it seriously. I went up to my room, put on a topcoat and slipped a pistol into my pocket. I spent a moment at the desk in the lobby buying postage stamps from the concierge and then stepped out into the alley between the Palazzo Pisani and the Gritti. You know the place. The alley opens into a piazza in front of the Zobenigo. You turn right, cross over a small bridge and come into the Largo Ventidue Marzo, which brings you slap against the facade of the Basilica of San Moisè. Even by day, it is a quiet route. There are few shops and nothing to see except the Basilica, and the stale backwater under the bridge is jammed with gondolas and barges. But at night, with choking fog, and every window shuttered, it was like a city of the dead.

I paused a moment under the light and heard a murmur of voices from the left; boatmen, probably, waiting to ferry some of the diners back home. I could not see them, but I could hear the boats bumping against the piles. I began to walk, not fast, but steadily, holding to the wall for direction, listening for the sound of other footfalls. Nothing, except the wash of the canal and the sound of distant music and the wail of foghorns from the basin at Mestre. When I turned out of the Piazza Zobenigo, I stopped and listened again. This time I heard, or thought I heard, the faint slap-slap of rubber soles, running tiptoe on the cobbles; but the sound was so vague, so muted by the mist, that it could have been an illusion. I began to walk, faster now, towards the vague yellow glow that marked the hump of the bridge. Then, from behind me, I heard a long, high whistle. I stopped, flattened myself against the wall, took the pistol from my pocket and slipped off the safety catch. The situation was clear now. Behind me was one man. Ahead, where the canal cut across the alley, there would be two, one at either corner of the *traghetto*. Before I reached the bridge they would close the trap and kill me inside it.

Backed against the wall, I began to ease myself slowly along it, feeling for a doorway or any projection of the wall that would give me the slightest shelter. I heard rubber shoes make a few swift, running steps. I saw a faint movement near the bridge, which might have been a man, but could just as easily have been a swirl of mist. Then my fingers slid off the rough surface of the wall and groped in emptiness. It was not a doorway. It was an open archway, low and narrow, leading back into the courtyard of a palace or a tenement. Thanks be to God! Now they would have to come for me. I slid down on one knee and peered out cautiously. It was perhaps ten seconds before they began to move, two hugging the wall on my side, the third moving down the opposite side of the alley. This was the one I must take first, if I could see clearly enough to hit him.

They moved irregularly, in a series of short runs, first one, then the others, never in the same sequence. I had to have them near. I dared not let them come too close, in case they were armed with grenades or a nail-bomb. Then, mercifully, the man on the opposite side made a run that brought him into range. I could not see him clearly. I had to guess him between a barred window and the deeper shadow of a doorway. I took careful aim and fired. In the narrow space the explosion was deafening. He did not fire back. He turned and ran. The others ran, too. I fired two more shots, wild into the mist. Then, because shutters were opening and heads were showing at lighted windows, I, too, bolted down the alley and over the bridge. I did not stop running until I reached the shelter of Harry's Bar.

Mercifully, the bar was busy, so my breathless entrance attracted no attention at all. I ordered a large drink, carried it to the telephone booth and called Manzini at the hotel. They called him away from his coffee and I told him:

"Thanks for the warning. I nearly did fall into the canal."

"What happened?"

"A well-laid trap. Three men. I fired shots. They got away."

"Where are you now?"

"Where you sent me. I haven't met the lady yet."

"Come to my room when you get back."

"How's our mutual friend?"

"Smug as a cat. I think I'll stir him up a little. Until later, eh?"

I carried my drink back to the bar, nudged myself onto a stool and waited for a slack moment to chat to the barman. When I asked him about Gisela Pestalozzi, he grinned.

"Interested in a little fun, eh? Well, she's expensive, but she's got the best girls in town."

"How expensive?"

"Sixty to a hundred thousand a night in season. At this time, maybe less, but you'll have to haggle. Still, they've all got their own apartments, and that's something in this weather. Where are you staying?"

"Friends of the family. Very stuffy people."

"Eh! Then Gisela's your best bet."

"How will I know her?"

"She sits over in the far corner. Big redhead in her middle forties. Wears lots of junk: bangles, neck chains, big earrings, that sort of thing. You can't miss her. She's an old cow, but always good for a laugh. Give you a tip, though. Don't cross her. She's got lots of friends."

"Police?"

"A few. More of the other kind."

"Thanks. . . . And here's something for the service."

"Thank you. Staying long in Venice?"

"I doubt it. Why?"

"Well, as I say, I wouldn't want to cross Gisela; but if you're interested, I have a few numbers of my own. . . ."

"Thanks. I'll remember. Pour me another drink and send it over to the corner."

I spread myself over the banquette. The waiter brought

the drink and I sipped it slowly while I thought about the
Cavaliere Bruno Manzini, called the Salamander. Everything he said was magical, but how much was true and
how much was fairy tale, I could not guess. Bruno Manzini, partisan hero, joined with the fascists and then called
on me, Colonel Nobody, to destroy them. I felt like a
whirling dervish, dancing himself into oblivion to prove
that God was God and all His works were a splendid
inconsequence.

Then Gisela Pestalozzi came in, scattering greetings and
perfume, and sat down beside me. She had rings on her
fingers and dangling bells in her ears and enough chains to
moor the *Galileo*. She had arms like a wrestler and
bosoms bountiful enough to feed a continent. Her hair
was titian red, her lips geranium, and her voice was like
pebbles in a gravel grinder. She was sweating profusely
and she fanned herself with a table napkin. She ignored
me for a full half minute, then she announced:

"This is my place, young man. You must be new here."

"And you must be Gisela?"

"That's right. How did you know?"

"A friend told me."

"What friend?"

"Can you lower your voice a little, please?"

"Why should I? It's my voice. It's my place. If you
want to talk business, that's another thing."

"I want to talk business."

"Sixty thousand a night, dinner and drinks extra. Yes
or no?"

"No. The Salamander sent me."

"Eh!" She collapsed like a vast balloon and her voice
dropped ten decibels. "Why didn't you say so straight
off? What do you need?"

"A safe house."

"How long?"

"I don't know yet. Weeks, months."

"With or without?"

"With or without what?"

"A woman, of course. What else?"

"Without."

"Two rooms, kitchen and bath. Fully furnished, light, heat and telephone. Two hundred thousand a month. Suit you?"

"It's a murderous price."

"It's a safe house. Private entrance. No porter and two other exits."

"Where?"

"A hundred meters from San Marco."

"Quality?"

"Well, it's not the Cà' d'Oro, but it's comfortable."

"Where do I get the key?"

"From me. With a month in advance and a month's deposit."

"I'll think about it. Where do I find you when you're not here?"

"The Salamander has my number."

"Good. A drink?"

"What's your name?"

"I change it every day. Just call me lover."

"Do you want a girl?"

"Not tonight."

"Then move over, lover! This is working hours."

"*Ciao,* Gisela! We'll be seeing each other."

And that was it, pointless and purposeless as everything else that was happening to me. I left my drink unfinished on the table and paid a sleepy boatman one thousand lire to deliver me two hundred meters down the canal at the front door of the Gritti, which, being a civilized hotel, has a good telephone service and booths where you need not discuss your business with the world and his girl friend. I ordered a call to Stefanelli in Rome and, two minutes later, I had him on the line. In ten seconds I knew that I was not a welcome caller.

"Steffi, this is Matucci."

"I remember the name. Yes?"

"I'm in Venice, Steffi."

"Happy you. Happy Venice."

"Steffi, stop clowning, for Christ's sake! This is serious."

"I know. I am out of a job. Every *fascista* in the

Service has jumped two grades and you are eating lobster in Venice. It can get more serious?"

"I want to see you."

"I'm at home all the time—midnight to midnight."

"Listen, please!"

"No! You listen. You sold out, little brother! You took a long leave and a lush sinecure and now you're on the payroll of private industry. You're a *stronzo,* Matucci. The worst I've ever known."

"Where did you hear all this?"

"Does it matter?"

"Yes, it does. And if you hang up, Steffi, I'll spit on your grave. Now tell me!"

"I heard it from the great talking horse himself, our dear Director, on the day he retired me. I quote: 'You are still active, Stefanelli. Why don't you emulate your colleague, Matucci, and direct your talents, your very considerable talents, to civilian occupation?' I still quote: 'The rewards are very great, as Matucci will tell you. We had our disagreements, but we were able to resolve them, and I venture to suggest that Matucci will end a very rich man.' End of quote. Do you want to hear any more?"

"No, thanks. Did you get my telegram?"

"I got it."

"But you didn't believe it?"

"No."

"Will you do me one favour?"

"Flowers for your funeral, maybe."

"Save your money. It could be sooner than you think. Go talk to Raquela Rabin instead. Ask her what we discussed the day I went to see her."

"And then?"

"I'll call once more. Then, if you want, you can call me all the names in the book. Good night, Steffi."

After that I went upstairs to talk to Bruno Manzini. I was surprised to find that the Director was still with him, but the atmosphere had changed. They were terse with me and tense with each other. Manzini plunged straight into interrogation.

"Tell us what happened, Matucci."

I told them. I drew a map on the hotel notepaper to make it clear. I made it even clearer that someone had set me up like a clay pigeon and I wasn't very happy about it. Manzini cut me off in the middle of this theme and said flatly:

"I have already told your Director what happened at the lodge."

"I see."

"And I have conveyed to him our suspicion that both these attempts were officially inspired."

"And I am shocked at the suggestion, Matucci." He looked it, too. For the first time I caught a hint of unease under his sardonic mask. "Did you really believe that, after we had settled an amicable arrangement, after I had agreed to your return to Italy and your private employment with my old friend, I would put out a contract for your life?"

"It had to be you or Leporello. You were kept constantly informed by the Cavaliere. You knew I had an appointment at his lodge. You knew I was coming to dinner here tonight. Knowing the trade as we both do, it's not too illogical, is it?"

"From my point of view, Matucci, it's madness. I would stamp you out with no compunction at all if I had to; but, as things are, I have a vested interest in keeping you alive."

"I will not work with fools," said Bruno Manzini flatly. "I will not tolerate threats against my staff. You will talk sense into that upstart Leporello."

"Please!" said the Director softly. "Please, Bruno. We're too old for tantrums. I will deal with it. . . . Sleep well, Matucci."

When he had gone, Bruno Manzini lay back in his chair and surveyed me with ironic amusement.

"Well, my Dante, what did you make of that?"

"I think he's telling the truth."

"I know he is. And I know he's worried. If he can't control Leporello now, he'll never be able to do it afterwards. . . . All profit, my Dante! When thieves fall out, it's gold in the pockets of the godly."

I laughed. What else could I do? I laughed until tears ran down my cheeks, while the old man sat chuckling in his chair like a spider who had just made a meal of a gadfly.

◆ ◆

THERE were lions at the gates, twin beasts of lichened stone, supporting beneath their upraised paws an illegible escutcheon. The gates were of black iron, scrolled and curlicued, twice the height of a man. The gatekeeper was a dwarfish manikin who came running to the door of the car to greet his master with a simian chatter of dialect. Beyond the gate a gravelled drive wound through an avenue of cypresses and opened into a geometer's fantasy of flower beds and miniature hedgerows, beyond which a stairway of white marble led to the villa, a small Palladian jewel, light and beautiful even under the grey sky and the steady drenching rain.

This was Pedognana, country seat of the Cavaliere Bruno Manzini, and he displayed it to me with childlike pride.

"Home, my Dante! The one place in all the world where I am truly myself. My mother bought it, in the good years, and sold it in the bad ones. When I made my first real money, I bought it again, and I have held it ever since. The arms over the gate are the ones my mother invented for herself. You can still make out the salamander if you look closely enough. I defaced it in the partisan days, because this was my headquarters until the Germans arrested me and shoved me into jail. There's everything here: orchards, farmland, mulberries for the silkworms, rice on the river flats, grapes and olives on the foothills. Something of the old life, too, as you will see for yourself. Come inside. . . ."

In the pillared entrance, under a dome resplendent with Tiepolo fantasies, the household was assembled: Gualtiero, the factor, six feet tall and solid as an oak tree; Lanfranco, majordomo of the villa; Don Egidio, chaplain to the estate; Donna Edda, the housekeeper, a stout coun-

try-apple woman, full of flounce and fluster; and with them
a small hierarchy of maids, gardeners and grooms. Manzini saluted them all by name, and I had perforce to
repeat the salutation, so that, by the time the ceremony
was over, I was convinced that I had been translated into
the nineteenth century.

The greetings over, I was consigned to the care of
Donna Edda, who bustled me upstairs with such a fervour
of welcome that I felt giddy. The splendour of the room
overwhelmed me—the canopied bed, the vast buhl desk,
the fire blazing behind the brass screen, the bookcase that
climbed to the ceiling, full of leather-bound tomes. Suddenly it was all too much, and I wondered irrationally
whether this were not a tactic: to stifle me with grandeur
and bind me like another serf to his service. However,
he put himself at pains to explain himself and the scope
of his design.

". . . Try to understand, Dante Alighieri. I am a free
man. I understand liberty in the Anglo-Saxon way, because my mother was a Scot and a free woman in her
own right. She fought Pantaleone to establish an estate
for me and he did it. She made a long nose at society,
but she never complained when society looked down its
nose at her. But freedom like this is a rare state of mind.
People have to grow to it, be educated to it. And this
country is still only half educated, in parts not educated
at all. Many prefer tyranny to freedom, because tyrants
can be corrupted while liberty demands a drastic innocence, a daily battle like that of Sant' Antonio with the
demons. . . . I am not innocent; neither are you; but we
don't want to be whores all our lives. Remember Raquela
Rabin? . . . Well, that's a story that says it all. We were
lovers, as you know. We parted . . . each for the same
reason. I bowed to social pressures. She found herself
a more powerful protector—a vice-president of the Jewish
Council, a man high in Fascist affairs. You are too young
to remember, Dante Alighieri, but even the Jews believed
in the *Duce* and trusted till the last that he would save
them from the German holocausts. . . . In the end we
knew that we had both betrayed ourselves. Raquela went

to Auschwitz—a willing victim. I went underground to fight. . . . Remember the Bible? 'A man's enemies shall be those of his own household.' It is like that still. So I had to test you. I will go on testing you, because you have not yet been hung by the thumbs or been shocked with electrodes clipped to your testicles. . . . Forgive me. I am too vehement. I am still not as wise as I should like to be. . . ."

Later that evening, with maps and documents spread all over the table, we sketched the first plan of campaign. Once again I marvelled that so old a man could be so precise and ruthless in his designs.

"State the purpose of the exercise, Colonel."

"To convict Major-General Leporello of conspiracy to murder Avvocato Bandinelli and Agent Calvi. To discredit the Director by showing him joined in the conspiracy."

"And where do you begin?"

"With three facts: Leporello knew the location of the Pantaleone papers and my arrangements to guard them; his aide, Captain Roditi, appeared on Ponza with orders to claim the other documents; later the Director joined Leporello in a plot to establish military rule."

"Given those facts, where do you probe first?"

"At the weakest point. Captain Roditi."

"Next?"

"Leporello."

"Why not the Director? You know him better."

"As he stands, he's almost impregnable. He can justify any action by the secret needs of the Service."

"Come back to Leporello, then."

"I've never seen his dossier. We can build one easily enough, but it will take time. Apart from that, we have two versions of him: his own and the Director's."

"Quotes?"

"The Director: 'A patriot, a devout Catholic, a Christian Democrat and financially independent. Doubt he could be bought or frightened.' "

"His own?"

"Verbatim quote: 'My loyalties were to the Crown. I

never changed them—even when it might have been convenient to do so. I disliked the Fascists. I loathed the Germans; but even for that I could not make myself a turncoat soldier. Today I am able to be honest and proud.' Quote ends."

"Dio mio! A resolute virgin! I don't believe it."

"Neither do I. What is your impression of him?"

"Cold, ambitious, more than a little paranoid. But put him on that balcony in the Piazza Venezia and many people would go mad for him. I'd like to examine him in social circumstances. I'll invite him to a suitable gathering in Milan. He's based there, so that's easy. He'll bring his aide, so that should give you a starting point, too. We'd better install you in the apartment as soon as possible. Which raises another question, Dante *mio* . . . women!"

"Oh?"

"How do you propose to arrange yourself, for business and pleasure?"

"I'm organized for both."

"I believe you. However, I suggest you take an interest in the marriage market as well."

"You must be joking!"

"On the contrary. You're a bachelor, a full colonel, with interesting prospects. So you're a good candidate for any woman's guest list. Use that, my friend, especially here in the North, where money talks and those who have it gossip like nuns. Now . . . since gossip is important, let's discuss your cover story. You are appointed as my personal adviser on all aspects of industrial security. You enter at managerial level. You have free access to all plants and offices. You will be supplied with a company credit card and a car for your personal use. You will make as many friends as you can inside my companies and you will allay as far as possible any jealousies that may arise out of your privileged position. When I am absent from the country, as I am frequently, you will work at your own discretion and report to me in a code which I shall supply to you. My secretary will be instructed to inform you of my movements. If she does not know them—and they are sometimes secret—I shall inform you in advance. My banker arrives at ten tomorrow morning to open your account and establish a credit rating backed by me. Now, what else is on the list?"

"Personnel."

"Employ whomever you wish. But check with me before you use any of my staff. Next?"

"You've written here: 'The Church.'"

"Oh, yes. This is a delicate one, Matucci. Mother Church is up to her neck in Italian politics. We know that. She's a very old and very shrewd lady, and she has friends to the left and right as well as in the center. Sometimes it's hard to distinguish them, because the cassock makes all priests look alike and everybody in the Vatican uses the same language—with very subtle overtones that make all the difference to the meaning. If you find you're treading on a cassock, tread lightly until you know who's wearing it. . . . Are you religious, by the way?"

"I was baptized, communicated and confirmed and the good brothers beat me into unbelief. Why the question?"

"It helps to know what a man thinks about dying—his own or another's."

"I think about it as little as possible. I find that helps. You?"

"I'm old. It makes a difference."

"I see that it might."

"I've lived the discord, but I think I hear a harmony. I hear it plainest in the old words and the old signs of grace. Maybe it's an illusion, but I'd rather die with it than without it. . . . Still, each to his own. My God! I really must get you to a good tailor. That suit was cut by a pork butcher."

In the morning the banker came, and in the afternoon, whirled from Milan, a tailor, who measured me for more clothes than my father had worn in a lifetime. In between, and late into the dusk, I played my memory game on the microfilms and sweated over the mountain of material from the data bank. In the evening, with an odd feeling of trepidation, I called Stefanelli. This time he was his old truculent self.

"So, I apologize, Matucci; then what?"

"Then I say, don't mention it."

"Then what?"

"Then I say, how would you like to work for me? Good salary, expenses, a little travel."

"What sort of work?"

"Now, Steffi, if I were fool enough to tell you on an open line, you would be a fool to work for me."

"Oh? That sort of work."

"Yes, Steffi. What do you say?"

"I'll have to ask my wife."

"You're a millstone round her neck and you know it. She can't wait to get you out of the house."

"Now, that's a great truth, little brother. How soon?"

"A week. Ten days at most."

"How long?"

"No idea."

"How much?"

"Your Service salary."

"You've bought me."

"Good. I'll be in touch soon. And, Steffi, please . . ."

"I know. Don't tell me. Once there were three wise monkeys . . ."

"Steffi, you're a jewel."

"I am also stark raving mad. But I'll be madder still if I stay in this house too long."

"One more thing. Do I have any friends left?"

"Still a few. . . . Need something?"

"Yes. Roditi, Matteo, Captain of Carabinieri, aide to Major-General Leporello. Any background you can get."

"Should be easy enough."

"Thanks, Steffi. Soon, eh?"

"Shalom . . ."

I felt happier after that. I sat down and typed a short note to Lili, who was staying at a small hotel in the Bernese Oberland. The note would be carried across the border by a courier and posted inside Switzerland. There is no official censorship of mails in Italy, but letters do get opened and a lot of private information finds its way into the files. I could not say very much because Lili might still be under surveillance and someone just might go through her things. And it's hard to be very passionate when you sign a letter "Uncle Pavel." Still she would know I was well and she would be able to answer through the accommodation address in Chiasso, provided by Manzini.

For the next week I worked like a galley slave on notes and mnemonics, daily conferences with Manzini, broken only by sessions with the tailor, who arrived every two days with a new batch of fittings, and who by some miracle of Italian industry would have everything ready for delivery the day I took possession of the apartment. I was inclined to be flippant about the tailor, but Manzini became quite testy and read me a five-minute lecture on the subject.

"This isn't a joke, Matucci. And don't let that Tuscan snobbery of yours cloud your judgment. We're talking about some of the most potent people in the world today —the image makers, the dream merchants, the illusionists. Put eight hundred million people in black button-up tunics and what have you got?—Mao's China, and the whole world goggle-eyed at the wonder of it. I make textiles, Matucci, and I know what the fashion business means. . . . Tourism is our second most important industry—and if you took the bikini off the travel posters, it would slump by half overnight. Have you read that batch of cuttings I put on your desk this morning?"

"Not yet. Why?"

"Because the image makers are working on Leporello right at this moment. There are two picture stories, four excerpts from recent speeches on law and order and twenty-three other references on various themes. It's the beginning of a campaign, Matucci. They're testing the market before they strike a line. There's a big agency behind it—Publitalia—and if you check your notes you'll find the name of the man who owns it. . . . Now, for God's sake, stop being coy and let's attend to business!"

He was a rough old pirate, but I was beginning to love him. He had so much talent, so much zest and drive, that he made me feel sometimes like a country clod. No detail was too small for his attention: the names I should use on my false papers, the decoration of the apartment in Milan, the clubs at which he might present me, whether I should play tennis or take a few lessons in golf, and even the make of car I should drive. He instructed me in the workings of the bourse, so that I could talk stocks and bonds intelligently. He sketched me the histories of the great families, the Torlonia, the Pallavicini, the Doria, the Orsini. He read me the careers of the modern merchant adventurers and the follies of their wives and offspring. He showed me where the American money was, and the German and the Swiss, and how the oil war was fought, and how the tentacles of the Honourable Society reached even into the North. Over and over again he repeated the same lesson:

". . . Think always in the frame of history, Dante. It takes more than a hundred and fifty years to build a nation and a national consciousness. Once Mussolini was toppled, we were back to the days of the warring duke-doms. Even the Marxists are split. Now we are looking for another point of focus, and that's the appeal of the new fascism. What people don't see is that we have to grow out of disunity, not be bludgeoned out of it by new Blackshirts. If they try it . . . God! I hate to think of the consequences. . . !"

Then, abruptly, as always, he dropped the subject and took me out on a tour of the estate, reminiscing all the while about his youth and his relations with his father.

". . . He was the perfect mirror of his time, Dante: an unblushing pragmatist who was convinced that money and a title could command anything, even immortality. He believed in God but found Him agreeably absent from most human transactions. He believed in the Church as one of the more stable and useful human institutions. He believed in marriage as a social contract but not as a solace for a normal man's desires. Diplomacy was an art for gentlemen, but politics was a trade for arrivistes and rogues. He was happy to profit from it but he refused to engage himself in it, being content with a public affirmation of loyalty to the Crown and a private manipulation of conflicting parties to the sole and singular interest of Pantaleone. . . .

"I see you smile, my friend. You're right. I'm very like him. He was a good businessman, too. He invested in steel and electricity and shipbuilding and insurance and banks, and bought no stock at all in colonial adventures. As I told you, my mother fought him to make a settlement on me, and that was the foundation of what I have today. After that first meeting on the Pincio, he began to take an interest in me, and I accepted him as the best and most exciting of all my uncles. . . .

"Looking back now, I see his intentions very clearly. He wanted to get me out of the harem atmosphere of my mother's house and thrust me into a world of men. It was a wonderful world then, Matucci, especially if you didn't see the underside of it—and I was spared that for many years. Once each week I would go to the *salle d'armes,* where Pantaleone practised saber and épée with the master, Carducci. Sometimes, at first light, we would drive out along the Appia Antica to the stud at Tor Carbone where he bred racehorses from British and Irish stock. We would watch the morning gallops, make the rounds of the stables and then sit down to breakfast in the kitchen of the old farmhouse with the studmaster and the trainer. . . .

"On other days he would take me to visit the craftsmen who flourished under his patronage and that of his wealthy friends. They were wonderful men, Dante, all gone now. There was Ascoli, the antiquarian, a wizened old gnome who could take a handful of shards and rebuild them into an Etruscan urn and read you a whole history from it. There was Haro, the Spaniard, a gunsmith who lived over on the Prati and whom even the British ranked with their own masters. He had a pistol range in his cellar and pigeon traps and a line of butts in the fields where his gentlemen clients could test their skills. That was where I first learned to handle a gun and to care for it, too. . . . Eh! memory is a treacherous gift!"

"You look troubled. Something bothering you?"

"I've just recalled something. A lesson Pantaleone

taught me. I hated him for it. Now—God knows why—it makes me want to weep."

"Do you want to talk about it?"

"Why not? It's very short. One day at the gallops I slipped and fell in the mud. A stableboy laughed and I flew at him, clawing and punching and screaming in Romanaccio. Pantaleone hauled me away and cuffed me till my ears sang, and I was sobbing with pain. He was quite cold about it, brutal and deliberate. Then he told me: 'You will never do that again. The boy did you no harm. You looked a fool and he laughed. He could not hit back because he is a poor peasant who depends on me for work. You are supposed to be a gentleman. You acted like an animal out of control. You will go now and apologize.' I refused. He gave me a look of such contempt that I felt crushed. Then he walked away and left me. Later I did apologize, but by then he was gone and the farm people had to drive me back to Rome in a wine cart. I didn't see him for months afterwards. I thought he had rejected me because of my disobedience. I did not know until long afterwards that his wife had given him a legitimate son and that I had been relegated to the shadows. . . . That's all."

"Not quite all, I think."

"What do you mean?"

"The lesson wasn't lost. I was talking to Gualtiero, your factor. He told me you've turned this place into a cooperative, so that your people can have tenure after your death."

"Oh, that! Well, it's something, I suppose. I'm bowing to social necessity. Eh! Let's change the subject. Look at those blossoms, Dante. The whole hillside is in flower. You'll be gone soon. But I want you to know that you are welcome here whenever you choose to come. You're good for me."

"And you for me, Bruno. I'll be sorry to leave this place."

"Have you no land of your own?"

"None."

"Then buy yourself a plot, however small. Plough and

plant and love it a little. Every man needs one earth he can call his own."

"Perhaps, after this is over . . ."

The rest of the thought remained unspoken, but we both understood the big *perhaps*. If things went wrong, I should have all the earth I needed: two meters long, a meter and a half deep—a grave in the camposanto.

❦

THE apartment in Milan was the penthouse of a new block, built by Manzini, not far from the center of the city. I had two bedrooms, two bathrooms, an American-style kitchen, a large salon, a dining room and a study, as well as separate quarters for two servants. There was a terrace on three sides, planted with shrubs and spring flowers in urns. The only access was by private elevator whose entrance and interior could be scanned by closed-circuit television from inside the apartment. The servants had one key to the elevator. I had another. The doors of the apartment were equipped with double locks and chain bolts and the windows with steel shutters. There were two independent alarm systems, each connected by telephone circuit to the headquarters of the mobile squadron.

Everything in the place was new and designed for a rich and sociable bachelor: deep leather furniture, a well-stocked bar, a high-fidelity system, racks of records, a television set, bright modern canvases, books, new and old, for lonely nights. There was a typewriter, a Xerox copier, a tape machine, boxed notepaper with my name on it, two sets of visiting cards, one for civilian, the other for military occasions. Behind the bookshelves, concealed by a false panel, was a modern safe with an electronic locking device and an alarm connected to the central system. Even the telephone index on my desk was typed up to date with all the numbers I might need within Manzini's organization and with the addresses of tradesmen, doctor and dentist. Manzini made me free of it all with a smile of satisfaction.

"There, my dear Dante. All yours. Now you have

nothing to do but to work and divert yourself profitably. Let me introduce you to the servants."

There were two of them, twin brothers from Sardinia, small dark men, taciturn and dignified as grandees. They were named Pietro and Paolo, so that they could share the same feast day. Pietro was cook and butler. Paolo was houseman and valet. There was always one of them on duty night and day. They had served Manzini for ten years, and, if first impressions meant anything, they would keep me like a film star. Within ten minutes of my arrival, my suits were ranged in the closet, my toilet things laid out, my soiled clothes whisked out of sight. They came from Nuoro, Manzini told me, and they had served a prison term for banditry. He had hired them for a season on his yacht and then offered them a permanence. They were fiercely loyal and so discreet that they would not give the time of day to a stranger.

We toasted the enterprise and blessed the house with a glass of champagne and then, before he left, Manzini did a touching thing. He put his hands on my shoulders and embraced me, cheek to cheek, as if we were brothers. Then he loosened his tie and took from round his neck a thin gold chain with a medallion. He slipped it over my head and said, quietly:

"It's a Saint Christopher. I had him all through the war. You don't have to believe. Just wear him for me, eh?"

An instant later he was his old ironic self, with a wave and a gibe as he walked out the door.

"Let's have some style now, Dante Alighieri. *Freghiamo i noncredenti!* Let's bugger the ungodly. Good luck!"

It was the first obscenity I had ever heard him use; but somehow it gave me courage and the will to be up and doing. I telephoned Steffi and told him to heave his backside out of the chair and get himself to Milan as soon as possible. He told me he had managed to pull a file on Captain Matteo Roditi, but there was nothing in it worth a second thought. *Allora!* I would have to start digging for myself.

There is a club in Milan called the Duca di Gallodoro. It was founded by an Englishman who sold it, under pressure, to some Milanese bandits and then, I am told, married an American widow and went to live in Boston. I never bothered to check the story; but I did use the club whenever I came to Milan, because it was one of the few surviving places where you could eat reasonably well, dance in comfort and not be beaten into insensibility by shouting oafs with a million-watt amplifier. The drinks were honest, the girls better than average and the prices high enough to discourage the sweat-shirt brigade. It was also close enough to Headquarters for the officers of the Carabinieri to drop in for a drink and see the kind of citizens they were paid to protect. I decided to go there, alone for once, so that I could drift and gossip and make my escape before I got bored or the girls got too eager.

It was about ten-thirty when I arrived. The restaurant was full but the bar was slack, so I perched myself in my favourite corner and made small talk with Gianni, the barman, who knew everybody and told everything in a thick Genovese accent. He was kind enough to notice my new clothes and pay me what he thought was a compliment.

"Eh! Beautiful! English cloth, virgin lamb's wool. And the cut—perfect! What is this, Colonel—a legacy or a rich widow?"

"My life's savings, Gianni. I'm on leave. I thought I owed myself a present. What's going on in town?"

"The same, only more so. Strikes every third day. Students marching. Police on every street corner. Takings are down, too. Twenty percent last week. People are scared. They're buttoning their pockets and staying home to watch television. All this violence! There was another smash-and-grab raid this afternoon. Fabbri, the jeweller. Broad daylight and they got clean away. . . . Maybe we need a new *Duce* to pull things into line."

"Maybe."

"This new fellow's shaking things up, though. What's his name? Lep-something. That's it—Leporello. I hear your boys talking about him. They say he doesn't care how many heads get broken, so long as we have a quiet city. And he's right! He doesn't sit on his backside either. He's out and about every night with the patrols. They tell me he's training new riot squads, like the French have. You know, slam-bam, clear the streets and no questions asked. You must know him, though. Big fellow. Looks like a German. The boys call him old Iron-jaw."

"Good name. Do you know any of his staff?"

"Sure. Some of them come in here. Never on duty, though. He's stopped all that. One offense and out. That's the rule now, they tell me. He even wants to know the kind of women they hang around with. Ask some of the girls. They'll tell you. . . . Hullo, isn't this a friend of yours?"

He sidled up to the bar, all two meters and a hundred and twenty kilograms of him: Giorgione, Big George, Major Marinello, on the official lists of the Corps. He looked like a great spaniel with sad eyes and dewlaps; but when he saw me, he brightened a little and raised a big fist in greeting.

"Hello, Matucci. Good to see you."

"You, too, Giorgione."

"What are you doing in this town?"

"I'm on leave."

"Chasing a woman, I'll bet."

"Winding up to it. Let me buy you a drink."

"Thanks, I need it. Old Iron-jaw's been snapping at my heels all day."

"Big changes, eh?"

"Changes? God! He's ramming the whole United Nations down our necks. How the Greeks do it and the French and the Brazilians and the British and the Japanese. . . . *Salute!*"

"Chin-chin!"

"I tell you, Matucci, you should be glad you're seconded. This Leporello is a one-hundred-percent armour-plated bastard. And you should see the types he's getting around him. *Mamma mia!* He's bringing in brains, he says, computer boys and statisticians and, God help me, psychiatrists even! But that's not the end of it. He's building up a little private group of musclemen, for special duties! Something funny's going on. I wish I knew what

it was. . . . He's got that Roditi fellow running round
like a fart in a bottle. Do you know him?"

"I've met him. I don't know him."

"You haven't lost anything. He's a real weird one. . . .
God, I'm tired."

"Have another drink."

"Thanks."

"How do you mean, weird?"

"Oh, you know: big front, big secrets, the General
presents his compliments, sir . . . that sort of stuff. No
friends, except among the new bunch. I wouldn't trust
him very far."

"Does he ever come here?"

"No, no! This is girl territory, Matucci. You know that.
I think our friend Roditi sits down to pee."

"Any proof?"

"Proof? Hell, no! I'm running so fast these days, I
can't tell whether I'm married or single."

"Is Leporello that way, too?"

"I wouldn't say so. He's married, got two kids. Goes
to lunch with the Cardinal Archbishop. Very proper!"

"Why Roditi, then, and the other odd bunch?"

"I don't know. I think he just likes the idea of the elite
guard and all that stuff. . . . Say, what's your interest,
anyway? You've got a nice sweet job with SID; why
should you care what happens to us poor sweats? Hey,
wait a minute. . . ." He set down his glass and swivelled
himself round to face me. "Come on, Matucci, give, eh?"

"How would you like to take a walk, Giorgione?"

"Where?"

"My place. It's quiet and the drinks are free. Come on,
it's only half a dozen blocks; then you can put your feet
up."

"Well, all right. But don't think I'm letting you off the
hook, Matucci. I want to know . . ."

"Shut up, or I'll make you pay for the drinks."

The walk gave me time to think. For all his vast bulk
and his shambling ways, Giorgione was as cunning as a
badger. He would never make promotion, but he was one
of the mainstays of the division that dealt with fraud and

corrupt practices. If I wanted his help, I had to give him enough of the truth to keep him happy and discreet. Strangely enough the apartment helped. He smelled money and he smelled power and he had a healthy respect for both. Pietro helped, too. His cool, wooden-faced service would have cowed a Cardinal. So, when I judged Giorgione ready and relaxed, I gave him the story.

"Facts for the record, Giorgione. You can tell these to the street cleaner, if you like. I'm on leave. Four months. I'm working, all aboveboard, for a big company, as security adviser. This apartment goes with the job. Everything else is off the record—and I mean so far off you can't see it with a telescope."

"Listen, Matucci, I didn't mean to . . ."

"I know you didn't, Giorgione, and you may be able to help me. First, I'm still with SID, active, you understand. All this is a cover; and I don't want the boys wandering up for a drink or a visit of inspection."

"Understood."

"Second, I'm on a job I can't tell you about. Maximum security and dangerous. That you don't even guess at. Check?"

"Check."

"Third, we're interested in Roditi, too. I've been asked to check him out while I'm here and to do it without upsetting General Leporello. If he is a *finocchio,* we don't want him in a sensitive post. If he's a disruptive influence, that's another good reason for moving him out. So I have to move carefully; but because of this other business, I can't waste time. If you can help me, fine! If not, there's no harm done, provided you sit quiet, as I know you will. That's the story, Giorgione. . . ."

"Well, thanks for telling me. I appreciate it. What do you want to know about this fellow?"

"The full sheet, Giorgione. Or as much of it as you can get."

"You know I can't help you with eyewitness material. I'm too big and conspicuous."

"You tell me where and when. I'll arrange the rest of it. Two main points: what's his relationship with Leporello, and what, if anything, does he have to do with the musclemen? Any immediate thoughts?"

"Some, yes. Roditi's a bit of a muscleman himself. Cheerleader to the health and physical fitness squad. Works out every day in the gymnasium—weight lifting, judo, karate. Anything that's going, he's in it. Pistol shoots, automatic weapons training. . . . How he gets time for it all, I don't know. Then he's doing some kind of recruiting job round the country, inside the Corps, that is. From what I hear, they're setting up some kind of commando group. It sounds like that French lot—what were they called?"

"The Barbouzes?"

"That's it. Real thugs, from what I hear."

"Where do they train?"

"Oh, that's one of the biggest secrets. Nobody seems to know and the boys themselves won't talk. Still, I'll smell around a bit and let you know."

"Where does Roditi live?"

"I don't know that either, but it must be on file. I'll get Rita to dig it out. You remember Rita, don't you? Dark, gypsy type. Last time you were here, you and she . . ."

"Let's not go into that, Giorgione. And for God's sake, don't tell her I'm in town. . . . Now, you think Roditi's a *finocchio*. Any evidence?"

"Well, no. But no girl friends and all this body-building stuff. It points that way, doesn't it?"

"It might. Any boyfriends at Headquarters?"

"No. The women watch him like vixens at mating time. There are half a dozen who'd love to give him a tumble; but they haven't noticed anything."

"How does Leporello treat him?"

"Oh, very formally, but—how shall I say it?—very much like a man of confidence. You know the sort of thing. . . . 'If you need any further direction, Captain Roditi will make himself available . . . Captain Roditi will call you to arrange a conference . . .' I know he visits Leporello's home."

"Where's that?"

"On the road to Linate Airport. Big villa with a high stone wall."

"Does Leporello have any women working in his office?"

"Three. A senior secretary and two typists. Nothing for you there, Matucci. The secretary's a dragon and the two juniors are straight from the nunnery."

"What about Leporello's wife?"

"Never seen her. I don't think she's ever come to Headquarters. If she had, I'm sure we'd have heard of it."

"When he made this study trip, did his wife travel with him?"

"No . . . But Roditi did, by God! Yes, he did."

"It doesn't prove anything, Giorgione."

"You're right. It doesn't."

"What's the general feeling in the Corps about Leporello?"

"Well . . . I know I was sounding off about him at the bar. He is a bastard. He drives us like a slave master. And it's easier to get milk from a chicken than it is to wring a word of praise out of him. . . . But he is good. He's very good. And a lot of the things he's done are real improvements. How do we feel about him? You know the Service, Matucci. You can cut it like a deck of cards. There's the big middle group who do their job and don't ask questions, and gripe about everything just to affirm their rights. There's the bottom group that I call the earth-brothers. They serve and serve willingly in country posts and small communes and outlying provinces. They're pretty good guardians of the peace. They're close to the people and, all in all, sympathetic with them. Then you've got the top group, the hard-nose boys, everything by the book, we serve the State, and it's three years' hard labour if you poke us in the nose when you're drunk. They like Leporello. The middle group are uneasy about him. The earth-brothers loathe him. Not always for the right reason, mark you, because some of them can be pretty sloppy, as you know. But instinctively—did I say that right? I'm a little fuzzy—instinctively they mistrust him."

"What about you, Giorgione?"

"Me? I just hate his tripes. But that's natural, too. I'm good enough at my job, but look at me! I'm no great ornament to the Service. And Leporello makes me feel it all the time. God! It's late! My wife will kill me! How soon do you want this stuff?"

"Yesterday, if possible."

"How do I get it to you?"

"Phone me here. If I'm out, leave a message with the servants. Name a place and time and I'll meet you, or call you back if I can't make it. Thanks, Giorgione."

"Don't mention it. Good to see you again. Oh, Matucci, if you change your mind about Rita. . . ?"

"Do you think she fits this place, Giorgione?"

"Come to think of it, not quite. . . . Still, she's a nice girl. Take care now. There aren't too many of us good ones left."

He shambled out, a great, kindly freak of a man who was beginning to find his Gulliver's world too complicated to live in. He left me both pleased and worried. Roditi, my first quarry, was an unpopular type with a dubious reputation. Leporello was a hard-nose with an unhappy staff. Therefore the preliminary investigation could move quickly, and there would be plenty of enthusiastic helpers to dig up the dirt. On the other hand, the news about the new riot squads was very disquieting. It was a regressive step, a new threat to privacy and personal rights. It argued an official sanction for intimidation and police brutality.

Italian law was, in any case, heavily loaded in favour of the State and against the individual. Many of the old Fascist enactments were still on the books and could be invoked at will. We had never, God knows why, adopted the British system of *habeas corpus*. A man could be held almost indefinitely on a trumped-up charge; and a complaisant magistrate could delay inquiries and shuffle his documents till doomsday. Our judiciary was overworked, our documentation systems were hopelessly outdated. Our interrogation methods were brutal at the best of times, and our prison system a public shame. To compound all this, with an open or tacit brief of terror, and a deliberate exploitation of the Mediterranean vice of cruelty, was a leap back into the dark ages. I understood Manzini's anxious conviction that the twenty-third hour was past and the minute hand was climbing already to midnight.

I was restless now, itchy for company and action, so I flipped through my pocket book in search of another contact among the night owls. I settled on Patrizia Pompa, a Lesbian lady of singular beauty and metallic charm, who made a handsome living decorating the apartments of rich Milanese. To my certain knowledge, Patrizia never went to bed before three in the morning. In my salad days I had tried to get her there, and I was raw from the experience for a long time afterwards. However, we understood each other in the end, and we had managed to maintain over the years a prickly kind of friendship. I called her. She answered in that deep, husky voice that promised all sorts of wild experience. She sounded faintly hostile.

"Who the hell is this?"

"Dante Alighieri Matucci, sweetheart. Did I interrupt something?"

"Nothing important. What do you want at this hour?"

"Information—and a little company."

"You can have mine if you bring a bottle of whisky. . . . What sort of information?"

"Clubs for the gay boys. Know any?"

"A couple. Why?"

"I'm looking for a man."

"I didn't think you'd be looking for a girl, lover. What sort of answer is that?"

"He's a nasty man. I think he killed a friend of mine."

"Oh! Then try the Pavone and the Alcibiade. They're both open till four in the morning."

"Do they admit girls?"

"Only nice girls, lover—like me."

"Care to come along and hold my hand?"

"Why not? I am just bored enough to enjoy the sight of Matucci among the fennel-flowers."

"You've got a dirty mind, sweetheart."

"Don't say no till you've tried it, lover. I'll be ready in twenty minutes. Bring transport, eh? Where are you staying, by the way?"

"In a convent. Where else? See you!"

I picked her up in my own car, a red Mercedes sports model. She was dressed for the fray in a man-tailored suit with a white shirt and a flowing black cravat. When she saw my new rig, she chuckled.

"My God, Matucci, I believe you have passed over. You didn't do all this on a colonel's salary. Who's keeping you?"

"Sweetheart, you embarrass me."

"You'll be more embarrassed where you're going. Were you serious about. . . ?"

"Yes, I was. So listen, darling, and get the story straight. I'm an old friend and you're showing me the town."

"Suppose we meet someone you know."

"Same story. And if you get any telephone calls afterwards, you stick to it. Don't play funny games. It could be dangerous."

"With a friend like you, Matucci, I need extra life insurance."

"I'm the best insurance you've got, sweetheart. Who's going to touch you with a handsome youth like me around?"

It was a bad joke, and it got worse when we entered the Pavone—a smoky cellar dive near the Duomo. The bouncers at the door set the tone of the place: two muscle-bound Adonises from the local athletic club, with tight jeans and studded belts and high-necked sweaters. They made a couple of cute remarks, collected four thousand lire by way of entertainment tax and bowed us through. Inside there was more of the same, big boys and little boys, all in jeans and jumpers, and not a woman in sight. There was a fog you could cut with a knife, and just to help the atmosphere, a stuffed peacock with moulting tail feathers, preening himself on a pedestal in the center of the room. There were a piano player and a pock-marked youth with an electric guitar pounding out a steady rock beat, and the talk was a low secretive chatter that stopped dead as we entered and made our way to the bar. Then there was a chorus of whistles and catcalls, and Patrizia murmured in my ear:

"Somehow, lover, I think we've come to the wrong place."

It was going to cost us two drinks anyway, so we ordered and sipped them slowly until the boys had finished their fun and settled back to their whispering. Then we turned to face the room and I peered through the murk to distinguish a familiar face. The barman tapped me on the shoulder with a soft, fat finger.

"Looking for someone, darling?"

"Yes, a friend."

"What's he look like?"

"Big redhead with freckles. Looks like a German, but actually comes from Trento. Lovely boy. But I don't see him here."

"Does he have a name?"

"He told me it was Matteo."

"But not the rest of it."

"No . . ."

"You must miss him, darling."

"I do."

"How much do you miss him?"

I slid a ten-thousand-lire note across the counter and held it under my hand.

"That much . . . for a start."

"Well, I think I've seen him in here a few times. Can't be sure, you know. There's a bunch that drops in every couple of weeks, three or four together. I never had much to do with them because they're too quiet . . . and they're interested in very rough trade. If I see him again, what would you like me to do?"

"Give me a call at this number." I scribbled it on the back of a paper coaster and handed it to him. "It's worth another ten if I make contact."

"And when I ring, who do I ask for?"

"Just Dante. Like the poet, you know. My friend here is a poet. Aren't you, sweetheart?"

"I feel like a horse's arse," said Patrizia unhappily.

"You look like it too, darling," said the barman sweetly. "Why don't you go where you belong and leave us girls to our knitting?"

The Alcibiade was a different proposition altogether, strictly plush, strictly for the carriage trade—and there was a great deal of it to be had, in both sexes. The place was designed in a complete circle, like the Pantheon, with a bar at the end of one diameter and a curved stage at the other, and the tables ranged round a small dance floor at the center. It was air-conditioned, which was a mercy, because there was a lot of smoking going on and not all of it tobacco. The decor was ingenious and furiously expensive. The walls were covered in black velvet, broken at regular intervals by illuminated niches in each of which was a white plaster figure, half-life and fully sexed, representing a classic male hero of antiquity. Woman was honoured only on the black dome, where a snow-white Leda was mounted by a very sinuous swan.

The clients were the most elegant bunch I had seen in a long time: mostly young, but with a sprinkling of grey-haired males and mannish dowagers, with short hair and long cigarette holders. This time our entrance attracted no attention at all. The stage was occupied by three youths in baggy gold pants and turned-up slippers. One of them was playing a sitar, the other was tooting soulfully on a pipe, while the third was executing some kind of slow dance which left me cold as Narcissus by his lily pool.

The barman was a splendid boy, beautifully barbered and ineffably polite. The drinks cost an arm and a leg, but they were served in crystal goblets, with a fresh canapé to help the digestion.

Patrizia purred with satisfaction. "Lover, I'm glad you brought me. I think I've been out of circulation too long. If I strike it lucky, just pay the bill and leave me."

"Anything you say, sweetheart."

"Can you see your man?"

"Not yet. Wait till the act's over and the lights go up."

We waited a small eternity before the last notes faded

and the dancer sank like a tired petal to the floor, to a rather pallid applause. The lights were rather pallid, too, but they were bright enough to show me Captain Matteo Roditi, in a midnight-blue jacket, seated with two other young men, at a table on the edge of the dance floor.

I turned back to the bar and whispered to Patrizia:

"I've seen him."

"What do you want to do?"

"Talk to him . . . alone."

"I'll wait for you."

"Better you're not seen with me."

"This is exciting."

"It doesn't look it, but it's dangerous. Order another drink and fake your own arrangements."

I pressed some notes into her hand and then wandered down through the tables, like any other client surveying the local talent. Roditi and his friends were so busy with each other that they did not notice me until I stood over the table and offered my little greeting.

"Captain Roditi, isn't it?"

He didn't recognize me for a moment, then he leapt to his feet and stammered:

"Colonel Matucci! Forgive me, I didn't recognize you."

"Relax, Captain, we're not on parade now."

"What are you doing in Milan, sir?"

"Enjoying some leave."

"Forgive me, but I heard you were retired from the Service."

"It's under discussion. Nothing definite yet. I'm still on the active list. Won't you introduce me to your friends?"

"Oh, I'm sorry, sir. Franco Gozzoli, Giuseppe Balbo, Colonel Matucci."

"Are you gentlemen in the Service, too?"

He was quick, but not quick enough to intercept their swift looks of inquiry. "No sir, no. They're both in business here."

"What sort of business?"

"Oh—er—architectural draftsmen."

"How very interesting. Please sit down, gentlemen. Do you come here often, Captain?"

"Occasionally. It's a change from the usual kind of club. You, sir?"

"Oh, I just dropped in for a drink—cruising, you might say."

"Indeed. . . ?" He reacted instantly to the familiar word, and a faint hint of conspiracy crept into his smile. "Will you be staying long in Milan?"

"A few weeks, possibly. Why don't you come and have a drink with me one evening, Captain?"

"I'd like that, sir."

"Good. I'll call you at Headquarters. Please give my compliments to General Leporello. Tell him I hope to see him soon."

"I'll do that, sir, with pleasure."

"Good night, Roditi. Enjoy yourself."

As I walked past the bar, I saw Patrizia Pompa deep in talk with a small doll-like blonde in a green pants suit. She gave me a wink and a farewell twitch of the fingers. She didn't need me anymore; she was back in circulation again.

It was three in the morning when I got back to the apartment. I was desperately tired, but I could not sleep until I had set down a summary of the evening's encounters. We were in profit on several heads. In Giorgione I had a friend and a source of information. Roditi was vulnerable, by reason of his sexual interests. Leporello was unpopular with his staff, some of whom might be persuaded to inform against him. The debit column, however, was alarming. Leporello had in training an apparatus of terror which could operate at will inside or outside the law. Such a group attracted social delinquents and put enormous power into the hands of a political manipulator. If the manipulator achieved political success, the apparatus became an arm of government, self-perpetuating and self-justified. There was a debit against my personal account as well. If the murders in the Via Sicilia were the work of the apparatus, it would be difficult, if not impossible, to prove charges against Roditi and Leporello. If Leporello wanted me removed, he had a whole pack of well-trained bullyboys to stalk me into ambush.

It was a chill thought. It haunted me through a restless sleep and was still with me when I woke, blear-eyed and irritable, at ten in the morning.

  ❦ ❧

AT midday Steffi arrived, chirpy as a cricket. He brought me blessings from his wife, who, he claimed, was happy to be rid of him. He recited greetings from some of our colleagues in Rome and a litany of curses against the timeservers. He surveyed every inch of the apartment and concluded mournfully that only a whore could enjoy such luxury without a twinge of conscience. Purged at last of wisdom and bile, he listened in silence while I told him what had happened to me since our last meeting. Then, sober and subdued, he gave me his own version of events in Rome:

". . . We liberals are out of date, little brother. Every current flows against us. Every wind blows contrary. Just when we think we have a moment of quiet to water the flowers, the Arabs hijack another airliner, or the Zionists knock off an agent, or some twenty-year-old idiots hold up a bank or the police fire on demonstrators in some depressed province. If it's not happening inside the country, it's just next door. Look, a simple thing! When I arrived at the airport this morning, the computer system had broken down. A little mechanical fault, but suddenly there was chaos. The booking clerks wouldn't handle the inquiries. The airline officials went into hiding. And five thousand passengers on domestic and international flights didn't know whether they were coming or going. We're not like the English. We don't form a queue and read *The Times*. We shout and scream just for the merry hell of it. But someone only had to scream too loud or jostle too hard this morning, and there could have been a riot. . . . For what? A blown fuse that cost maybe a hundred lire. . . . That's the terror of it, Matucci. Nobody blames the fuse. Everybody wants a scapegoat who can be kicked into a bloody mess because the plane's late. They're daubing slogans on the bridges of Rome now: 'Death to the Fascists,' 'Down with the Marxists.' And where I live, it's 'Zionist pig!' I wonder if you know what you're really fighting, my friend?"

"Do you?"

"Sometimes I wish I didn't. *Simia quam similis . . .*"

"I don't know that one, Steffi."

"The ape, the ugliest of the beasts, how like to us! Ennius . . . We haven't changed much since his time, have we?"

"No, except we've got computers to multiply the vileness. Steffi, understand something. This is a damn dangerous project. I don't want you too close to me. You work from the Europa Hotel. We meet in a variety of places."

"What do you want me to do?"

"We're investigating murder. So it's old-fashioned detective work, Steffi. On Leporello and Roditi first. I want to know what they eat for breakfast and what brand of toothpaste they use. If you've got any friendly colleagues at Milan Headquarters, use them; but for God's sake, be careful."

"I should give you the same advice, little brother. The Director doesn't love you anymore."

"But he has a vested interest in keeping me alive. His own words, Steffi!"

"He didn't tell you what the interest was, did he?"

"No."

"So let me give you more bad news. He has a man working full-time on your record."

"Who told you this?"

"Rampolla. He was making a big joke of it. Some joke! You've sailed very close to the wind in your time, Matucci. You need a very sympathetic biographer to make you halfway respectable. At this moment they're writing a Black Book on you."

"I'm writing a Black Book of my own, Steffi."

"The big question for the big money—who gets into print first? One more item. . . . Woodpecker has been under interrogation every day since you left Rome. He's sold out his whole network. And your girl friend, Lili Anders, figures prominently in the transcript."

"They can't touch her now. The Swiss don't extradite for political offenses."

"They do for criminal acts."

"Oh, come on, Steffi. I know her dossier backwards. There's nothing like that against her."

"There wasn't when you last looked at it. There may be now. If you're fond of that woman, it's a thing to think about. . . ."

"Steffi, you make me feel like Job on his dunghill."

"So, bless the Lord for your afflictions, little brother, and pray loud and strong for His mercies. Also, don't underrate the Director. He wants you alive—but buried up to your neck in the same dunghill. . . . Do you have a drink in this bawdy house?"

"For news like that, I should feed you cyanide."

"Make it Scotch whisky and I'll give you a few good words for a change."

"The words first, you old vulture."

"Remember the letter bomb that was posted in Lili Anders' flat?"

"Yes?"

"The police sent us a forensic report on it. The report came across my desk, together with a nice clear set of prints, matched from their files. I brought a copy with me, in case they might be useful."

"And?"

"The prints belonged to Marco Vitucci, age twenty-eight, onetime steward with the Flotta Bernardo, wanted in Rome and Naples on several counts of larceny and robbery with violence."

"Never heard of him."

"Nor I. But it's a start—a link in the chain. The police are working actively to trace him. He is known to use two other names, for which he has false documents. The names are Turi Goldoni and Giuseppe Balbo. . . ."

"Say that last one again."

"Giuseppe Balbo."

"Steffi, you're a genius! You're a towering transcendental magician!"

"I know it, but since when have you discovered it?"

"Now . . . this minute! I told you I met Roditi last night at the Club Alcibiade. One of the boys with him was called Giuseppe Balbo."

"If it's the same one, that's almost enough to nail Roditi as well."

"Almost, but not quite. Not with the protection he's got. But it's a beautiful beginning and, since it's a police report, SID can't bury it. Steffi, the soup's beginning to cook . . . !"

"So please may I have my whisky?"

We talked it upside down and roundabout, through lunch and into the afternoon. We arranged codes, meeting places, a schedule of telephone contacts; then Steffi left to rest his aged bones at the hotel and plot his own campaign of investigation. I had just finished transcribing the new information onto tape when the telephone rang and Major-General Leporello came on the line. He was brisk but surprisingly cordial.

"Welcome to Milan, Colonel."

"Thank you, sir."

"Captain Roditi delivered your message. I should be delighted to see you."

"I simply wanted to pay my respects, sir. I know how busy you are."

"Dinner on Thursday. How would that suit?"

"Yes, sir. I'm free on that night."

"Good. My house at eight-thirty for nine. I'll send you a confirmation with directions how to get there. Strictly informal—a family foursome. Er—is there someone you would care to bring?"

"No, sir."

"Leave it to my wife, then—she's the party girl. You and I can have a private chat over the coffee. By the way, have you ever thought about my offer?"

"Yes, sir, I have."

"Let's talk about it again. Until Thursday, then."

"I look forward to it, General."

I had expected some approach—drinks in the Mess perhaps, coffee at the Club—but this was out of all character and proportion. Two weeks ago he wanted me dead;

now he wanted me to dinner. The two wishes were not necessarily in contradiction—there have been many notable treacheries at Italian dinner tables—but they were certainly anomalous. I could hardly wear sidearms to a family foursome, but I had only forty-eight hours to find a very long spoon.

Steffi's news had disturbed me profoundly, not because it was unexpected, but because, once again, I had lapsed into dangerous inattention, selecting only one issue and ignoring the whole complex of threats and problems behind it. The Black Book was an ingenious perversion, first designed by the Director as a training exercise and then refined into a technique of blackmail. The trick was to take a man's dossier and, by editing, emphasis and interpretation, distort it into a criminal caricature. For "bachelor" read "not interested in women," for "likes card games" read "known gambler," and you have the art in a nutshell. It's a filthy game, but it works, because every man has some guilts, and the simple exhibition of the dossier to the victim is a crushing display of cynical power.

I knew the game because I had played it often. I knew, too, that I was the easiest victim in the world, a secret agent working always on the outer margin of the law and sometimes a long way beyond it. Lili Anders was in a similar position, a known subversive, guest in a neutral country. It needed only a telephone call from the Director to his counterpart in Switzerland, and she, too, would be helpless as a leaf in a winter storm. I was still chewing on that sour thought when a courier arrived with two messages from Bruno Manzini.

The first was a note in which, apologizing for short notice, he requested me to dine with him this night at the Bankers' Club, in order, as he put it, "to meet money and see whether it smells or not." He suggested we meet in the cardroom half an hour before dinner for a private briefing. The second was a letter from Lili:

My dear,
    It is so long since I have written to a man that I hardly

know how to begin. I would guess that you, my careful
amorist, have never written letters to a woman at all.
Uncle Pavel doesn't count, because he doesn't exist; but
it was nice to hear from him just the same.

I am sitting on my balcony, bathed in sunshine, with a
marvellous vista of green valley and snow-covered peaks,
and farms that look like dolls' houses—all mine to enjoy.
And I am enjoying it, my dear, in a way I would never
have thought possible. I do very little. I walk. I read. I
have taken up petit point. I chat to the other guests. In
the evenings I play bridge. I am in bed by ten and I sleep
until the maid brings my breakfast. It is all so simple, I
wonder how I let it escape me for so long.

I worry sometimes, because I am still so transient and
insecure; but my lawyer, Herr Neumann, reassures me.
He is a little old man with white hair and gold pince-nez.
He calls me "young woman"—which is always a help. He
knows all about me now—except some very intimate
things—and he says that perhaps I may be able to apply
for political asylum. He has taken a lot of depositions
and is seeking advice from colleagues in Zurich. I rather
like the idea of asylum. It sounds almost like finding
refuge in a church, where everything is confessed and
everything is forgiven and you can begin again without
fear.

The people here are simple folk, sober and kind. The
guests are pleasant, too. There are a couple of elderly
ladies, one of whom is my bridge partner. There is a
honeymoon couple who make me envious sometimes; an
American professor, rather elderly, who is writing a book
on the Germanic migrations; and there is a very dashing
fellow from Lugano, who talks to me in Italian and buys
me a cocktail before dinner and keeps offering me whirl-
wind tours in his Maserati. I haven't accepted yet, but I
may soon. He's attentive. He's not bad-looking and quite
intelligent—an engineer or something on a construction
project ten miles from here.

And you, my Dante Alighieri, how are you? I don't ask
what you are doing because I know too much and can do
nothing to help. I love you and I miss you; but I dare not
let myself depend on the loving, and I must get used to
the missing. I tell you only that I dream of you often and

when I wake I half expect to find you there beside me.
As I write, I am jealous of every woman you meet or
will meet. I wonder if you are jealous of my engineer.
I'd like to think so.

Take care, my dear. Think gently of me as I do of you.
One fine tomorrow, perhaps I'll be

Yours, Lili

I read it three times, then tore it and burned the shreds
in the ashtray. I was jealous and I had no right to be. If
I wasn't in love, then I was as near to it as I had ever
been in my life. I couldn't risk the distraction. I couldn't
afford the luxury. Forget it then! There were too many
dangerous tomorrows to survive, and Lili's bright and
shining day might never come.

∓∎ ∎∓

THE Bankers' Club in Milan is only a whit less venerable
than the Chess Club in Rome. It is, however, much more
impressive because the focus of its power is clearer and
all its members are fluent in a single, international language—money. It is a religious language reserved to
priests and acolytes, like Church Latin or the time symbols of the Incas. It is precise, flexible, subtle and quite
unintelligible to the profane populace. It is proof of the
cyclic nature of history, because the first banks in the
world were the temples of Babylon, Greece and Rome,
where you could raise loans, make deposits, arrange credit
and have your coinage tested by assay under the vigilant
eyes of the local deity.

If you ask why a fellow like me should know or care
about such things, then I must remind you again that I
am a Tuscan, and that I was bred to the history of the
Bardi and the Frescobaldi and the Petruzzi, who were
bankers to the English crown in the fourteenth century,
and that my father was an old-line socialist, who talked
me blind about the need to nationalize the banks and put
the speculators out of business. I like money. Who doesn't?
I am also fascinated by its history, its forms, its potency,

why some men make it and most men lose it and even Charon, the ferryman, demands a coin to row you across the Styx into eternity.

So I found a certain propriety in the fact that my first entry into the world of Bruno Manzini should be made through the portals of the Bankers' Club. I was also curious to know why he had chosen so sensitive and sacrosanct a place to present me. I put the question to him in so many words, as we sat over cocktails in the cardroom, a privilege reserved to the most senior priesthood. He answered me, with a grin:

"It's an exercise in logic, my dear Dante. Here everyone has money. Money imposes discretion. Discretion conduces to free speech. Here, therefore, there is free speech—quite a lot of it, in fact. There are six of us who meet for dinner once a month. We talk about everything under the sun. Any member may bring a guest, provided he guarantees him as a safe man with a secret."

"Thanks for the compliment."

"I can pay you compliments any time, my dear Dante. There are two men I want you to meet tonight. One is Ludovisi from the Banca Centrale, the other is Frantisek, from the Opera Pontificia at the Vatican. He's one of the shrewdest bankers in the business. The fact that he's an American and a bishop is incidental. Both these men can be very useful to you."

"How?"

"They can tell you, quicker than anybody, where the big money is going, and why. There's another reason, too. Ludovisi is the brother-in-law of your Director." He chuckled and held up his hand. "No, don't be alarmed. They love each other like cat and dog. Ludovisi is suing for divorce. He blames his wife's family for the failure of the marriage. He's very eloquent and very well briefed on the subject. Frantisek, on the other hand, is a very complex character. He looks like a football player, talks Italian with a Brooklyn accent, has a golf handicap of five and stands in high favour with the reigning Pontiff. He helped to reorganize the Vatican's financial arrangements and negotiate the tax settlement with the Italian

Government. He's not a very good theologian. His philosophy is pure pragmatism. His noblest virtue is a fanatical loyalty to the Holy See. Still, he does smell the wind, and if he likes you, he can be a very powerful friend. The rest? Well, they're agreeable and well informed. One's a Liberal, the others are Christian Democrats of varying shades. Paolini's an out-and-out Fascist, but on a personal basis he's so agreeable you can almost forgive him."

"And what do you expect me to do?"

"Whatever you like. Talk, listen, argue. If you make a gaffe, don't worry; it's the privilege of the Club. Now, tell me, what have you been doing?"

He heard me out in silence and then gave a long, low whistle of satisfaction. "Good! Good! As you say, the soup is beginning to cook. What do you propose to do now?"

"Wait until I have more evidence, much more. It's a risk. You must understand that. I may lose Giuseppe Balbo, who is our only link with what happened in Rome. But if I take him now and hand him to the police, I may lose the big ones, Roditi and Leporello. You know the way things are. We need a brass-bound case before we open proceedings, and a notarized copy of every document in our own hands."

He frowned over that for a long while and then, finally, nodded agreement. "I hate the thought of losing a key witness, but the risk of premature action is even less palatable. These new riot squads worry me. It's only one step from those to the Brazilian Esquadras de la Muerte . . . police assassins. Let's take some soundings round the table tonight and see if there's any news floating around. I know Leporello is in high favor with the businessmen just now. He gave a talk here last week on the theme of Order and Progress. Very seductive, I hear. Very well received. I wonder why he's asked you to dinner and who the fourth guest will be. Woman bait?"

"Possibly. Though it hardly seems his style."

"If he's recruiting homosexual gymnasts and criminals, I shouldn't think he'd balk at simple seduction. Let's go in, shall we? The others should be here by now."

We were eight people at a round table so that there was no question of precedence. Protocol was honored by an opening grace from Bishop Frantisek, who indeed did look like a football player. His accent was appalling, but his grammar was faultless, his talk fluent and his manners affable. Ludovisi was the wit of the group, a lean, grey-eyed dandy, with a faun's grin and a fund of scandalous stories. The others, with the exception of Paolini, were typical of their breed, well barbered, well fed, eloquent about everything to do with money, agreeably cynical about any other human concern. Paolini I found an enigma. His manners were impeccable and he radiated charm, but his mind was closed to every logic but his own—which I must confess was hard to refute. His hobbyhorse was multinational companies, the great concerns which spanned the frontiers of the world and operated in all jurisdictions, with no allegiance to any.

". . . Four thousand companies making fifteen percent of gross world product, that's what we're talking about. They control more assets than many of the countries in which they operate. Look at General Motors! Twenty-eight billion dollars in annual sales. Royal Dutch Shell, twelve and a half billion. . . . What single government can regulate enterprises like that? No democracy, certainly. The lobby's too powerful, the leverage in employment and capital is too great, to say nothing of external pressures exercised through commerce and diplomacy. . . . And they're getting bigger all the time, like a fat man who can't stop eating. You fellows laugh at me and label me a Fascist, but show me any authority as strong and belligerent as a board of a giant company. De Gaulle saw it. The labour unions see it, and it's the best argument they have for Marxism. . . . Even the Americans are seeing it now, as the Japanese apply the lesson and build multinationals of their own . . ."

"So, what do you want?" Ludovisi cut in with a laugh. "A junta that can be bought quicker than a parliament, because there's no one left to ask questions? Come now! Be realistic."

"I am being realistic, my dear fellow. Look what happened in Greece. A few years ago you could hardly raise a dollar for investment. Now they've got some law and order, the money's pouring in. Even expatriate capital is coming back. And the Government controls the terms. That's a much better situation than we've got at this moment."

"Correction, old friend." The Monsignore cut in with a tart reminder. "The colonels suspended law and imposed order."

"It's a proper distinction," said Bruno Manzini mildly, "but I wonder if it really makes any difference to the man in the street. We've got so many laws that we can't enforce them, and we end up with government by regulation. We've got so many parties that the people are not represented at all, only factional interests."

Ludovisi gave him a quick questioning glance.

Paolini applauded. "Bravo! If Bruno here can see the light, why not the rest of you?"

"It's not the light," said Manzini, with an impish grin. "I think it may be a pillar of cloud with a very familiar demon inside it. Did anybody hear the speech General Leporello made here last week?"

"I did," said Paolini. "I thought he made excellent sense."

There seemed to be a tepid agreement on that from every one except Ludovisi, who threw up his hands in despair and groaned aloud. "My God! The fellow used every cliché in the handbook—'liberty is not license; the desire of the people for a peaceful society; provocative elements; strong security measures' . . . Oh, dear, dear, dear! It sounded like my brother-in-law talking with his tongue in his cheek. Paolini, have you met this fellow personally?"

"I have. I think he's the kind of man we need, resolute, clearheaded, absolutely incorruptible."

"I've yet to meet an incorruptible man. Has anyone else met this paragon?"

I saw, or thought I saw, a faint signal from Manzini, so I moved into the discussion.

"I know him."

The Monsignore's eyebrows went up and he leaned his bulky body across the table to question me. "And what's your opinion of him, Matucci?"

"I'd rather not make a judgment of him as a man. I will say he's embarked on a highly dangerous policy."

"What policy is that?"

"Surely you gentlemen know. It's all over town. I'm new here, but I get it in every bar. He's recruiting special riot squads on the lines of the French Barbouzes. It's a secret operation, and that worries me. I know where some of the recruits are coming from, and that worries me even more."

"Where do they come from, Matucci?"

"Resorts of known criminals and social delinquents."

"That's a serious statement." Paolini was visibly shocked.

"I know. I make it in the privacy of this gathering. I shall be presenting some evidence in support to Major-General Leporello himself next Thursday."

"Perhaps he knows it already," said Ludovisi grimly. "Have you thought of that? You mentioned the Barbouzes. You could also have mentioned the Esquadras de la Muerte in Brazil. It's a familiar pattern: pull the rowdies off the streets and set them breaking heads under legal sanction. If your information is correct, Matucci, I'd say we were in for a very bloody mess."

"I agree."

"I think we're making a morbid prejudgment." Paolini was too bland and urbane to be true. "Why don't we change the subject? No offense, Matucci, but you don't know my colleagues as well as I do. If you spread panic and alarm like that, you'll rattle the market for a month. Eh, Bruno?"

"I hope not." Manzini chuckled like a happy child. "I'm coming into the market myself tomorrow. The English have just come out with an electron welder that will join two plates of twenty-centimeter steel in a single welding pass. I want to buy rights in it and finance a local manufacture. Any of you fellows interested, or do I have to go to the Vatican? You'll come in, won't you,

Monsignore? Just what His Holiness needs to repair the rifts in the Church."

They all laughed at that and the tension relaxed.

As we moved from the dining room to take coffee in the salon, Ludovisi laid a hand on my arm and steered me towards the men's room. He was sober and pre-occupied. "That was bad news, Matucci. How sure are you?"

"Very sure."

"Do you know where it's pointing?"

"Yes."

"How do you know?"

"I work for SID as well as for Manzini."

"Then you know my brother-in-law."

"Yes."

"Where does he stand in this matter? Before you answer, it must be obvious that I don't like him. I think he's both devious and dangerous."

"As a serving officer, I couldn't comment. As a guest in your club, I would say that I agree with you. For the public record I would deny ever having made such a statement."

"Thank you. Here's my card. If ever I can help, please call me."

"Thank you, but I doubt you can help me with this mess."

"You keep an open mind. I'll keep an open door. D'accordo?"

At eleven-thirty the guests dispersed, but Manzini held me back for a final coffee in the cardroom. He was obviously tired. There were dark circles under his eyes and his skin had a curious yellow tinge. Even his waspish wit had deserted him. When I asked if he were unwell, he shrugged wearily.

"That dinner tonight . . . Truly, I could go out and cut my wrists in a bathtub! You shoved a live grenade under their noses and only two had sense enough to see it . . . The others didn't want to see it. . . . Have you never thought, friend, that if you die one night in a back street, you will be dying for men like these?"

"You must have thought about it, too."

"I did, many times. Remember my telling you about my uncle Freddie? I thought of him this evening when you were telling me about these types that Roditi is recruiting. Freddie could be vicious, too: mostly when he was short of money or frustrated in some affair, which happened more and more as he got older. He used to sponge on my mother, and if weeping didn't open her purse, he would try a little blackmail. . . . That's how I found out that Uncle Pantaleone was my father. I must have been——let me see——oh, about ten, I suppose. I had a new toy, a jack-in-the-box. I wanted to surprise Mamma with it. I crept into the salon where she was talking with Uncle Freddie and I hid behind the settee. I found myself in the middle of a bitter quarrel. Freddie wanted money. Mamma was refusing vehemently. Then Freddie threatened to spread the story of my parentage all over town. He must have been very desperate because never before had he shown me anything but kindness. Finally I couldn't stand it any longer. I burst out of my hiding place and begged them to stop quarrelling. I don't remember what was said but I do remember a long, strange silence and how ill Freddie looked and how I had never seen Mamma so fierce and angry . . . After that I never saw Freddie again. . . . I know what happened to him. I could read by then. I saw it in a newspaper. One night, not long afterwards, he was wandering drunk and maudlin along Lungotevere. He was accosted by a young sailor, who invited him onto a river barge. There he was bound, gagged and beaten until he died. A fowler discovered his body, ten days later, tangled in the reeds halfway to Ostia. . . . He wasn't very popular. Indeed, in his latter years, he was very disreputable. But he was well connected in England, so the police were diligent in their inquiries and they made a voluminous report to the British Consul. It seems the people who killed him were paid for the job . . ."

"By whom?"

"Oh, I didn't know that for a long time. Not until my mother died and I had to go through her papers and possessions. I found Freddie's signet ring with a tiny label

on it: 'In memoriam . . . Pantaleone.' My father was a
very thorough man, you see, and like me, he had a taste
for irony. . . . There's a sequel, my Dante. It may answer
the question you've been too polite to ask. When the
Gestapo had me in jail—I'd been under interrogation for
about a week, I think, and I wasn't in very good shape
—my half brother came to see me. He was Captain then:
very chic, very General Staff. He offered me a bargain.
In return for the list of the Salamander network, the
Gestapo would release me and I could live out the war
in comfortable retirement at the Pantaleone Villa in
Frascati. . . . I didn't spit in his eye, like a hero. I was
too sick and tired. I told him the story I have just told
you. I thought I was signing my death warrant, which
would have suited me very well at that moment. . . . But
my brother was only half the man my father was. I was
handed back to the interrogators. They worked on me for
another month. Then, one day, without warning, I was
released into house arrest. I was put into a closed car and
driven to Frascati. The servants at the villa nursed me.
My brother was away on army business. I couldn't leave
the house. And, anyway, I was unwell and I had no place
to go and no papers to take me. One day my brother came
to see me. He told me he had procured my release. He
told me why: he wanted to discharge his father's obliga-
tions to me! I'm afraid I did spit in his eye then; though,
looking back, I think he meant at least half of it. That
was the half that took me to his funeral. The other half
. . . Well, you see what I mean about motives for mar-
tyrdom, don't you? Sometimes they're simple, and sometimes they're very confused. . . ."

⊷§ §⊶

EARLY next morning, while I was still rubbing the sleep
out of my eyes, Giorgione telephoned me from his home.
He had good news. From a word dropped in the canteen
and a few careful inquiries from Rita in the file-room, he
had discovered the location of a new camp. He thought
it could be one of those used for the training of the riot

squads. He gave me a name and a map reference: Camerata, a small Lombard town in the mountains north of Bergamo, about an hour's run from Milan. He told me I would have no difficulty finding the place, but I might have difficulty getting inside. The location was classified as a maximum security area. He had other information, too. Captain Roditi lived, in some style, in a new apartment block not far from the Europa Hotel. The rents were higher than he could afford on a captain's stipend. So either he had private income, or someone was subsidizing him.

I called down blessings on Giorgione's tousled head and then sat down to a very meditative breakfast. After breakfast I rang Roditi's office to set our appointment for drinks. His sergeant told me Roditi had left for Turin with General Leporello and would not be back until Thursday afternoon. At nine Stefanelli called in. I told him we were going for a run into the country. I would pick him up at his hotel in thirty minutes. By ten we were out on the autostrada, cruising westward to the Bergamo exit.

My plan was simple but risky. As a serving officer of SID, I was still in possession of my official identity document, which would procure me entrance to any military or civilian installation and access to all documents, however classified. The risk was that the commanding officer could insist on his right to check the document back to its origin before admitting me to his area. I proposed, therefore, to drop Steffi off in Bergamo with instructions to telephone Manzini if I were detained beyond a reasonable time.

Steffi was not enthusiastic. "I think you're crazy, Matucci. If they do check your document, you're up to your neck in trouble."

"I know, Steffi; but the omens are good today. Leporello and Roditi are out of town. I think I can bluff my way past any questions."

"What's the reason for the visit—the official reason?"

"The best. I'm looking for a man named Marco Vitucci, wanted on charges of subversion and murder. We feel he

may have slipped through the screening into a sensitive
organization. I won't find Vitucci, of course. But if I do
find Giuseppe Balbo, then we're in big profit."

"Enough to buy you a beautiful tombstone, little brother."

"Relax, Steffi. It's a beautiful day. . . . I'll be back in a
couple of hours and I'll buy you the best lunch in Bergamo."

"And what am I supposed to do for two hours in
Bergamo?"

"Let's see . . . you could make a pilgrimage to the
house of Papa Giovanni. After all, he did make the Jews
respectable again, and a lot of people didn't like him for
it. . . . You could read some Tasso, you could listen to
some Donizetti, or even dance the *bergamasca,* if you
can find a girl old enough to remember it."

"Regular little tourist guide, aren't you, Matucci?"

"You wouldn't believe it, Steffi, but I was just that in
my student days—until I made an improper suggestion
to one of the clients. She was willing enough, but her
husband caught us holding hands in the Cappella Colleoni
and I lost my job. You might pay a little visit there, just
for my sake."

"I've got a much better idea, little brother. Let's keep
driving until we get to Switzerland. You can settle down
with your girl and I'll peddle cuckoo clocks to the tourists.
That way we both stay alive a little longer."

From Bergamo the road wound upwards through the
Brembo Valley, curving along the flanks of the Lombard
hills. I drove carefully, rehearsing myself for the touchy
moments of my first entry into the camp. At Camerata
I stopped to ask directions and ran against the first
security perimeter. The three people I asked knew there
was a camp somewhere but had no idea where it was.
Finally I had to call on the local police and produce my
card to the *brigadiere,* who drew me a map on a sheet
of yellow paper. Even then I nearly missed the turnoff,
a narrow corrugated defile enclosed at the end by a stockade of logs surmounted by a watchtower with a search-
light and a machine gun.

There were guards at the gate as well, two husky fellows who halted me ten yards from the entrance and demanded to know my business. I showed them my card and told them I wanted to see the Commandant. One of them took my card and went back to his box to telephone. I waited five minutes and then they waved me through the gates and closed them behind me.

Inside, the place was grim and unwelcoming: twin rows of log huts with a broad parade ground in between, and beyond, a vast basin, half cleared, half still under timber, which was obviously the training area. I parked my car outside the Commandant's office and went inside. A desk sergeant took my card and disappeared into the next room. I waited another five minutes before I was ushered into the presence of a slim, bullet-headed major, who looked as though he could straighten horseshoes and tear telephone books with his bare hands. His desk was a mess of papers and he was quite self-conscious about it. He fumbled with this sheet and that, as if he were still not sure what was written on them. His greeting was respectful, uneasy. .

"Major Zenobio at your service, Colonel. I'm afraid I had no notice of your visit."

"There were good reasons, Major."

"Oh?"

"General Leporello left for Turin early this morning. I was still waiting on information from Rome, which came through just before ten o'clock. I left immediately. I am required to report to the General on his return. In fact, we're dining together tomorrow evening. If you feel the need to check that, please telephone his secretary immediately. I'd like to get down to business."

He hesitated for a moment, took another look at my card, then closed it and handed it back to me. His tone was one degree less frigid. "No, I don't think we'll need that, Colonel. Now, your business is . . . ?"

"Reserved to you and me at this stage, Major. I have to insist on that from the outset."

"I understand."

He fumbled with the papers again, tossing them about

like confetti. For me, a man whose life depended on paper, it was a kind of sacrilege.

"Major, I'm looking for a man. The police want him for attempted murder. We want him because he is a known subversive, and we need to talk to him before anyone else."

"And you hope to find him here, Colonel?"

"There's a certain logic in the idea that appeals to my people. These new groups of yours constitute a sensitive project, highly political. Your recruiting methods are, shall we say, unorthodox. To put it more bluntly, it has been decided, as a matter of high policy, that even social delinquents are acceptable, provided that they can be retrained to certain essential skills. Correct?"

"Correct."

"Next. The project is secret, the requirements special. A man who wanted to go underground might well present himself for enlistment. If his dossier didn't look too disastrous, you would accept him."

"A question, Colonel. The project is secret. How does your man know about it?"

"Ah, that's one of the matters I have to discuss with the General tomorrow night. It doesn't affect you, Major, but it does affect another officer who has been less than discreet. . . . However, that's confidential until the General gives clearance. Take it for granted that the man would know and could present himself. . . . Now, we're not interested in the police side of it at all. But a known subversive, an active Marxist agent, inside this kind of group—well! You do see my point?"

"Too clearly, Colonel. What's the name of your man?"

"Marco Vitucci."

"Let's take a look at the nominal roll."

"We'll come to that in a moment. What other records do you keep on your troops?"

"Each man has a record card, which contains his personal details and the reports of the training staff."

"Photographs?"

"Each card carries a photograph, a thumbprint and a list of distinguishing marks. These are recorded also on the subject's identity document, which he carries at all times in addition to his civilian identification."

"Good. Now let's have a look at the nominal rolls."

It took him three minutes to find them under the mess on his desk and in his trays. It took only a minute to establish that in a list of four hundred men in two training groups there was no Marco Vitucci.

"Well, we do have one other alias." I thumbed ostentatiously through my notebook. "Here it is—Barone, Turi." That landed me among the B's. There was no Barone either; but I did light on the name Balbo, Giuseppe, and I pointed it out to the Major.

"Balbo, eh? Nothing to do with the case, of course. I was wondering if he's any relation to General Balbo, who marched with the *Duce?*"

The Major smiled for the first time. "I doubt it. But let's take a look, just for curiosity. Funny if it were, though. Balbo was one of the first quadrumvirate of fascism. We could be the new beginnings. . . . Here you are."

He opened a filing cabinet, took out a card and handed it to me. I scanned it carefully. The identification was clear. This was the same man I had met with Roditi in the Club Alcibiade. If the thumbprint tallied with the one on the police files, then I had everything I needed. I handed the card back to the Major, who tossed it onto the littered desk and then half buried it under the nominal rolls.

"No connection, I'm afraid. The old General was a Ferrarese. This one comes from Gaeta. Well, it was a pleasant fantasy. That's all, I think, Major. Painless for you, disappointing for me. Still, we'll keep trying. I wonder if I could ask you one favour?"

"Anything, Colonel."

"Could I have a cup of coffee?"

"Certainly."

He yelled for the sergeant, and when there was no answer, he went through the door at a run and I could hear him shouting across the parade ground. I slipped the Balbo card in my pocket and followed him out.

"Please, Major, don't disturb yourself. I'll be on my way. Just a reminder—this visit is strictly reserved."

"Of course, Colonel. Have a good journey."

He was glad to see me go, but not half so glad as I was to hear the gates of the stockade slam behind me. The moment I was out of sight of the watchtower, I stepped hard on the accelerator and drove fast and dangerously all the way to Bergamo. I snatched a plaintive Steffi from the square of the High Town and drove straight back to Milan. The prints on the Balbo card matched those which Steffi had brought from Rome. We made four Xerox copies and locked the original in the safe. Then we rang for Pietro and ordered champagne and a gourmet meal to celebrate this first real rape of the ungodly.

It was one of those jubilant hours that only a professional can understand and share. It was like winning a lottery or having the prettiest girl in the room wilt into your arms. I was the shrewdest fellow in the world, as racy a gambler as ever bet his wife's virtue on the turn of a card. But—*post coitum tristitia, post vinum capitis dolor!*—at four in the afternoon, sober but sleepy, we still did not know what to do with the Balbo document. Steffi, who had missed his siesta, summed it up irritably.

"*Ebbene!* We now have evidence to put one Giuseppe Balbo in prison for life. You don't want that. You want him here, in this room, singing like a lovebird, telling you all he knows about Roditi, and the letter bomb, and the murders in the Via Sicilia. Then you want Roditi here, singing another song about General Leporello. Then, when you've copied down the whole melody, what are you going to do with it? Like the rabbi who played golf on the Sabbath and got a hole-in-one, whom do you tell? And when you tell, who's going to want to believe you? And, much more important, who's going to do anything about it? Matucci, little brother, big woodenhead, you have to answer all those questions!"

"Give me time, Steffi, for God's sake!"

"You don't have time, little brother. Suppose your Major Zenobio has missed the card?"

"I'm hoping he hasn't. He's careless with papers."

"Suppose he rings Leporello to check on you?"

"I'm gambling he won't."

"Gambling, hoping! On a thread like that you could hang yourself."

"I know, I know! Let's take it one step at a time. I want doubt, confusion and panic. . . . What's the time?"

"Three-thirty. Why?"

"How far is it to Chiasso?"

"Less than fifty kilometers. Again, why?"

I grabbed the telephone and dialled Bruno Manzini's private number. When he came on the line, I told him what I wanted.

". . . A courier, Bruno. I want him now. He's to drive to Chiasso and post some letters. They have to be delivered in Milan with tomorrow's mail. And I'd like to see you as soon as possible, here, at the apartment. I'm sorry to bother you, but it's very urgent."

Crotchety he might be, but he always ran true to form. The courier would be with me in fifteen minutes. He himself would join me at six. Steffi was looking at me as if I were an amiable lunatic. I unlocked the safe, took out the Balbo document, rubbed it clean with a new handkerchief and laid it on the desk. Then I rang for Paolo and asked him to bring me a pair of his clean white gloves. Finally Steffi could bear it no longer.

"So, tell me, Matucci! Or do I just stand here and watch you make like Inspector Maigret?"

"Step one. We make two fresh copies of the Balbo document. This time without our fingerprints all over the copy paper. Step two. We clip Balbo's thumbprint off each copy. Step three. I type two identical notes to accompany the thumbprints. Step four. The said notes and thumbprints are posted to catch tonight's mail from southern Switzerland."

"And what will be in the notes?"

"Two names: Bandinelli, Calvi. A place: Via Sicilia, Rome. And the date on which they died."

"And who gets the notes?"

"Major-General Leporello and Captain Roditi—at their private addresses."

"And how long does it take them to run the print through records?"

"Forty-eight hours at least."

"And how long to tie everything back to you through a stolen card?"

"Another twenty-four. Those are inside limits. We might do better."

"Then what, little brother?"

"Then there is the beautiful scene, Steffi. I think we'll get Fellini to film it. I, Dante Alighieri Matucci, am standing solitary and noble in the middle of the Olympic Stadium. All the stands are full. All the spectators look exactly like the Director. They all have guns and they're all pointing at me. . . . What happens after that, I'm not sure."

"I'm sure, Matucci. I'm going home to Mother."

"Oh, no, you're not. Not tonight, anyway. At ten o'clock we are going to make a private visit to the apartment of Captain Matteo Roditi. How does that sound?"

"Like madness, little brother. Like old-fashioned dancing madness!"

&ঙ্গ ঙ্গ

BRUNO MANZINI arrived punctually at six. When he heard of my day's exploits, he was not amused. He gave me no tolerant elegies either. He was coldly and eloquently angry.

". . . Matucci, you shock me! You do not lack talent. You have vast experience. You have at least a rudimentary sense of politics. So this children's game you have played today is an incredible and inexcusable folly."

"Now, listen, Cavaliere. . . !"

"No! You hear me first! You have compromised yourself. You have compromised me. You have set in motion a whole train of events for which we are quite unprepared and for which we have no time to prepare! Good God, man! Have you learnt nothing? This is high politics. We are talking of revolution, Matucci, barricades in the streets, gunfire and bombs! Yet you behave like some fly-brained agent from a comic book! Truly I despair!"

"I think you despair too quickly, Cavaliere."

"Do you, indeed? Then show me half a grain of sense in this crackbrained escapade and I'll die happy."

"Then here it is. Locked in that safe, there is a document, perhaps the only existing document, which can tie Roditi and Leporello to a conspiracy of murder. I procured it by a risky act with awkward consequences, but . . ."

"Awkward! Mother of God! Is that what you call it?"

". . . But, Cavaliere, if you don't take risks in my business, you're left standing like a clown while people pour buckets of water over your head. Next point, we agreed on a policy of doubt and confusion. I have begun to create it . . ."

"Prematurely. Without foresight!"

"With hindsight then. We are dealing with conjurers, Cavaliere: people who can make files disappear, people who can suborn witnesses and silence politicians and buy perjurers with straw in their shoes—if we give them enough time. I am trying, rightly or wrongly, to deny them time. I'm a fly-brained agent, because I don't have the luxury to be Lorenzo de' Medici compassing the downfall of his enemies by slow and princely degrees. I'm the opportunist, because I have to be. You can sit in the Bankers' Club and plan the campaign. I have to fight the skirmishes and the street battles, and if I lose those, your campaign is so much scrap paper! . . . Eh! This is madness! Let's drop it!"

He stared at me for a long moment, bleak-faced and hostile; then he nodded slowly, as if assenting to some private proposition of his own. Then he set it down for me.

"*Ebbene!* You are right and I am right, and we are both equally wrong. Let's start from there and see what we can salvage."

"No, Cavaliere. Let's see what we can build."

A small reluctant smile twitched at the corners of his mouth. "You're a real woodenhead, Matucci. What am I to do with you?"

"Wear me, Cavaliere. Like a hair shirt, if you must,

but wear me. And give me some advice. We project from the evidence we have in hand. We establish a case that involves Balbo as an assassin, and Rodito and Leporello as conspirators. Where and how do we present our case? And how do we tie the Director into it? You say we're not prepared. I know we're not. So I need help against the high men, before they close ranks. Can you give it to me?"

"It's the Director who bothers you, isn't it?"

"Yes. He's got a perfect position. He can excuse everything he has done on the grounds that he was infiltrating a conspiracy that threatened the security of the State. He knows so many secrets that everyone's afraid of him, even his own minister."

"I'm not afraid of him, Dante."

"That's hardly enough. You have to have the lever that will topple him."

"We have the lever, my Dante. It's the fulcrum we need; and you, without knowing, may have provided it."

"I don't understand."

"I know you don't. And that is what makes me angry with you. In the fervour of a crusade, in the heat of a new situation, you slip out of gear. You change from logician to opportunist. You chase the marsh light and forget the balefires burning on the hills behind you. Remember what happened at the lodge? In Venice? The same thing is happening now. This is why you are vulnerable to such a man as the Director. You have every talent he has, and some he lacks, but you cannot or you will not focus them. So, always until now, you have been a tool of other men's designs. . . . I'm sorry if I've offended you, but I have so much regard for you that I cannot bear what you do to yourself. . . . Let me show you what I mean. When you left my brother's house on the morning after his death, you left an old servant weeping into his liquor. You had asked him to record telephone calls for you. He did that. You never went back to collect the messages. I did. I went there to see to the wants of an old man who had known my father. Because he was afraid, he told me that he had lied to you. He

was not awake when my brother came home from the
Chess Club. He was drunk and snoring. He lied because
he thought he would be blamed for not putting on the
alarms. They were off when he woke in the morning. . . .
No, please don't interrupt. Let me embarrass you a
moment longer. The night after my brother's funeral, I
had his body removed from the vault. An autopsy was
performed in the mortuary of a private clinic. My brother
did take barbiturates. He probably took quite a large
dose, but not enough to kill him. He was killed by an
injection of air into the femoral artery. The mark of the
syringe was clearly visible under the pubic hair. You see
what happened, Dante? You connived with the Director
to hush up a suicide. You were made an accomplice in
murder."

"Why didn't you tell me this before?"

For a full minute he said absolutely nothing. His eyes
were filmed over like those of a bird, so that he seemed
not to be looking at me, but away and beyond into some
immeasurable distance. He sat quite rigid, with his fingertips joined and laid against his thin pursed lips. When he
spoke, his voice was frosty, remote, like the first chill
wind of autumn.

"To teach you a lesson, Matucci. Trust no one. Not
even me. Don't believe that the old Adam is dead until
you've screwed down the coffin and seen the gravedigger
stamp the last sod on top of him."

He was right, of course. The old bastard was always
right. We Latins are the most illogical people in the
world. We mistrust our mothers when they give us the
teat. The only things we believe happily are unprovable
propositions like weeping Madonnas, and flying houses
and infallible Popes.

ᦕ ᦖ

OUR visit to Roditi's apartment began auspiciously. There
was a party on the sixth floor; the foyer was busy with
guests in evening dress and the porter had lost count of
the arrivals. Steffi and I rode with the partygoers as far

as the fifth floor and stepped out onto a deserted landing. We rang the bell of Roditi's apartment; and, when there was no answer, I used a picklock and opened the door in thirty seconds. It was as simple as shelling green peas.

The interior of the apartment was a surprise. I had expected an epicene elegance or perhaps a feminine clutter. I found, instead, a place as aseptic and impersonal as a hotel room. The furniture was Danish modern. The pictures, arranged in a severe symmetry, were all of soldiers in historic costumes. There was a cabinet for drinks and a stereo player with a collection of popular songs, film scores and American musicals. The desk was bare, except for a blotting pad of tooled leather and a leather cup full of ball-point pens and freshly sharpened pencils. The place was spotless and the teak furniture glowed with wax and recent polishing.

We began our search in the kitchen. We found coffee and bread and butter and cheese and a carton of milk. The dining room was furnished with linen, cutlery and glassware for six persons. Everything was of good quality, none of it distinguished. In the liquor cabinet there was one spare bottle of each drink and perhaps a dozen assorted mineral waters. The books in the salon were innocuous: paperback novels, a few biographies. There was no pornography, no sign of sexy prints or photographs. The drawers of the desk were unlocked. They contained notepaper and envelopes and a few blocks of ruled drafting paper. The bathroom revealed nothing except that the Captain's toiletries were expensive, though not exotic.

The bedroom was more rewarding. Roditi had ten suits and four uniforms, all made by an expensive tailor. His shirts were handmade and monogrammed. He was prolific in shoes, ties, scarves and costly accessories. He was either a very tidy man or he had a jewel of a maid because his drawers were set with mathematical precision and his dressing table was laid like a showpiece in a store.

In the right-hand drawer of the dressing table, face down, was a photograph in a silver frame. It was a portrait, obviously taken by a professional, of a woman in her early thirties, who bore a striking resemblance to Rafael's Donna Velata in the Pitti Gallery in Florence. There were the same dark eyes, large and lustrous, the same nose, a little large for perfect beauty, the same mouth, soft and enigmatic in repose. Even the hairstyle was similar: dark, straight tresses drawn back over her ears and braided behind the head. The photograph was inscribed in a bold, round hand: "To my dearest Matteo, for memory and for promise, Elena."

Beside the photograph I found a bundle of letters, more than thirty, held together by a rubber band. They were written in the same hand, signed with the same name. I read them and passed them one by one to Steffi. They were love letters, lyrical, tender, totally uninhibited in their celebration of the nights and days of a passionate affair. I have thumbed through many letters in my time, but these moved me deeply and I felt a sudden shame at my invasion of the privacy of this unknown woman. The letters were undated. There was no address. From the text and the references, it was clear that they had been written over a period of several years and that the last was written no more than a week ago. Elena was married, unhappily, to a husband older than herself. Roditi, whatever his other vices or virtues, was obviously a passionate and thoughtful lover. There was no reproach in any of the letters, only yearning and gratitude and a vivid, sensual poetry.

Even old Steffi was awed. He handed the last note back to me and said somberly, "Eh, Matucci! If you and I could move a woman like that . . ."

"It doesn't make sense, Steffi. A fellow like Roditi . . ."

"He makes sense to her, little brother, the most beautiful sense in the world."

"A *finocchio* like that! Never."

"No, hold it, Matucci. Maybe you're wrong from the beginning. You've seen him at the Alcibiade. You've heard —only heard, mark you—that someone like him chases rough trade at the Pavone. Giorgione told you he's a physical culture addict. That's all you've got. The rest is imagination and inference. This apartment now, does it smell of fennel flowers? Not to me. Does the lady sound cheated? Not to me. Maybe you have to rethink this fellow. . . . Hand me that photograph a minute."

He unfastened the clip at the back of the frame and slid out the photograph. On the back of it was the address of the photographer, together with a file number: A. Donati, Bologna, 673125. Steffi scribbled the notation in his notebook and put the photograph back in the frame.

"Tomorrow, Matucci, I should take a little trip to Bologna and trace that print, no?"

"Do that, Steffi. . . . Wait a minute, though. There's something strange."

"What?"

"We are looking at half a house, half a man. The place is incomplete, as though not enough important things have happened here yet. It's as neutral as a showroom."

"But whichever way you read him, Roditi's not neuter."

"Exactly."

"So why don't you take one of those letters from the middle of the bundle and let's haul our tails out of here. I feel like a criminal."

"Which is exactly what you are, Steffi. But you bring me back the lady's name tomorrow and I'll pin a medal on you."

We left the apartment pristine as we found it and rode down, innocent as babes, to the foyer. The porter was locked in his little booth watching television. We could have been trailing a bloodied corpse across the Carrara marble and he would not have blinked an eyelid.

It was only a little after eleven. The night was balmy and the streets were still lively with strollers and traffic. Steffi was tired, so I dropped him at his hotel. I was too restless to sleep. Bruno Manzini had taught me a rough lesson. My thinking was confused. My judgments were hasty. My actions were precipitate and dangerous. The Director had judged me long before and made me a facile actor in his sardonic dramas. Even Lili knew my weakness and would not commit to me until I had mastered it, if indeed I ever could.

The prospect of a solitary evening in the apartment

daunted me, so I drove across town to the Duca di Gallodoro, where at least I could share my loneliness and have it set to music.

They gave me a table in a shadowy corner. I ordered a drink and sat watching the shuffle of the dancers and the drift of the drinkers around the bar. A couple of girls wandered past with hopeful smiles, but I waved them away. I was too morose to endure their inevitable small talk and their constant thirst for bad champagne. I had been there for perhaps twenty minutes when two men came in and sat three tables away on my right. One was a big, sturdy fellow with the lumpy, battered face of a pugilist; the other was small, dark and dapper, with ferret eyes and a wide flashing smile.

The small one I knew. Everyone in the Corps knew him, at least by name and reputation. They called him the Surgeon because, they said, he would cut the brain out of a living man and dissect it for the last morsel of information. They even had a proverb about him: Fall into the hands of God, not into the Surgeon's paws! The suspect who had jumped or been pushed from the high window had been under his studious care. The big fellow was obviously his bodyguard—and probably his assistant butcher. I sat back farther into the shadows lest he see me and salute me and I be forced to acknowledge him.

A few moments later the band stopped playing and the dancers drifted back to their tables. A microphone was set up in the middle of the floor and a master of ceremonies announced the presence of the eminent and well-beloved Patti Pavese, who would sing for us. Then all the lights went out and there were five seconds of darkness until a spot splashed in the center of the dance floor and revealed the singer in a splendour of fishnet and sequins. She looked better than she sang, but the audience loved her and clapped handsomely. When she delivered her big number, *"Una Manciata d'Amore,"* they went wild and called her back for two repeats of the chorus and sang the last one with her.

When the lights went up again, I glanced across at the Surgeon. He was lying slumped across the table in a welter of spilled liquor. His bodyguard was sprawled sideways on the banquette. They had both been shot in the head by a small-caliber pistol. I tossed a pair of notes on the table and made for the entrance. I was halfway to the door before I heard a woman's scream and the commotion that followed it.

꧁ ꧂

THE killing of the Surgeon made headlines in the morning press, and the foreign agencies made a big meal of it as well. The police announced a nationwide hunt for the assassins and appealed for information from the public, especially from anyone who had left the Duca di Gallodoro before the arrival of the police.

Manzini, who had telephoned me at breakfast and bidden me on a tour of his factories in Milan, was gloomy and dispirited.

". . . A fellow like that is better dead, but there are fifty others waiting to step into his shoes. So nothing is solved. The factions are polarized still more. The tyrants look so múch more attractive to a sacred and dispirited people. Watch, Dante. Watch and listen! Note the tension, the undercurrent of unrest and suspicion. You will see the groups of workers coalesce, each wary of the other, each on the lookout for spies and provocative agents. These are good people, Dante. We have fewer labour troubles than most, because we sign reasonable agreements and keep them. I am not hated as the *padrone;* I am even respected, I think. But as a man I am remote as the moon. I personify power. I am identified with all the excesses of power in this country. I had a telephone call from Rome this morning. The Government is considering a new regulation that will give the police even wider powers of search and arrest. They are talking of ninety-two hours' preventive detention on mere suspicion. . . . Preventive detention! That's madness! It puts us back forty years. Your Surgeon is the symbol of the terror necessary to control the restless man. In the old days he would have worn a mask and carried a headsman's axe. In part

I am guilty of him, too. I have guards on my gates and plant detectives to stop pilfering. Forgive me, I am morbid today. We will have lunch with the managers and then I will show you something a little more cheerful."

We drove ten miles outside the city towards Como and turned off the main road into a private parkland where twenty bungalows, all new, were grouped around a central building, which looked rather like a clubhouse, set about with lawns and flower gardens. Manzini explained it to me with ironic deprecation.

". . . A sop to my pirate's conscience, Dante. One of the things I hope may earn me a late reprieve from damnation. It's a home for mongoloid children who cannot be cared for within their own families. They tend to have a short life-span, as you may know. If they are submitted to undue stress, for example, in an old-fashioned institution, some of them may become violent and antisocial. So we've tried here to reproduce a family situation. Each house has six to ten children under the care of a married couple. The central building contains classrooms, a clinic, a recreation hall and staff quarters. We're experimenting all the time, and this place has become a prototype for others in different parts of Italy. In this country the Church used to be the fountain of charity, but too many of the old orders of monks and nuns have become sclerotic and outdated. As for the State institutions, the less said the better. I have seen orphanages, my friend, where children did not learn to speak until they were seven and eight years old because no one ever talked to them. . . . Here we are both teaching and learning, and every week there is some small revelation that makes it all worthwhile."

To me, the greatest revelation of all was the old man himself. The staff adored him, men and women alike. Each one had something special to show him: a therapy project, a piece of recent equipment, a diet chart, a game that seemed to have a special fascination for their charges. With the children he was like a happy grandfather. He fondled them, kissed them, squatted on the floor and played games with their blocks and models. He drew

comic pictures on a blackboard and even pounded out a
tune on the piano. He swung one tiny mite on his shoulders and carried him round the place, while half a dozen
others tugged at his coattails for attention. There was
nothing organized about the chanted chorus of welcome
or farewell. He came and went as the patriarch of a frail
family which without him would have remained ungath-
ered and forgotten. The odd thing was that he needed to
justify himself—and to me of all people.

". . . There is a man in Rome, Dante, a priest I know,
who deals only with monsters. I mean it, literally. Man
still begets and women still throw monstrosities with one
eye and three arms and half a brain and two hearts. Some
of them survive. God only knows why and He never explains, though I think He should if He wants us to believe
in mercy and loving-kindness and all the rest! However,
this man told me once that he was, perhaps, the only one
in all the world who could truly affirm miracles. Now,
you have to understand, Dante, that the creatures we talk
about are truly subhuman, beyond reason, beyond imagining, beyond even compassion. But this man told me
that, sometimes at the strangest moments, he would feel,
see, hear a response that shook the foundations of his
sanity. These vegetables, these monstrous nothings knew!
They knew. . . ! For how long and how much? Eh! Impossible to say; but for one flash of time there was light-
ning on Tabor. This work I do is far easier than his. It
costs me nothing but money. The rest is pure joy. I go
back to the anthill changed, if only a little. I know that
life is not all vendetta and woe to the vanquished. The
mystery is that we still must fight, to hold room even for
so small a loving. If we didn't, they would burn the monsters and sterilize those babies of mine and hand them
over to the brutes of the world for anatomical experi-
ment. . . . You are seeing Leporello tonight?"

"Yes."

"Worried?"

"A little. If he opens a door, I have to walk through
it, even if I'm not sure what's on the other side. You may
not approve what I do."

"Do you care whether l approve or not?"

"Yes, I care."

"A warning, Dante Alighieri. Shut the door on today. Forget it until a calmer time. We are going back into the jungle. You cannot afford illusions."

"What illusions, Bruno?"

"That the Salamander will always survive. That's a myth, a beautiful legend, like the Holy Grail and the Golden Apples of the Hesperides. I've had my warning, Dante. I have a mitral stenosis which will kill me—probably sooner than later. If I go before this is finished, you will be alone. What then?"

"Another test, Bruno?"

"No. A simple question."

"Answer one: I finish my leave and go back to SID, an obedient servant. Answer two: I take the job which Leporello will offer me at dinner tonight."

"Answer three?"

"I emigrate and live happily ever after, mining bauxite in Australia."

"Is that all?"

"No. There's one more possibility. Write me into your will. Leave me the engraver's plate from which you print your cards. I'll set up in business as the Salamander. Who knows? I may write a new legend before they hose me out from the ashes."

It was a bad joke, but he laughed at it. I laughed, too —at the wondrous spectacle of Dante Alighieri Matucci, perched on his dunghill, flapping his wings and crowing defiance at principalities and thrones and dominations and all the dark powers of this sunlit Latin world.

❧ ❧

I GAVE great thought to the manner in which I should dress for Leporello's dinner. The suit should be sober, but not too sober lest I look like some pettifogging clerk come to dine with the bank manager. Modish? Yes. The ladies like a man who has a little colour about him, and the General would not want another grey mouse on his staff. The shirt, white cambric, with gold cuff links, just for a hint of money. The General should know where the bidding started. It was all *figura* . . . the thing we live by here in Italy. The inwardness is something else. The women share it with their confessors. We males disclose it to our friends or, given grace and time in our advancing years, to God, who, by then may have lost interest in such trifling matters.

My car was polished; Pietro had seen to that. There was no cloud on the brightwork, no speck of dust in the interior. There was a basket of flowers for my hostess and a bottle of old brandy for my host, to honour my first footing in their house. If my dinner companion proved willing, there was champagne in the refrigerator and coffee on the stove and sweet music would flood the place at the touch of a switch. All in all—saving the ravages of time and middle age—the *figura* was not bad. Pietro flicked the last speck of fluff from my lapels and swept me out into the night.

I drove carefully, because there were police at every intersection and trucks full of Carabinieri parked at strategic points. The murder of the Surgeon was no small matter in this city of a million and a half people, restive under the twin threats of violence and repression. I was stopped twice on the way and a third time at the gates of Leporello's villa, where two Carabinieri checked my papers, waved me inside and closed the gates behind me. Leporello was taking himself and his job very seriously. There were two plainclothesmen inside the grounds. One of them opened the door of the car and delivered me, unscathed, at the front door, where a maid took charge of me and led me into the salon.

Leporello was alone. Even in civilian clothes he was an impressive figure, tall, straight and formal to the point of stiffness. Still, his greeting was warm, his handshake firm and welcoming. He apologized for the ladies, who were chatting upstairs. They would join us presently. A manservant offered drinks, whisky or champagne. We toasted each other. Leporello made a joking reference to the guards and the security men. I told him I thought it wise and necessary to take precautions. I asked about his investigation into the murder of the Surgeon. He frowned and shrugged.

"You know how it is, Colonel. The murder took place in a crowded nightclub, while the attention of the clients was focussed on a popular performer. Most of the place was in darkness. The assassins used silenced pistols, small caliber, low velocity. Where do we begin?"

I was lavish with sympathy for his problem. I wished fervently that I could offer some constructive suggestion. I was happy to be on leave and dispensed from responsibility. He smiled faintly and said that we must discuss that over the brandy. Then the ladies came—and it was as if the roof had fallen on my unwary head. The woman in Roditi's photograph was the wife of General Leporello.

I stammered God knows what by way of greeting and bent over her hand in a panic of embarrassment. It is one thing to look into a woman's cleavage when you know beyond all doubt that she has put it on show for you. It is quite another to look into her eyes when you have read all her secrets in a bundle of love letters. You feel the small shameful triumph of the voyeur and you wonder that she cannot read it in your face. You feel a guilt that makes you withdraw from her touch, a fear that some unguarded word may expose the secret knowledge that you possess.

Fortunately for me, my table partner provided an adequate diversion. Laura Balestra was a lively *biondina,* with big bedroom eyes and a little-girl smile and a talent for amusing chitchat. She loved dressy men. She hated stuffy soldiers. She had an uncle in Bolivia who mined emeralds and lavished them on mistresses in six different countries. She had just come back from Austria where she had almost, but not quite, fallen in love with a ski instructor. Didn't I love Elena's dress and wasn't this a beautiful villa? And why anyone would want to live in Milan, she couldn't imagine. She much preferred Florence, but then Mamma was ailing and she had to play duenna for Papa, who was enjoying his second youth in a rather embarrassing fashion. . . . And dear, oh dear, she did carry on, didn't she?

She did, but I was so grateful I wanted to kiss her, and thought I would afterwards. Then she turned to Leporello and left me to make my halting way with the lady of the love letters.

I will say it once and be done with it: she was a beautiful woman; she wakened the old Adam in me the moment I set eyes on her. The photographer had flattered her a little because he had caught her in a moment of repose and contentment. I wondered how a ramrod like Leporello had managed to marry her. She was wondering about me, too. Her first question was a challenge.

"You're older than I expected, Colonel."

"I try hard to conceal it, madam."

"I didn't mean that. My husband likes to surround himself with very young officers."

"Oh? I've only met one member of the staff, Captain Roditi."

"Do you know him well?"

"Hardly at all. We've met only three times and we've had very little to say to each other."

"He's rather exceptional. He's been with my husband nearly seven years now. Are you married, Colonel?"

"No."

"Not interested?"

"Very dubious—about marriage, that is."

"My husband tells me he's invited you to join his staff."

"Yes."

"You don't like the idea?"

"I have some reservations. I'll be discussing them with the General."

"You're very tactful."

"And you're very beautiful, madam. Do you know the Veiled Lady?"

"I'm afraid not. Should I?"

"Rafael painted her. She's in the Pitti. You're her living image, even to the hairstyle."

"Thank you for the compliment."

"I'm sure you get many, from all those dashing young officers."

"Very few, Colonel. I'm a respectable married woman with two children."

"Girls or boys?"

"Twin girls. They'll be six next March."

"Summer children! That's nice."

"Summer or winter, does it make any difference?"

"Isn't there a proverb that says, 'Spring loving's the brightest, but summer's the sweetest'?"

"I've never heard it. Is that your experience, Colonel?"

"Well, yes. I suppose it is."

"You must tell me about it one day."

"I'd be delighted, but I never tell names or write letters."

"Very gallant—and very discreet."

"In my business I have to be discreet."

"Oh, yes, you're something in intelligence, aren't you?"

"That's right."

"Do you like your work?"

"Not always. It destroys one's illusions too quickly."

"Do you have any left, Colonel?"

"Some. . . . And you?"

"Ask me some other time."

"I'll do that. It's a promise."

Dinner was announced at that moment, so there was no chance to finish the gambit. But if I guessed my lady right, she was playing the old game of spite-my-husband, and playing it very recklessly indeed. Leporello, on the other hand, was punctiliously polite, though never casual or intimate. For a man who was normally brusque and imperative, his attitude to his wife was surprisingly deferential. It was as if he had acquired the habit of stepping round arguments and avoiding the simplest discussions. I had the curious impression that he was afraid of her and that she, knowing it, was prepared to push him to the limit of endurance. At table he concentrated his first attention on me. He was persuasive and complimentary. He wished most earnestly to have me on his staff. Men with my training and experience were precious. He hoped the

women might persuade me if his own eloquence were
not enough. Laura Balestra was on his side, teasing and
inconsequent. Elena Leporello played her own game, flat-
tering me and denigrating her husband in a dozen subtle
ways. By the time we had finished the pasta, I was tired
of their comedy. I began to devise one of my own.

"By the way, General, did you know someone tried to
kill me in Venice?"

He was a very good actor. He choked on his wine and,
as he set down the glass, he spilled the dregs on the table-
cloth. The women were shocked and excited. Leporello
silenced them with a gesture and demanded a full account
of the affair.

I shrugged it off. "Well, I'd just had dinner with my
Director and the Cavaliere Manzini. I was on my way to
Harry's Bar to meet a girl. I was waylaid by three men
who tried to bottle me up in an alley. I fired some shots.
They ran away."

"You reported the matter to the Director, of course?"

"Yes. . . . He told me he would make some inquiries
and come back to me."

"But you haven't heard from him yet?"

"Not yet."

"This worries me, Colonel. It seems this kind of violence is becoming epidemic. You heard what happened
here in Milan last night?"

"I was there, General."

He was not acting now. He gaped at me, fish-eyed.

I explained with elaborate discretion. "You won't find
my name in your reports because I slipped out before
the panic started—to avoid embarrassing questions. I was
sitting three tables away.

"And you saw nothing?"

"Only the bodies when the lights went up. It was
obviously a professional job. I shouldn't think you'll get
far with normal inquiries. Myself, I wouldn't be inclined
to push them too hard."

"That's an odd thing so say, Colonel."

"Not really, General. Let's face it, both sides are in

profit. The Left have their victim. You're rid of a discreditable nuisance."

Elena Leporello was quick to see the point and turn it against us both. "That sounds like a loaded proposition, Colonel."

"Not at all. It's a statement of fact—unless you want me to say that your husband approved of sadism in police interrogations. However, I agree it's not the sort of thing one shouts about in public."

Leporello brightened at that and added a vigorous approval. "Very proper, Matucci. . . . Very proper. Our public image is very important at this time."

"And what do you think of the image, Colonel?" Elena Leporello was a very persistent adversary. "I get the impression it's rather tarnished just now."

"In some respects, yes. On the other hand, your husband's reputation is growing."

"His reputation for what, Colonel?"

"Firm policy, decisive action. . . . I was at the Bankers' Club the night before last. Your speech on Order and Progress made a big impression, General. I've heard other talk as I've been moving around. There's a great deal of popular support for your program. These riot squads you are training . . ."

"Where did you hear about those, Colonel?"

"They're being talked about in every bar and club in town, General."

"It's supposed to be a secret project."

"I assure you it isn't anymore."

"Could you name me any places where you've heard this talk?"

"Certainly. The Duca di Gallodoro, the Hilton Bar, the Club Alcibiade . . ."

The mention of the Alcibiade produced a variety of reactions. Elena looked blank. The General developed a sudden interest in the strawberry flan.

Laura Balestra quizzed me pertly. "The Club Alcibiade? And what were you doing there, Colonel?"

"Just looking."

"Did you find what you were looking for?"

"Yes, I did, as a matter of fact. I found a man I've been chasing for weeks."

"I didn't think you'd find a man within a kilometer of the place."

"Indeed, yes. I was there. Captain Roditi was there . . ."

"Matteo?"

It was Elena who asked the question, and she addressed it, not to me, but to Leporello, who smiled over it as if it were the first real victory of the evening.

"Don't ask me, my dear. I wasn't there. . . . Now, if you don't mind, the Colonel and I will take coffee in the library. We'll join you when we've had our talk."

No sooner were we settled and private than his manner changed, dramatically. He was every inch the soldier again: curt, decisive, dogmatic, as if he were addressing a staff conference.

"Matucci, the time has come for us to be frank with each other."

"I'd welcome that, sir."

"Your Director thinks you're a troublemaker. I think you and I would get on well together. Why do you hesitate to join me?"

"Two reasons to begin with: I want to finish my leave. I want to test myself in civilian employment."

"With Bruno Manzini."

"Yes."

"He's an old rogue—and dangerous."

"Dangerous?"

"He's a bad enemy. He has blackmailed a number of people into suicide. Before you leave this evening, I shall give you copies of two dossiers. I should like you to study them carefully and return them to me. I make no further comment. You will come to your own conclusions."

"You seem sure they'll agree with yours."

"We'll see. . . . If you decide to join me, you may finish your leave without curtailment."

"That's very fair."

"Now, as to the appointment itself. There is no establishment as yet, no title, no table of organization. You would be required to set up a completely new section, subject only to me and to my personal directives. You would model this section on the Service of Defense Information, with such variations as your experience dictated and we agreed together. Interested?"

"So far, very. What would be the purpose of this section?"

"Political intelligence, in the widest sense. If certain events take place, if certain projects mature, the scope of the work would be greatly enlarged, and your position would be one of considerable power."

"Can you specify the events and the projects, General?"

"I can, but not yet."

"May I ask why?"

"Because I must first be sure, Colonel, where your loyalties lie."

"I should have thought that was obvious, General."

"Indeed?"

"Yes, sir. We are both commissioned officers in the same Corps. We took the same oath of service. That specifies everything very clearly, I think."

"Unfortunately, it doesn't. It does not specify, for instance, your political affiliation."

"Am I required to have one?"

"For this post, yes."

"Then you should nominate it, General."

"I need a very conservative man."

"That could be a contradiction in terms. Intelligence deals both with the actual and the possible. I could quote my Director at length on that subject."

"Would it help if I told you that your Director has become a very conservative man?"

"I already know that, sir."

"What do you know?"

"The meeting was held at the Villa Baldassare, was it not?"

"How the devil . . . ?"

"I dined with the Director and with Bruno Manzini in Venice."

"What did they tell you?"

"I could not depose that they told me anything. Let's

say I became aware of certain situations and arrangements. For instance, there was a discussion as to whether I should be eliminated. There were two votes against, one for killing me—your vote, General. So you see, I'm rather puzzled by this offer of yours."

I had thought to shake him. I was disappointed. Whatever he was as a husband, in his character of soldier and strategist he was impregnable. He reproved me quietly:

"Why? You know the trade. We're all at risk. I voted yes. Then I changed my mind."

"Why?"

"I have never trusted your Director. I have always regarded him as a useful but fickle ally. So, when I left the meeting at the Villa Baldassare, I thought very carefully. I concluded I had need of a rival and an ultimate substitute for the Director . . . You, my dear Colonel. Simple, isn't it?"

"Too simple."

"Why so?"

"Everyone carries life insurance, except me. Manzini has wealth and influence. The Director has a presidential appointment. You have general rank in the Carabinieri. Me? I'm out on the limb of the cherry tree."

"Join me and you will have my personal protection. Don't underrate that, Colonel."

"I don't. But I was thinking of the Surgeon."

"What about him?"

"He's dead."

"I wasn't protecting him."

"Oh, I see."

"You said it yourself: the man was a discreditable nuisance. . . . More brandy?"

"Thank you. . . . Do you mind if I ask a few questions?"

"Please!"

"This aide of yours, Captain Roditi . . . explain him to me."

I had touched him on the raw. His head jerked up. He was suddenly tense and threatening. "I think you should explain yourself, Colonel."

"Ebbene! You want me to join you. I am interested, but I am not prepared to walk blind into a new situation. I have studied you, General, as you have studied me. I hear that this Roditi is a court favourite. He is resented. Because of him you are resented, too. I want to know why."

He considered the question for a long time. He turned it over and over, as if it were a piece of putty from which he might mould an answer that would suit me. Finally he said:

"Roditi is dispensable. You come, he goes, if that's what you want."

"What was he doing at the Club Alcibiade?"

"He recruits there."

"And at the Pavone?"

"Yes."

"I'm curious to know why you're using these types."

"We need men without ties, with no ambition beyond money and the companionship of their own kind. They, too, will be dispensable in time, like the Congo mercenaries."

"General, if you were sitting in my chair, would you accept that answer?"

"If I were sitting in your chair, Matucci, I should not expect to have all the words spelt out for me."

"Fair comment, General. I accept it. However, you must be patient with me. You offer me patronage, protection. I have to know where the power lies, and the weakness, too."

"I'm listening."

"Your marriage is obviously unhappy."

"Is it so obvious?"

"To me, yes. A man like you, with ambitions like yours, cannot afford an enemy in the house. You must be very lonely, General."

"I am. I confess that these are desert days for me, Matucci. But I am prepared to endure them a while longer."

"So, you lean on Roditi?"

"More than I should, perhaps. He's become like a son to me. But I need someone much stronger, much wiser. You, my friend."

"But you're still not prepared to trust me. . . . Please, General, let's not play games. There's a dossier on you at SID. The Director knows what's in it. I don't, because he has always reserved it to himself. That's why you wouldn't move until you had him as an ally. You still don't trust him, and you want to set me up against him. I'm impotent unless I know as much as he does. I can't protect you unless I know what weapons he can use against you. . . . Now, why don't you think about that? If you still want me, we can meet again and discuss final questions. After that we can sign transfer papers."

"You might decide not to join me after all."

"And you might decide to withdraw your protection. In which case I could end like the Surgeon, with a bullet in the head. If that happened. . . ?"

"Yes, Colonel?"

"There is a data bank in Switzerland which would immediately circulate a lot of information to the press and other interested parties."

"Blackmail, Colonel?"

"No, General. That begins when I try to extort money or preferment. I have done neither. I have simply taken out insurance. But, talking of blackmail, are you sure you yourself are not a victim?"

"I told you once, Colonel, I tell you again. My life is an open book."

"That's the public record, General. The secret one is what they hit you with on the day when you're proclaimed saviour of the country. . . . Look, I didn't ask for the job. You offered it. If you're unhappy with my terms, let's forget it."

"Let's define them more clearly."

"Full disclosure on both sides?"

"Very well. I'll be in touch with you again in a few days. Meantime, you can study the Manzini dossiers. . . . More brandy?"

"No, thank you. I should be getting home. It's been a long day."

"Not too unprofitable, I hope?"

"Far from it, General. I think we've come a long way towards an understanding."

"Good. . . . By the way, would you mind dropping Laura in town? Otherwise I'll have to call a staff car. I don't like taxis calling at the house here."

"No trouble at all. I'll be delighted."

"I like her. She's a cheerful soul. A little stupid, perhaps, but rich in her own right—and still unattached. A word to the wise, eh?"

Cheerful she was, and more than a little drunk, and she chattered like a featherbrain; but stupid she wasn't. As we drove back to town, she gave me a zany but revealing commentary on the dinner party.

"Meow-meow-meow! Talk about the cat in the pigeon loft! You were very naughty tonight, Dante. You know you were. You've still got feathers all over your whiskers. You're the first man I've seen who was able to handle Elena in one of her moods. Eek! She really had her claws out for Marcantonio tonight. . . . Not that I blame her really. He's no joy in bed and no fun anywhere else, as far as I can see. . . . You don't really want to work for him, do you? I can't see you fitting into that bunch of *finocchi* he's got around him. But then, I don't know you very well, do I? And you never did say what you were doing at the Alcibiade. And what was Matteo Roditi doing there? You didn't see Elena's face when you dropped that hot brick. I thought she was going to burst a gusset and pop that big bosom of hers in the gravy. You know they're lovers, of course? My dear man, everybody knows—even the General. If my arithmetic's right, Roditi has to be the father of the twins. . . . Why? Oh, come on, Matucci! Why do you think the old boy uses Matteo to do all his dirty work. . . . Me? I'm the little friend of all the world. But I am Elena's friend first. And I'll make a bet with you. If she doesn't call you in the next twenty-four hours, I'll give you a night in bed myself. . . ."

"No bet. You're already invited."

"I hate to be rushed."

"No rush. There's champagne and caviar and soft music and . . ."

"And Elena will hate me ever after."

"Who's to tell, *bambina?*"

"That's right, who's to tell? She'll still ring you, though. She's wild for you, Matucci. I know her."

"You told me she was wild for Roditi."

"Oh, that's special. The others—and there have been others—are her revenge on her husband. If you're going to join him, she'll get you to bed, if she has to scream rape and murder to do it."

"She sounds like a candidate for the *manicomio!*"

"Wouldn't you be if you were married to a middle-aged *finocchio* with delusions of grandeur?"

"God forbid!"

"Amen! Now, tell me about your love life, Colonel. I'd like to know what I'm getting into before I have too much champagne."

As it turned out, three glasses were more than enough. She passed out cold to the music of Henry Mancini. I undressed her, tucked her into the big double bed, hung up her clothes, stuck a get-well note to the bathroom mirror and closed the door on her.

❖ ❗

IT was now one in the morning in Milan, where, if her citizens are to be believed, money will buy you anything, day or night. My needs were essentially simple: an atomizer and a one-eyed notary, deaf and dumb, insomniac and avaricious. I record, as a matter of historic interest, that, even with my contacts, it took me an hour to find him, twenty minutes to haggle with him and a hundred thousand lire in cash to coax him out of the house.

I can be flippant about it now, but at that moment in time I was desperate. To explain: I wanted to take a legal deposition from a witness. I was prepared to exercise duress, threats, intimidation and physical violence, if necessary. So I needed a notary with a stack of *carta bollata* and a rubber stamp, and a flexible conscience.

At three-fifteen, armed and accompanied by the said notary, I presented myself at the apartment of Captain Matteo Roditi. The Captain was out, absent, abroad about the business of his master—or his mistress, as the case might be. I entered the apartment, closed the notary in the bedroom to doze a while, made myself a cup of coffee in the kitchen and settled down to wait. At three forty-five, red-eyed and almost sober, Roditi came home. I pushed him against the wall while I patted him for concealed weapons. Then I sat him in the Danish armchair and perched myself on the desk, with the pistol and the atomizer beside me. After that I was able to talk to him like a country uncle.

"Captain, you don't know me very well. You may therefore be tempted to believe I am playing games. I am not. If you don't give me truthful answers, I'm going to kill you. I shall spray cyanic acid gas in your face and you will be dead in four seconds. If you cooperate, I may offer you a way out of the mess you're in now. Clear?"

"Yes."

"In your bedroom there is the signed photograph of a woman and a bundle of love letters from a woman called Elena. Who is Elena?"

"She's the wife of General Leporello."

"How long have you been lovers?"

"About six years."

"Are you the father of her children?"

"I believe so."

"Does the General know of your association?"

"Yes."

"And condones it?"

"Yes."

"Tell me why?"

"It gives him a hold over both of us."

"Explain that."

"He is the legal father of the children. His name is on

the registration of birth. He could remove them from Elena's care and custody."

"And what is his hold over you?"

"I have performed services for him which put me in legal jeopardy."

"What services?"

"I have procured for him."

"Inside or outside the Service?"

"Both. I have another apartment, near the Duomo. The lease is in my name. He uses that as a meeting place. I pay the people and make sure there's no trouble afterwards."

"How do you do that?"

"Threats mostly. Action, if necessary."

"You have people beaten up, that sort of thing?"

"Yes."

"I'll need names and dates and places, but we'll come to that later. Do you know Major Zenobio, the Commandant of Camerata?"

"Yes."

"Have you heard from him today?"

"There was a message to call him. I haven't done it yet."

"Did you get a letter from Chiasso today?"

"Yes."

"Did the General get one?"

"Yes."

"What did you do about them?"

"I passed them to forensics to check the fingerprint and the typewritten sheet."

"Have you had any answers yet?"

"No."

"When would you expect the answers?"

"Tomorrow or the next day."

"Did you know whose print it was?"

"I had an idea. I wasn't sure."

"Whose?"

"It could have belonged to Balbo."

"Did he kill Bandinelli and Calvi?"

"Yes."

"Did he plant a letter bomb in the apartment of one Lili Anders?"

"Yes."

"Who gave the orders?"

"I did."

"Who gave you your orders?"

"The General."

"Where are the Pantaleone papers?"

"I gave them to Leporello."

"Where are they now?"

"I don't know. Possibly at his house."

"Where is Giuseppe Balbo?"

"I think he's dead."

"You think. . . !"

"I was told to take him to the Club Alcibiade tonight and make sure we left at two forty-five."

"Who told you?"

"The General."

"Because of the letter from Chiasso?"

"Yes."

"Who was going to do the job?"

"I don't know. I wasn't told."

"Any ideas?"

"Leporello talked of killing two birds with one shot —the Surgeon and Balbo."

"Very neat. Did you ever think he might want to get rid of you one day?"

"Yes."

"Did you never take out any insurance?"

"Yes, I did. I had the other apartment bugged. There are tapes and photographs."

"Where are they?"

"Elena has one set. I have another in safe deposit at the Banca Centrale."

"I'll need the key and an authorization of access."

"Very well."

"How do you feel about Elena now?"

"I love her, for God's sake! Why else do you think I've stayed in this rotten business?"

"Because you didn't want to get out. . . . When Leporello brought off his coup, you'd be a very big man."

"What are you going to do now?"

"Not I, Roditi, you! You're going to write a deposition. There's a little man in your bedroom who will notarize the document. When that's done, we'll talk about the rest of it. . . . Now, there's the *carta bollata,* there's the pen. I'll dictate. You write."

It took half an hour to compose the document and half a minute to stamp and notarize it. I sent the notary on his drowsy way, had Roditi write a letter to his bank, stuffed the documents into my breast pocket and settled down to a more cozy chat. Roditi was utterly defeated, sallow and trembling, so I let him have a whisky to revive himself while I laid out the deal.

". . . Your deposition buys you a life sentence, Roditi. A phone call from me to Leporello gets you killed before morning. So you're going absent without leave. You'll pack a bag. I'll drive you to a safe place in the country and you'll stay there until I've built the last brick into my case against Leporello. You'll be interrogated. You'll make more depositions than you've ever dreamed of. But at least you won't be in jail, and waiting for some cell mate to put a skewer in your back. Then, before the case breaks, you'll have twenty-four hours to get out of the country with Elena and the children. . . . It's the best I can do. Take it or leave it."

"It's no good. It won't work."

"Why not?"

"It just won't, that's all."

"Have you got a better idea?"

"Yes. Leave me free until you've finished your case. I can bluff it out. That's one thing I'm good at. I can feed you information—better information than you would get any other way. Things are starting to happen, Matucci, and they're going to happen very fast. . . ."

"What sort of things?"

"I can't tell you yet. But I will as soon as I know."

"I'm sorry. I don't like it. Pack your bag now."

"I'm not going."

"Then you're going to tell me why."

"All right. You've been followed all the evening. While your car was at the General's house, they fixed a bleeper on it."

"Which means they know where I am now?"

"Yes, yes."

"And they're waiting for me downstairs?"

"I don't know."

"Then let's take a walk and find out. If they're not there, we'll take a little drive—to Balbo's place first, then over to the General's house. . . . If we have to finish it now, let's finish it. On your feet!"

"I'm not going. You can kill me here if you like, but I'm not going."

"So, that's why it was all so easy, eh? They cut me down as I walk out the front door! Or they've taped the car with plastic and when I switch on the ignition, it blows me sky-high. Now, little man, which is it?"

"I don't know. I swear I don't know."

"Then let's find out."

I fished out my pocket book and found the number of the SID agency in Milan. I dialled it and spoke to the duty officer, quoting my identification number.

". . . I am questioning a suspect. My car is parked outside the building. It's a red Mercedes with a Milan number plate. I know it has been bugged. It may have been planted with an explosive device. It is also possible there may be an attempt to assassinate me as I leave the building. The suspect is an officer of Carabinieri, so I'd rather not have them brought in. Can you manage it by yourselves? And without making a fuss? I don't care about the car, you can deliver that for me when it's clean. But I'll need another vehicle at disposal when I leave. When you're ready, send a man up to the apartment to let me know. Code word *Dragon*. . . . That's right—*dragon*. Don't let him forget it. He might get shot as he comes in. . . . Thanks. Hurry it up, please. Oh, and just for safety, check me back on this number as soon as I hang up."

He checked back and told me the boys would be with me in thirty minutes. It was a long time to wait and a lot could happen in that time. I switched off the lights and crossed to the window and parted the drapes. It was already happening. Three police cars were already parked outside the building, a third was turning into the street. Already the men were piling out of them and grouping themselves round the officer in command. The plot was very clear now. Arrest and search and ninety-two hours' detention on any charge in the book. I could think of two that would stick—breaking and entering and withholding information from the police on the killing of the Surgeon. By the time I got out, if I ever got out, the depositions would have disappeared into thin air. I hauled Roditi to his feet, thrust a wadded handkerchief into his mouth, poked my gun into his kidneys and hustled him out of the apartment.

There was no way down except by the elevators or the concrete stairs. Either way would land me in the arms of the Carabinieri. We went up. We climbed four flights until we came to a door that gave access to the roof and the water tanks on top of it. The door was locked. It took me a minute to pick the lock. I pushed Roditi out onto the roof and relocked the door from the outside. Then I leaned him face against the door and chopped him hard on the back of the skull. He went down like a sack. I dragged him into the shelter of the water tanks and took the gag out of his mouth. I didn't want him to choke just yet. He had a lot more talking to do, if ever I could get out of this very neat trap.

I made a cautious circuit of the roof and found that the two adjoining buildings were similar in height and construction. It would be an easy matter to climb across the parapets and make my escape through the third building. It would be quite impossible if I had to take Roditi with me. I left him, and a few minutes later I found myself in a deserted office block. I waited, frozen and disconsolate, in a toilet, wondering what had happened to Roditi and why no one had bothered to check the rooftop.

When the workers began to arrive in the morning, I walked out into the crowded, sunlit streets and took a taxi to Steffi's hotel.

&c &

FOR all his cavils and quirks, Steffi in crisis was a treasure. While I bathed and shaved, he strolled around to the Xerox offices and made copies of the depositions on a coin-in-the-slot machine. Then he went to the Milan office of his bank, cashed a check and deposited the original document for safekeeping against my signature or his own. After that he surged, larger than life, into Manzini's office and demanded to see the old man. He presented my compliments, a photostat copy and a secondhand account of the night's events. The pair of them came back to the hotel for breakfast, chatting as if they had known each other all their lives.

Breakfast, however, was a sober meal. Manzini telephoned the editor of his newspaper and came back with three stories which would feature in the afternoon editions. The lead story dealt with a gun battle in which one Giuseppe Balbo, a suspect in the murders at the Duca di Gallodoro, had been killed by police officers while resisting arrest. Also on the front page was the account of a mysterious occurrence in a fashionable apartment block. Answering an anonymous telephone call, the details of which could not yet be released, the police had visited an apartment on the fifth floor occupied by Captain Matteo Roditi, personal aide to Major-General Leporello. The apartment was empty and in disorder. There was no sign of the Captain, who, at the time of going to press, was still missing. The police had already detained one man who was known to have visited the apartment in the early hours of the morning. They were also seeking to question a certain Dante Alighieri Matucci, member of a government agency, whose car was parked outside the building and whose fingerprints were found in the apartment of the missing man. There was a full and accurate description of me and a photograph obviously supplied by wire from the files of SID.

". . . And that, gentlemen," said Manzini flatly, "disposes of our case. Balbo is dead. Roditi is dead or in protective custody. Your notary is now under the lamps, and by the time they have finished with him, he will sign whatever they want. Roditi's deposition is worthless, because they will produce a counter-deposition proving duress. You, my Dante, are now a man on the run. If they take you . . . *Buona notte!* It's the Matteotti affair all over again."

"You're forgetting something, Bruno. I have a key and an authority that will open Roditi's safe deposit at the Banca Centrale. If he was telling me the truth, there's enough material there to finish Leporello at one stroke."

"There are three *if*'s in that proposition, Dante. If Roditi was telling the truth. . . . If Leporello hasn't already got a judicial order to open the box. . . . If you could open it yourself. . . . Remember, you have to present identification. An hour from now your description will be all over the streets of Milan. Which means also we have to get you out of here fast."

"Let me answer first. I believe Roditi was telling the truth. I don't believe he would hand his last insurance to Leporello."

"Not even if he were threatened with death? You broke him easily."

"Only because he thought he was protected. If he sold out to Leporello, he would know he was leaving his woman and her children defenseless. I think he would cling to one last hope—that I, or someone else, might bring Leporello down."

"I agree," said Steffi vehemently. "One crumb of hope keeps a man going for a long time."

"Access to the box, then." Manzini was still gloomy. "How do you manage that?"

"What does a banker need—not at the moment itself —but on his record after the customer is gone?"

"A signature and a note of the document of identification."

"You have my document of identification. You have a very good calligrapher in Carlo Metaponte, who did your salamander card. And you have your friend Ludovisi at the Banca Centrale who promised his help if ever we needed it. Well, Bruno. . . ?"

"It depends on Ludovisi, doesn't it?"

"That's right."

"I'll try him. Let me have your documents and the key. . . . Now, Matucci, what are we going to do with you?"

"I'll have to go underground. For that I'll need the false papers which are in the safe at the apartment."

"I'll go there and get them. Meantime, where do we put you?"

"Where's your car?"

"Parked in front of the hotel. The doorman's been paid."

"Could you get me out to Pedognana and keep me there for a couple of days?"

"Not in the house. I think we might have a visit from the Carabinieri. On the estate, certainly, if you don't mind a little peasant living. What about Stefanelli here?"

"I'll stay in town, Cavaliere. This big oaf needs me more than he admits."

"I don't like it, Steffi. It's a very rough game now."

"So, what do you need if not someone who understands the trade? Besides, who cares about an old sorehead on a holiday he can't enjoy?"

"Thanks, Steffi. When I call, I'm Rabin. It should be a lucky name for us all."

Manzini ignored the reference. He was still wrestling with a private problem. He asked abruptly, "Suppose Ludovisi won't play. What then?"

"There's one last hope . . . Leporello's wife."

"When she reads that report, she'll think you killed or kidnapped Roditi."

"The report came from her husband. I don't think she'd believe him if he told her the day of the week."

"It's an awful gamble."

"I know a worse one," said Steffi somberly. "Leporello for *Duce* and the bullyboys keeping order with truncheons and castor oil."

❧ ☙

I spent four days at Pedognana, three of them lodged in the attic of the factor's house. The Carabinieri came once and spent an afternoon prowling the estate. I spent that same afternoon in a barn loft and emerged with a beautiful dose of hay fever. On the fourth day Manzini arrived with my documents and a suitcase of ready-to-wear clothes to fit my new identity as one Aldo Carnera. Thorough as ever, he had procured me a back-dated employment as a travelling salesman with one of his small offshoot companies. I would never have to put in an appearance, but if anyone checked back, my false name and personal details were on file.

He brought discouraging news, too. Ludovisi was in New York at a conference. He was flying from New York to Mexico City and thence to Buenos Aires. He was not expected back for ten days. Manzini was fretful. All his careful plans to introduce me into society, to elevate me to the status of a diplomatic agent, were now in ruins. I was back in the underworld from which he had taken me. I was, by presumption, disreputable, and because of me, he, too, had fallen into some discredit with the Movement. He was excluded from its inner councils. The Director had sent him a caustic little note suggesting that, until his credit was restored, he might confine his activities to financial contribution, of which the Movement stood in constant need.

We dined together that night and I tried to coax him back into his anecdotal mood, but he refused to be drawn until I mentioned the two dossiers which Leporello had given to me, but which I had not had an opportunity to read. All I remembered were the names: Hans Helmut Ziegler and Emanuele Salatri. He mused over them for a few moments and then threw up his hands, casting off ill humour like a cloak.

"Eh, why not? What is the past for, if not to renew our hope in the future? Hans Helmut Ziegler. . . . That one goes a long way back. It began, let me see, in nineteen thirty. I was in São Paulo then, spending my first big money, making my first investment in the New World. In those days, my Dante, there were more Italians than Brazilians in São Paulo. Most of them were migrants, but some like myself were investors—in sugar and coffee land, in textiles and pharmaceuticals, small companies at first, but immensely profitable. Those were wild days. I was coining money and spending it and coining more. . . . And the women, *Dio!* They dropped into your hands like ripe papayas.

"One night in a gambling club I was standing next to a young fellow about my own age. He was Brazilian and he was playing higher than I was on roulette. I was having a run of luck. He was losing and chasing his losses. In the end, about midnight, he was cleaned out. He looked so disconsolate, so utterly despairing, I couldn't bear it. I put my hand on his sleeve and invited him to stay and share a stake with me—just for luck, my luck if not his. For a moment I thought he was going to strike me. Then he laughed and said, 'Why not? It's fool's money.' Well, to cut it short, I put a big green chip on thirty-five. It won. We split the money and walked away from the table, arm in arm, friends for life. His name was Paulo Pereira Pinto and he is now one of the best bankers in Brazil. When he got his first directorship he sent me an emerald, five carats, square-cut, as a souvenir of that night. I had the emerald set in a brooch for Raquela Rabin.

". . . That's the first part of the story. The second part is much later. Hans Helmut Ziegler was the Gestapo man who worked me over in prison. He loved his job and he was expert at it. A dialogue with him in the interrogation cell was like a confrontation with the evil one himself. Even now, old as I am, I remember him with terror and loathing. After the war he disappeared, swallowed up in the chaos. In 1965 the daughter of my old friend Pinto was left a widow with two young children. A year later she remarried and Pinto sent me the wedding photograph.

The man she had married was Hans Helmut Ziegler. . . . It took two years' work and twenty thousand dollars to build a dossier on him. I sent it to him with a salamander card. He couldn't even manage a clean exit. He drove himself over a cliff at one hundred and fifty kilometers an hour. Old Pinto read the dossier and thought the Israelis had killed him. He was glad to be rid of Ziegler. He didn't want the Zionists operating in his bailiwick. He called in the police, who sent the dossier to Interpol. Eventually they found their way to me, by way of the Italian authorities—which is, I suppose, how the dossier came into Leporello's hands. You may not believe it, but Pinto and I are still friends. . . .

"That ought to be the end of the story, my Dante, but it isn't. In the days before the Black Sabbath, the Jews of Rome believed they had a deal with the Germans to ransom themselves. A fund was set up to which everyone contributed in gold and jewellry. Women even gave their wedding rings. All to no avail. The Germans took the gold and took the people as well. . . . However, one of the collectors was a man called Emanuele Salatri. It was to him that Raquela gave the emerald brooch. Salatri never delivered what he had collected. He simply vanished with the loot. In 1969 there was an important auction of jewelry in Zurich. Among the pieces advertised in the catalogue was that brooch. I was therefore in a position to trace its provenance. I traced it through two other owners to Emanuele Salatri, who was then a prosperous gem dealer in Hatton Garden in London. I sent him a dossier and a card. He blew his brains out. Once again the dossier was traced back to me. Once again nothing could be done about it because I had committed no crime. I gave the brooch back to Raquela. She would not accept it. There was blood on it, she said, and it would bring no joy to anyone. I sold it to Bulgari, who broke it up and reset the stone.

". . . Old history! Am I wrong to dig it up? I have thought so many times, but always I have come back to the same question: why should the villains flourish while the victims still suffer the effects of their villainies? This is your question now, Matucci. It is one of the ironies of history that Leporello could wade through a whole ocean of crimes and still prove a potent and even a good ruler. But even if he did, should we still suffer him? Even if he came now in sackcloth with a halter round his neck, should we, in the same breath, forgive him and consecrate him to power? I cannot see it. I cannot. . . .

"There's one more story, my Dante, and then we must go to bed. Come over to the window. You see those far hills and the cluster of light at the top? . . . That's Vincolata. It's nothing much of anything, a little hill town with maybe five hundred people inside its old walls. In the Partisan days I used it as an observation point, and sometimes I slept there in the house of a widow woman called Bassi.

"One day we ambushed a small German detachment a kilometer from the town and killed two men. There were immediate reprisals. The Germans arrested twenty men, young and old, as hostages and ordered them to be shot in the square of Vincolata. The officer in charge of the firing squad was a young Austrian Oberleutnant named Loeffler. . . . You can imagine the horror of such an event in a small place like Vincolata. Twenty men. . . . It is a loss and a trauma that can never be repaired. They were my people. They had suffered because of orders I had given. So, I promised, one day justice would be done.

". . . Loeffler survived the war, went back to Austria and entered the pastoral priesthood. It takes us different ways, you see. Me, it made an instrument of vengeance; him, it turned into an apostle. I had lost Loeffler by then, and the more I came back here and saw the peace of this place, the less I wanted to disturb it.

". . . Late in the sixties I was in Austria, negotiating a contract for iron ore. In the local press I read the news that the Right Reverend Franziskus Loeffler, parish priest of Oberalp, had been nominated to a bishopric and would be consecrated in Rome by the Holy Father. I wasn't sure if it was the same man, so I went to see him. It was the same Franziskus Loeffler, and I didn't like him. I

found him shallow, stubborn, vain, the kind of church-
man I have always resented, half tyrant, half father-figure.
I told him why I had come. I asked him whether he did
not consider his elevation to a bishopric an affront to his
coreligionists in Vincolata.

"I could not come within a hand's touch of him. He
was so secure in his conversion, it was as if he carried a
private brief from the Almighty. I went away angry and
bitter. I wrote to the Vatican. I incited a press campaign
against the nomination and suggested that Loeffler could
and should be extradited to Italy to stand trial as a war
criminal. Loeffler declined his nomination, resigned his
parish and retired into obscurity.

"There is, however, an epilogue. About eighteen months
ago the parish priest of Vincolata came to see me and
asked as a special favor that I attend his Sunday Mass.
Loeffler was there. He was dressed in clerical grey, with
a white collar and a black tie, and was kneeling in the
front pew, by the nave. After the recitation of the Con-
fiteor, he stood up, faced the congregation and announced
very simply: 'I am Franziskus Loeffler. I attended the
execution of your relatives and friends during the war. I
gave the firing order. I am here to beg your pardon if
you feel you can give it. If not, I am prepared to offer
myself for whatever retribution you may exact. I cannot
bring back the dead. I wish I could. Please forgive me.'
He knelt down again and the Mass went on. Afterwards
I waited to see what the folks of Vincolata would do. . . .
Nothing, my Dante! Absolutely nothing! They ignored
him. They walked away and left him in what must have
been the cruelest solitude of his life.

". . . What could I do? I invited him home for lunch.
I still didn't like him; but he was a bigger man than I, for
whom the simplest apology is like drawing a tooth. Afterwards I thought he would probably have made a very
good bishop. . . . I'm sorry you won't meet him now.
I'd have liked to know your opinion. . . . See you in the
morning, my Dante. Sleep well!"

I didn't sleep. I sat up late and, desperately lonely,
wrote a letter to Lili; not from Uncle Pavel this time,

but from Dante Alighieri Matucci, fugitive, who tomorrow must go back to the half-world of those who cannot conform or will not submit to the discipline of the ant heap.

My dearest Lili,

This letter is from your puppet-man, who has discovered, late and painfully, how little he can control his own destiny.

It is very late. The moon is full and high and all the land is silver. It is very still, so still that I can almost hear the mice breathing behind the panelling of my bedroom. The fire is almost dead and I am beginning to be cold; but I do not want to go to bed, because you will not be there and I cannot dream you back. I tore up your last letter because I wanted to put you out of my mind until all this business was finished. It was no use. I cannot forget you. I cannot bear the empty room in my heart. I am jealous that you may have found someone else to take my place in yours.

I love you, Lili. There now! It is said. I love you. I have clowned the words before. I have lied them and traded them. This is the first time there has ever been a truth in them. Will you marry me, Lili? If I call you one day, to some tiny place that is hardly a name on a map, will you come and join hands and lips and body with me for always and a day more than always? Don't answer until you are sure, because when you are sure and I am free, I shall follow you to the last frontiers and home again.

Home? I have no home now, Lili. I am a man on the run. Things have gone badly for us, but there is still hope of a good outcome. Tomorrow I must leave this pleasant refuge and go back into the underworld, where the beggars plot against the tyrants and the tyrants use beggars for spies. I am looking for a legacy, left by a man I think is dead. If I find it, everything will be simple. If not, you may see me in Switzerland sooner than you expect.

I am afraid, but not too afraid, because I am learning slowly to live with the man who lives in my skin. I haven't seen him full-face yet. That, too, will come. The Salamander still flourishes; and I am learning from him, too, the arts of survival. . . . You will smile, but I never thought I could survive so long without a woman's company. Perhaps the truth is that my woman is never so far absent that I am without her utterly.

Strange how the words come back: *Quella che 'mparadisa la mia mente!* . . . she who makes my mind a paradise. My namesake wrote some very good things in his day. A pity he didn't write more about the body. That's very lonely just now.

Always yours,
Dante Alighieri

I have the letter still, because it was returned to me in circumstances which belong later in this record.

❧ ☙

I CAME back to Milan in the early afternoon and settled myself in a modest *pensione* near the Ambrosian Library. It was clean, comfortable and economical, the right sort of lodging for a travelling salesman whose only visible possessions were a cardboard valise and a leather attaché case, with a combination lock just to impress the customers.

After I had unpacked, I strolled out to look at the Sforza Castle, the vast fortress of red brick built by Francesco, Fourth Duke of Milan and founder of the Sforza dynasty. He began as a simple *condottiere* with a horse and a sword and three pieces of advice from his father: never beat a servant, never ride a horse with a hard mouth and never make love to another man's wife. He made himself the sword arm of Filippo Visconti, last of the line, fathered twenty-two bastards, married Filippo's daughter and, when the Visconti died, rode into a starving city with all his men-at-arms festooned with bread. He died of the dropsy in 1466, but the bastion he built is still the pride of Milan.

They were wild men in those days; but their genius and their vices perpetuate themselves in the Italians of today, and all who deal with us do well to understand it. To the foreigner, we look like characters out of an opera, exaggerated and larger than life. The reverse is true. The opera is only a pale shadow of our history, and our history repeats itself in shorter cycles than theirs. Filippo Visconti, for instance, was just like the Surgeon. He, too, threw people out of windows. He conjured up plots and spies and filled the city with soldiers of fortune to protect him. Galeazzo Maria was murdered in the Church of St. Stephen by three young men who went to Mass first to tell St. Stephen they were sorry for messing up his church. Where Leonardo wrote his Atlantic Codex, the Pirelli building stands, as a monument to Leonardo's successors.

Aimless thoughts, perhaps, from a man too disengaged for safety, in a city where every policeman had his name. And yet not aimless, not so irrelevant. Major-General Leporello was vaulting higher than the Visconti and the Sforza had even dreamed. They were content with duchies and provinces. He wanted all Italy under his fist. He had arms and communications beyond their imagining and he had no Emperor or Pope breathing down his neck.

As I wandered through the galleries and corridors of the fortress, I wondered how I should best approach Elena Leporello. She was my last chance: the last filly in the last race. If I lost on her I might just as well head for the Alps. I could write her a note. Her husband or a household spy might intercept it. I could accost her in the street. She might scream for the nearest policeman. I could telephone. She might, and probably would, slam down the receiver in my ear. I decided to telephone. I bribed a custodian to let me use the telephone in his office. A maidservant answered. I asked:

"May I speak with the General, please?"

"I regret. The General is not at home. I suggest you try Headquarters."

"This is Headquarters. Is the Signora at home?"

I waited a very long moment, and when Elena Leporello came on the line, I talked fast and eloquently:

"Please, madam, whatever I say, do not hang up until I have finished. This is Dante Alighieri Matucci. There is an order out for my arrest. I have been in hiding for several days. I read the papers. I do not know whether Captain

Roditi is alive, dead or going about his normal duties. Can you tell me, please?"

"I can't tell you, not at this moment."

"The reports give the impression that I either kidnapped him or murdered him. Neither is true. If he is alive, I must find him. Are you willing to talk to me?"

"Yes."

"When?"

"Any day between ten and six."

"Thank you. Now listen, carefully. At ten-thirty to-morrow morning go to the Ambrosian Library. Ask to see Petrarch's Virgil. The librarian will bring it to you. He will stay with you while you inspect it. A friend of mine will contact you then and bring you to me. Is that clear?"

"Yes, thank you."

"Are you being watched?"

"I don't know."

"If you think you are, don't keep the appointment. The same arrangement will stand for three days. If we have not made contact in that time, I will telephone again and make other arrangements."

"I understand."

"My friend will give you a recognition signal. He will ask, 'Are you Raquela Rabin?' You will answer, 'Yes!' Then do whatever he asks. Expect to be out of town for four or five hours."

"I understand that."

"I want to ask you some other questions. Just give me yes or no. . . . Can I trust Laura Balestra?"

"No."

"Can you trust your servants?"

"No."

"Will you trust me?"

"Until we meet—yes."

"Thank you. I will now repeat. The Ambrosian Library, ten-thirty for three days. Petrarch's Virgil. Are you Raquela Rabin?"

"Yes. Thank you. Good-bye."

So far, so good; but how far is far when you are dealing with a woman practised in intrigue? I put another slug in the telephone and dialled the number of Steffi's hotel.

"Steffi? This is Rabin. Shalom."

"And to you, too, old friend. How are you?"

"Surviving. Are you free for dinner?"

"When you get to my age, you're always free for dinner. Where?"

"Rent yourself a car. Pick me up at six at the entrance to the Sforza Castle."

"Who dines at six o'clock?"

"Nobody. We're going for a drive first. Do you like redheaded women?"

"With green hair even."

"Any news?"

"Only that I'm bored."

"That's good news. *Sbrigati eh!* Move it! There's a long way to go and the traffic's heavy."

It was six-thirty when he found me and another forty minutes before we were on the autostrada, bowling along at a hundred and twenty kilometers an hour in the direction of Venice. As we drove, through warm, soft air and a misty countryside of poplars and orchard trees, I told him of my conversation with Elena Leporello and what I proposed to do about it.

". . . If Roditi was telling the truth—and we always come back to that—then Elena Leporello has films and tapes that will hang Leporello higher than Haman's gibbet."

Steffi slewed himself round in the seat and regarded me with limpid, compassionate eyes. He smiled and nodded his head vigorously, up and down, up and down, like one of those silly Chinese mandarins. He admonished me with doleful patience.

"Matucci, little brother, it is as plain and large as the nose on my face that you have never been married. What do you know about this woman? She writes beautiful love letters to a frightened pimp who produces for her husband! She bitches her husband at a dinner party. What wife doesn't? You should hear mine sometimes, when I spill sauce on my tie or make a remark about one of the pretty

little tarts who work for her. And her girl friend says she
has fallen for you! Oy-oy-oy! How much is that to gamble
your life on? The trouble with you bachelors is that you
don't hear a word that's said between hullo and good-bye.
Now, listen, little brother. Keep your eyes on the road and
hear what an old married man has to tell you. This woman
is sick. Worse, she knows it and loves it. She needs a
husband she can kick around and humiliate. If he's a
big shot in his profession, so much the better. That's spice
for the turkey. She needs a lover of the same kind. Sure,
she writes him love notes . . . better than Petrarch even!
But she saddles him with two kids after a summer loving,
and the poor bastard takes it, because he is a poor
bastard and a rotten little pimp as well . . ."

"I know all that, Steffi, but . . ."

"But nothing, Matucci. Keep your eyes on the road
and let me finish. Now, you come waltzing to her party
all done up like a wedding cake. You're new, you're male.
Sure, she is interested. You're a challenge. She has to
prove she can pat you down and make you eat out of her
hand like the others. She's got something you want—no
matter that it isn't what she'd like you to want—and she's
going to make you sit up and beg for it. And beg, and
beg. . . . And if you won't beg, she'll turn you in, just to
show you who holds the whip. . . . So, you don't like it,
you don't have to buy it; but that's how I read the story
of Elena Leporello."

"Even if you're right, Steffi, it still doesn't solve my
problem. She's got something I want. How do I get it?"

"First question: where has she got it?"

"I don't know."

"Second question: who shares it with her?"

"I don't understand."

"A woman like that, with a wonderful dirty story and
pictures to match . . . You think she keeps it all to her
lonely self? Never in a million years! She has to tell it.
Else where's the fun?"

"Laura Balestra?"

"Possibly. Probably. What do you know about her?"

"Not much. I'm told she's rich. I know she's un-married."

"How old is she?"

"Oh, thirty . . . thirty-five."

"What else?"

"She's amusing and she likes to flirt, and I'd guess she likes to get drunk so she doesn't have to say yes and she can always blame the man when she wakes up in the wrong bed. I'd say she's an almost girl: almost in love and almost engaged and almost never likely to get married."

"She sounds a likely candidate for the scandal session. . . . Matucci, do you always drive like this? Please, I'm dyspeptic. Let me live to enjoy my dinner."

"So Laura knows where the stuff is hidden. She tells me. What then?"

"Then, little brother, you have the whip. You threaten the lady. If she doesn't hand over the material, you will tell her husband she has it."

"It would never work, Steffi."

"I told you. You'll never understand women . . . until you marry one and then it's too late!"

"Let me think about it."

"While you're thinking about it, here's a little bet. Ten thousand to a thousand the lady doesn't show at the Ambrosiana tomorrow."

"Done! Now what do you fancy for dinner?"

"First I would like a Bacardi cocktail, in company with a redheaded woman. . . ."

He got his Bacardi in Harry's Bar. He got his red-headed woman; but Gisela Pestalozzi was too much even for Steffi's jaded palate. Her appearance struck him dumb, her loud, bawdy talk reduced him to idiot confusion, so that I expected him at any moment to go into fugue and retreat under the table. However, the apartment she showed us was a little gem: with a front entrance that gave onto a quiet alley, a rear one from which you could step straight into a boat and an attic window from which you could climb over the rooftops, as long as the tiles would hold. The heating was more than adequate, the telephone worked, the furniture was worm-free and the linen was fresh. At our first meeting she had called the price at two hundred thousand a month. We settled on a hundred and fifty. There was no lease; the Salamander's name was good enough on both sides. I paid two months' rent in cash. She handed me the key and some advice by way of a bonus:

"If you want a boatman, call me. If you want to bribe a policeman, check with me before you hand over any money. If you're in trouble, stay out of Harry's Bar and use the phone. For false documents, there's a forty-eight-hour service. It costs less if you can give me more time. No wild parties. No brawls. You get resident's discount on my girls. . . . And you, old man, don't be shy. I've had eighty-year-old cripples throw away their crutches. . . ."

She left us with a clatter of baubles and a toss of that extraordinary hair.

Steffi collapsed into a chair and spluttered, "My God! She's straight out of the Wax Museum! . . . Safe house, indeed! With a man-eating monster like that, you'd be safer in a slaughter yard. But what do you want the place for?"

"Don't laugh, Steffi! After tomorrow you may be on the run yourself."

Looking at him then, popeyed and speechless, I remembered one of the less useful facts of history. Pietro Aretino died in Venice. He was no mean pornographer himself, and he died of apoplexy, laughing at a dirty joke.

◆§ §◆

AT ten o'clock the next morning, dressed in a mechanic's cap and overalls and smeared with engine oil, I was tinkering with a scrubby Fiat, sixty meters from the entrance of the Ambrosian Library. There was nothing wrong with the engine; but I was nervous and twitchy, half hoping that Steffi would win his bet and I could call the whole thing off with a good conscience. At ten-fifteen Steffi himself marched down the street, looking for all the world like an elderly professor who could decipher fifteenth-century cursive or decide a disputed interpreta-

tion at the drop of his black fedora. He was whistling
"The Hills Are in Flower," which, if you could recognize
the tune, was a sign that, so far at least, there were no
poliziotti on the horizon.

At ten twenty-five Elena Leporello drove up in a white
Lancia. She was alone, which was another good sign. She
locked the car, put the keys in her handbag and, without
a backward glance, walked into the library, calm and
unflustered as any Milanese matron out for a morning's
shopping. I straightened up, wiped my hands on the grease
rag, lit a cigarette and surveyed the street up and down
from the entrance. There was the usual passage of people.
There were no suspicious loiterers, no convergence of
cars or men that would indicate the imminent arrest of a
dangerous character. *Ebbene!* There was nothing to do
but wait and the waiting could be fairly long, because the
inspection of Petrarch's Virgil is one of the most serious
ceremonies at the Ambrosiana.

The volume is huge. The chief librarian himself must
authorize the inspection. An attendant, reverent and
watchful, must stand beside you as you turn the pages,
illuminated by Simone Martini of Siena. If you cannot
read the inscription, written in the poet's own hand, the
attendant will translate it for you:

> Laura, with all her illustrious virtues and long celebrated
> in my poems, first appeared before my eyes, in my young
> manhood, on the sixth day of April, in the year of our
> Lord 1327 in the early morning, in the Church of St.
> Claire in Avignon ...

I have always had a sentiment for the ceremony. In my
days as a tourist guide I found a reading of Petrarch in
the original worked wonders with impressionable young
women. Now, impatient and sweating with nervousness,
I cursed myself for an idiot. I tossed away my cigarette,
closed the hood of the car and sat inside, watching the
entrance through the rear-vision mirror.

At ten fifty-five Steffi came out with Elena Leporello.
They got into the Lancia and drove off. I followed far

enough behind to see whether any shadow car had joined our cavalcade. In the howling chaos of Milan's traffic it was difficult to be sure of anything, even my own sanity. I saw, or thought I saw, one or two likely followers, but they dropped away. When we came onto the autostrada, I hung well back, letting the cars build up between me and the Lancia; but by the time we passed the Verona exit, I was fairly confident that we were free of shadows. By Padua I was sure of it. I let them drive far ahead of me all the way to Mestre. Steffi's instructions were to cross to Venice, buy the lady a sandwich in St. Mark's Square and leave when I made my appearance. He would then go to the safe house and wait for me. Elena Leporello could drive back to Milan alone. I hoped the strategy might establish in her mind the fact that I had left Milan and was holed up somewhere in the city of the Doges.

I went straight to the house, washed and tidied myself and then, dressed in slacks and a green pullover, walked around to St. Mark's Square. Steffi saw me coming and left before I reached the table.

Elena Leporello gave me a frosty welcome. "I hope, Colonel, there is some sense in this sordid little drama."

"I hope, madam, you will help me make sense of it. Have you heard from Captain Roditi?"

"Not a word."

"Does your husband know where he is?"

"No. He has a team of investigators working night and day on the case. He says he knows what happened at Matteo's apartment. You forced him to write a false and incriminating document, then had him killed or kidnapped."

"And how does he know that?"

"From the notary who witnessed the document in Matteo's apartment. He's been arrested and he has signed a confession."

"Has your husband seen the document?"

"He hasn't said so."

"Then how does he know it's false and incriminating?"

"Obviously the notary told him."

"The notary didn't read the document. He simply stamped and signed it."

"But a document does exist?"

"Yes."

"Is it incriminating?"

"Yes . . . but not false. Would you like to see it?"

"Please."

I handed her a photostat copy of Roditi's confession and watched her closely as she read it. The colour drained from her face. She trembled violently and I thought for a moment she was going to faint. I put out a hand to steady her, but she rejected me with a gesture and continued her reading. By the time she had finished, she was in control of herself again, and the sudden mastery of her emotions was frightening to see. She folded the document carefully and handed it back to me. Then she faced me, cold-eyed and contemptuous.

"That's a tissue of lies, Colonel—monstrous, horrible lies."

"That is Roditi's handwriting."

"But you dictated it; the notary heard you from the bedroom."

"I dictated it after interrogation. Did he hear that, too?"

"He heard your threats, he must have heard the rest of it."

"Are you sure, madam, that everything is false?"

"Everything!"

"Then you and Roditi were not lovers?"

"Of course not."

"I read your letters, madam. I saw your signed photograph. Roditi kept them in the drawer of his dressing table."

"No, Colonel. There are no letters."

"You mean they were removed on your husband's orders. Not all. I have one in my pocket now. I can tell you that the photograph was taken by Donati in Bologna. He made an extra copy for me. . . . Let me tell you something else. Roditi, your lover, was a friend of Giuseppe Balbo, who was killed by the police a few nights ago. I met them together in the Alcibiade. No, madam. The statement doesn't lie. I'm not lying. You are. Why? Are you afraid of your husband? Of what he may do to you or the children?"

"No, Colonel."

"Then listen to me, please. Roditi told me you have material, photographs and tapes which prove against your husband all the charges in that document."

"I have no such material, Colonel."

"But, if your letters mean anything, you loved Roditi. He loved you. He told me so."

"Old love is cold comfort, Colonel."

"He also told me that the tapes and photographs were your only insurance against your husband."

"I have no such material. And I need no insurance."

"Why? Because Roditi's dead?"

"You said that, not I."

"Or because his evidence is discredited and your husband's giving up his little games for the time being? . . . What about you? What sort of a woman are you?"

"I'll tell you the sort of woman I am, Colonel. If my husband is clever enough to handle this mess, then he's clever enough to climb right to the top of the tree. I want to be there, too. If my husband can't make it . . . Boh! There's always another day for me."

"You can settle that question now, madam. There's a policeman over there, and two Carabinieri at the entrance to St. Mark's. Call them. Tell them who I am and have me arrested."

"No, my dear Colonel, I'm not quite sure yet how clever you are and whether you're a match for my husband. It's a game, don't you see? I'm the privileged spectator; I just sit back and enjoy it. I could even enjoy an hour in bed with you, now, if you're interested, and your place isn't too far. . . . No? Another time, perhaps. I'm much better than Laura, you know. . . . By the way, did you hear what happened to her?"

"What?"

"She drove her car into a tree last night. She drinks too much, as you well know. I've warned her many times; my husband has, too."

"Is she badly hurt?"

"The doctors think she'll live, but she could end up as a vegetable. . . . Pity! She was such a pretty girl. Good-bye, Colonel."

She offered me her hand. I could not take it. I would not even stand to salute her going. I sat and watched her walk across the square, head high, hips swinging, jaunty as any girl on the beat. The pigeons rose in clouds as she passed and the waiter, counting my change, sighed dolefully at the waste of so much woman. He was a Venetian, but he had forgotten the cynical wisdom of his forebears. When they sent an ambassador abroad, they let him take his cook. They made him leave his wife at home.

❧ ☙

IT was all defeat and disaster, and there seemed no way to mend it. Steffi summed it up in a terse valediction.

". . . Checkmate! You have no place to go, little brother. Your last hope—and that's a slim one—is the safe-deposit box. I wish I could help you. I can't. I'm going back to Rome. If there's something you need, call me. But take a little advice. . . . Cut out now and join your girl in Switzerland. Let Manzini handle the rest of it. Here you're in a trap. Worse, you're in a vacuum, which is demoralizing. You know the system. They've immobilized you. All they have to do is wait. Sooner or later you'll make a small mistake and they'll spring the trap. I'm fond of you, Matucci—God knows why, because you've given me grief and ulcers! I don't want to see you lopped before you've had a chance to grow up. . . ."

When he had gone, I called Manzini, who was equally gloomy. He told me he had been contemplating a press campaign to stir up the muddy waters, but that the risks were too great: risk of libel action, risk that old laws might be invoked to stop publication, risk that timid friends on the Quirinal might be lost by untimely action, risk of fomenting public disorder. He, too, suggested I move out to Switzerland. He sounded tired and spiritless, and I wondered about the state of his health.

When I put down the phone, I found myself suddenly in the grip of a violent reaction. I cursed and swore and slammed about the apartment in a frenzy of frustration. It was incredible that with so much evidence we could do nothing. It was monstrous that one man could manipulate an arm of the law to make it an instrument of crime. It shamed me that a bastard like Leporello could turn me into a fugitive while his bitch of a wife sat laughing and offering to go to bed with me. And, for a last straw, here I was, in an empty house, with no food or liquor, and suddenly afraid to poke my nose outside the door. To hell with it! I wasn't a criminal. Why should I behave like one? To hell with the whole rotten crew! I would stay!

. . . How I was going to stay was another matter. I needed to think that one out over a meal and a bottle of wine. I didn't bother to change. I strolled down the Calle dei Fabbri and found myself a simple place where the food smelled good and the waiter was friendly. The night was balmy, so I sat outside where I could look at the girls of Venice, who are better in the flesh than Titian ever painted them. I ordered a risotto and a dish of seafood and a bottle of Barolo and settled down like any honest citizen to enjoy my supper. It was a good meal and I relished every mouthful. I was relaxed and happy over my coffee, when two Carabinieri picked me up like an orange and carted me off to the Questura.

They were very polite. They spared me all the usual routine and took me straight to the Commandant. The Commandant looked at my papers and asked me if I was the person therein described: Aldo Carnera, travelling salesman. I assured him I was. I asked whether I was charged with any offense. He assured me I was not. It was simply a question of the green pullover. Had I been in St. Mark's Square that afternoon? I had. Ah! That explained everything.

It told me exactly nothing and I begged to know whether there was anything special about a green pullover. He admitted that he could see nothing special in it, except that he himself was not overly fond of green. However

. . . at three in the afternoon a woman, who declined to give her name, had telephoned the Questura with the information that she had identified a man wearing such a garment as one Dante Alighieri Matucci, wanted for questioning in Milan. She had seen his photograph in the papers.

Now, the Commandant had been informed of the Matucci affair, which was a highly political matter in which he did not wish to embroil himself. He understood that an agent of a secret service often carried a false identification. So, if in fact I was Colonel Matucci, the matter of the forged papers could be easily dealt with. Then he brought out a photograph of me and a set of fingerprints from the SID files. I smiled and he smiled and we agreed that it was the luck of the game.

He offered me a cup of coffee. I asked whether I might make a telephone call. He smiled again and produced an order stating that, when and if Dante Alighieri Matucci were apprehended, he should be held incommunicado, pending instructions from Milan Headquarters. He was going to telephone Milan now. He hated to do this to a senior colleague in the Service. He hoped I understood that there was nothing personal. He begged me to make myself comfortable until he returned.

A wink being as good as a nod to a bland elephant, I used the telephone on his desk, asked for an outside line and dialled an interurban call to Manzini's Milan apartment. The old man was out. His manservant took the message. It was a disappointment, but at least Manzini would know what had happened to me. There was one other crumb of comfort. The Surgeon was dead and I should be spared his tender attentions.

The Commandant was gone a long time. He came back looking grave and preoccupied. He told me that I was now formally under arrest and that I should surrender all my personal belongings, for which he would issue a receipt. His orders were to detain me overnight at the Questura and send me, in the morning, to Milan.

A *brigadiere* escorted me to the detention cell. A turnkey locked me in. About fifteen minutes later the *bri-*

gadiere returned, accompanied by a guard and a man in a white coat carrying a kidney dish covered with a towel. He introduced himself as the police surgeon and asked me to roll up my sleeve. He told me he wanted to give me a sedative. I protested vigorously against this invasion of my rights and my person. The surgeon suggested it would be simpler if I complied, otherwise he would be forced to put me under restraint. I did as I was told. I rolled up my sleeve and twisted it into a tourniquet. I made a fist and presented my arm for the injection. I winced at the prick of the needle and began counting one-two-three. . . .

Then all the lights went out.

BOOK III

We have changed all that.

—MOLIÈRE: *Le Médecin Malgré Lui*

I WOKE—or dreamed I woke—in absolute darkness and absolute silence. I was—or dreamed I was—floating in undetermined space in a timeless continuum. I was not sad; I was not happy; I was not in pain; I simply was. At first that was enough: the floating and the dreaming and the simply being. Then I began to be uneasy, faintly at first, then more and more acutely. Something was absent. I could not define what it was. I could not define anything. My mind was a swirl of mist. I was groping, without hands, into nowhere.

The mist dispersed slowly in drifts and eddies. Slowly and intermittently I began to collect the scattered parts of myself. My thumb encountered my fingertips. My tongue met my palate. My eyelids blinked. Somewhere out in the fog my feet brushed one against another. Then the parts became a whole and I was aware that my body and I were still together. I was able to lift my hand—both my hands—and run them over my face and shoulders and breast and belly and genitals. I was there, naked and lying on a hard, flat surface, warm to the touch.

Then panic engulfed me. I was buried alive. I was blind. I was deaf. I was dumb. When I cried out, no sound would issue from my parched, constricted throat. I broke out into a sweat of terror and curled myself into a fetal ball, huddling away from the horror of nothingness. The panic rose and fell, endlessly, like waves on a beach, but slowly, slowly, it subsided to a ripple, constant, threatening, but, mercifully, no longer a madness. The mist about my mind was tendrils now and cobwebs, but at least I knew I had a mind and must, somehow, begin to use it.

First I directed my body to uncurl itself; and, reluctantly, my body obeyed. Then I asked my fingers to explore my immediate ambience. The slab on which I lay felt like marble or smooth stone. It terminated a few centimeters either side of my body, and above it and all around there was empty space. Below it my fingers encountered a floor, not paved, but rough to the touch. The floor was colder than my slab. How far it stretched, I did not know. Enough that I had found a foothold in reality.

Now I must make a search of my inward self, testing for time holds and memory pegs. This was more difficult. Inside my skull was a kaleidoscope that made patterns, fragmented them, rearranged them, dissolved them into monochrome fluid. I was lifted on a wave of panic, dropped into despair, tumbled over and over in an undertow, floated free again.

At last one picture held, one peg was firm: a woman walking through a cloud of pigeons, a man in a green pullover sitting at a table watching her. I could go forward from that. I could go back from it. I found myself weeping quietly in the dark. The tears were good. They fell like oil on the panic waters. When they were spent, I knew that I was still a man. I knew, and I knew that I knew, what had happened to me and what would happen very soon.

If you walk through the museums of the world you will find a variety of instruments of torture: racks, thumbscrews, barbed whips, iron maidens, pincers, branding irons, machines for electric shocks. The most potent instruments of all you will never see. They are darkness and silence. Each is an absence, a negation. Darkness is a negation of light. Silence is a negation of sound. Evil, said Thomas Aquinas, is an absence of good. My namesake, Dante Alighieri, wrote a poem about hell which has become one of the world's classics. I stand now to witness that he did not know what he was talking about. Hell is nothing but a dark and silent room. Damnation means to be locked inside it—alone.

Please let me explain. It is necessary to me. Come the day of the tyrants, it may be necessary for you, too, to understand it. Do you know the word *parameter*? Many people use it, too few understand its meaning or its importance. The dictionary defines it as "a quantity constant in the case considered, but varying in different cases." Admit it now: the definition means little, if anything, to you. But suppose one night you went to sleep and when you woke in the morning the campanile or the oak tree that was always framed in your window was not there. Suppose you opened the door to your kitchen and found instead a rose garden. The constant quantities in your life would be gone. You would be lost. You would say: I do not know where I am. If the changes continued day after day, you would become a victim of their inconstancy. You would say in the end: I do not know who I am.

But suppose. . . . Suppose, suddenly, all the constants are gone: the steeple and the kitchen and the sunrise and the sunset and the sun and the moon and the stars and even the light. . . ? Suppose the inconstants, too, are taken away: the cars in the street, the doves in the cabbage garden, the dripping tap, the passing clouds, the wind, the sound of rain, the vagrant human voices. . . ? Then you are damned beyond redemption.

This is what happens when you close a man inside a dark and silent room and leave him. He has nothing against which he can measure himself except the confines of the floor, and the monotony of that measurement helps to drive him mad. He has no sense of height, no sense of time. He is cut off from his past. He has no expectation of the future. His present is darkness and silence. He cannot divert himself with the minutest things —a fly buzzing against a windowpane, an ant crawling across the floor, dust motes in a sunbeam. His only points of reference are the contours of his body, the fixed contours of the walls and the floor and his sleeping place, and the little world of memory inside his own skull case. And these are less, much less, than enough to keep him sane.

I can tell you what happens because it happened to me. It was planned to happen. It was contrived, inflicted, as the subtlest vengeance any man could contrive against another. . . . You are alone in this dark and silent nowhere. You say to yourself: I know who I am. I know what they are trying to do to me. I will not let them do it. I will retreat into my skull case and live there, feeding on memory and hope and faith and love, the whole capital of a lifetime. I will hold fast to the facts I know: that this nowhere is, in truth, a somewhere; that outside there are humans and animals and solid, tangible things. I know that they will have to feed me, or at least give me something to drink. This perpetual non-motion is as impossible as perpetual motion. Something has to break, sometime; else why would they take all this trouble to torment me. Someone will come, if only to gloat. Otherwise it would have been simpler to put a bullet in my head and toss me in a ditch.

. . . Eh-eh-eh! It is all illusion. Nobody comes. The silence and the darkness remain unbroken. You discover, in your first circuit of the walls, that they have left three plastic demijohns of water, enough to keep you alive for a long, long time. You discover other things, too. The world inside your skull case becomes quickly confused. You grasp for one memory and find another. Pictures flash by and you cannot hold them in focus. You lean on hope and collapse into weeping despair. You try to pray and find yourself cursing. You recite poems and hear yourself babbling nonsense. After three days, though you have long since forgotten time, you are hallucinating constantly, and, even if anybody came, you would not know whether they were real or not.

This is the trick of it, you see. They do come, but you do not know. They scoop you up from the floor and pump barbiturates into you to continue the hallucination. They drip enough glucose into your veins to keep you alive, and they feed you with new fears to drive you closer and closer to the cliff edge of permanent derangement. I learned later that I was there fifteen days. When they brought me out, I was blind for a while, and dumb and ataxic, shambling like an animal, bearded and filthy from my own droppings. They put me under deep sedation for forty-eight hours, and when I came out of it, I was sure I had died and arrived, by some cosmic mistake, in Paradise.

❦ ❧

THERE was so much light, I could only bear it for the shortest while and then must close my eyes and shut it out. There were flowers on a table. I remember that they were iris, blue and yellow and plum purple. Always, when I opened my eyes, there was a pretty nurse in the room, sometimes close to the bed, sometimes sitting in an armchair, reading. For a time I thought she was Lili; but later, when I could concentrate a little, she told me her name was Claudia and that I had been very ill, but now I was getting better.

Whenever the light began to fade, I would become restless and fretful, scared that it would go out altogether. But it never did. Always another nurse came in and turned on the lamps, and even when I slept there was always a small light burning. The night nurse was not so pretty as Claudia, but she was very gentle and solicitous. She was very patient, too. Sometimes I talked and talked until I couldn't stop myself. At others, I was morose and silent, staring at the small circle of light on the ceiling, hating myself, hating everything, unable to change the fixed and horrible trend of my thoughts. When I talked, she listened. When I was silent, she talked, a steady stream of soothing, meaningless gossip that lulled me at last into a doze.

Every day the doctor came and examined me and chatted for a little while about my illness, which he said was a psychic dysfunction induced by my experience in confinement. It would cure itself, he told me. All it needed was time and patience, a little sedation and the simple therapy of human communication. A couple more days of complete rest and he would let me walk in the garden. When I asked him where I was, he told me I was in his clinic and left it at that.

I told him I was troubled with nightmares. He nodded sagely and said that this, too, was a curative process: the subconscious mind working on the intolerable to make it tolerable. I told him that I had difficulty remembering, that I could not concentrate even on a page of print, and that to reason through the simplest proposition was an enormous effort. He explained that this was the natural response of an organism taxed beyond endurance. It simply refused to function until it was rested and ready. When I asked whether I was still under arrest, he smiled and told me that I was free, but that I needed to be prepared if I were to enjoy the freedom I had.

It was all pleasantly vague; but gradually, one by one, new parameters were established and I began to take a more confident hold on the realities around me. The distant realities were still vague. I thought often about Lili and Manzini and Steffi, but I could not grasp them as present or regret them too much as absent. They would come, or I would go to them, in some near future, which I did not need, as yet, to determine by days or weeks. My whole concept of time was still rather uncertain. I never once asked the date or the time of day. The inimical realities, Leporello, his wife, the Director, were so vague as to be almost irrelevant. In some fashion, which I could not yet describe, I had survived them. I had walked through them as if they were a paper wall and come out on the other side. When I looked back I saw only tattered images blown by the wind.

When they allowed me out of bed for the first time, I was astonished to find how weak and insecure I was. My sense of balance had been impaired and I felt as though

I were listing, now to one side, then to the other. If I turned my head too suddenly, I became dizzy. And the first short walk to the window left me weak and trembling. Even the view outside proved a shock. I saw it first in a single dimension. Then, quite suddenly, it solidified and fell into perspective.

There was a belvedere, set with cane chairs and bright umbrellas. Beyond the belvedere was a lawn, broken by flower gardens, and then an unbroken wall of cypresses, dark against a limpid sky. It was pleasant to look at, but it told me nothing. There were no people, no landmarks. After a few moments I was bored with it and glad to go back to bed. Claudia sponged my damp forehead and smoothed my pillows and closed my eyes with the tips of her fingers and told me to go to sleep.

When I woke, the night-light was burning and Bruno Manzini was standing at the foot of my bed. He came to me and took my hands between his own and held them a long time in a wordless greeting. Suddenly, and without reason, I was weeping. Manzini took the handkerchief from his breast pocket and wiped the tears from my cheeks. Then he perched himself on the edge of the bed and talked me back to composure.

". . . Eh! It's been a rough road, hasn't it, my Dante? But you've survived it. Another ten days will see you out of here. Then I'm taking you home with me to Pedognana. You'd like that, wouldn't you?"

"Yes, I would. I feel so weak and lost. I don't know what's the matter with me."

"You've had your season in hell, my friend. It takes time to recover from that."

"I suppose so. Where is this place?"

"Near Como. It's a small psychiatric clinic. I finance it. . . . Oh, don't worry, you're quite sane; but you wouldn't have been if they'd held you much longer."

"How did I get here?"

"I brought you. It took me ten days and a lot of bribery to find where they were holding you. Then I had to get a judicial order for your release. That was harder;

but we managed it. You're on provisional liberty, of course. Charges still lie against you."

"I can't imagine why Leporello let me go."

"He was convinced you were broken beyond repair. And the Movement would have lost a large check from me. He may still get you into court. Fortunately, we now have medical evidence of the treatment to which you were submitted, and I don't think he wants that revealed just yet."

"You've no idea what it's like . . . no idea . . ."

"It's over now—finished. I am proud of you, my Dante."

"Everything's in pieces. I—I can't put them together."

"You put it all together before this happened. We have everything in our hands. Your notes on the microfilms, the tapes and the photographs from the bank. We can break Leporello now—and the Director after him."

"Do you know what happened to Roditi?"

"Oh, yes. He's on indefinite sick leave. They put him through the treatment, too. He's no danger to Leporello now and no use to anyone else."

"I'm afraid I'm not going to be much use to you, either."

"Listen to me, my Dante, and listen well. . . . You are a lucky man, too lucky to have pity for yourself. You cannot surrender now. You will not; because if you do, you hand the victory to Leporello and all you have suffered will be useless. Also, you have cost me an enormous sum of money. . . . Come, man! I have been where you are now. I have climbed the dark mountain and come down into sunlight on the other side. You will, too. . . ."

"I'm so tired . . ."

"Try a little hating, my friend. It's the best stimulant in the world."

"It's all too big and complicated. I just want to drop it and get out."

"Easy now, relax. We'll talk about it another time. I'll see you again in a few days."

I was glad to see him go. I wanted to feel sorry for

myself. I deserved a little pity and this terrible old man had none. I would put him out of my mind. Later, when I was well, I would shut him out of my life.

Next day I was stronger and I sat for an hour on the terrace looking at the pictures in the scandal magazine. The day after, I made my first circuit of the garden with Claudia and found that I could walk without staggering and talk without confusion and fatigue. In the evening I watched a cabaret show on television and found myself laughing at the comedian and beating time to the music and wondering why my nurse wasn't there to share the pleasure with me.

My sedatives were withdrawn that night for the first time, and I was swirled through a series of disconnected dreams, so that I woke red-eyed and irritable, but aware that I had gained much ground on the climb up the dark mountain. After that I walked in the garden every morning, ambling like a monk in meditation, from one end of the lawn to the other, soaking up the sun and the colour of the flowers, knowing that the parameters were holding firm and I was beginning to be a man again. I was reading print now, colour magazines and light novels, which I never finished because my concentration still waned after an hour. The newspapers were brought to me, but I did not open them. Newspapers were today. Newspapers were a responsibility which I was not yet ready to shoulder.

Then Manzini came to see me again. He brought a bottle of champagne and a pot of fresh caviar, and we made a picnic on the terrace and afterwards strolled around the garden. He approved the change in me, but I was wary of him. I did not want him to disturb my still precarious comfort. He did not disturb it. He shattered it with a single stroke.

"I have bad news for you, my Dante. Lili Anders is back in Italy. She is in prison in the Mantellate in Rome."

"No . . . it can't be true."

"It is. Your Director called me yesterday to announce the good news. He asked me to pass it on to you."

"But why? How? Did the Swiss deport her?"

"She came back of her own accord. She entered the

country by way of the Brenner and was arrested by the border police."

"But that's madness! I don't understand it!"

"It seems you called her back, by telegram."

"How could I? I've been out of action for nearly four weeks."

"That's the way the Director tells it. Your telegram said she was free to return. You would meet her in Bolzano and you would make immediate arrangements to get married. She was carrying the telegram in her handbag. She produced it when the frontier police looked her up in the Black Book and questioned her."

"It was a trap!"

"Of course. But she walked into it."

"We've got to get her out."

"How, my Dante? You collected the evidence against her. You prepared her dossier. You broke her network and jailed her master, the Woodpecker. You can hardly refute your own testimony, can you?"

"But the Director promised to let her go."

"He did. She came back. Illegal entry, for a start."

"Mother of God! What a stinking, filthy mess! I've got to get out of here, Bruno!"

"I'm not sure that's wise."

"I don't give a curse whether it's wise or not. I can discharge myself. Let's go back. I'll do it now."

"If that's what you want, so be it."

We were halfway back across the lawn when a sudden thought stopped me dead in my tracks. I caught his arm and, heedless of his age and his infirmity, swung him around to face me. I challenged him brutally:

"Did you arrange this, Bruno?"

There was not a tremor in him. He stood straight and firm as a pine tree, staring me down. His eyes were cold. His mouth, under that great eagle's beak, was tight as a trap.

"Do you think me capable of it?"

"Yes, I do."

"Good. Then you have learned something."

"Did you do it?"

"I might have—if I had thought it useful. In fact, I did not. I think you did, sometime in those fifteen days of dysfunction and hallucination. I know that you told things about me, because I had to lie about them later. I know we nearly missed the safe-deposit box, because Leporello did get a judicial order to open it the day after we had extracted the contents."

"Oh, Christ, I'm sorry!"

"Don't be sorry. Think about those who made a traitor out of you against your will."

"I'll kill the bastards."

"They'll expect you to try. They'll be waiting for you. And if they take you a second time, there'll be no escape. . . . No, Dante, this time we'll do it my way. . . . Now, let's talk to the doctor. You're not setting foot outside the gate until he tells me you're ready."

The doctor was hesitant and very dubious. He was prepared to let me go only on condition that I understood the risks. I was still convalescent. There were still dysfunctions which would become acute again under stress. My memory would play tricks. My concentration would be limited for a long time. I would be subject to fits of depression and anxiety. I should not throw away too quickly the crutch of sedatives and tranquilizers. For the rest, I should trust to nature and not try to force myself too fast along the road.

It was easy to say, impossible to do, with the guilt of Lili's betrayal nagging at me like an aching tooth. The moment we drove out the gates of the clinic and into the sunny countryside of Lombardy, I lapsed into deep despondency. It was Lili who should be at liberty and not I. It was Lili who should be travelling in luxury with the sun on her face and all the world smiling back at her. Instead, she was penned with thieves and prostitutes and child-slayers in a medieval hellhole on the banks of the Tiber.

Manzini let me brood a while and then faced me with a blunt question. "How serious are you about this woman of yours?"

"I love her."

"Enough to marry her?"

"I've already asked her."

"When?"

"I wrote her just before I left Pedognana last time. I gave you the letter to mail through Chiasso."

"I thought you were supposed to be her uncle Pavel."

"I wasn't when I wrote the letter."

"Wasn't that rather foolish?"

"On the face of it, yes."

"So, you don't know whether she wants to marry you or not?"

"No. . . . Why?"

"A vague thought. Let me play with it a while. . . . There's something else more important. I think we know the date of the *colpo di stato*."

"When?"

"October thirty-first, mid-autumn. The tourists have gone home. Diplomats have returned from the summer holidays. Training programs have been completed. Transport still functions freely, which it doesn't in mid-winter. More importantly, the word is being whispered among the initiates . . . and it checks with dates mentioned in your notes on the microfilms."

"That's five months ahead."

"Never count on time, Dante. It runs away too quickly. Opinion is hardening on both sides. Leporello is a splendid organizer, and you are not the only one he has eliminated or immobilized. The Milan bomb cases have not been brought to trial. Several important witnesses have disappeared; others have been systematically intimidated. No, we have to move before summer."

"What do you want me to do?"

"For the moment, exactly what the doctor has ordered —rest and recuperate. However, there is one thing which you can do without prejudice to your health."

"What's that?"

"Entertain your friends. I presume you do have friends of your own rank and standing in the Corps?"

"Some, yes. But they're scattered up and down the

country. I'm a bad correspondent. It's hard to keep in touch."

"Now you will have time. Write a few letters. Make some direct calls. You've been ill. You've been in personal strife. You would like to see them sometime at Pedognana. We have plenty of guest rooms. There is riding and shooting . . . They'll come."

"What are you looking for now, Bruno?"

"A praetorian guard. Ten men would be enough, so long as they were resolute and understood what was at stake. On your own showing, there's quite a large amount of disaffection from Leporello and his policies."

"If you're asking me to stage a revolt of the armed forces, Bruno, forget it. I'm not very bright at this moment, but that's mystical madness."

"Who said anything about revolt? On the contrary, we need men proud of the traditions of the Corps, jealous of its honour and its oath; old-fashioned patriots, who don't like seeing their fellow citizens kicked in the teeth and justice denied by perjured witness."

"Buy me a tub and a lamp, Bruno. I might have a better chance."

"We're bitter today, aren't we, my Dante? But I agree. Go play Diogenes. But find me ten good men willing to put their heads on the block for one night. . . . Oh, by the way, I brought your clothes back from the apartment. You've lost some weight, but they'll still fit. I can't bear that rubbish you're wearing now."

He would not tell me any more and I was too tired to press him. I lay back in the seat and dozed fitfully until we drove through the gates of Pedognana.

At cocktails that evening I discovered there was another guest at the villa: the Principessa Pia Faubiani, prima donna of Roman fashion, mistress of Bruno Manzini. She was slim, dark, leggy, flat-busted and, if you favour the pinched and glacial *modella,* very attractive. At first meeting I did not favour her at all. I was edgy, jealous of my privacy and in no mood to lavish on her the attention which she very obviously demanded. I was also mistrustful, because of Manzini's equivocal description of his relations with her. However, this was his house and he could open it to whom he liked. The least I could do was to exert myself to be agreeable.

I was amply rewarded for my pains. Pia Faubiani was a witty and intelligent woman, with enough malice to survive in the rough world she exploited, and more than enough affection and good humour to spend on her friends. I was glad I wasn't married to her—her claws were too sharp for comfort; but for playmate and boon companion . . . yes, without a second thought.

She was wearing the salamander pin from Fosco's exhibition, and when I commented on it, she announced cheerfully, "It's a parting gift. This is my first and last season with Bruno."

Manzini chuckled and held up his glass in a toast. "You're too young and I'm too old, my lover, and I hate to be second best at anything. Besides, the way you're going, you'll need a bank of your own, just to pay the interest bills. This woman, Dante, is the best designer and the worst accountant in the business. I keep telling her she'll either marry a gold mine or end in debtors' prison."

"I was thinking of a convent, darling, now that you've deserted me."

"I've never deserted a woman in my life and you know it. I've just retired from the field—with honour."

"With honour! Listen to the man! You're an old fox, Bruno! *Buon giorno—buona notte—ciao, bambina*—and you're over the hills and far away, licking your chops as you go. This man, Dante, has had as many mistresses as I've had birthdays, and I don't think he's ever been in love in his life. . . . Have you ever been in love, Dante?"

"Handle him gently, Pia. He's in love and his woman's in jail."

"Oh, I'm sorry. . . ."

"So you're going to cheer him up for me."

It was obviously as much of a shock to her as it was to me. She sat with a morsel of cream cake poised precariously on the end of her fork and gaped at Manzini. "I am? I'm glad you told me, darling."

"If you drop that cake, you'll spoil a very expensive dress. Put it in your mouth, like a good girl. . . . No wonder God gets bored, Dante. Nobody ever gives him any surprises. Now. where was I? Oh, yes: what you, my Pia, are going to do for me. When do you open your show in Bologna?"

"Next Wednesday."

"And in Milan and Turin?"

"Each one ten days after the other."

"After that you're free."

"Well, not exactly free, darling. I have to go back to Rome and . . ."

"I know, but you'd come for at least a couple of days, wouldn't you? For last season's sake?"

"Of course, but why?"

"I want you to hostess a party for me, here, at Pedognana. I've been promising to introduce Dante to people ever since he came to Milan. He's had a rough time, as I told you, and I think he needs some diversion."

"Please, Bruno! A party's the last thing I need."

"It may be the last one you'll get, if you go to trial. Besides, there's a month yet to get used to the idea. Enjoy, man! Enjoy! They'll be toasting our funerals soon enough. . . . You'll do it for me, won't you, Pia?"

"You know I will."

"And if you see this fellow moping around like a barn-yard owl, take him out, introduce him to your girls, seduce him yourself if you like . . . But bounce him out of his miseries, understand?"

"Your servant, Cavaliere."

"I wish you were, my love. I think we'd have lasted longer. Still, it's been fun, hasn't it. . . ?"

She laid a hand on his and said gently, "It's been fun, *caro*. And I'm sorry about . . ."

"Enough, please! I've had a good life and I'm very grateful for it. Also, I'm tougher than they think. . . . And I'll tell you something, my Pia. I have been in love, twice, in my life. That's more than enough for any man."

"I know about Raquela, darling. That's something even I wouldn't joke about. But who was the other one?"

"My wife."

We both stared at him then. He gave us an odd, embarrassed little smile and a shrug of apology.

"I'm sorry. I wasn't trying to surprise you this time. I've been thinking a lot about her lately, wondering if we'll meet again, and if we do will we recognize each other. . . . I married her in Paris in 1934. She was nineteen years old. I was thirty-five. I had travelled all over the world and I thought she was the most beautiful creature in it. I brought her back here to Pedognana and she fell in love with the place at first sight. Ask some of the old ones and you'll find they still remember her riding the rounds with the factor, kneeling in the chapel on Sunday, with all the children about her.

"She was born to the land. Her people farmed a big estate near Poitiers. This place flowered under her hand in those two strange years. . . . You're too young to remember it, my Pia, but they were very strange. We had an empire then. We took Addis Ababa and annexed Ethiopia. Ciano became foreign minister, Farouk became King of Egypt, Germany occupied the Rhineland, and Charlie Chaplin made *Modern Times*. . . . But here at Pedognana we were almost able to forget the madness that was going on around us. We were ludicrously happy. My affairs were prospering. If things went wrong in Europe, I had capital planted and growing abroad, and, best of all, Marie Claire became pregnant. For a man like me, who had never known a family life, this was like the announcement of the Second Coming. I was out of my mind with delight. I was bubbling with wild plans for my son's future—because, of course, it had to be a son.

"In the fourth month of her pregnancy Marie Claire fell sick and died within a week, of cerebrospinal meningitis. . . . She's buried in the chapel here on the estate. I know you're not a praying man, Dante, but you'd have seen the inscription if you'd bent that stubborn neck of yours. Marie Claire, beloved wife of Bruno Manzini. Born

Paris, April 20, 1915. Died Pedognana, June 17, 1936. Requiescat . . . Boh! Long ago and far away. Let's have coffee in the study. It's cozier there."

When the coffee was brought, he refused it and announced abruptly that he was going to bed. Pia Faubiani made a move to go with him, but he pushed her gently back into the chair and bent to kiss her on the forehead. His tone was very tender.

"Stay here, my love. I'm very tired tonight."

"But darling . . ."

"Don't worry. I'll sleep. Tomorrow we'll talk about the party. . . . Good night, my Dante. Think about the praetorian guard, won't you? It's very important. Golden dreams to you both."

When he had gone, Pia Faubiani kicked off her shoes, curled herself in the armchair and gave a deep sigh of relaxation and contentment. "*Dio!* I'm so glad it's ended like this! He's one man in the world I wouldn't want to hurt. I never thought I'd let any man dismiss me, but that one—God bless him—is very particular."

"I know what you mean."

"You're rather particular, too, Dante Alighieri. I can't quite read you yet."

"Don't try, Pia. I'm a mess just now. You'd get the wrong reading, anyway."

"Bruno loves you."

"I know. He's told me."

"How do you feel about him?"

"I don't know. I admire him very much. I wish sometimes I could be like him. I fight him often. I never quite understand him. . . . How sick is he?"

"He's not sick at all, really. He's an old man. His heart's tired and wearing itself out. He could go quickly and he knows it. I think he's more afraid of lingering too long. His big regret is that he doesn't have a son. . . . Wasn't that a sad little story about his wife?"

"Very. It's the shortest story I've ever heard him tell. . . . What are you going to do now?"

"Me? The same, with someone else's money. I'm a

pretty hardy plant, you know. Give me a little sun and I can grow anywhere. Tell me about yourself."

"What's to tell? I am an intelligence man who thought he could break the system. Instead the system broke me."

"You don't believe that."

"I do. Look at my hands. I can't hold a glass steady. Do you know why? I'm scared to go to bed and switch off the light. I know it will pass, but I'm still scared."

"Did they hurt you in prison?"

"No. Nobody touched me. Would you like another brandy?"

"Yes, please. I don't want to go to bed either."

"What are you afraid of?"

"If I told you, you wouldn't believe me."

"Try me."

"Getting old and raddled like Coco Chanel and having some bright boy write a musical about me."

"I promise you, Pia *mia,* it will never happen."

"Can you swear that?"

"On the bones of my ancestors."

"Then I'll make you a promise, too, Dante. You'll sleep well tonight."

And I did sleep well. I had no nightmares, either. In the morning across the breakfast table Bruno Manzini blessed us with a grin and a Venetian proverb: *"El leto xe' una medicina . . .* Bed is a medicine." As usual, the old monster was right.

~§ §~

I FOUND I could not write letters, so I made telephone calls from one end of the country to the other. I talked to men who had once been friends and were no longer. I talked to friends who were delighted to gossip but were always too busy to make a train journey to a place so outlandish as Pedognana. There were others who said they would be delighted to come but found it hard to set a date. There were a few, six only, who expressed a care for an old friend and a concern about what they heard had been done to him. These would give up their leave and come on various days to have a meal and a chat with me. I wondered, with growing disillusion, why there were so few of them. As we sat in the study, examining papers and photographs and tapes, Manzini gave me his own answer:

"Cattle smell the wind, my Dante. They turn their tails to it and wait for it to pass. Reeds bend with the wind and sing whatever music it plays on them. Chaff blows away in the gusts and only the good grain settles. Be grateful, however small the harvest. I talked to Frantisek at the Vatican today. If you want, he will visit your Lili in the Mantellate. If she wants to marry you, we can perhaps arrange for you to visit her so that you can become betrothed in the prison. The regulations provide for that, but you must be very sure what you want. You cannot live a lifetime on guilt and pity. Besides, you have to face the fact that we may not get her out. The law in this country is a madness out of the Dark Ages. People can rot in prison for years without a trial. And there is nothing so destructive as a disappointed hope. So think carefully before you lay new burdens on the girl. . . ."

I knew I must. I knew equally that I could not determine myself to a lifetime of lonely fidelity. I was not proud to admit it—God help me!—but the fact was there, brutal and inescapable. I tried to put it out of my mind and concentrate on the work in hand, which was the collation of all the material at our disposal to see if it added up to a case which would unseat Leporello and the Director.

There were two problems. My notes on the microfilms from Ponza were third-hand material collated from memory. Even the originals had belonged to Pantaleone and represented his plans for a military coup, not those of Leporello. From an intelligence point of view, my material was valuable. From a judicial one, it was quite invalid. All we had left, therefore, were the photographs and tapes of Leporello's sexual activities in Roditi's apartment in Milan. With these we could make a scandal; but, in Italy at least, the scandal could be suppressed because the law forbids the publication of obscene material. We could publish the material outside the country, but then we would be open to suspicion of forgery and the accusation of political chicanery. However, we might yet be forced to take that risk.

Whether we could make a case out of the obscene material was even more problematic. Photographs can be forged very easily. Roditi could testify to their authenticity, but Roditi had succumbed to the brainwashing and was no longer a competent witness. The tapes were even more dubious evidence. Leporello could be identifid by a voice print, but the defense could claim that the tapes themselves had been edited and thus constituted a forgery.

There was another problem, too. Sexual misdemeanour is the commonest human aberration, and while everyone loves scandal, public sympathy is generally on the side of the offender—unless children are involved, which in this case they were not. If we could identify Leporello's partners as junior members of his own service, then we would have a case, and a strong one, to have him cashiered. . . . But, as Manzini pointed out, this was a long way from murder and political conspiracy, and the high men, including the Director, would still go untouched. Roditi could have proved murder. Balbo had committed it. But Balbo was dead and Roditi lost to us.

At the end of an hour's discussion we decided to concentrate our case on the photographs. I borrowed a magnifying glass from Manzini and settled down to study them minutely. There were more than thirty in all, some of them clear, some of them out of focus, some so contorted in their poses that it was impossible to identify the participants. We had Leporello. There was no doubt of that. I was concerned to see if I could identify any of his partners. The problem was that we had only contact prints of thirty-five-millimeter size and each one had to be examined minutely. It would have been easier in a studio, with full equipment available, but the material was so explosive we dared not yet commit it to other hands.

Finally I was lucky. In one frame there was a man whom I could almost certainly identify—Giuseppe Balbo. In another there was a face which, though less clear, was very familiar to me. I groped vainly for the name, but my memory, jolted and jarred by my experience, failed me every time. I called Manzini and showed him what I had found.

He was jubilant. "If that's Balbo, then we have all we need. A known criminal, probably a murderer, whom we can identify from a thumbprint and your testimony, and who was killed by Leporello's men in Leporello's zone of command. Yes, that would do it! The other one. . . . Well, he'll come back to you. . . . Now, listen! We can't afford to let this stuff out of our hands. We'll have to bring all the equipment we need into the villa. Can you do the job?"

"No, only the basics. This needs an expert. One we can trust."

"Then let's bring one in from outside. I'll call my people in Zurich and they can find a man and fly him down. We're coming closer, my Dante . . . two steps closer. Maybe your party will be a victory celebration after all. I'll call Zurich now. You lock that stuff away. We mustn't scandalize the servants."

It was still an hour to lunchtime, so I walked out onto the terrace and paced up and down, trying to reason calmly about Lili's situation. Wherever I looked, there was no way out for her. Escape was impossible. Acquittal was unthinkable. There was enough material in my dossiers alone to convict her twenty times over. The Director could recommend deportation or exchange if he saw a political advantage in either. All his advantage lay in keeping her in Italy.

The afterthought was even less comforting. Lili knew her own plight better than I. The thing she feared most was now a present reality: the small room, the lights, the questions that came from nowhere. She could not bargain even for a respite. I had robbed her of the last face cards in the pack. Having once tasted liberty and hope, how would she tolerate despair?

Manzini came out to join me, rubbing his hands with satisfaction. The equipment we needed was already being packed in Milan. His expert would fly in from Zurich tomorrow. When the news failed to cheer me, he frowned and snapped at me:

"Matucci, stop it! I refuse to spoon-feed you anymore. Your Lili is no child. She will survive if she wishes. So long as she survives, there is hope. You do her no service with self-torment or self-denial either! Now, have you put a name to that face in the photograph?"

"Not yet."

"Keep trying. I have set the date of the party for four weeks from now. My secretary is working on the guest list and the invitations. It will be a gala affair. This old place needs some life put into it. So do I, for that matter—and you."

"Truly, Bruno, I don't see . . ."

"You don't see the nose on your own face, Dante Ali-ghieri! That's your problem. Look! You think you can go back to the Service again? Never—even if they wash you in the blood of the lamb and give you a new baptismal robe. So you have to start again. Where do you start? As a *spazzino,* sweeping up rubbish in the streets? Of course not. You want to begin as far up the ladder as you can. For that you need friends and recommendations. Hence the party. . . . And, because it's my party, too, it must be something everyone will want to attend and everyone will remember. *'Che vale petere . . . e poi culo stringere.* . . . If you're going to fart, don't tighten up. It strains the arse.' I've left a book in your bedroom; you might find it instructive. . . ."

The book was the *Ricordi* of Francesco Guicciardini, and I read it after dinner in the study, because Bruno retired early and Pia Faubiani had not returned from Bologna. My father was a great reader, and I had learned the habit from him; though latterly, between chasing in-formation and chasing women, I had fallen out of it. Now, like sick Satan, I was disposed to be contemplative, and I found the experience rather pleasant. I also found that Messer Francesco Guicciardini was very entertaining com-pany.

Like me, he was a Tuscan born, a Florentine, who at

twenty-nine was named by the Republic as ambassador
to the King of Spain. Pope Leo X, Medici of the Medici,
made him Governor of Reggio and Modena and Parma,
and Pope Clement VII made him Lieutenant General of
the Papal armies. He was utterly without mercy, but he
knew how to govern and he loved women of all kinds
and ages and conditions. The only man who could handle
him was Cosimo de' Medici, who climbed to power on
his shoulders and then kicked him into retirement. But
Guicciardini was a natural survivor. He retired grace-
fully, grew vines, wrote books and died peacefully of a
stroke at fifty-eight.

The *Ricordi* were his secret memorials, a kind of diary
of opinion and experience, which he was wise enough
never to expose in his lifetime and which were published
centuries after his demise. Manzini had marked several
passages and annotated them in his precise script.

"To be open and frank is a noble and generous thing,
but often harmful. On the other hand, it is useful and
often indispensable to dissemble and deceive, because men
are evil by nature." (So smile, my Dante. Show them you
are a man who has no care in the world, because you have
aces in your sleeve!)

"I do not blame those who, on fire with love of country, confront dangers to establish liberty . . . though I think
that what they do is very risky. Few revolutions succeed
and, even if they do, you find very often they didn't win
what you hoped . . ." (Which is why I draw back from
public disorder and seek rather to seduce the ungodly in
secret.)

"Nearly all men are more concerned for their own
interest than for glory and honour." (Remember this
when you come to confront the Director, who is a quite
unbearable patriot.)

"I believe that a good citizen . . . should maintain
friendly relations with the tyrant, not only for his own
security, but also for everyone else's good." (Which is
why I pay money to the Movement and dine the Director,
and plot with you to bring them down. You have wondered, and I know it!)

"Do not take people too seriously when they prate the advantages of freedom. . . . If they could find a good job in a tyrannical state, they would rush to take it." (I would go further. If they could be tyrants themselves, they would climb over a mountain of skulls to arrive.)

"My position under several Pontiffs has forced me to seek their glorification for my own profit." (I wonder if the Director had this in mind when he cast his vote in favour of Leporello. Think about this as a motive for murder. Old Guicciardini had a lot of people executed in his time.)

"The past illuminates the future; the world has always been the same. . . . The same things come back with different names under different colours . . ." (You and I, my Dante, are trying to change the course of history. But let's not expect too much. The river is still the same.)

"Nobody knows his subjects as little as their ruler." (This is what we are betting on, you and I. They think they have bought me. They know they have frightened you. They do not understand we have not yet begun to fight back.)

It was at that point that I laid down the book and went upstairs to bed. I still could not turn out the light, but lay a long time, wakeful, staring at the ceiling, until Pia Faubiani came home from Bologna.

⋖ ⋗

NEXT day a variety of things began to happen at Pedognana. The artisans of the estate marched in force to the villa and in the space of a few hours converted an attic suite into a very passable photographic studio. The expert arrived from Zurich, was briefed, sworn to secrecy and set to work installing the new equipment which had arrived from Milan. Early in the evening Corrado Buoncompagni, the editor of Manzini's newspaper, arrived in company with a tubby little Torinese, whom he presented as Milo de Salis, the noted film director.

We were five at dinner that night—Manzini, Pia, Milo de Salis, Buoncompagni and myself. The photographer dined alone in his suite and continued working into the night. The meal turned into a council of war, at which Manzini exposed, for the first time, the scope of his design. I had seen him in many moods and acting out many roles, but I had never quite grasped him as the director of giant enterprises, a strategist of great and risky campaigns. Now, at last, I saw him plain and was amazed at the subtlety and the audacity of his genius. He was calm, dispassionate, unhurried, and yet he held us as no orator could have done.

". . . I ask no oaths of you, my friends. From this moment we are all conspirators. We are all at risk. All of you understand the nature of the risk. We shall have to use other people. That is unavoidable. We give them only the information they need to carry out their tasks. For the rest, we lie, conceal, confuse and obfuscate, so that the true issue is clear only to us, inside this room.

"I will define that issue. We are attempting to discredit and remove from power men who wish to impose by force, or threat of force, a government by dictation. We believe that this form of government is unacceptable to the vast majority of people. We know, however, that it can be imposed, as it has been in the past, and that with all the modern mechanisms of control it could be held in power for a very long time. Therefore, we must abort the *colpo di stato,* which we know is already planned.

"The means at our disposal are limited. They are limited by considerations of humanity and common prudence, and by the nature of the democratic process itself. We have in our hands explosive information which, if improperly handled, would confuse the public mind and lead to civil disorders, which themselves would provide the best excuse in the world for an imposed order. We cannot appeal directly to the people, who are already torn between the factions. We must appeal to those in power on the basis of their own self-interest, whether that interest be blind or enlightened. In other words, we work within the context of the history of this country and not of any other. Here the people speak but are not heard. Therefore, we do not attempt to manipulate the many-headed monster. Instead we threaten those who are afraid of the monster: ministers of state, big public functionaries, members of the elected assembly, industrialists like myself, all who have a vested interest in order and public security.

"The threat will not be overt, but implicit. It will not be protracted, but sudden and surprising. It will call for immediate action. The action must be such as to command the approval of all those who see themselves endangered. We must be prepared to take it.

"The preparations begin now. Corrado, commencing with Thursday's edition, you will reverse the editorial and news policy of the paper. We are no longer Centrists, we are swinging very rapidly to the Right. I know you don't like it. I know the staff won't. It's your job to keep them happy with the best lies you can tell. I don't think they'll go as far as a strike, but even if they do, it may help us. I want editorials that my Fascist friends will read and applaud. I want a big feature on the work of Major-General Leporello. Let's call it an accolade, modified by stringent and critical recommendations. In other words, let us not be cretinous or fulsome. I don't want to lose staff or circulation, but I want it known that I am prepared to support the Right under conditions. I want them to call me and invite me to lunch. Then I can invite them here instead.

"Milo, your job is more difficult, because of the time and the technical problems involved. Upstairs we have a mass of documents and notes collated by Matucci, of which the most important are the military maps and the campaign plans. In addition, we have a collection of obscene photographs and sound tapes. You have access to certain other material from film files and newsreels. You have three weeks in which to write, film and edit a ten-minute film based on all the material. The film will say that Major-General Leporello is a pederast with his own troops, a murderer and a conspirator against the security of the State. Matucci here will edit the film with you. He will also appear as commentator and final accuser. As an actor, he needs much direction. I trust you will succeed where I have failed.

"Matucci, you will work with Milo on the film. You will recruit and have at my disposal within the same three weeks a praetorian guard of senior officers who will agree to attend with you an official function and act with you if a certain unexpected crisis should arise. Now, this is the riskiest point of the plan, because it involves a nice consideration of how and when the nature of the crisis is to be revealed to them. I do not know your friends. I cannot pretend to decide how you will treat with them. I can tell you only this: if they fail us at the last moment, we may all be brought low, and the ungodly may survive, stronger than ever.

"Now, let me describe the moment at which our plan comes to fruition or disaster. I have just completed plans for one of the biggest ventures of my career, a chain of tourist hotels and marina developments around the southern coastline of the peninsula. This enterprise will bring a flow of tourists and dependent tourist industries into the depressed South. It is therefore of major interest to the Government. I am now able to announce that a consortium of Italian and foreign banks has agreed to finance the whole project. I propose to make that announcement at a gathering in this house a little over three weeks from now. The party will be private. No press will be invited, but Corrado will attend as my personal guest and as pipeline to the communications media. If we fail here, we shall, for our own protection, publish all the material we have.

"The guest list is already prepared. It includes senior ministers and functionaries—all the people of whom I have already spoken. Major-General Leporello and his wife are on that list, as is also the Director of SID. I believe that the tone of our new editorials and features will encourage them both to attend. . . .

"I am still not decided what will happen on that night. We shall have to wait until acceptances have been received before we can arrange a protocol and an order of ceremonies. I will consult with you from time to time before decisions are made. However, let me make one

thing clear to all of you. If we win, no one will thank
us. If we lose . . . Eh! We'd better take the next plane to
Rio!"

❦ ❧

THE next day I identified the second man in the Leporello
photographs. It was Captain Girolamo Carpi, onetime
aide to Pantaleone. This was a stunning surprise. It established a direct link between Leporello and Pantaleone. It
also revealed a yawning hiatus in my own information on
Carpi, since there was no hint of any deviate practices in
his Army dossier. I had hired him. I had dismissed him
and arranged for his safe exile to a training base in Sardinia. Now I had to rethink and, if possible, arrange for
his return to the mainland. Neither was going to be easy.
I was no longer on active duty. Therefore, I had no access
to files and could not make any formal requests to Army
authorities.

I took the news and the problem to Bruno Manzini.
He frowned over it for a long while and then announced:

"Dante, this man could be the most important witness
we have. We must get him here, question him, break him
and, if possible, get him on the film in time for our
function. How do we do that, without showing our cards
to the Army?"

"I go to Sardinia with the photograph in my pocket
and frighten him into talking."

"No, Dante. I can't risk you outside the gates of Pedognana."

"If we could get Carpi posted to Bologna, we could
arrange access easily enough. You must have friends in
the Army high enough to swing a transfer."

"I have. The problem is how far I can trust any of
them at a time like this. . . . Leave this with me, Dante,
I need to think about it quietly. What about your praetorians?"

"One is coming tomorrow, two more over the weekend,
the others during the following week."

"Have you decided what you're going to tell them?"

"I can't decide that until I've talked to them. How important is the number?"

"Less important than security. Ten field officers in full uniform would be very impressive, but I would rather have three, primed and resolute, than risk a single waverer."

"I'll report back to you after I've talked with each one."

"Let me ask you something else about Carpi. How did you come to use him in the first place?"

"Let me see now. . . . He was appointed as aide to your brother about eighteen months ago. About six months after that the Director called me and suggested we enlist Carpi as a domestic spy. He gave me Carpi's dossier, which showed that he was living beyond his means and was heavily in debt to a moneylender in Rome. I approached him with the proposition that if he worked for SID, we would pay his debts and give him a monthly stipend as well. He leapt at the offer. . . ."

"But his dossier was given to you by the Director. You didn't call for it yourself from the Army?"

"No."

"And knowing the Director's way with dossiers, what does that suggest to you?"

"It could have been doctored before I saw it."

"Exactly. Now I will tell you something else, my Dante. The Director knew my half brother quite well. You remember he was selling his art collection?"

"Yes. He was in correspondence with Del Giudice."

"And your Director was bidding against me for certain items."

"I thought he wasn't interested in old masters."

"He isn't—except as negotiable currency. He buys them as non-exportable commodities. He sells at a big profit to another dealer, not as honest as Del Giudice. This dealer has them copied by an expert, gets an export license for the copy and sends the original out of the country. Three of my father's paintings have gone on this route. This was the substance of my talk with Pantaleone on the night of his death."

"Can you prove that?"

"Yes. But don't delude yourself, Dante. It's a good point for a dossier. It is not enough to bring down the Director, who is in a strictly legal position. We have to prove murder."

"For what motive?"

"Profit—on every level. Pantaleone dies. Leporello replaces him as military leader. Since Leporello has organized the murder, the Director moves in as head of state, just to keep the record pure. Don't you see? It's the classic method. They are like bull-leapers, vaulting over the horns. The one who vaults the last beast and gives it the last pat on the rump is champion. Yes, we need your Captain Carpi. Somehow I will get him here. . . . Tell me, how are you feeling?"

"Better. You were right. Bed is good medicine, and hate's a better one. What are our chances?"

"*Così così* . . . fifty-fifty. It all depends on the mood of the gathering. If they walk out, we are sunk. If they stay, we shall win. It's an opera, my Dante, staged for an operatic people. Everyone knows the score backwards. It's a question of how well it is staged and sung. . . . I know this is positively my last performance. I hope I can hit the high note and hold it till the last chord and take the final bow. I hope . . . that's all. But if you see me wilting, prop me up until the curtain comes down. . . . Dante, even if I can get Carpi here, there will be no time for a full inquiry. You may have to bluff with him."

"I don't relish that. Let's wait and see whether you can get him and what I can do with him. . . . There's something that's bothering me, Bruno."

"Oh, what's that?"

"You're going to have a hundred, a hundred and fifty highly sophisticated men and women who come to your house for a celebration party. How are you going to get them to sit for ten minutes through a very sordid film, which impugns some of their fellow guests, casts suspicion on others and makes them all feel very uncomfortable?"

"Would you believe, my Dante, I have been so bothered by that same question that I have a certain Professor

Mueller flying in tomorrow from Munich. He is an acknowledged expert on mass psychology and group manipulation. I want to pose the problem to him in the most precise terms and in the ambience where it will arise. I should have preferred someone more familiar with our own Latin character, but I dare not use any of our own people. The old story, my friend: 'A man's enemies shall be those of his own household.' Sad, isn't it?"

"That's strange . . ."

"What?"

"Pantaleone used the same words to Lili Anders."

"In what connection?"

"Let me think now. . . . I want to get it right, and my memory still plays tricks. Oh, yes. Apparently Pantaleone had a habit of making cryptic remarks and then refusing to explain them. Lili linked two such remarks: 'There is no simple future for me, because my past is too complicated,' and the words you have just used."

"In what connection were these remarks made?"

"As I understood it, in connection with the Salamander."

"Could he have been referring to Carpi, who was a domestic spy?"

"Very possibly."

"Think about it, Dante. Think of Carpi as an intimate of Leporello, as an emissary of the Director, as a man with free access to the Pantaleone apartment . . . as the man who killed my half brother."

"And myself as the man who employed him. That's very pretty!"

"I'm glad you've seen the point. You told me the Director was preparing a black book on you. If we indict Carpi, you could be in bother, too."

"Bruno, let's face it now. You can stay me up with apples and pomegranates, you can surround me with angelic choirs. I'm still up to my neck in the *merda*. I'm the man who started all this. I'm the man who must finish it. That's the way I'm constructing the film with Milo. If things go wrong, you must walk away from me."

He lifted his white head and gave me a small enigmatic smile. "Dante, son of my heart, never underscore the obvious. If we lose, I can't afford you. If we win—touch wood!—we shall both be very busy men. Too busy for dramatic gestures. . . ."

The next three weeks were a period of mounting panic, suppressed only by the calm generalship of Manzini. The ballroom of the villa was invaded by an army of painters, decorators and electricians. A barn was transformed into a studio, offices and cutting room for Milo and his crew. Manzini worked, sometimes at home with a battery of secretaries, sometimes in Milan, from whence he would return, grey-faced and tired, but always with some new word of encouragement. His guest list was filling up. His press campaign had been well received by the Right. Leporello and the Director had consented to come. This minister or that had sent him words of personal greeting.

Milo and I quarrelled our way through the film, he concerned with the visual impact of his work, I troubled always by the legal logic of the case we must present. My friends came, one by one, to visit me, and I probed them like a confessor before I dared a single hint of the project on which we were embarked. All of them were troubled by the situation of the Republic and the divisions within the armed forces. They themselves were divided on the remedies. In the end there were only four to whom I felt I could commit with any real confidence. To these I proposed as follows:

"You will be invited as guests to an official ceremony here at the villa. It's a big occasion and you will wear formal mess uniform. I guarantee you each a pretty girl as escort. Now, here's the reason. The place is going to be full of important people, ministers, functionaries, that sort of thing. There'll be the usual contingent of security men in attendance, but we don't want them inside the dining room. That's why I want you there, looking like happy guests. . . . We've been told something may happen on that night. I can't tell you what it is. I don't want you to ask. I want you to trust me and come for friendship's sake . . . and maybe for the sake of all the things we've talked about. You are committed to nothing beyond attendance. You will receive the same invitation card as every other guest. Now, can you accept that or not? If you can, will you accept one other condition? This is a State secret and you'll have to keep it like that."

They accepted and I believed them. They were friends of the heart, close as family, which is the one thing on which you can depend in this troubled, disparate land of mine. When I told Manzini, he nodded a curt agreement and dismissed the matter. This was my province. I was on my own responsibility. When I asked him about Carpi, he frowned and shook his head:

"Nothing yet. Tomorrow I am flying to Rome to see a friend of mine in the Ministry of Defense. There is a risk involved and some very devious staff work. But I hope we shall get him here in time."

In the event, he was disappointed. The last week passed in a flurry of frantic activity. On the day of the great dinner party Captain Carpi had still not arrived.

❦ ❧

AT the final council of war, which was held at three o'clock in the afternoon, it was decided that I should not attend the function at all, but should present myself only in its closing moments. The reason was simple and perfectly valid. My presence could prove an embarrassment to Leporello and the Director and introduce a dangerous note of uneasiness into a gathering whose success depended upon a careful contrivance of atmosphere.

After the meeting Manzini walked us round on a final tour of inspection. In the foyer the guests would be received by four of Pia's girls and led to the first reception room, to be presented to Manzini and Pia and circulate for cocktails round a huge illuminated projection of the development—a large-scale relief map of the boot of Italy, showing the tourist arteries and the location of the development sites, and a series of models showing the completed installations.

After cocktails they would proceed to the ballroom, which had been converted into a dining room for the occasion. The place was ablaze with flowers and the lighting was contrived to flatter the least beautiful of women. The seating was unusual for such a function: a series of small rectangular tables, each seating three persons a side, so that the guests faced each other in a small closed community. At one end of each table was a silver bucket in which were six flat rectangular packages wrapped in gold paper and tied with ribbon—party favours for each guest. At the other end of each table was a small television set of the most advanced design, connected by closed circuit to a central control in an adjoining room. The host's table at the far end of the room was arranged as a horseshoe, with the television receiver placed between the points of the shoe.

Each guest was supplied with a program card, illuminated by Carlo Metaponte, and, for a final impudent irony, the place cards were set in small silver mounts in the shape of a salamander. The program was simple: a toast to the President and the Republic, an opening address by the Minister for Tourism, a reply by Bruno Manzini and the showing of a short television film on the new development, produced and directed by Milo de Salis.

There were other refinements, too: three television scanners were placed at various points in the room. Two were focussed on the tables where Leporello and the Director were to be seated. The third covered the room, so that all the proceedings could be monitored and recorded on tape for later evidence. Leporello and the Director were seated at opposite sides of the room, out of each other's line of vision. One of my praetorians was seated at each of their tables, with another at the table next in line. What Manzini had spent in terms of money was staggering. What he had spent of imagination and ingenuity was unbelievable from a man of his years. When the tour was over, he took me back to his study, poured brandy for both of us and made a last toast to the venture.

". . . I will not say good luck, my Dante. What has brought us to this point is believing and working and daring. What happens tonight will depend on how nicely we have calculated the interaction of small groups of people submitted to a sudden and shocking experience. According to Mueller, we are gambling that their curiosity will overcome their repugnance and hold them seated until the end. However, he does say there will be a crisis point at which either Leporello or the Director may attempt to leave, calculating that a sudden move may upset the audience. You must prevent that at all costs. You will be armed, of course, but for a threat only. There must be no violence. What happens at the end, of course, is in the hands of God . . . and though you may not believe it, Dante, He has to have an interest in tonight's affair. . . . Perhaps that should be my toast: I pray that He may hold you safe, my Dante, and bring you to a quiet harbour."

I said amen to that, and it was the closest I had come to praying for a long time. We drank and set down our glasses. Then Manzini sprang his last surprise.

"Dante, my friend, have you thought about tomorrow?"

"Tomorrow?"

"Yes. It will come, you know—unless we both die in our sleep."

"So?"

"So if our strategy succeeds, you will have the Director and Leporello under arrest on a variety of charges. How will you proceed from that point?"

"According to the book. Deposition by the arresting officer, deposition by the accused. Documents forwarded to the magistrate. Examination by the magistrate, indictment, submission of pleas by the defense and public trial."

"Which will, of course, make an international scandal?"

"Yes."

"And have profound political consequences?"

"Inevitably."

"Consequences for which neither the Government nor the country are as yet prepared."

"True."

"Read me the consequences as you see them."

"We shall have aborted a fascist coup. We shall have damaged public faith in the senior bureaucracy. We shall have given vast new strength to the Left. . . . On the other hand, we shall have affirmed that the State is capable of purging and regulating itself to the benefit of the people."

"And the final outcome?"

"Potentially healthy."

"Potentially?"

"That's my best estimate."

"Which leaves us still at risk—grave risk."

"Yes."

"The first risk is yours. You have passed the film. You will make the arrest, you will prefer the charges. You must file the indictment. Is the case complete?"

"Against Leporello, yes. Against the Director, no. A good lawyer could win it for him."

"And then you would go to the wall."

"Obviously."

"Are you ready for that?"

"I hope so."

"You could avoid it."

"How?"

"Accidents happen—fortunate accidents."

"I know. . . . 'The prisoner was shot while attempting to escape.' 'The prisoner suffered a cardiac seizure while under normal interrogation and the police surgeon deposed to a long-standing mitral defect.' 'The suspect was granted provisional liberty on the instance of his attorneys and failed to appear at the court hearing. . . .' No, Bruno! Not this time! Not for me. Not for you. Not for the Minister or the President himself."

"Not for the people either? Your people, my Dante."

"The people belong to themselves. I am the only man who belongs to me. You taught me that lesson, Bruno. I can't unlearn it now."

He gave me a long, quizzical look, grinned and dismissed the matter with a shrug. Then he went to his desk, unlocked a drawer and brought out a small velvet box. He handed it to me and said simply:

"It's a gift. I hope you like it."

I opened the box and found, slotted in the velvet bed, a gold signet ring. The symbol engraved on the seal was a crowned salamander.

My emotions were still unsteady, and I was deeply moved. Manzini, however, would not indulge me in any expressions of gratitude. He stood towering over me, like a sardonic sage, and read me his last cautionary tale.

". . . We are the victims of those who love us, my Dante. They dream our destinies and plunge us into nightmares. They plot fabulous voyages and blame us when the voyages end in shipwreck. Yet we have no recourse, because we, too, are born dreamers and conspirators. . . . My father robbed me of his name and the inheritance of his history and thought to recompense me with the foundations of the fortune which I have today. Your father dreamed his noble dreams of a new world, and his family suffered for them. In the end you, my Dante, came to wear the uniform of the men who arrested him.

"Yet each of us learned the same lesson: there are no guarantees; there is no permanence; life is a riddle propounded by a divine comedian, whose answer is so simple, we never see it until it is too late. I have never told you this, but after the war when we were, for a long while, a nation of beggars, subsisting on reconstruction funds from America, making all sorts of shabby bargains which today we are trying to undo, I toyed with the idea of quitting Europe altogether and investing what remained of my life and my fortune in the New World. Here I was entangled by history, caught like a lamb in a bramblebush, torn and scarred and totally confused. There, I felt I could be another man, a builder looking only to the future. . . .

"I came back here to Pedognana. One evening I walked down to the chapel and sat a long time looking at the slab which covered Marie Claire's grave. I tried to talk to her. There was no answer, because that is the nature of the divine riddle: the eloquence of those who do not understand it, the silence of those who have solved it at last. I wept then, the last tears I have ever shed. Old Don Egidio came in. You've met him. He's the typical peasant priest, not very learned, slipshod and cross-grained, something of a tippler, too, but with it all, very shrewd.

"He did not try to comfort me. He knew me too well for that. He knew that I should have rejected him as a man too ignorant to understand the complexity of my condition. He sat down beside me and told me the tale of the puppy with the straw tail. . . . You have never heard it? It's very simple. There was once a puppy who was born with a short tail. He was very ashamed of his defect, so he made himself a long and beautiful tail of golden straw. He was proud of himself then. He wagged his tail twice as vigorously as any dog in the village. He strutted and preened himself and was courted by all the bitches. Then one day, as he lay by the fire in his master's cottage, his tail caught fire. . . . He couldn't get rid of it, of course. He ran around yelping until his master tossed him in the pond to put out the flames.

"After that he had another problem. His real tail was still shorter and now his rump was scarred and all the other dogs laughed at him. What did he do? He had been very happy with his straw tail, so he made himself another one; but ever afterwards he was careful to stay away from the fire. . . . He could, of course, have made another choice. He could have shed his false tail and worn his scars and slept comfortably through the winter, close as he wanted to the fire.

". . . The moral, you would think, was obvious. Not to Don Egidio. His conclusion was quite different: man is not a puppy dog; he embraces all elements and is embraced by all and can survive them all; he can write his own bargain with life; the only thing he cannot haggle over is the final price: death and solitude. . . . You will be lonely tonight, my Dante. You will be lonely afterwards, because there is no credit for anyone in the company of the public executioner. The ring I have given you

is a symbol, not a talisman. The only magical thing about
it is the love that goes with the giving. Remember that
when I leave you, as I shall, as I must. . . ."

⊷ ∾

I HAD a long wait ahead of me. The guests would not
arrive until eight-thirty. They would not sit down to dinner until nine-thirty, when I would go down to the control
room and follow the proceedings on closed circuit with
Milo and his crew. The moment Manzini finished his
speech, the lights would be extinguished and the television screens illuminated. I would move immediately
to the ballroom, take up my post inside and lock the door.
If anyone tried to leave, unless it were a woman, I would
detain them until the end of the screening. It still lacked
twenty minutes to six. I went to my room, set the alarm
for eight, read a few pages of Guicciardini and lapsed into
a deep and dreamless sleep.

I woke refreshed and strangely calm. I shaved carefully,
bathed and put on my new uniform. When I looked at
myself in the mirror, I saw a man I hardly recognized: a
serving officer of a corps whose oath still had a ring of
royalty about it, whose tradition of service, however be-
smirched by individuals, still carried a blazon of honour.
The badges of rank I had earned myself. I, the son of a
political exile, could claim some service to the country for
which he, in his own way, had sacrificed himself. For all
the sordid shifts of my trade, I could still feel some pride
and a small, hesitant affection for the man inside my skin.
Enough! It was time to go.

As I walked down the stairs into the empty foyer, the
majordomo opened the front door and let in Captain
Carpi. For a moment he did not recognize me, and when
he did, he was nonplussed. He told me that he had been
sent from Sardinia with urgent dispatches to be delivered
personally into the hands of Major-General Leporello.
His plane had been delayed at Cagliari, and he had been
forced to hire a car to bring him out to Pedognana. I
told him the General was at dinner but that I would take

him in as soon as the function was over. He asked me
what I was doing. I told him I was on special duty. That
seemed to satisfy him. He was quite in the dark about the
whole affair. All he knew was that his commanding officer
had called him, told him he was to act as courier on a
special mission and sent him on his puzzled way. I wondered what devious staff work had gone into that ma-
neuver. I took him into the control room, fed him a glass
of champagne and a canapé and drew Milo aside to warn
him not to make any indiscreet comment. Then we settled
down to watch the show, while I tried frantically to figure
how I should make use of this very untimely arrival. By
the time Manzini stood up to announce the presidential
toast, I had made my decision.

The Minister of Tourism made an elegant and witty
speech, a little long, perhaps, but then he had important
people to impress: his colleague, the Minister of the Interior, among them. He noted the variety and the magnitude of Manzini's enterprises. He praised the boldness of
his vision, which he said made a lot of people blink and
others close their eyes and wait for the thunderclap. He
complimented the bankers on their foresight and their
confidence in the economy of the country and its political
stability. He was grateful for the lavish welcome extended
by the Cavaliere to his guests. He saw it as the symbol
of the welcome extended by Italy to the millions who
came visiting each year. He wished the project well, assured all the participants of the benevolence of the Government, added a flourish or two of metaphor and sat
down to polite applause.

Then Bruno Manzini stood up and began his own
speech.

"I thank the Minister for his kind words. I thank him
for his confidence in our enterprise, which is itself an act
of faith in the future of this beloved country of ours. This
act of faith is more sincere, because my colleagues and
I have committed huge sums of money to Italian development at a time when, despite the optimism of my good
friend, the country is divided on many issues. I can say
this here, in this gathering, because there are no press to

report my remarks, and you are intelligent men and women concerned, as I am, for the future of this country and its children. The decisions of which I speak are very deep. Some of them are historic; some of them are political; some are social. We are one people under one flag, but we are also many peoples with many different histories. We have too many parties and too little consensus to achieve easily a government for the people and by the people. Too much wealth is concentrated in too few hands, my own among them. However, to attempt to reconcile these differences, as some seek to do, by violent and sinister means is a dangerous folly; so dangerous, indeed, that it could negate at one stroke all that we have achieved since the war, all that we hope to build in the coming years. . . ."

They applauded him then. It was a proposition they could all accept because they didn't have to examine it too closely. Divisions they knew, and violence they knew; and they all had sinister symbolic scapegoats to carry their sins into the wilderness of forgetting. Manzini hushed them, slowly, with a smile and a gesture. His manner changed. He was happy now, and teasing.

". . . Have you ever thought of this, my friends: right through our history, dinners have been important occasions. That's strange, because we are not gross feeders, like the Germans, nor big drinkers like the French. We enjoy the food and we enjoy the wine and we enjoy the company of beautiful women, of whom there are so many here tonight. But the fact is, we do make history at mealtimes. There was Trimalchio's supper. You all remember that: very gross, very disgusting, even when dignified by the art of the great Petronius. Then there was the fatal supper of the Tolomei and the Salimbeni, which those of you here who are privileged to be Tuscans will remember. That one ended in murder. But I assure you all, dear friends, there will be no murder here tonight. Then there were the *cenacoli* of the Blessed Catherine of Siena, where souls were elevated by spiritual discourse and bodies were mortified by a very restricted diet. Saving the reverence of Monsignor Frantisek, who is here with us tonight as unofficial representative of the Holy Father, I regret we have not attained to this degree of spiritual perfection. However, I dare to think that this is an historic occasion.

". . . In the silver buckets at the end of each table you will find a number of packages. If the gentlemen will pass them round the tables, please . . . No, no, don't open them yet. They will make no sense until you have seen the film—which is not, I must tell you, the one promised on your program. . . . This one is a privileged document. The press does not know of its existence. The public will never see it—only you, my friends and compatriots. You will find it a strange experience. Some of you, especially the ladies, may be discomfited and embarrassed. I beg you to be patient and tolerant until the film justifies itself. . . . Now, if you will turn your chairs a little, you should all have a comfortable view of the television screens at the end of each table."

This was the cue. In the movement that followed, two of my praetorians stood up and leaned casually against the wall—a single pace would bring them to Leporello and Baldassare. Some of the other men did the same, so that the whole thing had the air of a casual and comfortable reshuffle. Manzini went on:

"If any one of you hesitates to share this experience with us, I beg him or her to leave now. . . . You are all resolved? Good! In a moment the television screens will light up, and this room will be plunged into darkness. I think you will all agree with me that secrets should be told in the dark and enjoyed in the light."

That was my signal. I hurried Carpi out of the control room and we reached the dining room just as the lights went down and the television screens lit up. I locked the door, put the key in my breast pocket and focussed on the nearest screen.

Milo de Salis had settled on a film method that was as simple as a child's primer and as devastating as a death sentence. It consisted of a series of direct and unqualified statements, in image and commentary. The image was too distant for comfort, but I knew the commentary by heart.

". . . This is a photograph of Major-General Massimo Pantaleone, who died in Rome this year, on Carnival night.

"This is the death certificate which states that he died of natural causes. . . . In fact, he died of an injection of air into his femoral artery. He was murdered. . . ."

There was a gasp of surprise, a rustle of movement, a flurry of whispers, then silence, as the commentary began again.

"This is a photograph of the later autopsy report, signed by three very reputable physicians.

"This is a photograph of an office block in the Via Sicilia, where the General's papers were stored after his death. The papers were stolen and two men were murdered—Avvocato Bandinelli and Agent Calvi of the Service of Defense Information. . . .

"This is the identity card of the man who murdered them: Giuseppe Balbo, a criminal who used a number of aliases.

"Among the General's papers were these maps: Turin . . . Milan . . . Rome . . . Naples . . . Taranto . . . These are military maps which have since beeen altered in detail but not in substance. They show how, on the thirty-first of October of this year, a military junta plan to overthrow the legitimate Government of Italy and establish a government by dictation.

"The moving arrows illustrate how the plan would operate.

"The maps and plans you have just seen are in the possession of this next man, Major-General Leporello, who is a guest here tonight."

Once again there was a stir as all heads were turned to identify Leporello. They could not see him in the dim light, so once again the image and the commentary commanded their attention.

"This is a recent photograph of General Leporello's aide, Captain Matteo Roditi. He is at present under psychiatric care because he was tortured into insanity to prevent his giving testimony in court.

"This is another photograph of Giuseppe Balbo, murderer, who was shot down while resisting arrest by General Leporello's men.

"This is the Club Alcibiade, a resort of deviates, where Captain Roditi met often with Giuseppe Balbo, who was, strange to say, an enlisted member of the Carabinieri, under General Leporello's own command.

"This woman, shopping with her children in Milan, is the wife of Major-General Leporello.

"This is a love letter, one of thirty, which she wrote to Captain Roditi, her husband's aide and true father of her children. Their love affair was condoned by the General, for good reasons."

This was the crisis point which Mueller had predicted. Leporello could not defend himself; he would and must defend his wife. Instantly he was on his feet, his tall frame monstrous in the half-dark. He shouted, "This is an outrage against an innocent woman. I demand . . ."

He demanded nothing. My praetorian was at his side with a pistol rammed into his ribs.

Manzini's voice rang like a trumpet blast from the rostrum. "Sit down, General! Ladies and gentlemen, I beg that you control yourselves. We are not here to insult a woman but to prevent an imminent bloodshed."

There was a gasp of horror which I could feel physically. They did not settle immediately. They watched and waited until Leporello subsided into his chair, then, lost and leaderless, they submitted in silence to the last brutal revelations.

"These next photographs will distress you, but I beg you to look at them carefully. This one shows Major-General Leporello engaged in a sexual act with Giuseppe Balbo, murderer.

"This one shows him in another act with the man identified as the personal aide, and probable murderer, of the late Major-General Pantaleone. His name is Captain Girolamo Carpi.

"This man, Major-General Leporello, ladies and gentlemen, was chosen to lead the *colpo di stato*. He himself, however, would never have assumed power. There was another man behind him . . .

". . . This man—Prince Filippo Baldassare, Director of the Service of Defense Information. This man plotted the death of Pantaleone, hired Carpi to kill him and then arranged for Leporello to replace him."

Again the audience slewed round in the darkness to identify Baldassare. I was one of the few who could see him. He sat calm and unmoved, sipping brandy from a crystal goblet.

"Who am I? I am Colonel Dante Alighieri Matucci of the same service. I collected this information. I, too, was imprisoned and submitted to psychological torture to prevent my revealing it. I take full responsibility for the substance and the presentation of this film. I depose it as true and I shall offer to the appropriate authorities, documents in support."

The screens went dark. The lights went up and a hundred and fifty people sat there, dumb and ashamed to look at each other. I moved forward into the silent room with Carpi, like a sleepwalker, at my side. I had one moment of blind panic. Then I found words.

"The officers present will place the General and Prince Baldassare under arrest."

I did pray then. I said, "Dear Christ, please make them move, please! . . ." They moved. They placed their hands on the shoulders of the two men. The act was final and complete. Now I had to speak again. I heard myself say:

"Cavaliere, ladies and gentlemen, I have with me, under arrest, Captain Girolamo Carpi, who will testify in the proper place to his part in this affair."

Then, from his own table, Bruno Manzini took command. "My countrymen! You have been insulted tonight. You have been shocked and shamed. You may choose never to pardon me for the pain I have inflicted upon you. I will not apologize. I tell you only that it is a small price to pay to prevent the bloodshed and the misery of a civil uprising and the oppression of a new tyranny. . . .

Now, may I ask you to retire to the salon, where coffee and liqueurs will be served."

They got up slowly and moved away blank-faced, like automatons, each carrying the supper gift, a dossier of the damned, with a complimentary card from the Salamander. Elena Leporello left, too, and she passed me without a glance of recognition. Finally there was no one left but the praetorians and the accused and Manzini and the Minister for the Interior and myself.

Manzini and the Minister stepped from the high table and walked slowly down the room towards me. They stopped. They faced me, bleak and expressionless. The Minister said:

"Thank you, Colonel. You will do what has to be done with those gentlemen. I shall wait here. You will report to me before you leave."

Bruno Manzini said nothing. He did exactly as he had promised. He walked away.

❧ ☙

IT was an eerie moment. Three prisoners, five jailers, silent among the debris of a rich man's feast. We were like actors, frozen on an empty stage, waiting for the Director to move us. Then I understood that I was the Director and that, without me, the play would neither continue nor conclude. I must move. I must speak. I must decide. I heard the words as if they issued from the mouth of another man.

"Prince Baldassare, General Leporello, will you please remain seated. You other gentlemen, will you please conduct Captain Carpi to the monitor room and wait there till I call you."

The praetorians linked arms with Captain Carpi and led him, mute and unprotesting, from the room. Those standing guard over the Director and Leporello left their posts and walked out. If I read their looks aright, they were very glad to be gone. When the door closed behind them I was, at last, alone with my enemies. I felt no triumph, only a strange sense of disillusion and of loss,

and a vague humiliation as though my best-told joke had
fallen flat. Both men sat bolt-upright in their chairs, hands
flat upon the tables, their faces averted from me. They
were so far apart that unless I stood far away like a
ringmaster or a theatrical tyrant I could not address them
together or even compass them with a single glance. I
had to confront them, one by one, face to human face. I
went to Leporello first. I straddled a chair in front of
him and found myself staring into a death mask. I told
him:

"General, it is your privilege to be held under arrest, in
barracks under custody of service officers, and you may
elect to be tried under military law. If you waive this
privilege you become immediately subject to civil process.
Which do you choose?"

He did not answer. He sat like a stone man, cold and
motionless.

I tried again. "General, there are formalities. I want
to make them as simple and easy as possible. If you
would like to speak to your wife, I can have her brought
to you. Afterwards, as you know, it will not be easy. If
you are unwell, I can call a doctor. For your own sake,
General, I advise you to answer me."

He had not even heard me. His lips were locked, his
eyes blank as pebbles. I stretched out a hand and laid it
on his wrist. There was pulse, but nothing more. The
muscles were rigid as iron; there was no twitch of recognition or aversion. Then I heard the Director's voice, cool
and ironic as always:

"Classic figure, Matucci. Total withdrawal. You'll get
nothing out of him tonight—if ever. To cover yourself,
I'd call a doctor and have the wife present when he makes
his diagnosis."

I swung round to see him, calm and smiling, sipping a
glass of brandy and puffing a cigar. He raised his glass in
a toast:

"My compliments, Matucci. . . . Trial by television! I
wonder why I never thought of that. It's hardly a democratic process, but it's very effective."

He poured a goblet of wine and pushed it across the

table towards me. "Sit down! Relax. I'm a cooperative
witness. You can afford to be pleasant to me. I imagine
you've had rather a tense evening. Still, you must be very
satisfied. You've got everything now, except the fellow
singing 'Sic transit' and burning flax under your nose.
What's the next move?"

"You know the code as well as I do, sir."

"And I know the trade better, Matucci. You made
your case against Leporello—though I doubt he'll ever
stand to answer it. The man was always a psychotic, in
full flight from reality. Tonight you pushed him over the
edge and I doubt he'll ever come back. Even if he does,
a good lawyer will plead him unfit and the State will, in
its own interest, concur. Against me, what have you got?
Carpi, a man with straw in his shoes, who will be frightened, suborned or eliminated before you get a line of
decent testimony out of him. Still, it's your case, and you
must make it, win or lose. Unless, of course . . ."

"What?"

"Unless you are open to a little lesson in statecraft.
You were always weak in that discipline, as I told you.
That's what held you back in your career."

"If you're proposing a deal, the answer's no."

"My dear Matucci! Why do you always underrate me?
Do you think I would be so naïve as to propose a deal to
a man both righteous and triumphant? On the contrary,
I invite you to a mature consideration of realities. . . .
Statecraft has nothing to do with morals, has nothing to
do with justice relative or absolute. It is the art and craft
of controlling large masses of people, of holding them in
precarious equilibrium with one another and with their
neighbours. All means are open to the statesman and he
must be prepared to use them all in their seasons from
the headsman's axe to the circus holiday. He must never
overrate his triumph or lose courage in temporary adver-
sity. From time to time he needs a victim, if he is to avoid
a holocaust. Clemency for him is not a virtue but a
strategy. . . . Only the aim is constant, to hold the many-
headed monster in control, to calm him when he growls,
to curb him when he gets too playful, to wonder at his

visions but sedate him before they turn into nightmares.
. . . You, Matucci, are still a servant of the State. . . .
You are not yet a statesman. Tonight you have the opportunity to become one." He broke off, sipped his brandy,
drew on his cigar and smiled at me through the eddies
of fragrant smoke. I said nothing, and after a while he
began on a new tack.

"At this moment, Matucci, you are in a position of
great strength. You have forestalled a military coup. You
have discredited the authors of it. You have two important
victims to toss to the lions, Leporello and myself. In
Manzini you have a powerful friend. In the Minister you
have an important patron who is waiting only for you to
give him the right advice. . . . Think about the Minister,
Matucci. He is a politician—a thinking reed, blown by
every gust of popular vociferation, by every whisper in
the corridors of the Assembly. What does he want? What
would you want if you were in his shoes? A discreet and
well-managed triumph or a platter full of bleeding
heads. . . ? One head is useful. You can stick it on a pike
and display it for a warning to the populace. More than
one is a carnage. . . . Which head would you select for the
pike? In my view—which I admit could be prejudiced—
the one with the fewest brains. You've got it, over there.
. . . Mine is worth much more to you and the Minister if
you leave it on my shoulders. I am discredited, so I can't
do any harm unless you bring me to trial—when, my dear
Matucci, I can promise you scandals that will be shouted
from Moscow to the Golden Gate. On the other hand, if
clemency were offered, I should respond to it gratefully.
I would remove myself from the scene and leave a rich
legacy of information to my successor. . . . Do I make
myself clear?"

I was ashamed for him then. For a moment he had
been eloquent. Now he was merely plausible. I told him
bluntly, "I must be equally clear. I have no authority to
offer clemency."

"My dear fellow, I know that. I will go further. It
would be useless and dangerous for you to treat with me

at all. You should and you must treat only with the Minister."

"What are you asking of me then?"

"I want to speak to the Minister privately, now."

"He may not want to speak with you."

"He will. And afterwards he will ask to see you."

"And?"

"All I ask is that you give him an honest professional answer to any questions he asks you."

"Can you be sure I'll do that?"

"No. I hope you will. You have no reason to love me. I would not blame you if you pressed to the limit the advantage that you have now. In fact I'd be rather surprised if you didn't. However, I've read you the lesson; make what you like of it. Will you convey my request to the Minister?"

"Give me a hand with Leporello; we'll get him to a bedroom. I'll call a doctor and then I'll see the Minister."

∵∵ ∴∴

THE interview between Prince Baldassare and the Minister lasted more than three hours. I was not present. I was closeted with Professor Malpensa, of the Army Psychiatric Unit in Bologna, who had been roused from his bed and brought by helicopter to Pedognana. With him was Dr. Lambrusco, a guest at the party and Manzini's personal physician. I had asked them to examine Leporello separately and in concert and then render me a joint diagnosis. They expressed it in writing: ". . . a catatonic or psuedo-catatonic state, expressive of a profound fugal impulse induced by guilt and shock. It is our joint recommendation that the patient be institutionalized for clinical observation. It is our opinion that the patient is at present incapable of rational communication, and that to submit him to interrogation or confinement would be pointless and dangerous. Prognosis, doubtful."

I accepted the document, signed the General into the hands of Professor Malpensa, who flew him back to

Bologna. Then I went in search of Manzini. His guests had gone long since, and he was sitting alone in the drawing room. He was grey about the gills but still alert and cheerful. He greeted me with a smile and a grim, dry chuckle: "Well, Matucci, we did it!"

"Yes. . . . It's very quiet now."

"What did you expect? Garlands and a triumph?"

"Blessed is he who expects nothing, because he is sure to get it. . . . I think I'd like a brandy."

"Help yourself." He gestured in the direction of the study. "Our friend Baldassare is trying to strike a bargain with the Minister."

"I know."

"Would it surprise you to know that I have recommended it?"

"In what terms, Bruno?"

"I have represented that without the cooperation and connivance of the Director we should never have been able to stage this evening's drama."

"That's not true."

"I know it. You know it. The Minister knows it. But it happens to be a fiction that fits the moment. Objections?"

"None."

"You approve?"

"I don't approve. I think it's expedient."

"You're learning, my Dante."

"The hard way. How much of tonight's affair will reach the press?"

"By direct report, nothing. By leaks and gossip, quite a lot. It's unfortunate, but inevitable."

"Could you reach your editor now?"

"Of course. Why?"

"I'd like him ready to file a report to the wire services. We've missed the morning editions, but we'll make the evening papers and the international correspondents will have it on the teletype when the bureaus open in the morning."

"What do you have in mind?"

"I can't tell you until I've spoken with the Minister."

He gave me a swift appraising glance and then a nod of satisfaction. *"Bene!* At last I can approve you, Dante Alighieri. For a long time I wondered . . ."

"Wondered what?"

"How much of you was man and how much a confection of circumstance. Forgive me! How does one know whether a nut is sound until one cracks the shell? You are a man full of contradictions, my Dante. You are coward and hero. You are wise and foolish. You are soft as putty and hard as iron. A friend can buy you with a smile. A purse of gold will not corrupt you. How you will end, God knows; but I am happy to know I have not wasted myself on you. . . . Excuse me, I'll call my editor."

He was gone perhaps three minutes when the door of the study opened and the Minister came out. When he saw that I was alone, he announced brusquely:

"I have some questions to ask you, Colonel."

"At your service, sir."

"I need direct answers: yes or no."

"I understand, sir."

"The charges which you made public tonight, are they true?"

"Yes."

"Can you sustain them in court?"

"I can sustain those against General Leporello. Those against Prince Baldassare will be more difficult to prove."

"Could you guarantee a conviction in his case?"

"Guarantee, no."

"But you would be willing to proceed?"

"As an officer of Public Security, yes."

"You have qualified that statement. Why?"

I handed him the medical report on Leporello and waited in silence while he read it. He folded it and handed it back to me. "I repeat the question, Colonel. Why did you qualify your last statement?"

"Because, sir, I am commissioned to act and advise as an officer of Public Security. I have not been asked to tender an opinion of a political nature."

"I take your point. I now ask you to offer, without prejudice, a political opinion. We have, thanks to your efforts, averted a national crisis. How should we act to avoid a national scandal?"

"We have two important men under arrest, sir. One is clearly incompetent by reason of a psychotic condition. The case against the other is incomplete; and even if we could complete it we should risk embarrassing revelations prejudicial to public security. We should risk also deep and divisive enmities in the Republic and between the Republic and her allies. I would advise, with deference and respect, that Prince Baldassare be permitted to retire from public life and remove himself within twelve hours from the confines of the Republic."

"Could that be done without raising a public outcry?"

"There would be hostile comment, a great deal of it. There would be political embarrassment. In my view that would be a lesser evil than a celebrated and scandalous trial."

"What are you personal feelings about Prince Baldassare?"

"I admire his talent greatly. I have learnt much from him. I disapprove his politics and his personal ambitions. I have very private reasons for wishing to see him brought down."

"What are those reasons?"

"He has imprisoned a woman, once a foreign agent, with whom I am in love. He has damaged my career. He has conspired to submit me to psychological torture from which I am only recently recovered."

"But you would still recommend his release?"

"As a political expedient, yes."

"Would you arrange it and supervise it?"

"What you mean, sir, is will I accept personal responsibility for it?"

"Yes."

"And will I, by consequence, absolve the Ministry and the Government and place myself in jeopardy?"

"You express it very accurately, Colonel."

"We could, of course, do it another way, sir."

"How?"

"You give me a ministerial directive. I execute it. Very simple."

"Too simple, Colonel, and you know it. A politician cannot afford to be a patriot. The moment he is elected, he abjures the luxury. I know it's a difficult decision. Would you like a little time to think about it?"

"There is no time, sir."

"A condition then? A gift to sweeten the risk?"

"No, sir. I'm not for sale—not anymore. I'll do it. I'll get him across the border tonight. The Cavaliere Manzini will help me to handle the press."

"Thank you, Colonel."

"Is there anything else?"

"One other matter. I should like you to report to me as soon as possible in Rome. We have to begin cleaning house."

"May I remind you, sir, that I am still on provisional liberty, under charges laid by General Leporello."

"The charges will be withdrawn. As of this moment you are restored to active duty."

"Answerable to whom?"

"To me, Colonel. By the time you return to Rome I trust to be able to confirm your appointment as Director."

He meant it as an accolade—manna in the hungry desert of a bureaucrat's career. Instead it tasted like Dead Sea fruit, dust and ashes on the tongue. For a moment I had felt like a patriot; then, for reward, he had made me a whore again. Still, that was the rule of the game. I had no choice but to play it or toss the cards back onto the table. I bowed and smiled and said, "Thank you, sir. You do me great honour."

"Thank you, Colonel. Good night."

◦⋘§ §⋙◦

IT was strange sitting in the Director's chair. For a man so elegant, he kept a very dingy office. There were no ornaments, no pictures, no photographs, not even a lictor's

axe. The only symbols of power were the grey filing
cabinets and the scrambler telephone and the intercom
switchboard, which would bring twenty people running
to attend me. Old Steffi sat on the other side of the desk,
cocked his parrot head at me and cackled:

"Eh-eh-eh! So, you've arrived, Matucci! How does it
feel? Does your backside fit the seat of the mighty? And
what now, little brother? What's the policy? Left, Right
or Center?"

"Middle of the road, Steffi. *Tolleranza*. I think we all
need to breathe a little."

"Same as before, eh? Until somebody tosses a bomb in
Turin, or the police fire on rioters in Catanzaro and the
boys up top get panicky and scream for action. I wonder
how tolerant you'll be then! . . . Well, *speriamo bene!*
Here's hoping!"

"Come on, Steffi, give me time!"

"I can give you time. All the time you want. But what
about them? . . . What about you?"

"Please, old friend. . . !"

"So, I'm still without a job and my nose is twisted out
of joint. I'm sorry. What do you want me to do?"

"I've called the Commandant at the Mantellate. He's
expecting you. You present the Minister's letter and mine.
Lili is released to you. You deliver her to her apartment.
I'll be there when you arrive."

He stared at me as if I were some curious animal,
kicked up from under a stone. There was contempt in his
eyes and a kind of wondering sorrow.

"My God! What kind of a man are you, Matucci? She's
your woman, why don't you fetch her yourself? What
have you got in those veins of yours, ice water?"

I was angry then, bitterly and desperately angry. I
poured out on him all the pent-up fury of the last months.

"I'll tell you what kind of a man I am, Steffi. I bleed
like everyone else. I bruise like everyone else. I'm sick and
tired of being pushed and shoved and used and misused
and misjudged and misread by every clot who thinks he
knows the secrets of the universe. I'm sick of all the smug

bastards like yourself who think they can sum me up in a line and pay me off like a whore after an hour in bed. I'm sick of friends who make like father confessors and expect me to walk round ever afterwards in sackcloth and ashes. You want to know why I'm not going to the prison? I'll tell you! Because the first time Lili sees me I'll be in company with the Commandant and a notary and a turnkey with a pistol at his belt. I'll look exactly the way they do and I don't want her to see me like that; because that's not the kind of man I am . . . at least not to her. I'll want to take her in my arms and kiss her and comfort her and I won't be able to do that while every whore and pickpocket in the gallery makes a dirty joke of it and every little jack-in-office smiles behind his hand. . . . I won't submit her to that. I asked you to go because I thought you were my friend. Instead you sit there and insult me and make lousy ghetto jokes as if God gave you the right to be the conscience of the world. Now get the hell out of here! I'll find someone else."

He did not move. He sat there, downcast, his lips working as if he could not frame coherent words. Finally he faced me and there was compassion in his look and a new kind of respect. He said quietly, "I'm an old fool with a bird's brain and a frog's mouth. I'm sorry. I'll be glad to do it for you."

"Thank you."

"You're scared, aren't you?"

"Yes, Steffi, I'm scared."

"Piano, piano, eh! . . . Take it very easy!"

Even for a Director, formalities are long in Rome. Functionaries come and go, but the great paper machine goes round and round, churning out hundreds and thousands and millions of reams of *carta bollata,* signed and countersigned and stamped and sealed and stuffed into pigeonholes and dumped into subterranean repositories, until one fine or cloudy day some poor devil goes to jail and stays there while they dig, or say they dig, for the one line of evidence that may prove him incorrect.

I filled the apartment with baskets of flowers. I had champagne cooling in a bucket and canapés on a silver tray and a whole refrigerator full of food. I had documents from the Comune to put up the marriage banns on Capitol Hill. I had even an emerald betrothal ring, especially designed by Bulgari. I still had to wait an hour and a half before Lili came home.

The ring at the door was like camel bells in the desert. When I opened it she was standing alone and very still. I swept her into my arms and was astonished at how light she was. I kissed her and hugged her and wondered where all the passion had gone. I sat her in the armchair and served her like a princess. And then I looked at her. . . . She was so pale, she was almost transparent. She had shrunk to skin and bone. Her clothes hung on her like scarecrow garments. Her mouth was pinched, her hands fluttered nervously. Her eyes, those eloquent eyes, were glazed and dull as pebbles. She ate and drank, not hungrily, but mechanically, and when I laid my hands on her brow and her cheeks, she submitted but did not respond. I knelt beside her and begged.

"Tell me, Lili, what happened? What did they do to you?"

"Not much. Sometimes they questioned me. Most times they left me alone."

"Lili, you know I didn't send the telegram . . ."

She stared at me blankly. "What telegram?"

"I was told you came back because of a telegram from me."

"There was no telegram."

"Then why did you come back?"

"I got your letter. I used to read it every night before I went to bed. One night it wasn't there. I thought I had mislaid it. The next day I was out walking. My friend from Lugano stopped and offered me a lift in his car. I got in. Someone put a pad over my face. The next thing I remember we were in Italy, near Bolzano. Then two other men took over and drove me here to Rome. That's all. Except they told me you were in prison, too."

"Oh, darling, darling . . . I'm so sorry."

"It doesn't matter."

"Listen, sweetheart. This is what's going to happen. I'm going to move in here with you. I'm going to nurse you and get you well and we're going to be married. The notice goes up on Capitol Hill tomorrow. After that, no problems! You're my wife. You're under the personal protection of the Director of SID, for ever and ever, amen. . . . How does that sound?"

"It sounds the most beautiful thing in the world, Dante Alighieri. But I don't want it."

As I stared at her, not understanding, I saw the first flush of life in her cheeks, the first dawning of emotion in her eyes. She put out her hands, not soft now, but thin and creped like raw silk, and cupped them round my face. Then she told me, very gently:

"Dante, I know you love me. Your letter was the most touching compliment I have ever read in my life; but I'm going to give it back to you. I couldn't bear to keep it. I don't want to destroy it."

"But you said the letter was gone."

"They gave it back to me in prison. I don't know why, but they did. They do strange things, cruel and kind, and you never know which will be next. I love you, too, Dante. I suppose I'll always love you . . . but not to marry, not to live with for ever and ever."

"Lili, please . . ."

"No, listen to me, Dante! You have to know. . . ! I don't understand you Italians anymore. You are so warm and kind; then, suddenly, you are devious and cold and so cruel, it makes my blood run cold. You smile at each other in the morning, and plot against each other at night. You have no loyalties, Dante—only to the family and to today. Outside the family, after today, everything is doubt and calculation. Oh, Dante Alighieri, I hate to hurt you, but I have to say it. You're the people who always survive, no matter what happens to you. That's a wonderful, a hopeful thing. But it is also very terrible, because you will trample each other down to get the last drop of water in the world. . . . Even you, my Dante, even your Bruno! I can't face that anymore. I want to live secure, with a little book that tells me what to do. I want to be sure that if I keep the rules, the rules will keep me safe—safer than marriage, Dante Alighieri, safer than promises, safer even than loving. In Switzerland I can do that. Not here . . . I cannot risk you anymore."

What could I say? It was all true. The ring on my finger symbolized it: the fabulous beast that survived the hottest fire. And yet it wasn't true. Not the way she said it. The book of rules wasn't the answer. Not for us, the sun-people. The light was too clear. It showed the crosswise writing on the palimpsest. How could we believe in permanence who walked to the office over the bones of dead emperors? We couldn't trust tomorrow; we could only make do with today. I knelt there a long time, face buried in her hands, whose pores still exuded the stale smell of prison. I pitied her. I loved her. I could find no words to comfort her or myself. Then I heard her say:

"Will you help me to pack, please, Dante, and see if you can get me a flight to Zurich. I'd like to leave as soon as I can."

It was then I discovered how important it was to be the Director. I was able to command a first-class seat on an overbooked aircraft. I was able to park the car in a prohibited zone at Fiumicino. I was offered free drinks in the distinguished visitors' lounge. I was able to walk Lili all the way to the aircraft and settle her in the seat and commend her to the good offices of the chief steward. All that came out of a small piece of card in a black leather folder, stamped with the arms of the Republic.

I didn't wait for the takeoff. I drove back to Rome and telephoned Pia Faubiani. She wasn't at home; she had gone to Venice to open her show there. I called an agency and commissioned them to find me a larger apartment in a more fashionable district. I needed a better *figura,* now that I should be dealing with high men and large affairs. I dined at my old place in Trastevere, but found it suddenly cramped and provincial. Even the musician seemed to have lost his touch. I went home early and tried to read a little of my namesake before I went to bed. I was too sleepy to concentrate on his ponderous imagery—

and besides, I didn't believe a word of him. . . . No, that's not true. There were three lines I had to believe:

... *"Nessun maggior dolore ..."*

And she said to me: "There is no greater grief
Than to remember happy times, in misery;
And your teacher knows it, too."